Mr.

Hamish Gleave

by

Richard Llewellyn

Mr.

Hamish Gleave

A novel by

Richard Llewellyn

Doubleday & Company, Inc., Garden City, New York, 1956

Library of Congress Catalog Card Number: 56–5588
Printed in the United States
Designed by Diana Klemin
First Edition

Mr.

Hamish Gleave

Epsom's white paint glimmered against scintillant grass as he had always remembered, and the bookmakers' shouts came on lulls of the wind, exactly like listening to a sea shell. He could hear his father's voice saying Always come here when you can. It's a very good thing to get away sometimes, and it's been the greatest possible help to me. I've often looked at this and thought to myself if my father hadn't been such a harebrained ass I'd own my estates in China and Ceylon, my plantations in Darjeeling, my shipping line, my London house, the place in Scotland, and that very nice acreage in Kent, and doubtless a good deal more beside. And I'd have my racing stable. But here we stand. I haven't exactly been a slacker, Hamish. To think I paid off all his debts twenty shillings in the pound, idiot that I was. What else could I have done? Tell me. That's why your mother's never had a decent piece of jewellery to her name. Hang it, the only time we were ever able to afford anything in the way of a holiday abroad was in 1913. Just getting on my feet. Then the war. It wasn't gambling, it wasn't anything of the sort that broke me. Do try to remember that. It was simply the sort of filthy luck that dogged your grandfather. What a different life we all might have had. Damn him. I really don't mean that, of course. But damn him just the same. Wicked old fool he was. Really, wicked. What?

That weary voice in its always-bitter rind of affectionate hatred seemed to have paused there over the years, real as a statue. It was odd and rather sad to think both Mummy and Father gone. He often wondered what sort of a show the pair of them had managed to get into Up There. Stupid to think like that, but there it was. If there was anything in it, of course. Theology and that sort of thing had always been rather beyond him. He liked to think of there being some sort of Bourne and so forth for the real triers. They both had been all that, every scrap. Even his school fees had come off their table and their backs. He knew it too well. But—his father's voice again—damn it, the fellow's got to have it. We produced him, and he mustn't disgrace us. He can't go to Eton. Which infuriates me to intoxication. But if we can't, we can't. He'll have to pig it somewhere else. Poor wretch.

The breeze cut between the knees and navel and around the neck as he remembered it had on the first and last time they stood there. A starched collar gave the breeze plenty of play almost to the point of producing a piped note. But—Father again—I simply will not wear an overcoat. I don't care what the weather's like. I'd rather freeze. And as for those brutes and their damned mackintoshes, great God. Never have been thought of in my day. Sign of the times, I suppose. Mackintoshes. A fine name. Always reminds me of the moors. Grouse. You've never—well, there it is.

He had since, though. But going up as a guest was different from owning a shoot. Grandfather's had been among the largest. That thought rather saved the day. The feeling was much too much that of a poor relation. But he was used to it. He remembered poor old Fatty Mantell bursting out of a blind and running over to Geordie Kelsoe, almost purple in the face and tears streaming from his little blue eyes and screaming Damn you, you shot me. If you do it again, I'll bloody well shoot you. And of course he would. And poor Geordie standing there wondering whethere to be horribly rude or gustily apologetic or a little of both. A few years later and they were both under the same pile of stones in Tunisia, well shot by somebody else. Ironic, really.

But there it was.

The usual perfect summer weather almost occluded everything. Rainy skies drooped mist into the hollow, and a puddle or two shone here and there, almost a balance for the periodic golden gleam of horseflesh turning in the paddock. He preferred this height, to look down and see what might have been the scene, if not of annual triumph, then at least of a day to be wished for, as it were, with a horse carrying the Gleave colours (Sangue de Boeuf, gold hoops, blue cap), and a possibility of leading him in from the winning post with the congratulations and all the cheering and that sort of thing. Great days. He quite understood how his father had felt. It was different to be holding a winner's bridle and nodding at other people's cheers and smiles, rather than watching others playing the winning owner and having to do some of the smiling and cheering oneself. He knew those smiles of lips and teeth, and stretched nostrils and eyes almost unseeing with the slyest kind of envy, and the sort of comment made at the bar afterwards. By the wits. The moneyless wits, naturally.

Money. If only one had some money—Father again, as long as he could remember—God, the things one misses without money. And it was so utterly true.

The smoke from a gypsy's stove reminded him of the damned boiler at home. His fingernails were still a little black under the cuticle through messing about with it. Of all the mornings to go wrong. But the children had to be bathed, things had to be washed, and poor Vinny had her hands full, especially since it was the maid's day off. Still, things were doubtlessly going to get better, or as Vinny said, they might just as well stick their heads in an oven. Not that they would, but a point could be reached. One had to wrest one's mind away from that sort of thing. But there was solace in thought of death, sometimes. A Nirvana, a nothingness, no worries, simply an endlessly lightly-felt sleep.

The stand was filling with the top-hatted and their ladies, and the hangers-on. It amused him to see the number of raincoats—rarely called mackintoshes now, and he wondered why—and all the raised umbrellas. A gay venture into the mud, meek processions to the pari-mutual, jostling mobs in a fine aroma of casks and damp clothing at the bar, bookings of tables and glimpsings of menus—same old thing—he could sniff the oxtail and the more aseptic salmon mayonnaise and strawberries and cream from there—all signified that the Derby Day ritual had begun, and it would carry on to the last torn ticket, he supposed, but without him.

Merely stroll among them, but never dream of mixing—dear Father!—because if you haven't got it, you haven't got it, and there's an end to it. Don't be a try-to-be. Remember that except for your grandfather's mistakes—I can be charitable now—you'd be down there as son of one of the wealthiest men in the country—myself— and we'd probably have the winner in a stall at this precise moment. Always be the genuine article you are. Hamish Tyrwhitt Gleave is superior to the general and equal to the particular as far as lineage goes. We aren't titled, well and good. That was the Prince Charles Stuart debacle. Losing side's always unfortunate. But your grandfather would certainly have risen to an Earldom if he hadn't been Creation's most egregious ass. You'd have been down there now as Viscount—I suppose we'd have taken the name of our Scottish place Balteith—and I, the Earl of Glentallon, after the shipping line. To think of all our ships being sold like that. And everything else. God, really, life's been the most appalling farce. Why I haven't gone insane I shall never know.

He remembered his father's face, whitish and lined and inclined to shine in the summer day's heat of 1924—or '23?—and drips on his Adam's apple making a blotch on his collar, and a runnel shining from the pouch under his right eye trickling through his *Kaiser-Schnautte* moustache, grey, cut rather short, but unmistakeably Germanic. As if I cared what that cringing mob down there thinks. I'm one of the people they should have listened to. We never should have fought them. Never. We should have been together. England and Germany. That's the team. Unbeatable. What we haven't got, they have. And vice versa. We could have ruled the world. As it is, look at us. Those damned people across the water puling about the money they're supposed to have lent us. As if we hadn't paid in blood. First-class blood, too. Rather different from that rabble over there. It makes me frantic to think what we've missed. This country and Germany, think of it. Do you suppose those filthy Bolsheviks would have dared raise their heads? And think of the money coming in from those Lena shares year after year. It's robbed us of a great deal. But then, it's a mere drop in the bucket.

There was something gratifying about the rotten weather, because Vinny would feel rather better about things. She might have managed to come had she known. But he found he could take the day off only the afternoon before, which gave her no time to find someone to take care of the children, much less get herself something to wear. And as she said, what was the use of dragging all the way down there to meet people looking like a fin-de-siècle ragbag, when just a few minutes in one of those little shops off Bond Street would do the trick. He was glad she had stayed at home. The business of hiring finery went absolutely against his principles. For God's sake wear your own clothes even if they're falling off you, his father had so often said. Your mother looks simply awful, but at least her clothes are her own, bought and paid for. Only cads would dream of hiring a garment and appearing in public pretending to be something they never were or could be. Never try-to-be, Hamish. Do promise me that. Don't put yourself among a collection of prize-fighters and actors and that sort of person. They're merely hirelings, first and last.

Father had been harsh, but he was certain there was a great deal of truth in it. And, indeed, pretty well all he had seen since that time made it only too evident. Vinny was inclined to disagree. Make the best of it, and take what you can was her motto, and she never had the slightest compunction about wearing a dress and stole hired for the evening. He hated it, and always felt as if the tickets were showing. Still, and as she said, it always seemed to wash, but from his point of view that was mere commentary on the state of society.

Rain started, and it was getting rather chilly. He wondered if he could stroll down as far as the grandstand without getting soaked, instead of raising his umbrella and so ruining a perfect furl. Remember, Hamish, a number of little things mark a cad, and they're quite infallible. A cigarette stuck in the mouth, talked through and breathed through whatever the occasion, the use of the diminutive in place of Christian names, the pernicious sowing of Old Boy or Dear Boy or Old Chap in conversation, and the misuse of the umbrella. They always go, if you'll notice, with a bad shirt and footwear in disrepair. And I call any shirt bought from a pile a bad shirt. And footwear bought from the box begins and ends in disrepair.

It meant, then, strolling down in the rain.

A black-moustached gypsy with rings in his ears and sideburns bushing out of a cap sidled up holding out a sodden envelope. One hand held his jacket together at the neck, and he crouched, hoping perhaps that a note of misery might help him.

"Here y'are sir. Give us half a dollar for two winners 'stead of half a bar,"—zinc-filled teeth in a sizing grin—"Two nice 'uns here. Certs. I can see you're a toff."

"I'm not betting, thanks."

"Not on the Derby?"

"Not even on that."

"Listen, half a dollar. Be a toff. I got four young over there."

"Go away."

"Half a dollar won't hurt you. We'd get a stew out of it. Look at the day. We can't work. Half a dollar, guvnor. Go on, tip it out. Listen, four full bellies——"

"Would you please go away?"

"There's blokes down there, they look like toffs but they ain't. You can tell 'em a mile off. They puts 'em on of a mornin' and sends 'em back at night. They're snots, not toffs. You ain't one o' them, guv. Listen, make it two bob. Four of 'em. Ain't even got a fire. The wife'd say it over peat for you."

"Say it over what?"

"Over peat. Never heard of it, did you? We got the Rom ways, guvnor. Wife'll make a ring o' sugar on the peat and say the words while it's a-burnin'."

"There's no peat here."

"Turf does it. We don't live the wild 'un for nothink. Tell us the names o' y' young."

"How do you know I have any?"

"She see you comin' up. She says 'Tap him. He's a toff. But he's wide.'"

"Wide?"

"Got some nous. She knew, didn't she? She knew what you was. What's their names?"

"Robert and Hamish."

"Ah, Robert 'n' Aym-ish, eh? I'll remember. Couple o' bob does it."

That impulsion to help—that idiot feeling—an urge of noblesse oblige, perhaps—brought his fingers to separate a pound note. He held it out, looking away, hating the man's avidity and the muddy sacking tied about his feet.

"Here. And good luck."

"Oo, Jesus, the blessed Christ, a bar!"—open-mouthed, glaring, slavering—"I knew you was a bloody toff minute I set eyes on you. Keep us a week. She'll say it for you, guv. Robert 'n' Aym-ish. Dark blessin's on all o' yourn. And here, shove a bar on these two."

"Sell it to somebody else."

"No more today. Couple o' cozzers on me tobey."

"What's that?"

"Coppers. Blue 'uns. Up an' down here's me tobey. Where I work. Have a good day, guv. Don't forget. She'll say it for 'em."

He saw the name of one of the horses printed in mauve ink, Cylot, before the man folded the paper and jerked his cap-peak and slopped away.

Disgusting business, it had always seemed, begging. Hopeless to try to run things while that type of creature spawned. And four more to batten on the future. Poverty's own seed. Although, on a fine day Epsom took a lot of colour from the gypsies and their caravans. There seemed fewer, or perhaps memory was faulty or the police might have been busier. There again, Conscription could have had something to do with thinning them out or clearing them off. A couple of years solid discipline in one of the Services was just the thing for the shiftless. Not that he was at all sure that it was a good thing for everybody. He was grateful in many ways that he had managed to keep out. His was, indeed, as contra-oligarchic an outlook as any, but he certainly thought that too much mixing-up did no good whatever, and he was quite certain not merely that Jack was decidedly not as good as his Master, but that Jack had a proper place and should if necessary be made to stay there.

In fact, had that rule been followed all along, most of the trouble in London could never have occurred, and life would be, not easy of course, because one never expected ease in the affairs of Government, but at all events a more felicitous business, and by the compass of a firmament of planets far more efficient.

He preferred not to think about London. It was a day of memory, sacred in many ways, and he wanted nothing to impair his enjoyment.

In my day, one merely drove in and went to
one's box— poor Father—but now there was a business of getting
tickets, and of having to show them to people and so forth. He had
no desire to join the crush in the stands, or in any shape or form to
join anybody. All he wanted to do, and what he intended to do, was
to stroll about with the spirit of his father and his grandfather, and
look at what might have been a setting for a great day in every year
of his life.

Inside the enclosure was drab enough, in all conscience, although
a coat of paint here and there had brightened things, and the crowd
appeared cheerfully inclined, even if the day was a brute. Still, he
felt that had he been there in his proper station he might not have
noticed drabness. There would have been so much more to think
about, and do.

But there it was.

Peter Harrack came across—he would—and buttonholed him
in the Harrack manner. He wore a rather bewildered-looking morning coat that seemed to have little idea where to fit and a black
waistcoat trimmed with gold fleur-de-lys for some reason or other,
and a cricket-shirt-collar—as Father would have called it—and
a rather terrifying cravat, badly tied, naturally, and a pearl of sorts.
It was a moral certainty that his umbrella had any number of
tassels.

"Hamish, how very good to see you. Got anything exciting for the
sharks?"

"You know me much better. Racing's never been my forte."

"Pity. I thought you'd be bursting with information. Spot like
yours."

"Not the slightest interest. I'm merely taking the day off."

"Oh. Well, look here, if you'd like to win a little—children's shoes et cetera—that French horse, Flambeau——"

"I was told Cylot's got a chance."

"I thought if I tried hard enough——"

"Not at all. Just a tip."

"But isn't Toddy Berrish somewhere near you? That's his horse. He's got another running. But of course you knew."

"It's a week since we spoke. I thought he was in Paris."

"Flew his own plane over. Quite a number of Embassy people here, naturally. Vinny well?"

"Glowing, thanks. And your mother?"

"Oh, first-class. Going to the Grosvenor on Wednesday?"

"Probably."

"May see you there."

Long face, long hair, and sloppy underlip, patronizing idiot. Children's shoes, good God. People thought of the most ridiculous things to say. Trouble was, they rarely had enough to think about. Harrick was something, though not by any means too much, in the City. His mother's money got him the berth, and a good marriage made the salary something of a bursary. Talk had it that he and Beryl were living apart. But that was their business, and since it could have been something of an embarrassment, there seemed really no necessity to mention her. As it turned out, that must have been the form. Vinny had rather taken to her during the Bridge and Cocktail era at The Hague. It lasted until he put his foot down. Beryl could afford that sort of thing. Vinny could not—at any rate, as his wife—and at that time he had been a little sick of her mother's constant interference in the matter of cheques. Against maternal insistence that Vinny was entitled to any help at all times, he set the realities of her position as the wife of a diplomatist with, he thought then, a very fair chance of an important career. She simply could not be seen drinking and playing cards all over the place with all sorts of people. It was not merely improper, but extremely dangerous. Conversation was listened to and noted. Conduct was reported at higher levels of the Service. A bad wife was never an asset at any time, but in his line of country she could be utter ruination. Vinny was much too sensible not to see it, and Beryl had gone by the board. After that, there was Rome, and then Manila, and then Hamish came along. Bridge and Cocktails were a thing of the past. Of course, there were small parties now and again but he was extremely particular about their guests, always. It had been rather amusing to find that an invitation to a Gleave party was regarded as something of a cachet.

That, he knew without having to be told, was why the Peter Harracks were inclined to buttonhole, always deferentially, though with that gayish attempt at awkward familiarity which he resented more for their sakes, poor things, since it made conversation so difficult.

Others were walking on the grass but he preferred the pathway because somebody had to clean his shoes and the maid might be a little late, so the somebody would be himself. And he hated like the devil having to clean shoes. And that was another strange thing. Shoeblacks seemed to have disappeared. The few he had seen were not so much shoeblacks as beggars by default of any desire to clean, much less polish leather. But a dearth of shoeblacks illustrated the plight of all the bechristianed. Everybody had to wear a collar and tie to fit along the dotted lines of a patterned respectability, work in places where hourly wages came in a weekly envelope, and own a car to give them a feeling of being able to get away from it all.

He saw the Calton-Islip party before they saw him and turned away. George Calton-Islip had a great deal of money, a number of directorships, a horsey-theatrey wife, his third, and a certainty that one way or another he could get anything he wanted. That, said in a loud voice, had come over the desk a few times in the Intelligence summaries. Everybody knew he was prepared to pay for a knighthood so that his wife could register, at long last, as a lady. The Party treasurer was known to have him down as a fat touch for the next Election, and the whisper was out to try to put up with him. But he also had a habit of throwing entertainment at those he thought were In The Know, and because he had a lot of oil and shipping interests, officers of the Foreign Service were always certain of invitations to cocktail parties, that went on to dinner and a night club, and free theatre tickets sprayed from the secretary's office of his tulle-and-bathroomy wife, clipped with a message to enjoy yourselves, dears, we know you will, yrs, Ivy and G.

Kind of them, really. But they could be and often were a pest for many reasons. Invitations begat favours. Favours led to liberties. George Calton—the Islip was added by marriage to musical comedy —was not the sort of person to be friendly with. He used names in a loud voice, anywhere.

In turning, he almost knocked over Sir Mathew Kyle, his father's friend and godfather by proxy to himself.

"Hamish! You're absolutely the image of your father. What a shock!"

"Highly complimentary. I shall treasure that."

"No, no. I mean it. You're an older edition of your father as I remember him. We always remember people at their best or worst. I remember him best when things were well with him. Last year at Eton. He went to Cambridge. Mistake, some of us thought. Where's Vinny?"

"At home, mending socks."

"Poor darling. Not much in it for any of us these days, is there? I really don't know what you Whitehall fellows think you're doing."

Slight irritation replacing pleasure that even Sir Mathew, most kind, and at one time extremely able, could blame Civil Servants for the outcome of politics. It must have been three or four years since they last met. He looked far from well, a little humped, pinched in the cheeks, and his moustache seemed to have lost touch with the curling iron and sprouted instead of bristling. His top hat had been brushed over with talcum and frays hung out of his collar, and his morning coat was wrinkled and the cravat overlapped a waistcoat that was simply not clean. It was evident he no longer employed a man. Neither was he very particular. And in his eyes, faded hazel, a little yellowy and raw-rimmed, there was instant bright light as if he knew what was being thought, and then a smile of greyish, chewed-down teeth. After all he had not colonelled and brigadiered for nothing. He knew the inspective look too well.

"Thought I'd come down for a last fling. Can't afford it. Can't afford anything. Pensions don't go very far, I'm afraid. Nothing to stop M.P.'s voting to raise their own salaries, naturally. Those of us who served the Country for a lifetime, well, I mean, what are we except graveyard litter? I was at the House the other day. I listened to them. Never heard anything like it."

Rarely had he thought of Sir Mathew as an old man. Yet he must have been on toward seventy-five. There had always been that memory of Colonel Sir Mathew in Mess Dress, and rows of miniature medals and a jungle of spurs and the Hullo, there, young fellow! Ursula, do look at the way this chap's shot up!—all the way back before he left school, the night he overheard Lady Kyle tell his mother she had just parted with her diamonds and it felt exactly like tearing out her fingernails, and his father saying after they had gone that he thanked God he had never had the money to buy diamonds his wife would have to sell to maintain their position.

All, and the smell of jasmine coming in the window, and candles shining on silverware, and his mother pushing a pin in the hair on top of her head, and nodding, lived over, in grey light and a rain-wind, with a smell of mud in trodden grass, and horse sweat, and a gauzy drift of perfume from a hat dainty with marguerites, and a hand holding it delicate and tender, rarer than white enamel, roseate.

"They're not very bright, I'm afraid."

"They must have some brains somewhere, or they wouldn't get in, I suppose. But listening to them, I confess I doubted it. We're in a most awful state, you know."

"The Cabinet doesn't appear to think so."

"I know most of them by their Christian names. I doubt if it's possible to find in the entire length and breadth of the country a more tedious set of pifflers. How they ever got there keeps me awake at night——"

"They seem to do fairly well in local Elections——"

"But Hamish, you've forgotten who puts them in. Coming down this morning, I looked rather hard at all of them. My eyes are not what they were, but I saw enough. Truly. It's not our country any more. It really isn't. Even the Fighting Services are only part-time American condottieri. Those of us who once served His Majesty are now objects of American charity, so we're told."

"I think you're being a little hard——"

"Read the papers. Any move anywhere will upset the balance of something or other, and the deficit will have to be borne by the American taxpayer. He's as tired of it as I am. And what's to be done? Die as quickly as possible, and gratefully. One burden the less, what?"

"I wish I'd brought Vinny. She'd have chased you out of this."

"I don't doubt it. You were tremendously fortunate. As I——"

Startling, but the old face seemed to be losing its age, and the eyes shone as a boy's looking over an orchard wall. Memory came of Lady Kyle's black braids twisted with ribbands, and a contralto voice just the tiniest bit under one or two notes on the piano—I know perfectly well I'm singing flat. I can hear myself. I always say, now come along, old girl. Just a little bit up. No, no, no! Up, you ghastly creature! And his mother saying Oh, but my dear, you should hear me. In any case the piano's done nothing but breed mice ever since we had it. I don't think the people ever got their money for it, either. It was one of our rather dreary periods.—Strange, he remembered his mother best in relation to her friends. Sir Mathew turned away rather suddenly. Age was back, and the hump stretched the seam in his coat. His face was calm, too calm, and there was no smile.

"Had a wonderful life, really, I suppose. Mustn't complain. Rather too much on my own, that's all. I trot down there every week. Keep the grass in order, that sort of thing. I was rather lucky to get it. Overlooks the Thames. We've boated past there for years. Never dream of it at those times. Still, be there myself soon. Incredible to think her gone. Incredible."

The voice was Sir Mathew's, clear, a little friable, and the face was his, slightly crinkled under the eyelids. Yet he gave a curious feeling of being elsewhere. Even the solid body held sense of phantom.

"I think we ought to have what Father always called a philosophical drink, don't you?"

"No thank you, Hamish. Much as I'd love to. I'm strictly TT. Not because I don't like it. I can't afford it, that's all. The grave's got to be paid for, and I'm having quite a bit of trouble with the cottage. I do all the work myself, of course. God knows where the money goes. But it does. I'd like some of those fellows in the House to share my life for a few days. Only another fifty a year'd do it. A silly little pound a week more, think of it. After forty-seven years' service. And years of debt, of course. I seem to be talking the most awful rot, don't I? Hope I'm not getting senile."

"Hardly that. But I don't know how I'm to tell Vinny I let you off a happy little drink——"

"She'll understand perfectly. Do give her my love. And the sons. I often wish Colin had lived. He'd have been a little older than you. The Somme attended to that. I'd love to go over and see him before I pop off. They keep those cemeteries rather well, don't they?"

"There'd be trouble if they didn't."

"Mm. Well. Just as well he went, I suppose. 'Blow out, ye bugles,' what? I must say I don't envy any of you young fellows today. It's not the life I'd want. Why, some fellows are actually letting the public into their places, and taking shillings at the door. Amateur tavern-keepers. Never heard of such a thing. Look here, I'm talking my head off."

"Not at all. Why not adjourn for the drink?"

"No. I'm going to watch this race, and then I'm off home. It'll take me a couple of hours to get back. This may sound rather tiresome. But have you by any chance a standard of some sort in your garden?"

"A number of quite good ones, I'm told. I don't take much interest. I like them on the table, though. Vinny, of course, can't be kept from her gloves and trowel."

"Green thumb. Just like Ursula. What a marvel she was with a garden. I wish—asking a great deal, I know—I'd be most grateful for a cutting or two. I'd like to get the grave looking rather better than it is. I'd love to see a few standards blooming. She adored them."

"They'll go off to you before the weekend."

"Very kind of you. Really. Seems right, somehow. The son of our friends—what's the thing she always sang? 'Beautiful garden of roses.' Yes, that's it. Poor darling."

The crinkles under the eyelids were deeper and the eyes brightened perhaps with cold. Fortunately, the crowd shouted They're Off and it was simple to pretend some interest along the course. But Sir

Mathew turned about, and put his umbrella on his shoulder sabre-fashion, and smiled.

"Goodbye, Hamish. Got a shilling on this one. Must see it run. Love to Vinny. Take care."

He raised his hat. Sir Mathew lifted a finger to the brim of his—exactly like Father!—and high-cockalorumed off. He turned and walked the other way. He had no wish to see the jaunt petering out to the frail shamble he knew must come. There seemed, in thinking of Sir Mathew and all his once-redoubtable corps and their women, an ugly quirk of injustice, after so much lived through, and fought for, always selflessly in the main, that so little should be got for reward, with nobody to appeal to, and not much hope of redress anywhere. Even the powder sprinkled over the top hat to revive its condition had an echo of We Are The Lads Of The Old Brigade, the frontier guardians, sashed and medalled and mentioned in many a dispatch, and we scrape without saving, but we keep our mouths shut or something might be said about Bad Form, and appearance, after all, is our first duty.

But promise of duty toward a system which accepted so much as its right, and gave such a miserly little, could only come from the brainless, the helpless, the impelled, a new type of proletariat, willing to give its children into slavery of a peculiarly selfless order, and asking for nothing except to live, to serve, and to die. The loyal, the good, the trusting were everywhere, strongest pillars of authority that used them, depended upon them and when strength was gone, gave them leisure to pick the carcass of kinder years, and just enough to keep alive but not enough to live on.

A great deal of shouting, and a movement of the mob brought his mind back to the course. Cylot, he saw by the board, was first in a minor race. The pound the gypsy had told him to bet would have won eight in return, and Vinny would have been hugging herself to think the coal was paid for.

But there it was.

But here, damnation, came George Calton-Islip, and his wife Ivy, sinuous architect of the hyphenation, with their guests, as conscientiously wine-worn as one might expect.

"Da-a-a-wling!"—Ivy, hands out, mouth open—"Haven't seen you for ay-jez! Whea-ah hev you be-e-en?"

"Rather busy——"

"No use being busy all the time, chum."—George, through cigar smoke—"Now listen. We had a lovely party last night, didn't we, Iv'? You must have got the card. I happened to mention to your boss I'd been after some info about this Venezuela job. You know what I'm talking about, don't you? I'm not letting them Yanks get away with it. I told him straight. Listen. We can't talk here. Join us after, will you? We'll have a bite somewhere. Dorchister, probly."

"Sorry, I've promised. My wife's waiting for me."

"Listen. We'll phoner. We'll get a car out there and picker up."

"You've forgotten two hale and hearty Gleaves. She'd never find anybody to look after them."

"Gerraway. Listen. Ivy'll send one of the servants out there. Where's it near? Singapore?"

"Beaconsfield. Quite a long way. Sorry. Some other night——"

"Any naight, da-a-wling. You know how imp-o-ortant Georgie thinks this new thing is. Ca' get him to bed. Ooh ai say! Whattuv ai said?"

"Listen, Gleave"—forefinger dabbing his shoulder—"I'll get in touch in the morning. I don't want no playing about. They're not doing us out of more than I can help. I said to your boss, I'll fight this by meself, if necessary. But I'd like some help. You know what I'm talking about, don't you?"

"I have an idea."

"We can't wait for you people to make up your minds, you know. Business is a differnt story."

"Undoubtedly you're right. We're sometimes very thankful——"

"I bet. Some of your blokes are too light. Very light. No weight on the turns. Know what I mean?"

George Calton-Islip's reddish face cushioned a slightly veined and sherryish nose, and his eyes were full of a blue gutter-imp. He mouthed all he said around a cigar, and his tone meant that the crew with him should hear it, and afterwards, doubtless, he would tell them what a lot of squirts the people at the Foreign Office were, and how they all jumped when he cracked the whip, all the way down from the Secretary of State. That, too, had appeared in the Intelligence reports. And it had to be suffered. Mr. Calton-Islip seemed to think that any sort of insult was to be endured if it were slyly gutter-grinned and spoken with what he called a sensa yewmer.

"We're all inclined to be a little careful on the turns. We often have some very curious people to deal with. By all means get in touch in the morning. I don't doubt somebody'll be able to help you."

"You don't doubt, eh? Listen, Gleave. I know a couple of editors'd go mad over this. They'd have men out there in two ticks. What, d'you want a few questions in Parliament, do you? I can get 'em in there, you know. All I want's some help. National importance. I'll see I get it. Clear?"

"Quite."

"Quite. That does it. Come on, Iv'. He's lost a bit of dough and he's in a temper with everything. Stamp his foot in a minute. All jokes on one side, though. I'll get through to you tomorrow. So long, Gleave. You got my lighter, dear?"

So goes the little Gleavish world. Whether or not he wanted very badly to punch the man's nose was beside the point. The point was that Calton and his kind were in control of most things that mattered. The others in control worked rather differently and perhaps with better-schooled variants of English, but with the same sort of do-as-I-say, and dare no argument. Many a Senior Officer used the technique at conferences and screamed at any questioning of directives. Which told rather dismally that they were unsure of themselves, and they hoped that bloodshot rage might disguise it. If it also frightened off the opposition, so much the better. It nearly always did. A mixture of gold lace and screams often got things done, right or wrong mattered nothing. Calton was the supra-gold-laced-archscreamer. He could out-scream anybody, easily, and in fluent Billingsgate, and did, quite often, even, it was said, on the Cabinet level.

Sense of shock came in thinking of him, and then of Sir Mathew. Even if Sir Mathew had done his share of screaming, and he most certainly had, it had been a vastly different world to scream in, and an enormously different sort of scream. For a number of reasons among ten thousand, and it was not certain which combination was correct, Sir Mathew's world had gone and Calton's had come in its place. The question, thought about and weighed for some time, was not whether Calton's was worth serving, but whether there was not a far greater duty to destroy it.

He looked up at the boxes filled with male and female grins, flowered hats, top hats and binoculared faces, and at the seethe on the terrace. He thought of Hamish's and Robert's being led here in about fifteen years' time, trying to imagine what they would look like, how they might be dressed. He was touched to the quick at thought of those little chaps growing up. But this was not the sort of thing he wanted to show them, not the sort of life, not the sort of manner. It was foreign. Alien. Un-British. And if that were the answer, then it was useless to boggle. Obviously there had to be destruction as complete as that which Sir Mathew's world had suffered. All we want's another silly little pound a week.

He walked through the crowd to a gentlemen's lavatory before going into the bar for a philosophical drink. He tried not to walk in the wettish pathway, wondering why men usually careful at least of outward appearances could be so careless in their personal habits. The endward drip always seemed to go on the floor to be stepped in. He went to a bowl near the door, and spent a little time watching the more indeterminate among the enfranchised enter and look about, choosing with the care of treaty-makers the one chalice above all others to be honoured with the contents of their bladders. Some of them took moments on end and went to this one, and that, and

after all chose another on the opposite side. And all of them, doubtless, had opinions about most things, and all of them had a right to
vote, to approve or disapprove, and in exactly the same vacillant and
morbid way. Which, for some, seemed to give the world a great
deal of its charm.

A philosophical drink his father had always called the odd glass.
Sit down and ruminate at will and at ease. But never rub elbows.
Leave that sort of thing to others. The average dive, the ordinary
pub, the bar, per se, are not the sort of places to be found in. If you
must have a drink, then go somewhere that supplies a table and a
chair. Sit to your drink as a gentleman should. You'll find many to
disagree with you on that, and also upon the meaning of the term.
Take no notice. Pretension must always argue to sustain itself. The
truth requires no emphasis. Suspect the people inclined to be argu-
mentative. They live in a perpetual nebula of embarrassment. Have
your philosophical drink and think over your misdeeds in comfort.
And for God's sake order something drinkable. Never let me see you
drinking beer.

He ordered a half of a vintage he happened to know was fair,
wishing Vinny were there to share a bottle. A bottle he thought a
little too much for early afternoon, and the weather howled for hot
whisky in any case. But Father had always said he detested any interference with decently constituted spirits, and if hot water must be
displaced, then by all means let it jeopardize some such concoction
as a punch, or other coddle.

A mirror gave him a glimpse of himself in a stroll to the buffet. It
was gratifying to see that Grombie had caught him about right with
the scissors, which was just as well considering his prices. The morning coat had a good line and the right amount of devil for the waistcoat, that sat as it should without too much of anything, and the
trouser hung, and broke, in exactly the right way. Very satisfactory,
all in all. Nobody would notice he was wearing a dress shirt. He
needed linen rather badly, in fact. But, as Vinny was in the habit
of saying, every penny counts, especially with two children. On such
a day as this, though, there were excuses, although he was damned
if he would justify the pound note given to the gypsy. Arrant stu-
pidity in anyone else, of course, but if the fellow had four children

that was excuse enough. He had a very uncomfortable feeling that Vinny would have thought, and certainly would have said, a great deal more. But without any mention of a pound note.

Grey had not yet touched his fair hair, though why he had no idea. He had put up with more and worried more than many another older than he, but only Vinny could find the grey ones and crow. She had quite a number and never seemed to worry at all. His eyes were clear enough, a little too watchful, he feared, and far too prone to say what he had rather not put into words. But the famous stone-grey eye of his mother's line had passed to him and also to Hamish, though not, unfortunately, to Robert. (He had something between Vinny's gold-brown velvet and old tawny port. Very good to see in the sunshine.) Not many lines or creases, though there was that pull at the mouth. Disappointment rather than anything else, perhaps. London, again. He refused to think of it. All in all, nothing to shout about, no film star, of course, and from all he had seen of them, he was extremely grateful.

He chose a couple of sandwiches from the pâté tray, and went back to his table. The champagne was very good indeed, exactly what he wanted. Despite the dress shirt and a darn in the toe of one sock, he felt almost as he should. There was no vehicle in the enclosure to take him home, and his colours were not on the card, but one had to be satisfied with the best one could do. This was it, and thank heaven it was no worse.

A lonely day, some might have said, but he thought differently. A fellow had to get away from everything now and again to look on and think for himself. It had a salutary effect. He quite saw Father's point. There was something to be said for being part of a crowd and yet not of it. One saw so very much more. Critical faculties that only germinated at other times came to life and gave answers that the normal mind never dreamed of, and to put it mildly, received with something of a shock. People, for example.

A very odd crew seemed to have found their way in. All the men wore the enclosure uniform in endless varieties from the greenish-brown-about-the-shoulders heirloom to skimpy, too-much-roll-in-the-lapel and far-too-long-in-the-tails hired coatings, and untold ranges of striped circus-horse fore-and-aft trousers. Most of the cravats were ready made. Those that were not had an almost electric lilt. But nothing told quite such a tale as the tophats. They reared, straight-up or tilted bastions of the secondhand universe, and the faces under them stared out across a Promised Land, the one they could all attain with the price of a ticket to come in, rental for the uniform, and return fare with or without pocket money.

For the most part the women looked far too good for the sort of men they were with. Yet a closer watch gave them fewer points. Discounting lines, good legs, and the dressmakers' whims, most seemed taken by a studied vacuity, as if they were asking themselves how they appeared to others, and if this were the Good Time everybody had told them about, and what prayers should be said to pick a winner. Many—the obvious governess-kickers of yore—looked bad-tempered. Others, rather more expensively dressed, did their best to look bored, perhaps hoping to confer upon themselves some aspect of untouchability if only to escape the ruck.

The First World War, Father always said, altered form by depleting the stud, besides spendthrifting money and property until Society was little more than a convenient label for a fashionably-schooled and therefore well-accented debris. Some families still had a male line and their property. They were the fortunate. Others had names but no money to hold their property. Others had no name and a great deal of money and property through profits of war or merchandising. In a couple of generations they could be either landed gentry or back in the suburbs. Society as the Victorian conceived it no longer existed. There were cliques, no more. The lower the clique, the more self-important the members, and the higher, the more desperate the effort to keep others out. Always excepting those with the millions in any currency however earned, and whoever, whatever they might be.

And after a second World War—which Father would never under any circumstances have believed possible—here, animated if not noisy, was the product, a majority triumph for the Great Lord Copycat. His sibling, the Knuckly Ape, that curious part of the human mentality which impels its victims to do everything that others do from fear of missing something, was rather more on display than the horseflesh.

And that was part of what Father had meant.

See them once a year and make up your mind what things are coming to. Do it just as you might take yourself to the zoo. Then go home and think. My time has been taken up much too much with your grandfather's affairs. Fortunately you will never know that sort of worry. You have a clear road, so all you have to do is to think your way forward and make the right decisions. For God's sake be right. Take informed opinion, ask advice, enquire, read everything and give yourself time to digest it. Read all you can of British history, especially that written by Continentals. They have the more astringent viewpoint. Ours are mostly bootlickers and fakers. There are certainly many lessons to be learned and followed. Remember that British statesmen have made a reputation by doing the unexpected successfully. But they never made the mistake of doing unexpected things as juniors. Remember that, Hamish. Stifle your feelings and say nothing, do nothing, unless you are told. Statecraft and politics is nervy business, even worse than the Stock Exchange. A word will ruin you. Bad company will ruin you. A woman will ruin you quicker than any word or anybody. Above all, for God's sake, be careful of women.

He wondered what Father might have thought about Myril. Even thinking of her made his scalp tingle. He wanted to go to her then and there. But his promise was to absorb enough of Epsom to last for a year, and he stood by his promise. He could see her on the way home. Salivation before the meal, perhaps. And that, and everything it meant, was dangerous.

But danger was an extra condiment.

It was hard luck on Vinny. Worse than that, it was nothing short of brutal. But there was nothing, really nothing he could do. All the will power in the world did nothing against the shy mouth and breasts like blunted pears and thighs that poured the juices of seven goddesses and clipped him in the grasp of all the furies.

Hopeless in a gilt-edged sort of way.

And quite by accident. Or, at any rate, he was hopefully certain it was so.

Every movement, every word with

her he sifted afterwards, trying to find any trifle that might be suspicious. There had never been the slightest hint or stress or breath.
She was what she said she was, a saleswoman, one of three, at Chotouille Ltd., makers of women's sports clothes. Meeting her had been
as natural as smelling a rose. It was one of those oyster and champagne parties—(last kick of a dying mule, James Wittard had called
it, and Charles Roff had said it was outward sign that all was as it
should be)—with not very good oysters and execrable champagne,
at the staff party. Nothing at all suspicious about it. Everybody was
there with their guests. She sat in a corner by the piano, leaning back
in the shadow. Only her legs showed in the light, and one shoe was
half-off the foot beating time. She had eaten only one oyster. Her
glass was minus a sip, perhaps. That seemed to establish a palate, if
not sensibility. He saw the movement of her eyes in shadow. She was
about halfway good-looking, dark, with a pencil-line of moustache on
her upper lip. Her mouth was thin, nervous in itself, though when
she pouted there was fullness enough, and her teeth were irregular
but white. Her eyes were full in the lids, smallish until she opened
them wide in surprise or rarely in laughter, clear grey, almost always
in a dream, sombre, perhaps shaded by a smile of regret, or even by a
gibe at herself. She often laughed at herself and her dreams. Her
pretensions, she called them. She had an Oriental habit of thought
in that she was amused by things, rarely by people. The comic in
life she loved. The witticism passed her by. Her white Russian
father had been a physician at Port Arthur. They had escaped to Peiping, but the Chinese revolution sent the family to one town after
another. Myril had been taken all over the Asian continent, to India,

and Egypt, and Europe. Rebellion came on her nineteenth birthday in flight to London, and a skirmish with starvation and bitter landladies because she had no money and no permit to work. But Lucia Chotouille came over from Paris and opened a shop, and that solved all problems. Myril Gislan became director, saleswoman, accountant, window dresser, and model when necessary, and an allowance instead of a wage bypassed the work permit and made her a fairly happy human being. As happy, at any rate, as her nature allowed. The dense cruelties of her childhood, of having to watch her parents die of typhoid without treatment, of being taken here and there by relief societies' matrons, of a month of school now and three months then, and different languages to learn, customs to unlearn and relearn, cast-off clothing to wear, scraps from the table to eat, and finally as a maid-of-all-work in a Paris boarding house while she finished school, all left their marks.

But how she had managed, after all that, to become as she was seemed to him to be something of a speechless miracle. If only by her example, he thought he saw hope for the human scheme whatever its vicissitudes. She had not grown to be bitter, or in any degree frustrated. She had no hatreds, few dislikes, but many contempts. Having suffered all the indignities, she loved the settled peace of London and wanted the world to be like it. Her idols were the bobbies. She made an excuse to talk to them if only to stand within the fatherly benediction of the law. But in herself she was hard as stone. Music had no effect, ballet was a specialist exercise, and the theatre was puppetry. Film, television and wireless were all propaganda, and worthless. Books she rarely read, for having learned eight languages, she said she spoiled all of them and wanted no reminder. She hated newspapers of any kind, and magazines were only coloured throwaways for advertisers. She admired Grand Opera for its discipline of the human voice, no more. Her favourites were *Carmen* and *Boris Goudonov* as opposite sketches of times gone by, without regret. Her hands were like a nurse's, bony, short-nailed without polish, and they rested. She had no gestures. She managed her tallness with grace. Although she had the longest of all legs she never looked leggy. Her ankles were like a little girl's, chubby, yet they seemed to add symmetry, and in a funny, childish sort of way they made appear half-grown what was not only full-grown but opulent. She had cut her hair to save money at the hairdresser's, and then found out she had to go there oftener or look as if she had just crawled through a hedge, so now she was letting it curl just below the ears, dark, chestnutty, soft.

He felt he should be ashamed of dreaming time away in thinking of Myril when there were any number of other things to think about much more important. Unfortunately, there was that tingling in the scalp, and moisture behind the eyes and, not least, the strict discomfort of the male want.

The crowd and its noise passed him by. He was no longer interested. Perhaps the champagne had a little to do with it. He felt confident that there could be no loss in leaving this sort of existence. The jabbering, giggling congeries with nothing better to do than watch horses whipped for their entertainment were not worth serving.

"Hamish. What luck to find you!"—Arthur Gregory Todderton, Lord Berrish, Toddy to everybody, short and plump and shiny, baldish at forty, with an opaque blue eye that always seemed to be saying Let Me See Now, Where Was I? and quite a jolly smile at times—"I called before I left Paris——"

"I thought you were still enjoying your holiday——"

"Called back last night. Awful rockets flying. Look here, let's find a quiet corner. This is a little too open. Never saw such a gang. It's really getting deplorable."

All to the good if somebody else could see it. Toddy had become one of the Party's fairest hopes, first for inheriting millions on the death of his father, secondly by being nobody's fool, and thirdly for choosing Diplomacy as a career which he worked at where others with half his advantages fiddled. He was the sort of fellow to chew the lower joint of his thumb very gently while people were speaking and while he was thinking, and the opaque eyes looked at spots on the table, and shifted, up, down, and over there, as if something interesting were going on in each place. If he missed a point, he asked for a repetition and questioned until he was sure. At home, he inclined to the more liberal wing of the Party chiefly because he resented any encroachment on what he talked about as liberty of the individual, though that, on examination, turned out to be his own. His coat of arms—he was third of his line—bore the motto Faith and Go Forward, and his only grief was that his title prevented him from fighting an election and winning a seat in the House of Commons.

"Here'll do."—turning into a quiet place by the telephone booths —"Look here, I'm really very worried. We all are"—looking about to see who might be there. Nobody, in a nice, orangey sort of light, telephone books hanging open on the stand, empty booths, rumble of voices a thousand miles away, and Toddy's eyes, surprisingly not opaque, but a rather horrid, glistening blue—"I've been here forty-five minutes, that's all. I'm leaving after the race. I don't even feel like seeing it. That's how miserable the thing is. I tried to get you before I left."

"What the devil's wrong?"

"You know James Wittard, don't you? As well as I do——"

Shock, in a bare whisper. To remember something James had said only a short time before, and then to have his name pushed at one.

"Yes, I do."

"I can't believe it, but he's suspected of tucking things under the Curtain."

"What?"

"Exactly. The misfortune is that a lot of it's come from us. From me. Straight from my desk. I almost fainted. Some of the stuff I saw came from you——"

"Can't be right!"

"Wait until you see the files. Bob Abbatt brought them over this morning. Mp opposite number at Uncle Sam's. Nice chap. Thank God I hadn't gone. I've never seen the Ambassador in such a state. He's usually rather turgid. He left stains all over the woodwork. It might mean our jobs."

"What was it? My stuff, I mean?"

"A report from the Embassy in Washington on the disposition of bombers."

"Too near the bone——"

"And a précis of a talk with the President about withdrawal of troops——"

"I'm going back to the office——"

"Not only that. There's that very achey thing about what Uncle Sam intends to do if France should change Governments in a particular manner. The airfield situation in Morocco, for example. It's one of yours——"

"I know. I'm trying to stanch the blood——"

Plainly in mind, now, James Wittard, of the black cowlick hanging over one eyebrow, and the hand-knitted ties and tweed jackets, extremely Magdalen voice and a slight stammer on *m*'s and *d*'s rather unsoaped aroma and nicotine stains under his nose and on the fingers of both hands and a desk forever nauseous with cigarette-tin lids full of ash and ends.

"A filthy spy—"—Toddy, looking away, wiping his hands and his forehead—"I'd very willingly shoot him myself. I'm quite prepared to. Bastard fling of a syphilitic whore."

"Agreed. But what did the Ambassador do?"

'Spoke to Number 10. Mr. Wittard, bless his despicably raddled soul, is now the darling of Intelligence. They've got a net around him. Trying to find the others. How in God's name does it happen?"

"Why did you want to see me?"

"The Ambassador tried to talk to you. About our survey on U. S. Personnel."

"Safe enough."

"That's what I said. But it's not. I went over and saw the attaché from the Federal Bureau of Investigation. Most affable. Made it more horrifying. He told me all about it. They picked up somebody going into Eastern Germany——"

"I'm feeling rather weak. Look here, I'm off——"

"Take my car. Tell the chauffeur he can go home after you've finished with him. Get you there much quicker than the train. I'm flying back to Paris. And the sack. Sorry if I've mucked your day. Even if I won the damn' Derby I couldn't care less. To think there are such people on earth, much less among the people one works with. Christ."

"I'll telephone tonight. Tell you who's in the wreckage, and what's happening."

"Awfully grateful if you would. I can feel my head dripping on a pole."

"We'll outstare each other across the gateway."

"Traitor's Gate, no doubt."

"It's got to be thought about, I suppose. But who'll blame us?"

"I can think of a lot of people. The Management, certainly. Our delightful barnyard exhibit of a Secretary of State. He isn't here, you'll have noticed?"

"It's an ill wind. He might have to resign."

"The Government might have to. I'm taking the weathery view. That's how I feel. Sorry."

"It might take a little time to call my wife. Would you be very kind and see she's told I've gone back?"

"I'll see that's done. Off you go. This the number? Right."

Right, yes, absolutely right. Even with that shaking of nerves down the inner flanks and in the calves, still a thought came clear of Myril. When all the talking was over and the decisions were made and the last piece of paper was initialled, then he could go to her. Even then, he had a sudden and arctically guilty feeling that Vinny would find him out.

He stretched on the leather cushions, as
the car's upholsterer had meant him to, on the way back. There was
a lot to his liking in the friendly, busy silence of the Rolls-Royce. It
spoke of the accomplishments of his grandfather's generation, and
of the ambitions of his father's. But what it said about his own was
silken commentary of dispassion. As well-bred adults speak in the
presence of the half-grown, he seemed to hear the voices of the
designer, the engineer and their patron intent upon producing a
monument to their time. What they said was not so much above his
head as what they had done was beyond his reach. He earned a fair
salary, and he could look forward to increments with the years, and
a pension at the end of his career. But there would never be enough
in the bank to buy a Rolls-Royce. The small car in the garage was
burden enough, barely paid for, and neither ornament nor monument. It was a tool. Father had once said that the Rolls-Royce was
product of three principals with one principle, that the prime of the
best is only just good enough. The makeshift do-without-it philosophy
in that day was still in its proper place in the confines of squalor. The
patron's wish was paramount, and there were plenty of working men
far readier to make the splendid than the trashy, if only out of self-
respect.

He had never been able to see anything much wrong about patrons.
Social apostles flatulating upon the indignities of patronage had
always made him sick. Onward-And-Upward-With-The-Arts-Of-Me
First posturists seemed to have forgotten the patron Church that
gave them a language, to start with. Churchy talk of heaven and
hell and all the do-goods and their damned baskets of groceries had
never had much appeal, and he had no wish to think of any after-life.

But certainly he respected the Church for its service to scholars and artists and for a system of thinking that created a desire for decent standards of conduct and conditions of living. A lot of theorists seemed to forget that without that fallowing, they and their notions could not have existed. They made the further mistake of appearing to believe that those conditions must always exist, at least in the Western half of the world. It never seemed to trouble them that a pseudo-sophist and sports-fuddled mankind might refuse Churchist thinking as it once had refused paganism, and for the same reason, that some other way promised them more than they had.

Marxism of any kind seemed merely to have twisted the original Christian teaching of Be Better, into Be Better Off. Its followers took advantage of wilted Christianism, and without puerile inhibitions, went about turning Thou Shalt Nots into Thou Art Nots, and forthwith ruled the roost.

Curious to think that James Wittard might be one of them. He had been in the Service for about fifteen years and got his last promotion from Delhi to London, which, from all he was given to saying, was very far from what he had wanted. His appearance caused a few jokes, but eccentricities were welcomed in Englishmen of the New School even as they had been in the Old, the more since he was heir to his brother's baronetcy. He often lectured on Indian affairs, religions and what-not, and articles of his had reached *The Times*, but an appearance or two on television had made him something of a Sunday Night Lion. How he could be persuaded into playing traitor was a little like wondering how a princess might be induced to skip with the Crown jewels. It was unthinkable except as questionable and extremely clammy farce. But for Toddy Berrish to threaten to shoot as a traitor one of a family which had borne arms since the fourteenth century was very far from anything to do with comedy. No question about it, there was something very difficult in trying to imagine how a Wittard could become a traitor.

Although, reviewing the past couple of hours, he began to wonder if there were not some smell of traitordom in what he had himself been thinking. The majority of the people he had seen and disparaged undoubtedly were loyal subjects and certainly taxpayers. His salary and pension would come partially from their pockets. Singly he supposed they were nice enough to know, always excepting strumae of the Calton-Islip order. Perhaps a contempt for that kind had boiled over on the crowd. But the crowd was part and parcel of the Calton-Islips, a moneyed segment of an alleged democracy, most of them lovers of the rag-to-riches-by-any-means school with never a thought in their minds that it became possible only by advantages made for them by a reduced, if not almost extinct order of men and women.

He realized he had thought the entire crowd not worth serving. If that were his conviction, then he was thinking traitorously, and if he were honest, he ought to resign. He had no doubt that Calton-Islip wanted to do something drastic about the oil business in Caracas. If he succeeded, there would be more headlines about British leadership and a great deal of type about a windfall of dollars to the Treasury, pithy editorials about initiative, and Calton-Islip's merit as flag-bearer.—(You got my lighter, dear?)—There would be nothing, of course, about the rain of coin into the Calton-Islip coffers. That was business, a triumph of private enterprise and Mr. Calton-Islip's own bouncing baby. That he was helped at all times by officers of the Crown, and that without that help he would arrive nowhere, would nowhere be mentioned. He paid super-tax. He had rights. There were dollars to be earned. That covered that.

He wondered why he should victimize Calton-Islip. There were tens of thousands of his kidney. The fellow was only a product of his day, but he stuck out for the moment, that was all. That gutter-imp grin, as if he thought himself treating with half-wits or glorified office boys was a little hard to bear. The sensa yewmer came wrapped in a bludgeon. Being rude to him by way of reply was rather like drooling on an armoured duck, one, moreover, that hosed from the sewer by return.

But it went against the grain to give that sort of laundered ruffian any help, or to make effort of any kind. He acknowledged elements of traitorship in that. A near-miss traitor, perhaps.

He folded the whole thing up and put it away to talk about with Vinny. Resignation was certainly in his mind, but she had to be consulted. There was the future to be thought about. He wondered why it had not occurred to him to discuss it with Myril. But it was obvious why. Vinny was Vinny, the best, the truest of all trust itself. But Myril, he was certain, would not only have no sympathy but she might feel she had to tell somebody about it. He had no proof. Any distrust he had felt in the beginning had gone soon enough. He had never given her any inkling of the type of work he did, and she had neither asked any questions nor taken the slightest interest. He knew she had gone to the party as guest of one of the senior secretaries, Louise Hamble, a student at a language class where Myril earned pocket money as a teacher. If she had passed Security as far as that, there was little to worry about. But the habit of twenty years persisted. He said nothing to her about politics and never mentioned the Government at all. Their relationship was strictly of the dining table and bed, and their conversation was about nothing that he could remember except when she spoke of her experiences. Those he listened to very carefully because they told so much about her, besides showing the difference between the Intelligence reports of the time, and what happened to someone having to live through it. There was a radical difference. And that was one more reason he had found among many for treating all agents' reports with a certain reserve.

Rain teemed, draping the windows with silver lamé, and despite the frenetic salaams of the windshield-wiper, the chauffeur scraped the grass verge at a crawl, driving blind. As suddenly, the rain stopped. Trees cast rags of shadow down one side of the road. Ethereal tints of English green patched the fields and pasture, and a hidden sun lit knolls of birch in strange, pale gold, making them appear to float on hills of white mist blowing in the hollows.

The car moved on, and the rain smudged shape and colour. But the glimpse of ordered land and promise of harvest brought sense of another kind of reality. The island's solid earth called in its own telurgic voice for his allegiance. Not only that but it reminded him of responsibility. Eight and a half acres and the house near Beaconsfield were his on a mortgage. If he resigned, there was no immediate way of paying the balance that he could think of except by help from Vinny's mother, which was no help. What he might do for a living he had no idea. There was literally nothing he wanted to do except the work he had been trained for since he joined the Service. At some time in the future he could expect an ambassadorship and a knighthood. Then another dozen or so years of representation in one capital city after another. In all, a comfortable and honourable life with a not unimportant place in the world's affairs. Though not if he persisted in his present manner of thinking, and not if he crossed the Calton-Islips too often. Certainly not if he resigned.

All the "Scots Wha Hae" and "O England, My England" type of thing he looked upon as mawkish drivel. But however it might be deprecated, there was a fundament of true emotion there. Perhaps it was only to be properly expressed on state occasions, when listeners might yield themselves to a feeling that they were adding another solemn note to History and be content to sop their embarrassment in the anodynes of Augustan prose. There again, thought of the gutter-mind obtruded. More and more policy, whatever its prose, seemed to rest on the What's In It For Me Boys, instead of the old-fashioned ideal of what was best for the Country. But first there had to be explained what constituted the Country. And again, as so many times before, he was unable to define what he meant.

He inclined to blame the champagne for cloudy thinking. But cloudiness was not its fault. Cold sober, he had often tried to convince himself of what he meant when he spoke of the Country. It seemed simple enough. There was first an island and its people under the guardianship of the Crown, with all its adjuncts. That, in short, should have been enough of a definition. But there was also the far more important matter of its life, how it thought and what it did, not merely in its shops and factories, but as a family living in a family of nations. And what it did was entirely a matter to do with its politics. There were four main bodies of political thought, Conservative, Liberal, Labour and Communist, though Communists counted only for shock value, and little more. The electorate, of people living in the Country, were split fairly evenly down the middle between the Conservers and the Labourers. The Liberals spread between them, thin as paste in a railway station sandwich, and about as edifying. The party winning most votes chose a Cabinet of ministers to govern. Each Cabinet minister controlled a department. Each department functioned by the ruling party's policy. The policy was put in work by departmental Civil Servants, like himself, employed by the State and paid by the Treasury. When Governments resigned, former policies went out the window, and new ones were wheeled in. Whether he liked the new policies or not, he had to conform, or he could be transferred, or resign, or get the sack. Very few of his colleagues ventured to say anything out loud because of their bread and butter. Some of the seniors complained, but having got it off their chests, they settled down and fought just as hard for the new policy as the one it supplanted. Sometimes. In any event, disagreement with the Management always meant a black mark, and loss of plums when they came up, and a good deal of strain between one desk and another. (Far better—dear Father—to do nothing, say nothing, until one were told what, and what not to do.) But what, among it all, could be called the Country, he had no idea. What was best for the Country seemed to mean to some what was in the best interests of the party in power. What the Caltons meant by the Country was obviously that area bounded by the hemline of their pockets. What he tried to explain to himself, in thinking of the country, was the position once occupied by the best minds of his father's generation. Even then he was uncertain whether he was right or not. A great many things had happened during that time which were absolutely inimical to the Country's best interests as events had later proved.

It all boiled down to the fact that the Country existed, certainly. It could be seen, and walked on, and travelled about, and its affairs could be dealt with. But everybody had his own set of notions of what it was. For the majority it seemed to mean that if they were getting what they considered to be their proper share of the booty, then the Country was doing very well. But if booty were scarce, then the Country was in a shocking state, and it was time somebody did something about it.

There was, naturally, and quite apart, the monarchical ideal of lealty to the Sovereign. There again, the Sovereign was little more than regal catspaw for the politicians. Cabinet ministers dictated what speeches were to be spoken from the Throne. Any words put into the Sovereign's mouth for public utterance were always those of the party in power. The Country itself was very rarely even half-seen through them. Yet far beyond politics, the Royal House had its

place. About that edifice the topheaviest portion of Society's debris
built a wall, and the sentiment of others filled the moat. But the
Crown could be and had been expunged on occasion, though with
the Crown or not, the Country remained.

The car went over the rise of Westminster Bridge, and the House
of Commons appeared on the rainy panes blurred as his thoughts. He
wondered if any of the Members were any clearer in their minds
about what they meant by the Country when they spoke of the
Country-this, the Country-that, before going into the Lobby to
vote with the party.

Whitehall's façades glowed splendidly white in London's own
late-afternoon lemony-yellow light, and grass in St. Stephen's Square
shone brilliant rain-green, and scarlet buses threw deeper shades of
red across the roadway's shining blue, reminder enough that whatever was thought or done, the City lived on and so did the Country.
The chauffeur went down to the entrance and stopped without
effort or sound.

"His Lordship said I was to wait for orders, sir,"—bowing, cap off
—"I've got my dinner money——"

"You may go, thank you. A very good trip."

" 'k you, sir."

There was a certain amount of regret in leaving the car. Not only
that, but he had a curious feeling of having left substance behind.
He thought he saw why men able to afford Rolls-Royces appeared
to have a great deal of confidence in everything they said. The fact
of possession acted as a sort of strengthener. He thought immediately
of dear George Calton-etcetera, owner of two or three—(Listen, we'll
phoner. Picker up.)—and found his right fist gripping the umbrella.

"Been to the Derby, sir?"—the liftman, eyes on the cravat—"Got
back quick, didn't you?"

"Yes."

"Wasn't a very nice day for it, was it? I bet Lord Berrish don't
care, though. Last words he said to me when he was here, 'You can
stick a couple of bob on with confidence,' so I did."

"Did Lord Berrish's horse win the Derby?"

The liftman opened the gates, and stood to one side, and appeared
to be wondering what he should say.

"Yes, sir, both his horses won today, sir. Three lengths, the Derby was. You never see it, sir?"

"No, I didn't."

"All that way for nothink, eh? That's hard luck, sir."

Walking along the quiet corridor, grinning to think what the liftman might have to say when he got below. The lift stopped whining and there was almost complete silence. An extraordinary sound became apparent, and pulled him up. It seemed impossible, but somebody in Blaise Cramers' office was weeping. Sobbing. Wailing.

He went next door to his own office. There were three or four notes on the desk about telephone calls. The place looked too ordinarily dowdy for anything much to have happened. Blaise opened the inner door and put his head in. The weeping was loud, sniffy and almost croupy.

"So glad you're back, Hamish. Toddy told me he'd talked to you."

"I thought I'd better get here."

"You'll wish you'd stayed away. I didn't get the gale winds till I was sent for by Mr. Flap. And he surpassed himself."

Blaise—quiet, incisive, impeccable always in dress, courteous in a rare and old-fashioned and most likeable manner—looked deathly weary. His smooth white hair showed the frizz of a careful singeing but the drilled bristles of his moustache had been disturbed by his habit of wiping his mouth on a handerkerchief worn in his left cuff. He looked, and was, the perfect Under-Secretary. But of all the hundreds of times his photograph had appeared in the world's press, very few would have recognized him now. The languid air he affected, the drawl, the one-raised-eyebrow, one-side-of-the-mouth smile, were gone. He sensed the wreck. It was all in his eyes.

"Is it certain about——"

"Wittard? Yes. The Intelligence people are still with him. He's hooting at them. Wouldn't say a word to me."

"Who's that next door?"

"His brother. I asked him to come up. We went to school together. Poor devil. Can't think what he's going to do after this."

"It's a little too much to take in. I can understand some half-baked clerk or other imagining himself a hero for a cause. Something with a bee in its bonnet——"

"If you wish to learn a little about bees and bonnets, go down to the waiting room. There are half a dozen Security people there, and they've got that insect between them. Listen to it, and ask yourself a few questions about sanity when you come away."

"You think he's insane?"

"On the contrary. He knows exactly what he's doing, and what he's done. It's our sanity I'm worried about. Why on earth didn't we see it?"

Blaise took out his keys, polished friends of years, and looked at them, threw them up and caught them, and put them back in his pocket as if he wanted to be certain he was there with them, awake.

"Who's to be trusted?"—asking a pigeon outside on the window sill—"That's the shocking thing about this. Must we all start looking over our shoulders? Should we act as if we belonged to some third-rate Ruritanian hodgepodge with a spy in every desk drawer? Mr. Flap thought so. He's going to transfer everybody. Everybody. But not until everybody's passed Security. That's my news for you. Plus the fact that there's very little we wouldn't like others to know that hasn't found its way to the darker side of the Curtain. I think the Security people ought to be shot."

"That's what'll happen to Master James, I suppose?"

"I don't think shooting's enough. Hanging's much too good. Although I dread to think what's going to happen to his family. I've sent for a doctor to attend his brother."

"Aanything I ought to do?"

"Wait for your summons. It's coming. Mr. Flap's with the Prime Minister. Then he wants to see me. When I get back here, it'll almost certainly be to pack up and crawl into retirement. Mr. Flap was good enough to say that he'd never at any time had much use for me."

"I hope that got a sharpish reply?"

"One doesn't waste energy. I must say I never thought I'd have to endure that kind of thing when I entered the Service. However, that's rather a long time ago. I don't want to sound like Squire Pauncefoot, but who in his right senses would expect a Wittard to betray his name?"

"Did he admit it?"

"Walk down the corridor. Ask him yourself. You're entitled to. I'm afraid we're all in for a packet of trouble."

"Why?"

"Proving we weren't guilty of gross dereliction of duty. Everybody'll want scapegoats. Infinitely more important, is anybody going to trust us with a scrap of information worth a brass farthing after this? Wait. That's my telephone."

The door closed. It would thump like that never mind what took place. But the weeping had sounded like an ultimate of coarse laughter split by a sobbing retch. That curious sense of fear wavered in the muscles of his legs again. A voice screamed for moments on end. He pulled the door open. Blaise and another man were struggling with a third. He managed to tackle and pull down the kicking legs. Blaise and the other pinned the arms.

"You make me regret having asked you here,"—Blaise, gulping, straightening his waistcoat—"You've got to listen to me. Will you promise to behave?"

"Behave, my God behave! Yes. Very well. But you mustn't use drugs on me. I won't have it. My brother needs my help. I demand to see him. I demand you let me call my solicitor. He cannot be treated as a criminal."

"If you'll promise to be quiet, I'll see what can be done."

"You have my word."

Sir Alfred Wittard bundled in the chair rather like a heap of old shooting clothes. He looked too small for everything, and the struggle had made things worse. His eyes mourned in a purplish blotch and whitening hair touched his eyebrows, and a moustache straggled in his mouth. He lay held by his elbows against the arms of the chair with his legs anyhow and the toes of his boots turned in, and he wept again, ah-ah-ah, open-mouthed and wrung-eyed, and tears shone on his cheeks.

Blaise nodded, and they went out, leaving the doctor there.

The corridor seemed darker, longer, more silent than ever.

"Awful business," Blaise grumbled to himself. "I'll swear Alfred couldn't be got to emit a groan if you flayed him alive. But look what the thought of having a traitor for brother does. I don't know what the fellow deserves."

He tapped on the waiting-room door and went in. The lights were on, the blinds were down, and James Wittard looked as he always had, though much more cheerful. He sat back in the chair at the head of the table plucking with beaks of his thumbs and forefingers at the tips of his jacket lapels, always his habit in discussion.

"So glad you two managed to get here," he laughed, and raked back the cowlick with his fingers, and it was easy to see the family likeness. "I've been trying to convince these gentlemen that I wasn't employed by anybody. Really not. I received no money at any time. No bottles of sherry or fashionable clothing. Nothing. Neither have I the least idea who got what I gave away."

"Who did you give it to?" somebody asked.

"I'm afraid you'll have to find out."

"Look here," Blaise spoke across the table in a peculiarly harsh voice. "Your brother's in my office. I have no wish to talk to you. I want to know two things. First, what is the best way of getting him back to his home. Secondly, the name of his physician down there."

"Is he in need of attention?"

"I asked two questions."

"Hire a car. The address is Wittardsholme Abbey. Sussex."

"Wittardsholme Abbey. Sussex. I fully expected you to vomit when you said it. The physician?"

"Doctor Randall. And don't be theatrical. You've been vomiting nearly all your life on everything that might be expected of you. You're time-serving as you stand there. Does that micturating clod you dance for every day represent you, or anyone you know? Or are you taking your salary on the off-chance that things'll get better?"

Blaise looked away, with a certain restraint, at a tall grey-haired man.

"Sir Alfred Wittard wishes to know if he may call a solicitor to represent the family, Inspector," he said.

"Yes, sir. Tell him to go to Bow Street. He'll get instructions there. We'll complete this statement, first."

"This is the only statement anybody'll hear from me," James Wittard said, smiling and plucking away, completely at ease. "I want it known that what I did was in the best interests of people like myself who hate what England has come down to. A large plaything for a set of utter criminals, none of them English in any sense except that they shelter under the flag. Between them they've given away an Empire. They've gradually ruined those of us with something rather more than theories to maintain, and they've entirely ruined a working class that used to be the world's best. In the matter of class, that is to say, of social class, the same criminals have tried to impose an idea that there are none, whether working or otherwise. I say that demonstrably there are. I joined the Service, as many of my family have done before me, to further the cause of the England I was educated to cherish. I found I was serving a succession of Governments dedicated to ruin, accepting debt as an honour, and running cap in hand to dear Uncle for the odd dollar whenever things looked grim. Politically grim, that is. I got rather tired of it. Anything I gave away did no intrinsic harm to us, should I say, to England. Rest assured of it. But I had no intention of sitting there and letting others plan to wipe us out. That's the basic plan, whether you look to America or to Russia. We're too importantly in their way. They're both out to get rid of us——"

"I haven't the patience to listen to this," Blaise told the inspector. "Let me know when you've taken him off."

"It won't be very long," James Wittard said, in the calmest manner, and plucked his fingers away from both lapels, and held them on a level with his ears, thumbs and forefingers together and the other fingers raised, like peacocks' heads. "Do be kind to my brother. He's a dear soul. I'm glad the title lapses with him. What use will it be in a few years time? Unless, of course, we wake up. We shan't, I fear."

"That fear's as much a treason as anything you've ever done," Blaise said, and sounded as though he wished he had not.

"But don't you remember that epigram of Harington's?" James Wittard smiled, leaning back again. " 'Treason doth never prosper; what's the reason? Why, if it prosper, none dare call it treason.' Isn't that very apt for our day? Inspector Morriss, please remember that nobody in this building gave me the slightest help. I had no accomplice."

He turned toward the peacock's head on his right, touching his mouth with the tip of the thumb and forefinger. His teeth clenched and the smile jerked to a stare. All the police leapt about him in a scrum and the table tipped in a clatter.

Inspector Morriss stood, holding out a few crumbs of glass in the palm of his hand, and Wittard's tweed jacket, with loose stitching in the right-hand lapel, hooked on a little finger.

"Done a Goering on us, sir," he said, abashed as a schoolboy, almost in a blush. "That's why we never found it, look. Capsule sewn in the collar. Knew he'd want it one day."

"Come to my office as soon as you can," Blaise told him, smiling, hands in pockets, and turned to the door. "Hamish, that's what I'd call the most blessed fortune. There's just a chance we might pull the whole thing out of the fire!"

"What's the form?"

"We'll see what we can do with Alfred, first. Not a word!"

In the office he went across to Sir Alfred's chair, and rested his hands on the arms, bending over him.

"Alfred, you'll have to compose yourself. Your brother has suffered a severe heart attack. Doctor Bennet, would you be so good as to attend him? Mr. Gleave will show you the way."

The doctor took his bag and nodded thanks for direction, and hurried down to the lit patch of the open waiting-room door. It seemed useless to follow him, and a waste of time to go back into Blaise's office. A desire came for one of Father's philosophical drinks. James Wittard's smile was horribly clear. The tremor in his voice lay over the whisper of traffic outside. Had it been at any other time, in conversation with almost anybody, many would have agreed with all he said. There would certainly have been a debate of sorts. But nobody would have dreamed of calling him a traitor.

Blaise came in and carefully shut the door.

"Whole thing's settled,"—almost chewing satisfaction—"Alfred goes home with the doctor. The other thing's taken out of the basement to the mortuary. Certificate of heart failure. Saves the family, and we're absolutely clear. No newspapers, no fuss of any sort."

"Can we do that?"

"Can we?"—staring half-humorously, flourishing the handkerchief, wiping his mouth, and pushing the crumple back in his cuff—"My dear Hamish, it's done. Care for a walk? I think we deserve a drink

before we go upstairs. Miss Relph just gave me the message. Mr.
Flap wants to see us in forty-five minutes. Got your basket?"

"What for?"

"Strawberries. There'll be quite a generous harvest, I'm sure."

But if the strawberries were ever grown, they had no time to ripen. While he was having a wash and deciding what to do about going home in a morning coat and top hat at midnight, the telephone rang, and Miss Relph asked him, with the Secretary of State's compliments, to see Colonel Fadden of Military Intelligence, and other representatives. A large officer with a pale face and three rows of ribbons came in and asked him questions about receipts of despatches and diplomatic bags. There followed a monotony of questions and answers, and a lot of scribbling with a ball-pen, and a large measure of the Colonel's habit of pulling an earlobe. Somebody else came in after him, and then a Commander from the Admiralty. They all asked for much the same information, and he gave them much the same reply, and they all wrote copiously and looked very serious. That was about all he could afterwards recollect of them. Miss Relph sent in a plate of sandwiches and a pot of coffee at about eleven o'clock, and told him Vinny was on the telephone. The tone of his voice warned her not to take long. She asked how much he had won on Toddy's horse, and cheered when he told her, and said she had won twelve shillings for a sixpenny bet with the milkman. She went on to say that Robert had turned on the heater in the bathroom and had almost blown them all to kingdom-come, and that she would be on the first train with a suitcase for him. He asked her not to forget his socks this time, and if she could, to cut a lot of standards for Sir Mathew and send them down. Her private laugh told him she knew what he meant even if he did not, and she ended with a good night, darling, that sounded distinctly wistful and a long way off. It was indeed a long way to Beaconsfield, but she had been alone before and nothing could happen. But he got Miss Relph to telephone the local police station and ask them to keep an eye on the house. And the whole time he was looking at a couple of pudding-faced gentry from Security and trying to keep any feeling out of his voice. He made a note to tell Vinny that. But he knew she must have guessed.

All the staff had been called back by telegram. Miss Sells, his secretary, came in from a birthday party in a pretty pink dance frock. One officer after another came in, asked questions, took notes and went away. Diaries, journals, records, receipts and files stacked on the desk, tables, and on the floor. Just before Big Ben struck five in the morning, Blaise came in and raised his hands. Even he looked a little dishevelled.

"Start again at eight o'clock," he told Miss Sells and the messengers. "The cars are out there to take you home. You've done splendidly. Hamish, where are you sleeping?"

As if there were any question.

"On the couch," he said. "Looks as though we shall be here for the next two or three days."

It was a fair guess, but a day out. The tumult died away on Sunday afternoon, four days later. During that time nobody except members of the junior staff left the buildings. Miss Sells worked herself to a standstill, and so did everybody else, and Blaise sent the staff a valedictory message to say they had done nobly and that he was very proud of them. But they were four days behind in their daily work. That meant getting there early and finishing late until they caught up. He was sure he could depend upon them.

"Remarkable thing is, I'll swear not one of them has the slightest idea of what it was all about," he laughed while he put on his overcoat. "Just as well, what? But Uncle Sam's rather badly titubated about it all. I gather they're rather inclined to treat us like a lot of Frenchmen. I expect you'll find out tomorrow."

In his usual distant way, Blaise was giving warning that all was not well. However, tomorrow was the time to tackle it. Vinny's message said she had brought the car up to drive him back. He realized how tired he was when he stood on the steps looking to see where she had parked. He knew from her face that it showed.

She paused a little before she came to him, and he felt idiotically flattered to see that her eyes were wet. It was only four days but it seemed far longer. She appeared in that cool evening light exactly like somebody out of an album of photographs, not in the least changed, but clearer in details that had been forgotten. Her slimness surprised him for some reason. She made the old grey tweed look as if the Milo had found her arms and a good tailor. He knew she must have washed her hair because it was bunned in a net, gleaming winter-honey, under a handful of lilies or something plonked on top in her usual manner and held there by elastic. Hamish and Robert looked at him from her eyes, and because there was nobody about he kissed her rather more carelessly than he might, and she was certainly in no hurry.

"You look just like one of your brats when it's fallen down," she said. "I've had a glorious four days. They've driven me stark, staring, raving mad, and completely nuts. Questions, morning till night. Hamish wanted to know if you'd gone off with somebody else. I don't know where he got that. Darling, you're going straight to bed. If you want to nap, put my coat under your head. Do. I'd rather it didn't fall off."

"If it did at this moment, your fingers'd go into it like a well-hung pheasant. I couldn't sleep if you paid me. The cold luncheon today's the best idea you've ever had."

"Cooked it myself last night. Mrs. Taber's left our employ."

"Oh, Chr—why?"

"Drunk and disorderly. Well, not exactly. I noticed the bottle going down. And I didn't have a drop. Then I passed her on the stairs and I caught it. Oho! So I read the riot act, and off she traipsed. Breathing vengeance, of course."

"Who've we got now?"

"That rather nice old thing I've had my eye on in the village. I think I shall be very satisfied. Mrs. Lindley. She launders perfectly. You might even have something fit to wear. I'm really ashamed of that thing you've got on. That goes straight in the bin. I can't think what's happened to laundries. They must employ people to munch the things. I was very sorry to see that Mr. Wittard died. Rather sudden, wasn't it?"

"Very."

"A year younger than you. I'd like you to see a doctor, Hamie. I'm not being stupid. You're working much too hard. It isn't fair to you. Or to me. I shan't worry you about it, though. I'll bet if Mr. Wittard had been sensible he'd be alive now."

"May be entirely right."

"I'm not wearing the elastic legs today, Hamie. I had to go and make myself a cup of tea and sit down and have a quiet cigarette, I was so horrified."

"Where did you see it?"

"*The Times.* His brother said in a Personal he'd write to everybody who'd sent messages. I suppose you sent one?"

"Not yet."

"I thought he was awfully nice. I should think a brain like that would be a terrible loss. That Hindu lecture was quite the best thing I've ever heard. Two more like that and I'd be ignorant. Then there'd be a basis. I honestly believe nobody knows less than I do. Bobby's quite certain. He asked me what five times eight were. It's not the sort of thing to do without warning. I had to put five eights down, and add them up."

"And you got it wrong."

"Of course. You should have chosen somebody brainier."

Rage of dearness held, irresistible, far beyond any thinking or speaking and without design and with all desire to go as close as he could and put his arms around her, and kiss her cheek, and keep his lips there and feel her straighten, pretending she had to keep her eyes on the road.

"If I curled up, and put my head on your lap——"

"I'd love it. Sleep like a lamb. Not another word. You'll wake up at the front door. The Last of the Mohicans will most probably cleave you to the bone with his tomahawk and yell with glee. But you won't mind, will you?"

"Not the way I feel now. Is Bobby still Colonel Custer?"

"He's playing some game of his own. He's got a box of assorted stinks in that dark place in the potting shed. I'm petrified to go anywhere near there."

"Just as well. Supposing he turns out to be one of those physicist chaps? Wouldn't it be fun?"

"You forget I know his mother. There isn't much there to give him a start."

"I doubt if they'd pick any other. I wouldn't."

He closed his eyes, but if sleep were near, it kept well out of his way. Vinny rested her hand along the side of his jaw when she turned corners, holding him steady. He tried to throw out any thought of Myril, but she took off her clothes, and her stockings whispered in his mind, and he saw the golden-red aura of her body against the bars of the gasfire in her room. There had been no opportunity of calling her, and in any case, Security was far too strict.

He thought back over the days, of hour after hour of checking receipts and despatches and verifying signatures, trying to trace the defections of one man in a department of thousands. It was appalling to think how much damage was done, and how simply it had been managed without suspicion. Except for some careless agent's permitting himself to be caught going over the West German frontier, it would still have been going on. But never again, certainly if Security could help it. Everything from codes to methods of despatch were changed. Everybody on the staff, down to the boiler-men, were all in the machine. It would have caused him no surprise to find somebody in a car behind them, and he fully expected enquiries at home.

"Anybody called from anywhere? Any interesting letters?"

"One from Mumsy. She's very well. I thought you were sleeping?"

"Curiosity, that's all. I like to know who's been taking advantage of my absence."

"The milkman, the postman, the butcher, the fishmonger, the knife-grinder, and of course the grocer's boy. Then there was a funny old thing selling windmills for jampots."

"I'm not sure I'm in any mood for fantasy."

"Windmills made of paper for empty jampots. I got half a dozen and put them away for Christmas."

"Five pounds they're tearing round the garden with them by the time we get back."

"Taken. That's a beautifully silly bet. I put them in a marvellous place I cleared out in the attic. It's a sort of priest's hole they used to have long, long ago."

"That house can't be more than fifty years old."

"Well then, let's say some very shy parson went to earth up there."

"All right. I said I was going to sleep, so I'm going."

"Don't let this disturb you, darling. But you owe me five pounds, thank you."

His eyelids were too painful for sleep. If he sat up, he had to talk or listen. Lying down at least he could think. He saw no hope of getting in touch with Myril. He dare not try. He expected to be followed everywhere for the next month or so. Or for a day or two now and again. One could never be certain. A Security check was a deadly business. An inquisition without physical torture, perhaps. But torture to the nerves. It was ridiculous to take the slightest chance. He wished that he could. But lying there with his head cushioned by thighs which had mothered his sons, he was a little ashamed, if amused, to be thinking of somebody else's, passionately, greedily thinking, and remembering.

He sat up, stretching legs and arms.

"No use."

"You're overtired, that's all. Would you like to stop for a drink?"

"All right. Why not? Would you like one?"

"I wouldn't have asked if I didn't. I want to drink to having you home again. That house creaks like an old corset. I don't say I'm frightened. I only leap five feet every time I hear something."

"I'll be there tonight."

"I think it's a disgrace you're not there every night. They can't expect you to stay away from your home."

"Affairs of State."

"I shan't be rude, but a large pool of wee-wee on the State. That's all."

They turned into a Ye Olde something-or-other, full of chintz, copper pots, and lopsided dummy candles in iron candlesticks. He ordered whisky and soda for two. There were very few people in the bar. Nobody followed them into the carpark, and the traffic went booming on both ways. He wondered if he might chance a call.

58

Myril shut shop at about six but she did the books until seven or later.

"You're going to have a pill tonight, my lad. You're a much worse bag of nerves than I am."

"I'm perfectly all right. I was considering whether I oughtn't to book a table for luncheon at the Club tomorrow. If I wait until the morning they might be gone."

"Why don't you? Somebody special?"

"Hatton Dail who does more or less my job at the American Embassy here's bringing a chap called Abbatt from the Embassy in Paris. Toddy might come, too."

"Phone, darling. What's your secretary doing?"

"Poor girl. She's had a rotten time. I think I will——"

He looked for the telephone booth. It would be a toll-call, and wondered if he would have to give the waiter a number. That would be awkward. He hoped he could dial direct. He heard car tires slither in the carpark gravel and sat down.

"Forgotten the number? Where's your little book?"

"I don't need it in any case. There's a directory——"

Two men came in and went to the bar. The taller man almost deliberately took off a black hat and showed his grey hair and grey eyes and turned to look about the room. His glance touched and passed over Vinny, but there seemed no slightest degree of surprise in smiled recognition and an official sort of nod before he turned to talk to the man with him.

"Who on earth's that?"—Vinny, whispering—"Looks exactly like a policeman."

"That's exactly what he is,"—sitting back, devoutly thanking his stars and cursing himself at the same time—"Met him at the office. Can't get away from them, can we?"

"Aren't you going to phone?"

"No, I don't think so. You can do it in the morning. After I've gone."

She shivered.

"That sounded awful."

"After I've caught the train, then."

"Much more comfy. I'll drive you in. Table for four?"

"One o'clock."

"I wish it were me. I haven't been lunched or bunched for such a long time. I'm so looking forward to Thursday."

At any time before, or during, or after luncheon he could have wished Vinny were there if only to smile and shatter the glacier. Glacier it was and the thickest sort of ice from the start. The Americans arrived at ten thirty, without documents of any kind.

Missionary guests of head-hunters could not have been more courteous, or more distant, or more word-perfect or more didactic than those two in their presentation of the gospel according to Uncle Sam. Luncheon was an error, but he refused to listen to instinct. He knew afterwards that he should have called a thirty-minute break and carried on from there. Instead they went to the Club. But the Americans' cool distrust was too plain. Small talk died its small death, and the nature of their meeting flattened any attempt at humour.

Hatton Dail, from the Embassy in Grosvenor Square, propped himself against the chair, tall, black-crop-haired and black-almond-eyed, long-nosed, frown-mouthed, white-toothed and blue-chinned, and dressed in a grey suit without a waistcoat and a white shirt with a buttoned-down collar and a black silk tie held in a gold clip. He spoke in a soft and remorseful voice, and he went on speaking against any attempt at interruption for questioning until he was satisfied he had said all he had been told to say. It was evident he had committed whole tracts of instruction to memory. When answers to questions were outside his brief, he made a note and said he would refer back. It was like throwing a ball against a gigantic jelly. Nothing happened, nothing bounced. Mr. Dail closed up, played with a gold pencil, and looked at a print of the Guards calling the Roll in the snows of the Crimea.

Robert Jerome Abbatt, from the U. S. Embassy in Paris, wore a blue suit with a blue polka-dot bow. He also spoke at length in language prepared for him, clutching his right wrist with his left hand and resting his forearms on the table, tipping his head a little but keeping it still, and looking at Toddy and Dail out of the corners of his eyes, or across the table directly down his nose. A thin curl of fine, flaxen hair ran down the middle of his head, and his pale blue eyes shone with the barest I-told-you-so smile of suspicion not without a tinge of malice. He made it fairly clear that he thought somebody not in his team had been caught out. He finished his sermon just before luncheon. The journey by cab was made in complete silence except for some remarks about the traffic and the weather. Dail ordered eggs benedict and coffee. Abbatt said that all he wanted was a ham sandwich and a glass of milk. Toddy and he had a plate of cold roast beef and a glass of claret from the barrel.

Dail made an opening—which appeared to cost him as much effort as cutting through the toast—by congratulating Toddy on his Derby winner. Toddy plunged in from there. He took them on a bird's-eye tour of the horse and its pedigree, and ended by saying the winner had been kindly weighted, and the going had been just what the stable had looked for. Unfortunately he had been denied full glory of ownership. A call from Paris had taken him away when he should have been down on the course to lead the horse in.

"That's tough,"—Dail, smiling—"But that was the day, wasn't it? I got hauled out at 3 A.M. I didn't go to bed till noon Saturday."

"You mean you didn't get any sleep at all?"

"Didn't zip a lash. The Ambassador didn't either. Nobody did. Critical couple of days. We had everything alerted. Everything."

"That sort of stuff you can't get careless with,"—Abbatt, shutting one eye, biting his bottom lip, shaking his head just enough to make his curl fall on the other side—"Sitting on a powder keg——"

"I don't consider we were unduly careless,"—Toddy, using the most distant range of his Where-Was-I voice—"We weren't careless at all, in my opinion. Nobody can do very much about a traitor. He's like a horrible little flea that manages to hop on from somewhere. You've got to find him."

"Right,"—Abbatt, emphatically—"But if we knew, how come you missed him?"

"I wasn't aware we knew anything at all."

"Now look, Mr. Gleave,"—Abbatt, comfortably—"You knew the guy was a deviate."

"I haven't the slightest desire to controvert you,"—Toddy, pulling a slight face—"I must ask you to believe that we knew nothing of the sort. At least, I didn't. What's your conception of a deviate?"

"He was a homo,"—Abbatt, stolidly—"You only had to look at him."

"He cultivated a mannerism, possibly. Apart from that, I'm sure you're wrong."

"I have my opinion,"—Abbatt, summarily—"He's in the record as the co-inventor."

"It's easy to say that sort of thing now. Why wasn't it said while he was alive?"

"It didn't have to be,"—Abbatt, shrugging—"It was known, though."

"Who knew it?"—Toddy, smiling, unperturbed—"Which authority?"

"Ours,"—Abbatt, equally unperturbed—"I knew it. I met him a couple of times."

"But if you knew him, and had this opinion, then presumably you knew his position? But we weren't informed?"

"It's no part of our job to tell you your business, Mr. Gleave,"—Abbatt, turning, chidingly good-humoured—"It's not our business."

"But surely it is, if you know that secret information's going to somebody untrustworthy. Isn't it your duty? Or what's the purpose of our meeting? What's all the somersaulting been about in the past few days?"

"Don't tell me you're going to turn in a whitewash job,"—Abbatt, smiling—"The guy was a deviate. Any deviate's a risk. He shouldn't have been there in the first place."

"One moment,"—Toddy, bending forward, smiling—"Are there any more of our people here or in Paris on what must be your highly entertaining list of deviates?"

"That I wouldn't know,"—Abbatt, soberly, glancing at Dail—"Maybe——"

"You should let us have their names immediately,"—Toddy, incisively—"We must know exactly where we stand, and so should you, in this matter."

"Oh, we know where we stand,"—Abbatt, quietly and with greatest confidence—"We fired every last one of them. Best thing ever happened. Let 'em stick to theatre and ballet. Government's no place for that kind of people."

"But I asked you for names on our side,"—Toddy, in the same tone—"With the names, you might append the evidence. It's sometimes required."

"I don't believe that's in our province,"—Dail, looking at the knife-blade between his fingers—"You could apply to Security. I believe they'd tell the relevant authority. But I'm with Bob on this. They've done a lot of harm. Not only to us. Everybody else. They've got all the faults of bad women and none of the qualities of good men."

"Right,"—Abbatt, raising his forefinger—"You'd be surprised how far some of them travelled before they got riffed. Key-posts. No wonder things went cockeyed. You can't trust them."

Toddy began to chew the lower knuckle of his thumb, and his eyes went from a piece of tomato, to the pepper-pot, and to the edge of Dail's plate.

"I don't doubt for a moment, that all you say is correct,"—very distantly, after a moment.—"Nevertheless I think you're mistaken about the late Mr. Wittard. My information is that he was a great favourite with some of the ladies."

"Double-doored maybe,"—Abbatt, seriously—"It's no way to judge."

"I agree,"—Toddy, smiling again—"That's why I think it unwise to ascribe unnatural habits to a man who isn't here to defend himself. I'm not talking out of respect for the dead. I have the least respect of anyone here. But I see no reason for posthumous calumny."

"Why not?"—Abbatt, sitting up, a side glance, glacial— "Didn't the son-of-a-bitch sell anything he could lay his hands on?"

"No. At least there was no money involved in anything I've seen. And while I shan't defend his conduct, there's a limit."

"Mr. Gleave, I think you have to take into account public opinion,"

—Dail, trying to make out the hall-mark on the spoon handle—"This case didn't get the publicity it deserved because he died a lucky death right the moment he was picked up. That's luck. From my point of view, you can't say anything bad enough. It's the only way people are going to get mad. They have to be got mad, and kept mad."

"That's the way I feel,"—Abbatt, nodding, finding something of interest in the coffee cup—"It's the only way, if we're ever going to get people in a condition to fight. We've gone soft. They have to be given the word any way we can. Why do we have to worry about what we say about Commies?"

"There's this,"—Toddy, knocking a glass on the tablecloth to the rhythm of his speech—"Everybody who's caught helping the Russians whether he's English or what he is, always seems to be called a deviate. I've had a great deal to do with the Russians in one way or another, but I have yet to meet anybody on the male staff who wasn't almost painfully normal. If that's what we're discussing. Yet we're asked to believe that any foreigner taken into their employ's ipso facto a deviate. Every time somebody makes off, that's the excuse. I think it's not only bad psychology but a remarkable tribute to Russian perspicacity that they're able to find these people. It says very little for us."

"What does a Wittard have to say to you?"—Dail, smiling, watchful—"This is interesting. I read a file on him. Where he was born, the report cards he got at school, his university, the family, everything down to the fact he always slept on the floor. Even though he had a castle or something to live in. Why does somebody with a background like that, and the job he was in, not just renege, but go all the way down the line? You ask me why the Russians find these people? They happen to be on hand, don't they? Why shouldn't they find them?"

"The question is,"—Toddy, insistent—"Why is it always discovered after the event? Why not before?"

"It was known before,"—Dail, glancing at Abbatt's emphatic nod —"He was known to be a pervert."

"I cannot agree,"—Toddy, putting down the glass, impatient— "Because the fellow was given to odd neckwear and spoke largely of the Upanishads, and mumbo-jumbo on the Brahmaputra is no reason for calling him something he wasn't."

"Ever hear him speak?"—Abbatt, straight-faced—"Didn't that tell you something?"

"He had a slight impediment, is that what you mean?"

"Aw, now Mr. Gleave, impediment!"—Abbatt, closing his eyes— "That was an intercontinental, six-lane skyway lisp, if you want to know. He was cut out to be a momma. State of things in Denmark, now, it wouldn't have been too difficult. No, let's not flog a dead homo. That's hitting below the belt, what? I don't need to tell you where I'd have hit him."

"You'll probably deduce we didn't have too good a time the past few days,"—Dail, laughing, marvellous teeth—"Everything took a free kick. It wasn't comfortable."

"I sympathize, and I know Toddy does. We haven't gambolled in a bed of roses ourselves. You're angry and so are we. But we've also got to put up with a feeling of shame. He was a fellow-countryman. And there's nothing we can do."

"That's the devil of it,"—Toddy, quietly—"I may also mention that whatever you've called him, I'm quite certain is very flimsy stuff compared to what he's been called by some of us."

"Then I can't see what all the argument's been about,"—Abbatt, a bright blue stare—"That's what I say. What's it matter?"

"Because that particular statement's unfounded,"—Toddy, at his blandest, from behind his thumb—"And I see no reason for it."

"You mean it's such an honour, he can't be called a homosexual?" Abbatt, sitting up, staring— "This is a special reserve, or some new-type order of chivalry?"

"Not a bit,"—Toddy, even blander—"But it's as well not to confuse an issue. The fellow was a traitor, sound in mind and body. That makes his crime the worst in the calendar. To palliate it by describing him as an invalid—which is all those creatures are—is not only wrong but harmful, in my opinion. He had no excuse to offer."

"I get your point,"—Abbatt, half in relief—"I accept it, with reservations. I still think the Commies are way ahead of us. Or how did they get to him?"

"My original question,"—Dail, nodding—"How?"

"I don't think it's a bit of use asking us. If we knew how, we'd have had some inkling. We didn't. He wasn't satisfied with the present Government. That much we know."

"He was a rabid anti-American,"—Dail, looking up, seriously— "That might give you a lead. He got his secretary to talk if there was an American on the phone. It happened to me. But what makes him a traitor to you?"

"Maybe the guy had a painfully soft spot for one of those painfully normal Russkis,"—Abbatt, between gulps of coffee—"And what that vodka does to you. Had him hanging on by his babushka."

"I think we ought to have the names of any other people you suspect, don't you? Otherwise, it seems to me we're wasting our time."

"All right with me,"—Abbatt, looking at his watch—"That means I can make that afternoon plane back."

"In other words, you haven't any desire to hear what we have to say?"

"We said everything we came to say,"—Abbatt, hospitably— "I'll be glad to hear anything you have to tell us, Mr. Gleave."

It was reassuring to see Toddy's slight flush and to know that annoyance was shared.

"There's no point in talking merely to be listened to. Our meeting was to discuss the damage done, and ways of preventing a recurrence. All we have now is a list of your methods of doing things, and the things you find unsatisfactory about the way we do them. Are we, this afternoon, to be regaled with further suggestions for betterment?"

"Mr. Gleave, I've gone as far as my instructions allow,"—Dail, holding a table knife as he had held the gold pencil—"I have no suggestions at all. Do you, Bob?"

"No, I don't, Hatton,"—Abbatt, with a superb air of hurt efficiency—"Not another thing. It's up to those gentlemen. If they want to talk to us, I'll listen. I'm like paper. I'm very patient."

"Fortunately, so am I,"—Toddy, smiling a diplomatic smile— "A very good and very profitable meal, Hamish. Since there's apparently no meeting this afternoon, I'll walk back with you if I may, and get my overcoat."

"Thanks for the lunch, gentlemen,"—Dail, pushing back his chair—"Anything I can do, Mr. Gleave, just let me know."

"Any time at all,"—Abbatt, crumpling a napkin. "See you around, Toddy."

On the walk back, Toddy's bowler hat rested on his eyebrows and his left hand was jammed in his jacket pocket like a skipper on half-pay, and he poked his umbrella into the pavement with a tinny clack of a loose ferrule at every other step. The smile in his eyes reminded of a done-in runner's with plenty of heart but no stamina, trying his best not to show himself beaten.

The sentry's scarlet tunic outside St. James's Palace brought a remark about the colourfulness of automatonism, and what an inexpensive form of street decoration the guardsmen were.

"Highly utilitarian too. Make very good policemen. And of course they give foreigners an excellent impression. I like Paris. I quite enjoy working there. But I'd never be happy away from London for long. When I think of it, I always get that picture of St. James's. The crenellation, and the archway and the sentry. Something timeless about it. Pity if it's all blown up."

"I'm glad we've got the odd bomb if it's only for retaliation."

"They'll have to do a lot of second-thinking."

"I'd feel far happier if we had a few really large missiles."

"They're on the drawing board. The entire R.A.F.'s poised on the verge of the junkpile."

"I don't know what we'd do if we managed to put our heads into a big war. Depend on the Americans again, I suppose."

"Wickedly bad policy. Any change of climate there and we'd be in a hopeless position. Air should be the most important post in the Cabinet after the Chancellor. The War Office and the Admiralty are complete anachronisms."

"It'll take a little while before anybody finds out about it, I dare-say."

"If ever I headed a Government I'd close them both down the moment I held the Seals."

"Ambition take you as far as that?"

"Why not? Later on, of course. I don't see very much coming up. I shall certainly not stay in the Service. I suppose you know I saw Mr. Flap this morning? Fellow talks more utter rubbish than anyone I've ever met in my life. I'm rather sick of it."

"He was rude to Blaise. A measure of his worth, perhaps. Not that I mind rudeness when it's warranted. It's quite often the only way of getting things done."

"I don't like vulgarians. Particularly the sort who consider themselves privileged. They bank very heavily on one's personal sense of discipline."

"I'm seeing him this afternoon. I'm warned there's a saga in the offing."

"About the same as I caught, I expect. I won't spoil it for you. By the way, he's made up his mind that our agents aren't any good. I told him they're far better at their jobs than the Americans'. He's gone extremely pro-them. If he were a decently-bred cockney he'd be much pleasanter to deal with. I've never liked that Labour flavour in any case. I mean their outlook. I do not, cannot get along with them. Nothing snobbish. I hope. Or perhaps it is. I'm indifferent."

"You mentioned the Country. Ever thought what you mean by it? There's a great deal of Labour sympathy there."

"I don't think very much about them. Give them all three ha'pence an hour extra now and again, and back they go to their kennels. What I mean by the Country is the historic part of it I happen to be interested in. I suppose it's really nothing more than one's own sense of right and wrong for our people. Sort of national amour-propre, perhaps?"

"There's still a tangible Country beyond it, though."

"And a great deal of it's not us. Not. It needs alteration. Mr. Flap's part, for example. The moribund, the slavish Anglo-American hypocrisy. Mr. Wittard's part. The effete, and completely unreliable."

"Ever hear his opinion about things in general?"

"I'm deeply thankful to say that any thought I retain of him is tenuous in the extreme. I refuse to devote a moment of my time to it. Why do you?"

"It's often illuminating to find out how other minds think."

"The only one I'd care to investigate at the moment is Mr. Flap's. With an ordinary garden rake. All he can think about are treaties. Treaties!"

He swung the umbrella whippingly at a leaf on the pavement. It was a little amusing to find Toddy in a bad temper. The sudden cut told a great deal. But the smile was still there.

"You'd never met Bob Abbatt before, had you, Hamish?"

"No, and I'll make no exertion to ripen the acquaintance."

"Would you believe that until last week he was the best possible sort of chap to work with? I needn't tell you what I thought this morning. Or at luncheon. They've both had a thorough mauling. It's understandable, I suppose. Bob's got three children. I'm very glad we didn't quarrel."

"Diplomacy is partly the art of holding the other fellow's temper. I didn't like the remarks about Wittard. Unnecessary."

"It's more than that. How long is it since you were in Washington?"

"Four or five years."

"There's been a curious change. Not for the better. According to some, we all speak the language of Oberon."

"From Oberon, in Fairyland?"

"Exactly. I find it most unpleasant, because I speak a language I was taught, to be considered abnormal by others who speak a mere dialect."

"The people who make the suggestions are unpleasant. The bad-breath type. I don't know, it seems to be the fashion to talk about the cloacal side of things. Sprinkle their conversation with it. Part of the honest approach to life, possibly."

"Honest? Most of them walk about with an anus in their faces. They're found out the moment they begin to talk. Sickening. Even from people one might presume were intelligent. It's one good way of damaging someone they don't happen to like. And if the poor devil happens to speak with any impediment, he's got no defence at all. In view of the educational system it's not surprising, I suppose. The Americans are certainly not alone."

"What's this anti-British miasma? The old perennial?"

"Something much worse. I've caught quite a lot of it lately. And it's gathering headway, particularly among their Service people, and the Government generally. Anything British is not just suspect, but within a toucher of bad business."

"Always has been. If their politicians ever went wrong internationally, it was always our fault."

"It'll come into the open one of these days. Not very pleasantly, I'm afraid. I don't quite know what we shall do about it. Find new allies would be far the best thing. It won't be long till there's a distinctly Jewish cast to their politics. With a little help from the Catholics, we'll catch it. Moneybags and bigotry."

"You sound a little depressed."

"I am. I don't like people who dictate. Especially from a wrong premise. I'm hanged if I like this assumption that because they've got armaments and dollars that we must necessarily bend the knee. I won't."

"They've got quite a number of problems coming up at home that'll keep them busy very shortly. Negroes for one. It's fortunate they seem to have their own community law apart from the State and Federal. Rule by elders. Harkback to the tribal days, I expect. About the Jewish business, there's a healthy section of public opinion always against them. Not openly, but it wouldn't take long. About the Catholics, I'm not sure. Showmanship and a lot of money. Their voting strength I suppose isn't to be sneezed at."

"Politically-minded clergy are a pest. They supposedly take their instructions from God Almighty."

"They're saying in Italy they used to wear black to the waist-belt during the Fascist days. Now they wear black to their heels in a cassock era."

"They're bound to come a cropper. People can't eat novenas."

"It's the Pentagon style of thinking I don't like. The industrial brains behind it. If those maniacs have their way, Europe's the cockpit. Won't be anything left."

"What about us?"

"We shan't exist."

"Happy thought, isn't it?"

Rather more sun appeared to be looking for a gap in grey cloud, and walking was warmish, though pleasant enough. The Horse Guards parade ground was empty except for pigeons and sparrows, and an old man eating a sandwich and throwing them crumbs. Some harmony in the buildings, perhaps their age, or instant flight of thought about the things that had happened there caused a tug, even a pang that not only bricks and mortar but everything they stood for could be destroyed. At the same time, it was not by any means clear exactly what they did stand for. It would look the same under a Conservative as a Communist or any other Government. The birds undoubtedly would be there, without change of any feather. And old men would continue, doubtless to throw crumbs, whatever the Government, law, or the state of the Country.

It was a curious feeling to walk, apprehending the spacious unsafety of what might well be condemned ground. Though, if it came to that, there were very few areas in the entire country that were not.

"You saw the last report on Woomera, I suppose?"

"Yes. Not very pleasant."

"If we could only get the Russians to do something really worthwhile. Something more than a speech for the newspapers. Let's say, withdraw from Europe——"

"They won't, Toddy. For at least ten years, I should think. You'd have a locust swarm of the other boys straight in there with their cigars and sample cases. No. We've got the problem squarely in front of us. Bombs will move it certainly. But far beyond our ken."

"Helpless business. I'm sure we'd get things right if we were left to ourselves. But not while the Americans are jumping about the place."

"You seem to have it in for them."

"The Russians are half and half Asiatics. One expects difficulty and one's never disappointed. But there is daylight there. The Americans aren't Asiatic, and they're not difficult. They're monied, avaricious and intractable. There's no daylight there at all. They have what amounts to usufruct in Europe and certainly in this country. They're both forward bases and expendable. Why should they talk to us as if we mattered? We mightn't be here much longer."

The thought had never before occurred that a man like Toddy could be dangerous. There was no ducking the fact that he represented a considerable body of opinion. He was a fairly persuasive speaker, eloquent on occasion, and he had any number of friends in Fleet Street and the City. Perhaps the Americans knew about his views. Their agents missed very little, and that might explain, to some extent, what had happened at luncheon and before. Straw-plucking, perhaps.

"Have you any plan? Anything workable?"

"Beyond cutting our cable across the Atlantic, no. That might bring them to their senses. We'd take Europe with us. France, Germany and ourselves would hold the trumps. Of the three, we'd be on top. We've got the weapons for the moment. Not that we'd want to use them. Then let the Americans fight it out with the Russians. We'd be neutral. Let them wreck themselves. Sounds somewhat sketchy, but in detail it would work."

"I wonder."

"Anything rather than this sort of thing."

He appeared like an agile schoolboy trying to see some way of shoving his way through to score. Any effort, and any trick to outwit, or overcome.

"Not much dignity in that, is there?"

"We've always had far too much."

"Who'd trust us afterwards?"

"All the more intelligent people. The rest don't matter. After the first bomb drops somewhere, they'll keep their mouths shut. In any event, who trusts us now? Nothing but lip-service. What's your solution?"

"I doubt if I could give it in a couple of minutes."

"Same old cautious Scot. At least while we've got a few Hamishes we'll have somebody to rely on."

"Think so?"

"Certain. I don't know what else'll keep us going."

"You're thinking of flying back this evening, are you?"

"No, I don't think I will. I think I'll go down to Mappersley. Do a day's hacking about tomorrow. Take some of the taste of today out of my mouth. They'll scream their heads off in Paris. But what the hell."

And the last memory, though not quite as clear, was of Toddy laughing to think of what might be said of him. With the brim of his bowler almost touching the bridge of his nose, and a dark grey double-breasted suit, starched collar and Regimental tie, and a maroon carnation of perfect shape in his buttonhole, he appeared in head-up, closed-eyed laughter to exude the chrisms of Eton and Balliol, and vivid abstractions of the farms and trout-streams and hunting scarlet of Mappersley, a slop of skiffs and punts at Maidenhead, the noise of the stables and an array of silk and caps, and many a satisfactory meal under the Gainsboroughs in the dining room of the house in Belgrave Square.

Yet for all his contempt of traitordom it was apparent that he was just as much against present policy as any James Wittard. The difference was that James had not only talked. From somewhere or another he had found the courage and the means to do something about it, that could have put him in front of a firing squad or stood him on the hangman's trap. Dail's question recurred. There appeared no sufficient reason or any chain of reasons which would impel a Wittard to become a renegade. Birth and breeding, scholarship and choice of career were all against any possibility. His opinions, whole or in part, were held by the many. But his was not merely an opinion, a sort of safety-gauge for a general agin-the-Government steam to be let off in clubs or pubs for a breather, a fresh hold and then get on with it. His was a belief that led him into giving away what he knew would imperil the public safety.

Wittard at some time had passed a document or had divulged secret information, knowing in that moment, by that act, he forfeited his right to be called a loyal subject, and knew himself to be a traitor, a far worse word, in his language, than Cheat, and a much more horrible term than Murderer could ever be.

Yet the frustration of sitting at his desk day after day, reading messages in and out, probably knowing at times as much as all the originators put together, and seeing quite clearly what was going on from moment to moment, might have bred an unbalance. His was

not a patient spirit, and impatience breeds indiscipline unless curbed
by a respect for consequence. But if Wittard had thought it all out,
and had come to the conclusion that he and his class of people were
finished unless action of that kind were taken, then perhaps there
might be reason for his traitorship, and protection for his conscience
by telling himself that what he did harmed a Party Government but
not the Country at large. He ruined or wrecked a policy, but not a
people. He did his best to smash a system, never the State.

Or so he implied.

But it was not enough.

Traitors were traitors, and nobody knew it better, because of an
innate and touchiest sense of honour, than James Wittard. He must
have known and feared the word, and yet persisted. Why James Wittard would renege was a difficult question to answer, because all the
answers seemed essays in the fanciful, although there could be nothing more fanciful than his self-persuasion, expressed to Myril, that
all should be done to protect the creative moment.

Perhaps a germ worked there. The act of creation he had always
promulgated as the marrow of the British spirit, a desire to be, to
achieve, to lead, to fecundate in glory for Britain's sake. Watching
that spirit's being distorted, or stifled, or in any way prevented from
being what it must, perhaps might have seemed to him, in his rage,
to be excuse enough to call the distorters, stiflers and preventers, traitors, and himself patriot. A Wittard, with his contempt for what he
chose to call cheap politics and the people behind them, would
hardly concern himself with their opinions, and neither would he
care for the consequences. He was far too much a part of the "once
more to the breach, dear friends" tradition to care what anybody
thought or said about him once he made up his mind.

With that as basis, it was not difficult to follow his reasoning in
presenting material to the Russians. By seeking to strengthen them,
he was trying to level the balance weighed down so heavily on the
American side. In that manner, he might have hoped to create two
champions of equal strength, neither with more say in world affairs
than the other, and prevented from engaging in battle by mutual
respect if not a common fear. That condition, he could have thought,
would bring about a more healthy mental atmosphere in the world,

and a fair chance of survival not only for Great Britain as a country, but for his own class of people, and a further opportunity for expression of their point of view and even, perhaps, for their redintegration.

But it was useless to say that sort of thing to Toddy. James Wittard, of a much older family, became on that account a target for even loftier contempt, and what remained of the Berrish parvenu rejoiced in the downfall of its unacknowledged though obvious studsuperior.

"They're almost ready for you upstairs, sir,"—Miss Sells, when they reached the office—"You're down for fifteen minutes."

"Sounds like a dental appointment,"—Toddy, taking his overcoat —"About the same thing. I'll pop in and see Blaise. Good luck!"

"Have a good run tomorrow. I'll let you know how this goes."

"Do."

The corridor looked even darker, longer and wider. There was apprehension in the lift going up a floor, and a dryish mouth walking toward the suite occupied by Mr. Flap. But then came a sense of buoyancy. He had all the facts given by the Americans during the morning, and the conversation at luncheon. There were enough small shocks there to hold Mr. Flap from saying very much. In any event he was surprised to find himself, for no specific reason, distinctly more cheerful.

"The Sec'try will see you in just a moment, sir," Louise Hamble told him in the outer office.

Instantly there came a thought of Myril. He could almost see her pulling off her frock, and while he was going through the door the closing whisper over the carpet was almost the sound of his hand in caress along her thigh.

Mr. Flap looked up from signing a letter, nodded, and went on signing. He was sixtyish, spare, pale, with streaks of white hair here and there, and a small grizzly moustache. Edmund Charles Bracey looked anything but a Secretary of State for Foreign Affairs. But he was. And in any case he was no worse than some of the others. He had, it was rumoured, a brain. There was no telling. He liked to give the impression of briskness, as if it were an ingredient of capability. He also liked to do the talking. He seemed afraid to listen to another opinion in case he might be won over. But it was extremely unwise to cross him. Then he screamed like a drunken fishwife, and waved his arms when the words stopped coming, and stamped his feet when his arms stopped waving. Hence, Mr. Flap.

"Ah, Gleave, sit down. I hear you've got a lot of interesting things to tell me about. Start at the beginning."

Mr. Flap never missed saying it, and it never stopped being maddening. It was a command to lesser mortals to bow down. For that reason it was always politic to start well before the beginning of the matter in hand, or else there came a further command to paint the picture. For God's sake paint the picture or I shall never know where I am.

Mr. Flap sat back with his spectacles on his forehead and threaded his fingers and closed his eyes in the manner of a High Court judge. There was no point in waking him up, although Blaise had once dropped an ashtray without getting a move out of him. Far better to go on talking, and then send in a report.

The Wittard business was completely stale, but it was gone over step by step. Then the sermons of the morning in précis, and a reconstruction of the conversation over luncheon detail by detail. The moment he finished talking Mr. Flap startled him by opening his eyes. That was a lesson well learnt. Suspicion came that Mr. Flap was not always asleep.

"Very interesting, Gleave. Bears out what I've been thinking for a long time. I think their suggestions are right. Matter of fact, I'll have them circulated to all departments. Some ways they're streets ahead of us. Not so many cobwebs, and the red tape's a lot thinner."

"We've got a few things to say about that——"

"I don't think we ought to mess about with it. If that's the system they're using, then we use it. If anything goes wrong, it's their look out."

"There's a counter-proposition——"

"No, Gleave. Let's have it their way. It works. Ours didn't. We've been made to look a very umpty lot. I don't like it."

Mr. Flap got up and went to the window, and leaned against the curtains, hands in his trouser pockets, one foot crossed over the other. A boot dragged a lace, the trousers bagged, and the creases must have been slept into the coat. Memory came of Sir Mathew. How they ever got there keeps me awake at night. And Father. If a fellow can't look after himself, he won't look after very much else.

"I get a feeling in the back of my throat every time I look out of this window,"—Mr. Flap, talking almost to himself—"Even when I cross the road. I can't bear to think of seeing everything smashed up again. We're in a terrible position. Terrible. No other word for it. If that lot took it into their heads to come for us, I don't know where we'd be without an American or two."

"We all realize that, sir,"

"I often wonder if a lot of you do. That Wittard business I'll never get over as long as I live. Bloody swine. I agree with the Americans. We ought to have known it. But if you can't trust a man like that, where are you going to look next? I'm having a spring-clean, Gleave. It's going to mean hardship for you and your wife among others, but I can't help that. I believe you'll go to Japan. I'm not sure yet. It's not a punishment or anything like it. I think you've always done a good job of work. That's more than I can say for a few of them. Are you much of a friend of Lord Berrish's?"

"Yes, sir."

"Well, I'd like you to know this. Just because he's a lord-tom-noddy and he's got a million in the bank doesn't make him any different from the office-boy when he's working for me. I'm having none of it. You'll find a French agent's report about his carrying-on in the summary going out today. I just want to say this. The minute I find anybody talking anti-American here, I'll boot him out. I don't care who he is. The policy is full, and complete, co-operation with the United States. That's as far as we're concerned. Can I put it any plainer?"

"It's plain enough, I think, sir."

"Good. Now then. Mr. Calton-whatever-his-name-is has been worrying me one way and another. What have you done about it?"

"I telegraphed for the figures. I'm waiting for a reply."

"That's it. Let me know what happens. He can make a lot of trouble. Now, I've got a very serious letter here——"

Any letter from his constituency was a Very Serious Letter, although it had never been found out whether the paper itself was serious, or the contents, or a dash of both. Mr. Flap licked his fingers and eased up page after page in a file.

"Here we are. A young fellow, son of one of my voters, got himself pinched in Newport News. Charged with being drunk. Swears he wasn't, and there was a lot of fiddling about with the Consul. I don't doubt it's a lot of toffee, but find out about it, will you?"

"Yes, sir."

"I'll have you called tomorrow. And you can stand by for a trip to Geneva. You'll get notice of it tonight. Thank you, Gleave."

That was all. Apart from bowing out of the Presence, that was all. However, there were a couple of questions.

"It might be wise to find out a little about the technical people U.S.A.F.'s sending over here from France. There's a lot of activity——"

"I think it's just as well left to whoever's in charge of Security. Why should we waste time?"

"We ought to know what they're doing, oughtn't we? I don't want to be told at some later date that I was remiss——"

"You won't be. I garantee that. If there's too much poking about, they'll begin to wonder whose side we're on. I don't call that friendly, Gleave."

"There's no question of friendliness. There's a responsibility that I have for my side of things. As far as I'm concerned, this morning was nothing more than service of official notice that we can sing for any sort of information——"

"We'll get it in other ways, don't you fret. No, leave it alone. See the Treasury Report today, did you?"

"No, sir."

"Have a good look at it. They've spent one thousand two hundred and eighty-five million pounds in this country over the past six years. That's somewhere about four thousand million of their dollars. I suppose if you paid a bit of rent, you wouldn't like the landlord coming round peeping in your windows, would you?"

"I'm not ungrateful for the help they've given. But that's not my concern. I'm supposed to know what's happening——"

Mr. Flap threw his pen down and pulled off his spectacles.

"Either you'll damn' well do as I say or I'll get somebody else,"— staring across the desk, raised eyebrows, four complete wavy furrows— "The policy of this Government's full co-operation with the United States. D'y' understand the meaning of the word 'full'?"

"Yes, sir."

"Then don't let's have any more of it. That's enough!"

It was, indeed. Walk out, noticing that the secretaries were all diligently engaged, although they must have heard most of the last outburst, and stroll down the corridor trying to look as if nothing in particular had happened. Nod to Leonard Porrit—tall, limping from a wound won in Holland, always smiling, one tooth in front missing, just about the same age and seniority—coming along with a thick file.

"Hello, Hamish. Fireworks today?"

"A few rounds of grape."

"Old man's in a spitter, i'n' he? I caught the devil this morning. Lots of trouble at Bonn. I've just sent the report down to you. I couldn't get him to see a thing. I very nearly got the push."

"That's about what happened to me."

"If this goes on, we'll be the Fiftieth State in the Union. Junior to Hawaii. I understand that's pronounced Huh-woy-yuh. Then us. Wonder what'll happen when the Senator from Lower Britannia takes his seat. Everybody gets up and whoops out 'There Awwiz Be A Ninglun' probably? Dismal, i'n' it?"

"Not very bright. Dammit, I'm not against them. It's the way they go about things."

"Brash is their word. Uppish is ours. Still, there's not much to be done. Just have to wait for the big show. Coming nearer every day."

"Think so?"

"Certain. They're saying if you're on the outside of the blast zone —that's about ten miles from where it drops—you're perfectly safe behind a sheet of stout brown paper. So I've started carrying a sheet with me. Better to be ready for things. So Babs tells me. When it starts I shall wear a brown-paper poncho."

"What about your head?"

"Shan't worry about it. It's not much use, or I wouldn't be working here."

"I'm beginning to feel like that. Any clerk's good for my job."

"Ours not reason why, ours but to hew and cry. Going to the Grosvenor tomorrow, aren't you?"

"Yes. Vinny's very excited about it. She hasn't been out for years. Babs coming?"

"Oh, rather. Place looks like a slop-shop. She's going to machinate everybody with something she's tacked together out of one of Dior's old fishing-nets."

"She's quite a catch, herself."

"Thanks. I've often thought so. She's rather hard-roed at the moment."

"Oh? When's it to be?"

"Six months, eighteen days and some hours, I believe. Much more sensible to read in bed. Less expensive."

"Let's make a table tomorrow night?"

"Let's."

The postbag was fairly heavy, and between dictation and writing notes, six o'clock came long before its time. Miss Sells was grateful to be sent home. The reports from Bonn brought reminder of the early days of 1939. New names and new schemes gave more or less the same impression as the old names and the old schemes. And the same old feeling of helplessness in the middle of rot. Thought of going to Japan had the strangeness of a move backwards in time, a return to youth.

There seemed nothing more sensible to do with a headache than to take it home. Just before he left, one of the night staff delivered orders and air tickets for the journey to Geneva. That meant at least three days away from home. Not that he minded. It was something of a holiday and he liked the place. The meeting was nothing but a session or two of chinwag about travel documents for the governmentally-employed going from place to place. Nothing in it except a lot of negotiation. Considering that for nearly the whole of free Europe only a passport was needed, it seemed absurd to raise barriers anywhere else. But it was understandable that the American countries had many more problems, not the least that free frontiers would bring ten thousand ships year after year loaded to the gunwales with every kind and colour. It seemed ludicrous, despite all the talk of distrust and dislike of Americans in general, that their continent was still terminal for the dreams of millions.

He walked down the stairway to stretch his legs. The foyer was fairly chilly and he stopped to put on his overcoat. One or two people passed by. His mind was somewhere between stopping for a philosophical drink at the Club, or going on to the station and having one there, and the details of the situation in Bonn, and the fact that he would have to tell Vinny about selling up and going to Japan, though certainly not until after the ball at the Grosvenor.

A hand caught the collar of his overcoat and gave it the exact amount of pull to get it on. But in turning to say thanks, the words snapped in greater surprise. Kevin Chalmers, last seen in Manila, thirty-five or so, tall, broad and bronzed, wearing a covert coat, a spotted muffler and tweeds, with his bowler on the back of his head, grinned behind a Present Arms with his umbrella.

"Old Faithful, ready for your disrespection, sir, please!"

"Kevin! When did you get back?"

"Got off the plane a couple of hours ago. Broke the record from

New York to Shannon. That's Chalmers form, of course. Just saw
Flappy. Two minutes, burnt to a cinder. I'm catching a plane to
Paris. I just spoke to Toddy."

"Coming back this way?"

"I'm back this way. I did rather a lot of weaving with a car a
couple of nights ago. A little squiffed, I'm afraid. They didn't like it.
Washington being what it is, here I am. Robbed of seniority, sworn
at, sent to Paris in a very junior capacity, no friends, financially not
so much embarrassed as pursued, regarded as a very pariah upstairs,
and withal, I hope, incorrigible. One thumbnail sketch, K. Chalmers,
complete. How's Vinny? The boys?"

"Very well, thanks. Sorry about this. Didn't I hear you were getting
married?"

"Yes. She was in the car with me, matter of fact. Quite a blow. If
she'd kept her delightful mouth shut, we might have been all right.
They have an extraordinary habit of saying what's in their minds.
Most of it distinctly uncomplimentary."

"Couldn't you stop her?"

"I'd had about four gallons of a positively toxic firedamp called a
Gibson. It's served with onions, which should tell you. I was under
the impression that we were invaded by at least half a dozen cops.
His name, I discovered later, was Maloney. Indicative?"

"Better sign the pledge."

"It's signed. Her father jawed for a solid hour. Astonishing thing
is, one couldn't think of anything to say. He's forbidden the marriage."

"Not very pleasant for her."

"Mary? I wouldn't go through that fifteen minutes at the airport
again for the Mint. Her mother remained my friend, I'm thankful
to say. Bless her."

"I suppose she'll come over?"

"I hope so. Or I shall have to work my way over before the mast.
One becomes rather attached."

"Indeed. Let's try one in here. Or have you time to come to the
Club?"

"Don't want to see anybody, thanks. In here's perfect."

The place was fairly quiet with not many lights. A malty smell of beer pushed through a muffle of sawdust, and something roasty filtered in from the kitchen.

"Extraordinary how one changes,"—Kevin, looking about the room —"I once thought there was nothing like an old pub. Now you can keep it. Some chaps still cry in their tea about them. Not I. Give me the American style every time. It's new, it's clean, of the age."

"Only in some places."

"The majority. One can find a hole-in-the-wall anywhere. But why? This sort of old, beery den I've grown away from."

"Swallow, and let's find another more suitable."

"Fifty thousand apologies, Hamish. But damn it, we are so far behind the times."

"You seem taken with America. Love?"

"Not altogether. It's difficult to say. I like so much of what they do. This is about the only time I've regretted having to leave a place. However, Paris calls. I hear all's none too well there?"

"Few rents in the fabric. Get the story from Toddy."

"Good chap. Won a lot of money on his horse in the Derby. Put it all on a plug for the Oaks. Lost the lot. Heigh-ho. Sure you won't have another?"

"No, thanks. Just time to catch the train. Give Toddy my regards, and say that Mr. Flap didn't disappoint me."

Kevin looked at the last drop, and drank it, and put the glass on the counter with the slight crack of an auctioneer's gavel.

"That's what really worries me, Hamish. A complete ass of that sort talking to me. I don't mind it from somebody I can respect. But that mollusc. It never hit me until today. Damn it, I refuse to be introspective. Come over when you can. Let's have a party. Lots of things I'd like to get out of my system."

"I'll let you know. 'Bye, Kevin."

Kevin whistled at a passing cab, and ran for it, wagging goodbye with the umbrella. Further along toward the bus-stop, a telephone box showed red in the headlights. The wish was alive to talk to Myril. Not only to talk, to see. All he had to do, as so many times before, was to take the Tube to Bond Street, walk along to South Audley Street, and go down the alley beside the shop to the back door.

But it was too risky, the trip or the call. There were only two people on the other side of the Cenotaph, and in the wide, lamplit distance of Whitehall not more than a dozen. But it was not worth it. There might be somebody watching him from a doorway. To risk being shadowed was absurd. In fact there was very little sanity about any of it, wish, desire, or waste of time. In anybody else he might have called it unbalanced. But thinking of Myril was really very normal. The insane part about it was that he might be, and probably was being followed.

There it was.

And here came the bus for another weary jolting to the same old smelly station, and an hour, via hard-arse because First Class was too expensive, home.

Vinny walking into the Grosvenor foyer for the Highland Ball might have looked more beautiful at other times but he was quite unable to remember when. Ten years at least had gone in some mysterious touch of a wand. She looked early-twenties, entirely kissable in a wonderfully melting sort of way, and the family diamond on her finger was a match, but only just, for the bonfires in her eyes. Her dress—new for a change, and ruinously costly—was almost the tone of her hair, a sort of russet, with a shawl of the Gleave tartan pinned to one shoulder, and sitting next to Babs Porrit in something ashy-blue under a lot of black lace, she made one of a very eyeable pair. Leonard thought so, too. Babs' gleaming black head, camellia-petal skin and Arabian-nights eyes went very well with Vinny's more restrained, perhaps, but extremely taking wild-rose daintiness, yet there was a hint of stability about her that Babs lacked. He noticed that everybody looked at Babs first, but at Vinny longest.

They had a table away from the band. Miguel O'Patrick, an Argentinian trade attaché, and Magi his wife made the third pair, and Bejian Emyenkov and his wife Frolla, cultural attachés, ostensibly from Hungary, made a fourth. Bejian spent most of his time at the British Museum library copying from old music books, and Frolla's only interests seemed to be youth education and cooking. They were known to be a couple of Russian ex-schoolteachers, with no political record of any kind, and neither were they at all sympathetic to Communism in theory, although they never had much to say about it. Which said far more. There had been a startling incident at one of Charles Roff's parties, when Beji got himself a little tiddly and said in his excellent English how much he would enjoy making

sopranos out of the unnameables in the Kremlin. But poor Frolla
in a pathetic state of fright got hold of him in time, and whisked
him off. Next morning all the male guests were called upon, one
after another, in their offices, and Beji asked them to be generous
and never to mention a word of what he had said. And Frolla had
done the same with all the wives, going out as far as Beaconsfield to
have a word with Vinny. As if any of it were necessary.

They were a nice enough couple in their way. They dressed well.
But as Vinny said, with that scale of pay and allowances, she could
have headed the ten-best-dressed. Frolla was a big girl, pale blonde—
she called it dirty-platinum—and pale grey eyes, with not a line in
her face although she must have been thirty-five. She had the
shoulders of a timberjack, a figure with barely an undulation, and a
peasant's legs. She looked magnificent in a bathing suit. She looked
equally good in black faille with pearls, that Vinny said must have
cost the earth. Beji was a head shorter, bald, with the eyes of a
musician, black and somnolent, and he was very proud of his paunch,
which Frolla was in the habit of patting when he grew a little loud
as he quite often did, as if she were excusing mental afflatus by ex-
cess of tub.

Miguel and Magi O'Patrick were both rarely tall, dark-haired,
tanned, and dark-eyed, blazingly good-looking, mid-thirties, with six
children, and from the way they held hands, still trying and enjoying
every moment. Vinny said that watching them was like a hormone
bath, and Babs said it was perfectly all right thank you, but the
Porrits were doing splendidly without aids of any sort. Vinny said
it must be that attractive Porrit Limp, and Babs said she had yet to
find anything limp about it.

Beji tried to explain that in Russian to Frolla, and she almost
stopped the show with a yell, and covered her face, and went into
a coughing fit that lasted through two glasses of champagne. Vinny
said that if Beji had anything amusing to tell her that would require
a couple of glassfuls to cure, she was quite prepared to listen. Beji
said that the only amusing things he knew in Russian were all about
music, and quite intranslatable. Babs said she had the same trouble
in Ireland, and let it go at that.

Charles Roff came over to dance with Vinny. He was short and fairly stout, and he wore tortoise-shell-rimmed spectacles under bushy white eyebrows which gave him a look of fixed amazement. Charles was known to be one of the few top cipherists with a command of about twenty languages. Vinny loved him in all of them. His daughter stayed at Beaconsfield for three years running on holiday from school, and always cried for at least a week before she went back. Charles thought it did her good emotionally. Vinny was not sure, but she was certain it did more good to have Zena with her and the boys than send her off to God-knows-who to look after her. Charles' wife had left him some years before. God, he said, could sometimes be very kind.

Vinny wanted a daughter. That was all. She was a little frightened of the expense, but she said she was prepared to go without a lot of things to round off the family with a girl.

Looking at her, he was quite certain she was right. But perhaps the news about Japan would make her change her mind. It was sickening to think about. He had a feeling that Leonard was a little distrait, too, sitting at ease, well groomed, letting tiredness show now that Babs was dancing with Beji, but smiling and frowning, as if he were trying to repress laughter by reminding himself of tragedy. A funny mixture.

"Taking Babs for a holiday this year?"

"Not sure. Depends where we are."

"Things happening?"

" 'fraid so. Heard tonight."

"I heard yesterday. Japan, probably."

"Peru."

"You're lucky."

"I suppose we are. But we've just paid for the blasted house. And all the furniture. We'll never get anything near what we've spent."

"Our problem. We'll have to apply to the Fund, that's all. Told Babs?"

"Not yet. And I'm damned if I know how to."

"I'm taking Sunday morning for it. How about a little bottle?"

"Might be just as well. The girls'll be furious."

"All right. But we've got to stand the worry for the next few days, haven't we?"

They strolled among the crowd lit by frilled table-lights, and colours raying on the dance-floor turning dress-shirt-fronts into oblongs of pinks, greens, blues and primroses. There were plenty of decorations among the men and a surprising number among the women. Whether it was the music and the risible babble of a thousand people, and light falling on the white perfection of a woman's upper arm, and glinting across a torso of black sequins showing bone, muscle and omphalos, perhaps all had something to do with deflecting the normal course of his mind.

But he came awake, in a freeze not perhaps of horror, but something very much like it.

Myril was laughing at him.

Her hair was loose and she wore no jewellery. Her dress sheened dull red, bosomed, tight to the waist and with yards of skirt to the floor and a row of tiny buttons ran all the way down from the décolletage.

Leonard gave him a look as if to say Aha, There, and walked on, kind fellow, toward the buffet.

"What are you doing here?"

"I am with Louise and a party. The kilt is so beautiful."

"You know better than that. Only women are beautiful. You, for one. Kilts are passable, or comical."

"But handsome is not a good word, either. I like something that says how I feel. Handsome is as handsome does. Nothing. When I look at you I cannot speak. I have not seen you in a kilt. I forget my language. Aymie, we shall dance? Please? Aymie. Ami. Amo. Amore."

"I shan't decline. Tell me where your table is, and I'll come across for you. The one after this."

"The number is 18. I shall wait. I dance with nobody till you come."

She passed, bracken-sweet, with some heavy vestige of the gynaeceum in her eyes, in her hair, in her voice, something not of the senses, but from the mind, deeper, more vivid reflection, perhaps, of his thoughts of her. And yet wholebodiedly herself, graceful senior of all the shadows she sent to play behind his eyes.

The room was getting uncomfortably warm. He walked into the buffet and found Leonard watching the waiter opening a very good bottle indeed.

"Good lord, can we afford this?"

"I always put a little aside for private bibbling. I can't dance, so I get the room going round me instead of me round it. That was an esculent morsel?"

"Mmmmm. I'm worried."

"Thank God I don't know anybody like that. With Babs here, at any rate. She'd have me on the ropes, bucket in hand."

"That's why I'm worried. Vinny's not the angel she might look. On form, she has all the instincts of a punch-drunk cruiser-weight. Head down and both hands."

"Babs comes out of her corner with rather more circumspection. With a fireiron. She taught me to sprint. Any ideas?"

"One dance."

"I think you're going to need the full tank. Act careless-like. Women'll forgive you anything if they think you were drunk at the time. That's the ticket, Hamie. Drunk and impossible."

"I've got to drive home. Cheers."

"Lots of bubbles. That's the cash. She's not in the Service, is she?"

"No."

"Oh."

Fat headed feeling having to explain things, not wanting to, and yet knowing there to be nothing wrong. Well, not really.

"She's a language teacher."

Leonard almost spurted over his drink, pulled out a handkerchief, and kept his face absolutely impassive.

"But you speak excellent Japanese, don't you?"

"Oh, she's not teaching me."

"Pity."

"I mean, damn it, we met at the Club. There's nothing in it."

"What I saw could hardly be described as that. Awfully well-gunned forrard, I thought. Makes fortunes for them in the cinema. Don't have to open their mouths. Any more than usual, anyway."

"Not that, Leonard. Please. She isn't—she's—look here, she's rather—damn it, that's not the sort of thing I want said."

Sudden, stunning anger and the room going black, cloudy black, and clearing, and a hopeless and shocking thought of having made a complete fool of himself. The sweat on his forehead felt much colder than the glass in his hand.

Leonard had seen it. The tip of his tongue touched the inside of his bottom lip, and he stared at the candelabrum for a moment and he raised his glass and drank.

"Difficult to say one's sorry after fracturing somebody's tympanum. Sorry. More?"

"Thanks. Must be a little wound-up. I suppose it's the over-all pootling about."

"Like to know what I think?"

"Yes."

"You might be in love."

Dodging it for a long time. Now he could deny it or not. Love. Four letters, one syllable and an entirely new cosmos. Another perspective. Not a bit of use denying it. She was out there, in red, waiting. And Vinny was there. A reluctant witness, shadowy, dangerous.

"I suppose I am. Passing phase, I think."

"Hope so. Extraordinary the messes one gets into, i'n it? Nice messes, though. I once advanced somewhat gingerly into midstream with a West African girl. Black as your hat. A more exquisite and delightful companion I defy you to find. I'm still a little in love with her. Not a hair on her body. Funny. One never missed it. Another bottle, I think."

"I've got to dance."

"You make it sound like a rattle of tumbrils. Have your dance. Report back for your share, flushed with guilt or not. I'm partial to gross natures, and poached eggs with haddock."

Through the buffet's crowd and down the steps, head clearing a little, thankfully, and the band ranting with a blast like a hot breath, winding in and out among the tables to the one with 18 on its card.

She sat by herself, a robin on a snowy lawn, at a round expanse set for a dozen. Everybody else was dancing. She got up to meet him, and took his arm. No words, no look. They waited for space on the floor, and went in, pushed along whether they liked it or not. They danced apart, with space between, looking across, not at each other. One hand lay on his sleeve, and his guiding hand barely touched the satin bodice. He held the other hand only by the fingers. She moved easily, turned, stepped. Discretion and a sense of occasion were both hers, and he was quite sure that nobody looking at them would suspect the slightest thing. Two people dancing in a style to be commended for elegance, as much for a soi-disant air of having never known that by taking off a couple of layers of cloth they would be naked, or that below the waist was flame and snuffer or orgasm.

Nobody would notice.

But he was appalled to see the sidelong smile, dark, a smoulder gleaming through the fall of her hair. Appalled because there was no mistaking it. And instead of pivoting by herself, she was yielding in the turn, coming closer, and her hand went further around his shoulder, and her body came gently and by degrees hard against him. There was little enough he could do even had he wanted to. A sense of danger turned in a moment to complete and almost drunken disregard for opinion of any kind.

"Aymie, let us go outside."

"We can't. My wife's here."

"For ten minutes. Into the park. It is a glorious night. We could look up at the trees and count the stars. For ten minutes?"

"Darling, listen to me. We can't do that sort of thing——"

"Yes, we can. It is across the road. We sit down under a big oak tree."

"And somebody calls the police."

"Don't joke with me. What shall I do? You have a wife. It is simple for you. Come with me. Aymie. Shall I tear this dress off? If you will not, I scream!"

Her hand beating on his shoulder, and her mouth against his ear, but the whisper had changed to a raw, breathy rasp.

The band stopped by some unheard-of blessing. Almost with force, he pulled away and led her through couples to a space between the tables.

"We must use common sense——"

"Common se—!"

"Myril. Either you pull yourself together or I can never see you again. I don't care what sort of a scene you make."

"I don't make a scene. Nothing. But I had this—passion. You know? Day after day. When will you come? If you said tonight, I could worship you."

"Darling, look how impossible it is. Try to see it. Please. If I can tomorrow, I will."

"I don't know what I can do."

Her head leaned, and the dark hair fell across her face. Her eyes were dry, wide, glittering, fearful, and yet apprised of love, and the languor of her body showed in the lines of the red dress, the more marked by the long white glove she pulled taut, rounding it over the pride of her hip.

"Myril, I didn't think you were like this."

"You make me to be so. What can I do? Suicide?"

"Please listen. Please? Let me telephone you tomorrow. I rely upon your sympathy if nothing else. My wife's here. If she weren't, all right."

She moved, and licked her mouth, and breathed in, shutting her eyes, wrestling her arms as if someone's hands were running over them.

"I can do nothing. You know what I have said. How I feel. Aymie. Tell me. Do you always want me?"

"As much as you want me."

"So, then. I suffer half. You keep your promise? Before you sleep, you feel my kiss. Good night, Aymie. You make me savage."

She walked ahead of him, and he put her in her chair. Half a dozen other people were talking at the table but nobody looked up. He felt a sense of desolation in leaving her there.

"Share a bottle of champagne with Miss Hamble, won't you?"

"Oh, yes! And I drink to you. This is wonderful!"

He gave the order to the waiter, but the whole time he could see her smiling at him. He waved, and went back, watching the buckles on his shoes, to the buffet, stone cold sober.

Leonard lifted his glass, and waited until another glass was poured.

"Scouts have been here from the Gleave clan. I told them you were pleating your kilt. Longish job."

"Thanks. Here's peace on the billowing main."

"Hear, hear. I've just had a talk with Blaise. He's very fed up."

"Don't blame him."

"Doesn't like the way Toddy and yourself were treated."

"Can't do anything."

"Expects to go to the United Nations."

"Good for him. Hard on the pocket, but it's the best place to be."

"I didn't think you liked America at all."

"That's quite wrong. Never had a better time. Vinny loved it."

"Where did I get the impression——"

"Certainly not from me. Need a lot of money there, that's all."

"That's another thing Blaise said. The Select Committee says we're all getting a lot too much. They're cutting allowances. I think we'd better have another bottle, don't you? While we can. And toast something very rude in their direction?"

"Let's have it inside. Get awful stick from Vinny, otherwise."

They found Beryl Harrack talking to Charles Roff and Babs. Vinny was going round with Beji. Frolla came back with Miguel at about the same time. A couple of bottles appeared, and somebody toasted Beryl on the service of divorce papers.

"I shall be so glad to be free again. Nothing bitter, you know. Very friendly. Peter's been rather a darling about it."

"Going to lead the gay life?"

"No. I'm sick of it. This is my last party. I'm off to Australia. A new husband and a sheep farm. Here's to it!"

Beryl looked thinner than she had been for many a year, but her hair was golden as ever and her eyes had just the same sparkle. She had almost no bosom at all—she called them cockers' ears—but a small waist saved the day somewhat, and her filibeg of McArris tartan did a great deal for her.

"Hamie, I thought Vinny looked marvelous."

"She's very well. So are the boys."

"She told me. I'm looking forward to some of my own. Wish me luck."

The band started again, and somebody came to fetch her. He heard his name and turned. Blaise, talking to Charles Roff, held up a paper.

"Hamish, this from the House. Mr. Flap understands there's a telegram in from Washington about Caracas, and wants to know what it is. Know anything about it?"

"Must have come in after I'd gone."

"Our great friend, Mr. Calton-Shum-Shah, is on both his horses about it. I could say he shall have it first thing in the morning."

"Unless I get it done tonight——"

"Certainly not. Why should you be dragged away?"

"Oh, I don't know. Save a few ragged ends."

"No doubt about that. May I act as Legate and Plenipotentiary to the Court of Vinny?"

"Wish you would. She'll never believe me."

Vinny left the dance-floor on Beji's arm. She looked brilliantly happy. A background of balloons and coloured lights and murmurous laughter seemed absolutely right for her. Blaise showed her the message and spoke for a little in his gravest manner, and although she looked stricken she came over immediately and jerked her thumb a couple of times en route.

"Back to the sulphur pit, Hamie darling. You'll miss that last train. Shall I book a room here?"

"Aren't you going to wait for me?"

"Blaise said it might take hours. Mrs. Lindley's going home at one. I ought to be there soon after, darling. Supposing something happened?"

A kiss of her cheek, and the other cheek, and a touch for her mouth.

She smiled at him.

"Give me time to get home and ring me. Or I'll ring you."

"One or the other. Drive for the four of us. I'll kiss you good night later."

He might have been mistaken, but in turning toward Blaise he thought he saw tears. But that was Vinny's way. Everybody waved, laughed, called sympathy, and off he went. Leonard winked as he passed, pretty far out at sea. Blaise was inclined to frown

"Leonard's rather overdoing it, isn't he?"

"It's not often."

"I wish he devoted as much time as you do. I'm very grateful for this. I'll say good night, Hamish. I'll telephone and say you're on your way."

"Good night, Blaise. It's nothing. Truly."

Nothing, except something sent gloriously, blissfully from the dearest niche in heaven. Randy health made him stretch. All he had to do was to get to the office, dissect the information, get the night staff to type it, and send it across to the House of Commons. That was part one.

He had a suit and a change in the wardrobe. Once into that, he could hop across the road, take a cab up to Hyde Park corner, pay it off, walk down to the second turning on the right, find the mews entrance, and ring three times at the white door.

Myril.

Really too simple.

But after he had been at work for almost an hour, Miss Relph telephoned to say that Mr. Calton-Islip had just come from the House and would take it as a personal favour if Mr. Gleave could see him. He shook his head at some invisible he wanted to punch, and told her to send him up.

Mr. Calton-Islip loomed in evening dress with a top hat and a white orchid in his buttonhole, and a cigar long enough to climb out on and fish off. His clothes and linen were excellent but they hung on him, and he wore the top hat with the aplomb of a doorman. Neither did he take it off.

" 'Evening, Gleave. Very kind of you, this. I say, you do look a bit of all right, don't you? I didn't know you were Scotch?"

"Yes. I'm a Scotsman."

"I'm a Smokesman, myself. Londoner. The Ol' Smoke. I wasn't born in the sound of Bow Bells, so I'm an East Ender, you might say."

"Do sit down. This won't take long."

"Take your time. I'm in no hurry. I never knew you people worked at night."

"We often have to."

"I suppose you sting 'em for a nice bit of overtime?"

"We aren't entitled to it, unfortunately."

" 'bout time you got yourself a Union. I can just see you picketing this dump. Togged up like that? I can see the girls tickling your ol' knee there, eh?"

"Some of them like a little fun."

"Yes. I've had some myself. Nothing like it at times. It's a bit parky in here, isn't it?"

"Parky?"

"Cold. Like sleeping out in the park. Ever done that? I have. Don't you feel a bit chilly?"

"It's not exactly warm."

"Listen. I've got my car outside. Come up to my place and work there. My car'll drop you home."

"I think I'd rather work here, thanks."

"Listen, that stuff's for me, isn't it? Well, then. Come home and work in comfort. By the fire. It's only up the road. Park Lane. Don't catch your death of cold hanging about here. They ought to give you some decent offices to work in. You'll pardon me saying so, but this is a pigsty alongside our offices. I always say if you want people to work, give them a proper place to work in."

"Just give me about fifteen minutes here. Then I'll get it typed rough and we'll go over it."

"Don't say another word. I got a paper."

Mr. Calton-Islip pulled an evening paper out of his hip pocket and his spectacles out of a breast pocket, and sat down in a chair that might once have served a company touring the Midlands with *Tristan and Isolde*. He had a good look at it, and at the other furniture, at the walls and prints, at the ceiling and windows, and finally at the desk.

At that time, columns of figures were being added in the rough, and balanced. Fortunately, figures had never been the slightest trouble—(both the boys had the same gift—to the delight of their form-master, and of course their grandfather had been a magician)—and there was rarely need to do any thinking to add a column, and changing currencies was simply a matter of dividing. That completed the draft, and he rang the bell for the messenger.

"Gleave, I've been watching you."

"Really?"

"I'm going to check your totals with a calculator. If those sums are right, I'll give up."

"Why?"

"I didn't think—I mean—don't take this the wrong way, will you? I never thought you had the noddle. I reckoned I was good at a page of figures. Listen. This place'll give me the bronchitis. Come on home. Stay ten minutes. The car'll take you wherever you want to go. Let me have your scribbling-pad, there, will you?"

Park Lane was halfway to Myril's. Going by Calton-Islip's car would throw anybody off the scent. If there were anybody. There was no real certainty of there not being.

"Give me time to change. I'll meet you downstairs with the documents."

"You're my kind, fella. Now we're talking!"

While he dressed he put a call through to Vinny, but there was no reply and he asked the operator to keep ringing and connect the call to Calton-Islip's number.

Calton-Islip wanted him to share the rug in the car, but he tried to explain that a Scotsman's were the last sort of knees to require wrapping.

"Wonder why that is?"

"Same reason, I suppose, that we eat salt in our porridge instead of sugar."

"Can't stomach porridge. We used to call it skilly. I went to a Ragged School. Stuck it till I was eight. Then I got a job on a barrow. Nothing you can tell me about fruit 'n' veg. When I see these blokes in the Ministry of Agri-how-de-do playing with it, I have to laugh. Honest. I go back home, and I die laughing. Gover'ment? I should say so!"

"I thought you were a great admirer."

"Who? Me?"

Calton-Islip sat back and covered his face.

"I don't know, Gleave. I get very downhearted at times. I feel like chucking everything up and going to Jamaica or somewhere, out of it. Iv' wants to. She's had enough."

"Why don't you?"

"I like working. It's a fact. I'd go mad if I didn't have an office and a couple of deals going on somewhere."

"I suppose this one at Caracas will be fairly large?"

"Nothing very much. It's the effect of it on prices somewhere else that's important. I got a much bigger one going in Arabia at the moment. No, Gleave. I didn't want these figures really. I only wanted to see what you'd come up with. I've got my own figures. The right ones. But the taxes'll get paid on these. Always do things official. Then it's right, see?"

"Laws are made for intelligent men to ignore."

"No, fella. Make a difference. There's some laws the coppers are there to look after. They're the ones I hold with. But there's other laws that stop you making a penny or two. They're the ones I mean. What gets me narked, them sort of laws are put out by a lot of twots who couldn't make a sausage in business. If it wasn't for some of us payin' 'em, they'd all starve."

"What sort of Government do you prefer?"

"What's the use of a lot like we've got? Gift of the gab, that's all. Put cobs on you. You want some blokes 'at know a bit about it running a show like this. Trade and profit. That's what keeps us going. Here we are."

Calton-Islip told the chauffeur to go back and wait for an envelope and look slippy about it. He led the way into the vestibule of a block of flats. A porter took them up in a small salon of golden grilles and blue mirrors to the top of the building—"Always makes me feel like a bloody canary, this lift does. All it wants is a seedbox, I'd be right." —and along a corridor—"Twelve thousand a year, this lot, Gleave. Wait till you see my pictures. Say it myself, you'd have to pad a long way to find better. I just got another Rembrandt. He was a lad, wasn't he? Couldn't half slap the old paint about, though. Died broke. Must have knew some of the blokes I've come up against—" and the front door opened with a butler behind it looking as if he had just popped out of a Consistory.

"Ah, Moxon."

"Good evening, sir."

"This is Mr. Hamish Gleave."

"Good evening, sir."

" 'Evening, Mr. Calton-Islip——"

"Just call me George. We're at home now. Iv'! Iv-uyyy! Oops, dere, kitty-kitty-kitty!"

At what must have been the Calton-Islip open-season moose-call Mrs. Calton-Islip came from the far door streaming voile and pink ribbons like something out of Botticelli by Boots the Chemist, hair tied up in a pink bow, pot of cream in one hand, a mirror in the other, and a glistening face.

"Ah, da-a-awwlling! Ai didn't ikspect you. Whai, Mister Gleee-uv! Greecious!"

"All right, Iv'. Get it over with. We come back here to talk business. I'm not sure that place he works in hasn't give me the bronchitis again. Let's have a drop of something nice and hot, Moxon. One of your specials."

"Mulled wine, sir. Certainly."

"And, Moxon, ai'm sure we'd laike caviare and smoke' salmon, and that. Whatever you've got."

"Don't be too long, Moxon. Mr. Gleave hasn't got a lot of time. Now then, Iv' Hop it. This is business."

"Ai'll make an entrance with the drinks. Ikscu-u-use me!"

Calton-Islip took a midget calculator out of an ormulu escritoire, and sat down in a pink brocade and gilt chair, and brought the scribbled roughs out of a pocket. He seemed to take the greatest delight in pushing the tabs and winding the handle, and crossing off as he went.

The room was quiet. A fire of artificial logs glared in an open fireplace. Tiles of venetian mirror covered the chimney and a row of Dresden figures lined the mantel. Two gilt-and-black Moors held ashtrays on each side of the fireplace, and a beige and brown Berber rug separated two sofas in red-chrysanthemum covers. The other furniture was either Empire, Palace or Hippodrome, and any flat space held a knickknack, or vases and bowls of flowers. A couple of Renoirs, a Cézanne, and a Picasso were hung among a dozen others, and the Rembrandt crowded something out of Chelsea that looked as if the painter had chosen some unfortunate moment to fall flat on his face with a full palette.

"Ten out of ten—"—Calton-Islip, laughing at him—"Not a ha'penny out anywhere. I saw you do a bit of it, so I know there's no hanky-panky."

He took off the dress-coat and threw it on the chair, pulled up his shirt-sleeves, and sat down opposite.

"Listen, Gleave. I suppose you make a couple of thousand a year, do you?"

"Reasonably near."

"Wife. Two kids. You got to put them to school. Doesn't go far, does it?"

"Not very."

"What do you get out of it?"

"Out of—?"

"Come off it, now. Think I don't know what you think of me?"

"I wasn't aware——"

"You wasn't what? Listen, Gleave. Man to man. This is Park Lane, this is. My place. I happen to own this building. I told you I was born in the East End. It's no lie. It's only a fourpenny busride from here. That's all. It's took me thirty-eight years to do that ride and stay here. The only way they'll get me back's in a coffin. What I want to say is this."

He got up and put his hands in his pockets, and paced as far as the Rembrandt, and stood looking at it.

"I love this, Gleave. I can see the man behind it. I hope he can see me. George Calton-Islip's got three Rembrandts. Forty years ago I didn't have a hole in me pocket. I didn't have a pocket. Now Mr. Calton-Islip's got Rembrandts. 'Course, what makes me laugh is the Calton-Islip part of it. My name isn't Calton to start with."

"Not?"

"Definitely not. I was left on a doorstep. I got shoved in this Ragged School, they called 'em in those days. I was named Calton after one of the old girls there, and they give me George after the King. Marvellous old boy, he was. Iv' and me cried when he died."

"He was a great King."

"Took me a bit of time to get over it. He see the last of the good old days, he did. The days I never see. When I was coming up."

Calton sat on the stool behind the grand piano and played a chord, more chords. Ridiculous, but in the tone of his voice there was some reminder of Sir Matthew. Even of—of all people—Father.

"Then I met Iv'. Say what you like about her, she's this world's best. You know what she did? She was in a show—been on the stage years—Ivy Islip?—fill the house—and I got in a deal and lost me shirt. Know what she done? Lent me her savings. Every penny. We wasn't married. Just running about, that's all. Four thousand quid. I said, 'When you want this back?' She says, 'When you've made it.' I says, 'Think I can?' She says, 'I don't think you can't.' 'Want a receipt?' I says. 'Yes,' she says, 'Give us a kiss.' "

Calton got up, and walked toward the Chelsea blizzard.

"I can tell you this, Gleave. I've never even looked at another woman from that day to this. I'd give her the earth. She's got most of it. So I had her name shoved on mine. Calton-Islip. And she's the only part of it that's real. The rest's the Ragged School. 'Course some of my friends call me Calton-Cowslip. Not always Cowslip, either. But you can't have it two ways, can you? Unless you're funny-made."

He undid the buttons of his waistcoat, and turned about, biting the cigar, and looking at a vase of pink gladioli.

"I've never had no education, Gleave. For what I've had to do, I've never wanted it. But I've missed it. I can't talk nice. I haven't got it. If I try, I feel such a slop I've got to go out and be bloody rude to some poor bloke who don't know what it's all about. Then I have to part with a tenner for his feelings. So it comes expensive. Now, if I had your looks, and I could talk like you, I tell you straight I'd be the number one man in this country."

The number one man looked down, hands in pockets, waistcoat undone, trying to puff the cigar, with a diamond razzling fire from a cuff link.

"Think you'd get there? Conservative?"

"Prob'ly. Very prob'ly. They've got the City. That's where the Labour boys got clobbered. City never works with them. You can make all sorts of laws, can't you? But you can't get blokes to work with you if they don't want to. When a bloke's agin you, he's agin you. Don't expect nothing out of him."

"What would you do?"

"Get the City working with me. Make it worth their while. Like they're doing now, only a million times better."

"Got a programme?"

"No. And I wouldn't have till I got in there. I'd get some brains round me, first. You can't work with a lot of slops. Now listen. What are you getting out of what you're doing?"

Calton had his face not more than a foot away, staring over his spectacles in the grey-green quintessential grin of a thousand generations of gutter-imps.

"Here you are, working day and night, earning somewhere about a couple of thousand a year, wife and two kids, where are you?"

"Perfectly happy, thanks. But I'm not sure I like——"

"Wait a minute. Don't get your temper up. How would you like to earn ten thousand a year?"

"Very much. In your Government?"

"No. In my office. Hand your notice in any time you like. Listen. I'd send you to Panama as our representative. You can fly anywhere from there. You'd have your own house, everything you want, cars, servants, all the exes, free. And ten thousand quid in the bank. In dollars. No taxes. Ten-year contract."

"I'd be disappointed to wake up."

"You're awake all right. What about it?"

A chime tolled near the fireplace. Calton went to the right-hand Moor and took a telephone out of a cupboard in its stomach.

"Hullo? Calton-Islip here. Who? Yes, Mrs. Gleave, he's here. Working very hard. Can't tell you what a pleasure it's been. Saved me a great deal. Oh, yes, I'm looking after him, dear."

He held out the receiver.

"Hullo, Vinny."

"Got home much later than I thought, darling. Do forgive me."

"As long as you got there safely. Everything all right?"

"Perfect. Such a lovely time. Didn't get a single thing on my dress. Isn't that lucky? Leonard got stinkingly sozzled. Babs was furious. There's trouble there."

"What sort?"

"Oh. He called Blaise a bottom-kisser. But he used another word."

"That's not like him."

"He said lots of other things. Nothing praiseworthy, I assure you."

"Mr. Calton-Islip's waiting."

"All right. What train shall I meet tomorrow?"

"I'll telephone. It'll be early. How would you like me to earn ten thousand a year working for Mr. Calton-Islip?"

"Let me get my curlers in, and I'll sleep on it."

"Like the idea? Appeal to you?"

Silence. A small sigh.

"I'm a little too tired, I suppose. I'll play dream-games with you tomorrow."

"The offer's firm enough. Ten thousand a year for ten years."

"I shan't sleep a wink. You'll say yes, of course?"

"We'll see. Good night, darling."

"'Night, my sweet. I booked a quiet, inside room for you, and turned the blankets down myself. And I managed to borrow some pajamas. And Hamish——"

"Yes?"

"Don't dare let that man out of your sight!"

Moxon served an extremely good mulled claret. Mrs. Calton-Islip came in wearing a greyish satin negligee, and a blue turban, and no make-up. Extremely ocular in an Afternoon-Of-The Fawnish sort of way, good figure and pretty legs that she had no hesitation in showing almost all of.

But a mind holds only so much, and behind everything, Myril's red dress made a languorous pose now and again, whirled, and vanished into the glare of the fireplace.

"I've knocked him cold. Haven't I, Hammish? That's the stuff!"

"Why are you offering me this? I've had no commercial experience at all."

"Let me worry about that. You've got a fine head for figures. You're no fool. I found that out. You can talk. You've got the—er—the——"

"Presuntz, da-a-wling."

"That's the word I mean. What more d'you want?"

"How would I know what to do?"

"You'd get your orders. You get 'em now, don't you? By Bracey and that lot? Do you any good? Ever asked yourself? What good are you doing yourself or anbody else where you are?"

Standing up at least got the blood flowing again. The claret brought a feeling of sleepiness, not quite a drowse, but thickish.

"I'm not sure of the answer. My wife's the deciding factor. She'd have to be very sure——"

"Listen, fella. The minute you sign that contract, there'll be ten thousand pounds in your bank account. Nobody can take that away from you. Unless the bank goes bust. That's the way I do business. That's why some of the best brains in the world work for me. Tell your wife that."

Follow Moxon to the door and get a hat and coat, and carry the coat over the arm.

"Sorry. I'm a little confused. Good night, Mr. Calton-Islip. Thank you for your hospitality——"

"But you didn't have a scrap of caviare or nothing!"

"He's got plenty of everything coming along, dear. He's working for king George from now on, eh, Hammish?"

"I'll let you know soon enough. And by the way, *Hay*-mish is the Scots."

"Oh, I see. *Hay*-mish. Ay, I like that, don't you, Iv'?"

"Think it's swee-eet, da-a-wling! Hey-hey, Hey-hey, *Hay*-mish!"

"She will have her little lark. Goo' night, Hamish. Call you tomorrow."

"Goo-od night, da-a-wling! Bring the waifie next taime!"

He sent the chauffeur away, and strolled, opening and closing his eyes in a cool wind, watching the tail light turn down to the garage. Not a soul moved anywhere, not even a cat.

It was a little disheartening to find himself unsure of going to see Myril. Perhaps too much thinking burned up so much in the dream that impending actuality no longer held lure. He stood outside the park, looking across at dark grass and trees black in the moon's blue. Less than half a mile away she waited, trusting him to keep a promise, though she would hardly expect him tonight, that was certain. To wake her out of sleep was a little cruel, and besides, undressing, going to bed, performing, and getting up to dress again and walking home with the milk all sounded a little superfluous. It was strange that the mind painted such inviting pictures at moments convenient to itself, and then at the last moment washed its hands of the whole thing. But it got more annoying when things started all over again, especially with that tormenting thought of lost opportunity.

After all, it was the same old thing in varying degrees of the wonderful, depending on co-energy. Vinny had been in a class by herself. Recently she had become rather more mature, casual, but still good on her night. Which made the Myril episode something of a non sequitur as far as he was concerned. Why she should make him feel as he did was something he had often tried to fathom. There were scores of really beautiful girls up and down the place. But they had as much effect as pieces of furniture. Nice to nod to, and that was that.

It could be, of course, that the stolen-sweets side of things had an appeal. Perhaps the knowledge that he was committing a social wrong added an extra shake of pepper. But had it been merely socially wrong, that would have been bad enough. It was made far worse because Vinny was involved. She could be badly hurt. Risking anything as atrocious should have been out of the question.

All that had brought him right past the front door of his hotel, to Hyde Park Corner. Myril lived just across the road. There seemed no point in deliberately turning round and going back. Might just as well go on and get it over with. There was, after all, something uninviting about that cold hotel bed. Myril liked to be warm, and was, and she liked lying on top of him which was no undue burden.

Here was the street, and a little further down, the turning. Nobody moving anywhere, not a light in any window, and except for the hum of a passing cab, not a sound. He turned on to the mews' cobbles, and walked in the shadow down to the white door, and rang three times.

Light shone in the glass, and the stairs creaked all the way down, and he heard a whisper. He tapped on the panes for reply. A chain rattled, and a bolt squeaked, and the door opened, a black line, and she laughed. He went in and carefully set the latch, and she raced him up the steep stairway, in a silhouette naked as his vision.

She knelt to light the gasfire, but she had some trouble with the matches and held them out to him, and turned on the tap for him to catch the flame. They moved together to put out the light, but he had the longer reach, and then they were mouth against mouth, part of the dream. But the weight and strength of her were real, the warmth was real, the muscle under his hands was real, the feel of milk-silk was real, her arms were real and so were the talons.

She held away.

"Wait. I boil some water. I will make some coffee. There is cognac if you want. I am cold."

"We'll attend to that."

"Ahhh! Aymie. You are here. I am not awake. I like the feeling to wake up not sleeping, not awake, but a little thinking, a little sleeping. I wish never to get up then. Darling, we drank your champagne, and every drop I drink I promise never to be a fool again. I was a fool. I was mad. Forgive me, Aymie. It is something stupid."

"I've completely forgotten it. Where are the glasses?"

"Behind you. In the cupboard. Don't you remember?"

"I'll get the geography right in a moment. Here we are."

He poured a couple of fingers in each glass, and took his own to the half-armchair that had the comfort of a bony spinster's lap. She came back wearing a towel gown with the hood over her head, looking like an El Greco, and she threw the pillow at his feet and sat, resting against him.

"I think if I were your wife I would not be so patient."

"What's that?"

"You think a woman cannot tell there is something?"

"I don't doubt she can. I'm quite sure my wife doesn't, though."

"I intended to make her see tonight. That is the madness. Why? How can I say? But I saw you didn't care. You didn't. Why not, Aymie?"

"One's forced not to notice that sort of thing. It's a scene. The theatre does it rather better. You'd have been put outside. Where would that leave you?"

"But would your wife not say something?"

"Very likely. And very uncomplimentary. But it takes a great deal more than that, you know."

"More than to know somebody else has what is yours?"

"I wouldn't put it as far as that."

"But suppose your wife——"

"We won't suppose anything of the sort. We will not discuss anything to do with my wife. As far as you are concerned, I am myself, a man, a lover if you like, and nothing more. Those are the terms. Now, shall we talk about something else?"

She drank a little of the cognac and looked into the flaming shells of the gasfire.

"Why have you come here?"

"To keep a promise."

"That is all?"

"To see you."

" 'See'?"

"To get into bed with you, then. As you agreed at the beginning. 'A woman likes a man. A man likes a woman. What harm shall we do? I will never come between you and your wife.' Didn't you say that?"

"Yes, I said it."

"Very well, then. Why all this?"

She shrugged.

"I told you I was mad. It will pass. These thoughts I think to myself. Nobody else. If I cannot speak them with you, what shall I do? I am not a Catholic. I cannot go to the Confessional and whisper in the Wooden Ear. I cannot tell a priest of my love. I cannot tell him how I feel or what I think. I cannot tell him of my torment. I cannot make him unhappy. I cannot test his strength. He cannot remonstrate with me. Or advise me. Or punish me. Punish? Who can punish as much as the body? What agony is more? I open myself. Who shall come with me?"

"Myril, isn't it possible to be just a little less—less body-sotted?"

"I don't like your word, Aymie. Think of yourself. What do you do when you come here? You spit into me, and you go. This is what you think? I am a thing to spit in. Spittoon? Yes? La Belle Cra-choir——"

Up, twirling in the towel gown, slipping out of it, herself, dark-crowned, pink-disked, dimpled, whitely smooth above the black panache, thighed, kneed and legged in rose and shadow, arms clasped behind the nape, and still, motionless, torso outthrust, hands sliding over breasts and down, hanging, and eyes staring, smiling, hidden in the dark hair, watching him.

He reached out and tweaked the glinting floccus, and pulled her on to his knees.

"Did a little over two weeks of my absence bring this on?"

"Partly. Yes, certainly. I had so much to think. Why didn't you come to me in your kilt? I love it. You wear something under it?"

"Rather. If only to protect us from the curious. Don't you wear something?"

"Sometimes. Sometimes not. It is nice sometimes to go out with nothing. To look at men and feel naked sometimes is nice inside."

"I'll have to remember that. Anybody ever take advantage?"

"Nobody. I say yes, or I say no."

"How many times do you have to say 'no'?"

"Oh, my dear! So many times. Travellers come into the shop. 'Would you care for a little dinner? A little drink? I would like to see how you look in this very special little gown. Take off your dress, darling. It's yours.' No, Aymie. For this sort of man, I have the spit. In his face."

"And what about 'yes'?"

"Of course. But I forget them. They are nothing. No. Not quite that I forget. When I take a man, he is all men, and I am loving not one man, but every man who wishes a woman. How shall I say this?"

"It's fairly plain. So I'm merely standing-in for the male sex, is that it?"

"Yes. I have my share of all men, and I go to work singing the next morning. Let me take off your things till you are like me."

She flipped his tie out of the knot, and drew it through the collar. She had a little struggle with the stud, and sighed impatience, and put her hands on her hips.

"Why do you wear starch, Aymie? Why not a comfortable shirt? See, the collar makes a mark."

"I don't feel it. I'm not a devotee of the soft collar. Especially not to work in. It isn't done."

"Oh, it isn't done! Everybody wears them. Why not? Jimmy Wittard wore always a soft collar. Not smart but comfortable. But he was a brilliant man. You knew him, Aymie? He died a few days ago. I was sorry. And poor Louise. She didn't want to go tonight. But I said, why not? If you live or die, the world is the same."

An enormous and terrifying patch of black spread slowly over the ceiling, and down the walls and all over the floor and the gasfire became a foggy lamp in a corner of his eye. He listened to a roar of something that might have been blood streaming through his head, and in among it all he heard himself, although by what volition he was at loss to know, asking how she came to meet Mr. Wittard. He found time to admire that distant self for the admirable way it had kept its head.

She stood at the table pouring more cognac.

"Oh, it was with Louise. They came often here. He cooked pilaff sometimes. A marvellous cook. And an extraordinary conversationalist. Such a knowledge. He believed as I do. No. Not as I do. He could say what I would like to think. What I think, but only he could say it. And he is dead. What a tragedy. Wait, I go to get a towel for you. And the coffee."

She went into the bathroom and shut the door. Sitting there, but without the smallest moment of desire to call on strength. A warning pulsed to be up, collect an overcoat, jacket, tie, hat, and take the stairs in threes and fling open the door, and run across the cobbles, down the street, over the road, through the park and into the hotel, and get up to the aseptic safety of that quiet room and lock the door, and there take an oath, never, never again.

It froze in his mind that any friend of Wittard's, or friend of any friend, whoever they might be, must come under close surveillance. And here he was. Even a thought of earning £10,000 a year elsewhere did nothing to alleviate fear, or whatever it was he felt at thought of being found here.

Wittard's name had never been mentioned before. But it seemed strange that if he and Louise Hamble had been her guests on occasion, something would not have been said.

She left the light on, and the door open, and came out with the coffee tray.

"Known Louise long?"

"About a year. A clever girl. But very hard to understand. She has plenty of money. But she works."

"Hard to understand?"

"For me, yes. If I had money I would live. See everything. Do what I must do."

"What's that?"

"Go back where I have been when I was a little girl and see if there are more as I was. And take them and look after them. I must do that. Drink your coffee, Aymie. We have a little drink after, but I wish it was champagne."

Nothing else for it. And after all, the name had slipped out in the most innocent sort of way. There was really no need to shoot off at a tangent. By far the best thing was to get it over with, and get out before daylight. And to that end there must be a little conversation, though his mind felt petrified.

"What are some of the things you'd like to say if you could?"

"You mean what I think? Oh. Come to bed. I tell you there."

"Couldn't you give me something to think about while I'm in the bathroom?"

"Let me see. Yes. I think it is for everybody to make life better."

"Extremely cogent."

"To make life better for everybody. Not just for themselves. It should be everybody's good. A share for everybody. It is us, we who know what is good who should do this."

"All right. I'll take that in."

"And this. When you find something which will bring more misery to people with already too much, you must try to destroy it. However it is possible."

Her eyes were clear, wide, fixed. Chill, or perhaps the emotion that vibrated in her voice, made her body tremble and her half-clenched hands shook against her shoulders.

"Did you ever sleep with Wittard?"

Her eyes became wider, and then she laughed.

"This is so much like a man, Aymie! Yes, I slept with him. Two, three times."

"Satisfactory?"

"Certainly. Or why more times than one? But when you came, no more. He was very sad."

"There's an opinion that he wasn't much of a man for the girls. Some people thought he was fonder of the boys."

"Oh, Aymie. Who says this? He was very kind. He knew a woman. He liked everything that is sensuous. He made me feel everything. Everything in me. Whose opinion is this?"

"People."

"People."

He turned away from rock in her voice and took his clothes to the bathroom. A coffee pot simmered on a gas ring under the heater. After all there was desire. The thought of her lying on the bed beyond the wall, docile recipient of whatever he had to offer that would take her to work singing in the morning, was in itself a challenge and some sort of aphrodisiac.

He cantered out with the towel in position of vantage, and found her sitting on the floor, chin on knee, hands clasped on her foot.

"You thought a little of what I said in the bathroom?"

"Oh, yes. I agree with it all. But we'll get closer agreement if you come over here."

She stood, and three long paces brought her beside him.

"Does it matter that I had lovers before you?"

"Why should it? 'A man likes a woman. A woman likes a man. What harm shall we do?' Remember? Why?"

"I wish I had said nothing. It is silly to talk of other men. Like speaking of fried potatoes years ago. Forget what I said. Let us be us. Yes, Aymie?"

"Yes. Let us be us. A share of us for each. For the good of each?"

"That is something I thought!"

"What?"

"Why do you come to me if you have another woman? You have a strong sex, Aymie. But so much?"

"Enough. Or don't you agree?"

"Yes, I agree. Aymie, I agree. Aymie. Amore. Yes, I agree——"

He turned her under him and kissed into her sighing mouth.

"That's why. What more? Could anything tell you more?"

"It is what Jimmy said. We should live only within a philosophy planned for the guardianship of the unknowing, and unthinking, and unprotected moment of creation. It is our highest duty, we, its children, we, the forgetful, the coarsened, the contemptuous, the unillumined."

"He said that?"

"Where you are, now. He said it."

"Funny thing to say. But you don't think like that?"

"I would like to. But to think is not enough. I have no real language. No real country. I have my body. Without this I am nothing. And the world? Nothing. Therefore my body is more important."

"And mine?"

"Oh, yes. I give one for one. Good exchange?"

"Excellent. Where does that damn' towel go to?"

"Here. I will make more coffee."

Blaise came in during the morning to present Mr.
Flap's compliments upon a devoted pursuit of duty. The old one-
side-of-the-mouth, one-eyebrow-up smile made all appear in order,
and he had nothing to say about Leonard except that wine did
something to the liver. There seemed no necessity to discuss the
Calton-Islip offer at that time. Apparently the gentleman had been
most gracious and Mr. Flap had said that Gleave "had done himself a bit of good." A couple of matters had cropped up to be talked
about in Paris on the way back from Geneva, which meant at least
a day longer on the trip and perhaps two or three. Vinny, doubtless,
would be livid at thought of his having what she called a week's free
holiday. Blaise agreed that an early finish was in order, and just
before noon he packed up for home. He took the bus to the station
and the conductor let him put the bag under the stairs. A porter
carried it to the train, and seemed a little disappointed to be told to
put it in a Third Class compartment, possibly because it meant less of
a tip. But the difference between First Class and Third sent Hamish
to a very good prep. And that was much more important.

There was an uncomfortable feeling that small savings were a
little ridiculous in view of the money that went on champagne and
new dresses and tickets for expensive outings. It had no explanation
that might suit a professor of logic. But Vinny agreed with him that
if the cork had to stay in all the time, then to hell with it. And there
it was.

A young woman with a baby got in, and an old man in a cap, and
a tall, thin negro with a new, grey felt hat perched on top of his head,
large eyes, a thin nose and enormous mauve lips. It occurred that
there might be a scurry in the barnyard if a negro's lips were red.

The old man had a pipe but no matches. The negro grinned with the shattering suddenness of a trapdoor's opening to show two rows of new enamel mugs, and handed over a box in fingers a pianist might have given his wits for, and took opportunity of squeezing his lips into a fleshy vortex and opening liquescent eyes to coo a little banana-talk for the benefit of the baby. The child lay back and bawled its head off. Mama turned it about, and did all the things mamas do. The old man got the pipe going and tamped it with the matchbox, and the negro looked out of the window, smileless with a touch of hurt.

"When they're that old, they don't understand,"—the old man, waving at the child with the matchbox—"Everything's a bogey. My ma kept me down the bottom of the bed for three months. That was the old style. Didn't do me no harm, did it?"

"The advent of the unusual,"—the negro, in a high voice and a surprising secondary-school accent—"I keep forgetting. It is very foolish. I hope you will pardon me for frightening the child."

"Oh, it's all right,"—the woman, smiling assurance—"She's like that with her father. Can't even go near her. Teething, that's what does it."

"Ah,"—the old man, puff, swallow—"That an' the mumps. I suppose you have 'em in your country, do you?"

"Oha, yes,"—the negro, laughing—"We have the normal ills common to us all. There is no difference."

"Where's that, might I ask?"—the old man, leaning forward—"I was in Africa."

"The British West Indies,"—the negro, laughing again—"Barbados."

"Ah,"—the old man, nodding—"I'd heard of it. Long way from home, ain't you?"

"This is my home,"—the negro, with great seriousness—"I live here now."

"I suppose it's a bit different, is it?"—the old man, puffing—"How long's it take to get out there?"

"Oha, two weeks, comfortably,"—the negro, laughing again—"No, it is not very different. The weather and the scenery, yes. The way of living, perhaps. Otherwise, no. There is more work here. That's all. It is possible to live. Live well. Everybody is very fortunate."

"I'm glad somebody's satisfied,"—the old man, looking out of the window—"Wish I could say the same, mate."

The train stopped, and the negro helped the mother out, and walked along the platform carrying her basket. The old man lifted a foot swollen out of its boot, with a V-piece cut away over the bunion, and rested it on the other knee.

"They're a danger, they are, y'know."

"Oh?"

"Yes. Work for nothing, they do. Ain't used to earning big money. Take anything. Ought to see 'em. Half a dozen families in a room. It's when they get after the women, though. Be surprised."

"Really."

"Donkey-rigged, they are. We ain't in it. Can't see it, meself. The colour'd put me off. Why don't it the girls?" ·

"Difficult to say."

"You're right. We'll have the lot of 'em over here 'fore long. I suppose then we all go over there, eh?"

"Very good solution. Do you like the sun?"

"Can't say I do, too much. Had plenty of it, though. My job's mostly been night work. 'Course, that's all done for now. Yes, all gone. Be surprised the changes."

Reading the paper brought a pause. The train slowed again, and the old man pulled his coat about him, and thumbed his pipe, and lay it carefully in his pocket, and went to the door.

"Yes, guv', I'm eighty-six. Seen a lot, I have. I bet you wish you was me when I was your age, eh?"

Looking into the old eyes and trying not to say yes, I wish I had lived then.

"Good as that, was it?"

"Oh, yes. I hear 'em talking now and again. I have a quiet nod to meself. Don't cost nothing, do it?"

"Nothing at all."

"Good job, too. I was at Khartum, I was. Right through South Africa. Mafeking. Done twelve in India and Burma. Finished off in China. I was a gunner. Right of the Line, and the pride of the British Army. That was us. Never let any of 'em forget it, neither. But what they done with it? Eh? Give it all away. I've often thought about that. All the lads, eh? Last man, last round. Still, no use grousing, is it? So long, guv'. Got to look a bit nippy, here. Me feet's wore out."

Fortunately there were only a couple of stops more, with a little extra speed in between. The seat was too hard and the shaking-about was a little too violent for easy reading, and too athletic for sequent thinking.

He saw Vinny turn into the station in time to park and wave him in. Her smile told him everything before he was out of the train.

"What's wrong?"

"Darling, don't be disappointed. Mummy's here."

"I'm going straight back——"

"Oh, no! You can't. She's in a very good mood. And she's bought the loveliest presents for us all——"

"She knows what to do with them——"

"That's unkind. It's only for a few days."

"Well, there's always a silver tra-la-la. I'm off for Geneva tomorrow——"

"Hamish, you absolute stinkpot. You're not!"

"Three or four days, that's all. Hadn't we better get a cup of coffee or something, and discuss things before we go home? There are one or two things. There's a transfer to Japan being hotted up. So I'm told."

Vinny had the key in the car door. She half-turned, looking up at him, neither frowning nor staring, and in her eyes was such hate, and contempt, and denial, that had he not been there he would never have believed her capable.

"This is going to be a most interesting cup of coffee,"—taking out the key—"On second thought, let's leave the car here. It's a nuisance parking. You told them you wouldn't, of course?"

"How could I?"

"Good God, what would we do with the house? What about this £10,000 a year thing?"

"That's what we want to talk about——"

"Take it!"

"Wait a moment, now. There's a question of pension——"

"Take it!"

"We've got to do more thinking than that, sweetheart. Look at the other side. I might find I wasn't up to scratch. Or didn't like it."

"Do you like the way you're being treated at the moment?"

"Can't say I do, no. But it's a particular form of Service——"

"What's your main objection? Working for commerce instead of Government? Some sort of a comedown?"

"No, not exactly. But it's not much of a thought, leaving merely to get more cash——"

Vinny stopped akimbo in the middle of the pavement, and people had to prance all round her.

"It's not often I catch you talking rubbish, my lad. But when you have ex-ambassadors going back to their jobs in banks, and generals and admirals and all the rest of them resigning and going on the Boards of companies, I really don't see why you should be accused of doing anything but following a well-greased path. Did they give a damn? A few hundred a year extra, darling Hamish. And that's what you're going to do, and not another word!"

She led the way into the café and went to the darkest corner. The table was tiny and their knees touched. Quietly, because she was not at all herself, and her chin was on her fists, and her eyes looked anywhere but at him, the events of the night before and that morning were retailed, with special reference to his pleasure at the room she had booked for him, and the comfort of the bed and the refreshment of a hot bath after a long bout of Calton-Islip.

"Iv' sounds rather nice."

"I think she is. Want to meet her?"

"I'm prepared to meet the devil himself as long as we don't have to go back to Japan. Or . . . I'm thoroughly sick, tired and mortally exhausted at the thought. I'm thirty-four. It was wonderful from twenty or so, on. Yes, I love travel. Yes, I love Japan. But I love those two little boys much more. I want a home. I intend to have a home."

"Others can't pick or choose. Supposing I were sent as Ambassador——"

"A long, long time yet, darling. By that time the boys will be in school. I'll be prepared to follow you. But I still want a place where we can put a few sticks of our own——"

"In other words, it's £10,000 a year, Panama, a free house, servants, cars——"

"And all the exes. That's right. And I'll see there are plenty, don't you worry. Just pretend you're an ambassador or a general, or something, and hand in your resignation."

"Don't forget we still have to go to Panama——"

"On £10,000 a year, darling."

"And the boys have to go to school——"

"We'll have what I always wanted, and that's a couple of really first-class tutors——"

"That'll run away with quite a lot——"

"All the exes, didn't the gentleman say? I'm the little bobbit who can make them. Let's pay for this awful wash, and go home to luncheon. Please God dear Mummy hasn't upset Mrs. Lindley. What an utter pet! How did I live without her? She's coming with us if I can help it. Panama's rather pleasant, isn't it? Smaile, Heemie. We'll soon be a couple of Cawlton-Aislips!"

Sunshine made the lane a ragged channel of gold and green, and wheat-ears fluffed above the hedgerows between white bursts of hemlock and spraying blackberry. The gate was open and he got out to close it with a pleasant sense of being home. The drive went through oak and beech, passing the greenhouse and potting sheds and the vegetable garden on the right, and the flower garden on the left. The house had been built for comfort. Five windows up, four down and a front door in the middle, flat-fronted in pointed brick, windows and door-surrounds painted white, with a varnished black front door and a hand-and-ball knocker in silver. Vinny had wanted window boxes, but watering them made dribbles down the brickwork and after a couple of months she had put them tidily along the garage walls. The dribbles stayed there, but she hoped that by next year the rambler would cover them.

The boys seemed to have shown sound common sense by going off with the Wolf Cubs for the afternoon. They were neither of them greatly taken by their grandmother. A smell of stewed plums and hot piecrust met them inside, and Vinny said something under her breath and ran to close the passageway into the kitchen.

"Why people won't shut doors I really don't know,"—impatiently opening windows—"Hate the smell of cooking in a house. Are you going to change? I expect Mummy's in the garden."

"I'll give her a filial peck, first, and see how long you'll give me after that,"—looking at ordered bookshelves, polished furniture, masses of flowers, black leather armchair by the fireplace and the current book exactly where he had left it—"That Mrs. Lindley seems to know what to do——"

"With a little help, darling. I used the vac in here this morning.

The gleam you see o'er every dam' thing's my own elbow grease. A servant's a servant, Hamie."

"Properly chastened, ma'am. May I escort you to the garden?"

Vinny's mother sat in state under the one pergola still in bloom. She received them seated, took his peck, and asked them to wait a moment while she made a note in the margin of the financial page of *The Times*. Delia looked exactly the same, early sixties, in a hat that should never have left the fruiterer's, and a general appearance of a slattern taking the day off in her mistress' clothes. She dressed with very good people, but the result was the same as if she relied on her friends. Never at any time did she suspect it. Nobody dared to take her on one side, first because she was incapable of listening, and secondly she believed nothing unless it were published in the Court Circular. Vinny's mother was not a favourite woman. Too handy with a word of advice in the early days, and cheques now and again for Vinny had never been gifts but only links in an attempt to keep her at heel. Her cheque-book was her Scripture. Nothing could happen without it. If one of the boys was ill—Oh, my dear, I must send a cheque—or if she found Vinny wearing something comfortable—Darling Vinsy-Wins mustn't go about looking like that. I must give you a cheque—and she had once seen him in a pair of run-down old tennis shoes—Hamie, my dear, how can you. I really must give you—and the acid raging which ensued had taken five years to patch, ten years to heal, and its memory still held, bringing silence between them and smiles held together with courtesy's glue.

She had no conversation beyond shares and shareholders, and chatter about the Court picked up at her club. A divorce had freed Vinny's father after five years of marriage, though how Vinny could have come from such a mother was a genetic mystery. Vinny's father had said she was product of an immaculate conception between himself and Undine, and had nothing to do with her mother except in the matter of transport. Delia kept estates in Scotland, Devon, and the South of France, and a house in London. She was wealthy by inheritance from her father, and a good marriage and divorce settlement, and had no compunction in putting a price on what others wanted and less in bargaining for what she had an eye on.

Not by any means had it been a runaway marriage, but Vinny, without a penny of her own, had been only too glad to escape. From childhood, through school and university it had always been Mumsy will have to go without to buy it for darling Vinsy-Wins, or if Vinsy-Wins is very good to Mumsy, until instead of asking for an English dictionary and having to go through hours of listening to how generous darling Mumsy would have to be with a few shillings to buy one, Vinny took Eng. Lit. with the one in the school library and ever after hated ragged pages and torn books.

Vinny had never, even to him, said anything unkind about her mother. She had no fear of her, and certainly no active dislike, but they rarely looked at each other and there was a feeling between them that if they did, they might scratch each other's eyes out.

Mrs. Lindley, small, spare, soap-polished, footy in large black felt carpet slippers, white hair in a black bow, blacked out from neck to ankles and whitely pinafored in between, served dishes from behind the chair, coughed into her shoulder—un-hum, par'me—and footed out at a stalker's lope.

He told them about the gypsy's promise to say it over peat, which brought fifteen minutes of balderdash from Delia on the awful habits of people and the waste, the sheer waste that went on. Vinny caught his eye a couple of times, smiled in the pupils, and when she could, led the way into the Window Room for coffee.

After the second sip, putting the cup in the saucer and resting the butt of her hand on the chair-arm and lightly clenching the fist as if it held a sceptre, Delia said she was thinking of altering her will. Vinny made encouraging noises—a sort of m-m-m?—and got up to take his coffee cup. Delia asked if they had any thoughts in the matter. He said he had none. Oh? None at all? None. Vinny said that surely she knew what she wanted to do with her own property? Delia said she was always open to suggestion and improvement. But if nobody had any, then she must use her own. But it was rather a pity about the boys.

He said there was no need to worry about them. Vinny said they were well looked after, and far luckier than millions of others. Delia took another sip, and said—into her cup—that they might have been infinitely better off if things had been done the right way. She meant that if her wishes had been followed with that supine adulation reserved for the wealthy, much more in the way of largesse would have been on tap.

He let it pass. He felt Vinny's eye on him, and half-smiled at a set of the Waverly Novels to let her know that he was far from rising to gadflies. The house could have been paid for, Delia said, opening a gold saccharine tablet box, the boys could have been entered for a *good* school, and their future would have been very well provided for.

Vinny raised her eyebrows, and asked if their future were so uncertain. Delia said that nothing was certain in these days. Nothing and nobody.

All this, he knew from old, was a way of trying to goad him into speech. Vinny seemed to know, and smiled that wonderful eyes-alight-teeth-alight smile. Delia said that she could see nothing to laugh about. There were any number of Researches and Foundations requiring money. She was thinking of making a Delia Hall Trust Foundation in memory of her father. Vinny wanted to know what the Trust would be for, and Delia said there was no necessity to explain where there was so little interest. And she put her cup down, and got up, and tugged at her skirts as if her crotch were full of them, and said she would rest for an hour or two.

Vinny looked rather serious for a little while after the stairs had stopped creaking. But then she smiled.

"It's awful. It's just as if I'd never known her, you know. I'm rather thankful you're off tomorrow. I don't think you'd last the weekend."

"I'll have to go tonight. That plane leaves at seven-thirty in the morning."

"Hamie! Oh, hang Mother!"

"For once she's blameless. I'll catch the ten-something and take the room I had last night."

"Promise you'll phone me?"

"Yes. What a pity she was born doited."

"That's why I'm so bright."

"You're an effulgence of the first order. Absolutely trillion candle-power. Nobody in the world like you."

"Not even the girl you danced with at the Grosvenor?'

He had to turn about to look at her.

"Who?"

"Oh, now come on, Hamie! Beryl Harrack met Mumsy and told her, and Mumsy told me. I think that's really why she's here. I phoned Beryl. A girl in a red dress, extremely expensive and obviously from Paris, and draped all over you and being rather sick-making, she said."

"Well, what about it?"

"Who is she?"

"A friend of one of the secretaries——"

"Known her long?"

"No."

"What's her name?"

"What does it matter what her name is?"

"I want to know. I don't like your being talked about."

"Who's Beryl to talk about anybody?"

"If she could tell Mumsy, she's told dozens of others. I want to be able to say I know her——"

"Because I have a casual dance——"

"That wasn't Beryl's description, and she was right behind you."

"Beryl always was the most——"

"She's entirely truthful. That much I'm sure of——"

"I'm not going to argue about Beryl's moral status. I'm simply saying that I shall not answer any questions prompted by anything she's said. I will not be a target for gossip——"

"If you make yourself one——"

"I wasn't aware that I had——"

"Who was she?"

"I've already told you. Nobody. Now, have we finished?"

Vinny picked up the coffee tray and went out. Something in her back said no, she was certainly very far from finished. And there was little doubt about it, if it came to handing out a prize, there was nobody in it for obstinacy except Vinny.

The armchair's former comfort had gone in favour of a fakir's bed of nails. Except through Louise Hamble, he saw no way of Vinny's getting hold of Myril. And please God, she never did. Care, great care was needed. No wonder darling Mumsy had threatened to change her will. It was a real sigh of relief to hear the boys outside.

And they hurled themselves at him, shrilling bundles of flailing arms and legs, and it took a roll or two on the lawn, and grass stains on the knees of his trousers before he could get a word in.

After all that he had to visit the rabbits, the white mice, and the pigeons, jointly owned, and the bees, which were Mummy's, and the wasps' nest, which was nobody's, and was driving Mrs. Lindley mad in the kitchen. After that he got a full half-hour of the afternoon's lesson in lighting a fire by rubbing wood against wood. The Cub-mistress appeared to have got smoke and flame every time, but for some reason both Robert and Hamish failed to make it work. That Daddy rubbed his palms raw in an effort to show them how was passed over in crusty silence. The Cub-mistress had done it. Daddy came a purler. That was the way it added up, and three utter dubs walked through the leaves toward the potting shed.

The stinks turned out to be a dark-room, filled with racks of jam jars, bottles and ex-officio cooking dishes, all of them holding something to do with photography. A curly handful of quite passable portraits of Vinny and Mrs. Lindley and others, taken by Hamish with his box camera, were offered for praise, and then Robert, feeling he was being left out, led the way upstairs to show a crane without a hoist—"'s'not supposed to, but look how it winds the string!"—and a new set of railway trains and miles of track and a pile of new picture books, brought by Grannie for them both. It had the taste of corked wine. The boys thought otherwise, and their faces said very plainly that they were sliding, if they were not already deep in the gilded clutch of darling Grannie.

Mrs. Lindley took them off to supper, with his promise of a bed-time tale about Sir Conkemall and Ososad, the Hebridean giant, and he was left in the empty playroom, watching trees black against the smoky red bars of the sunset, and listening to the chatter of homing birds.

Again, a vision of the boys growing up attacked him. He wondered if Father had ever thought in the same way about himself. There was something frightening about the idea of their having to go through the same old mill and landing up at thirty-nine, waiting for dead men's shoes, and having to put into practice dead men's thoughts. A memory of Myril came impersonally. The night before, and the morning's goodbye kiss, with a taste of coffee on her mouth, seemed to have happened to someone else. There was little recollection of pleasure and little sense of anything except that it had happened.

But the Beryl Harrack episode was a nuisance, and a warning, and a stopper, in one. Something sordid had happened to the entire business. A mistress was all very well for a wealthy man, with her own establishment and all the fal-lals. A mews flat, kitchen-bath, with blisterous paint flaking off the walls, grease in the gas-ring, and damp towels, was not in order.

He shut the whole thing out of his mind, and went to have a bath, and change, and do some packing ready for the trip. Vinny came in and kissed him without saying anything, and he took it that all was well. She finished the packing while he went along to the boys' bedroom to give them the latest development of a story that had gone on for at least five years, about Skalds, Fata Morganas, and Werewolves, always with a final battle between Sir Conk and Oso, which had to end with some cataclysm that stopped the fight and let them live for the next instalment.

Mother had her dinner on a tray. Over candles in the dining room, Vinny talked about their neighbours, the Cottons, and how kind they were to lend Hamish and Bobby ponies, and what a dear little thing the daughter was, and how she loved getting through the fence for ice cream and picnicking in the orchard. He listened and said the right thing in the specific pause. But a smell of guilt hung about the place, and he was glad to see the coffee tray. The News came on at nine o'clock. They listened to a weather report and headlines. Vinny sewed and appeared to be listening. But in the middle of an item about Germany, she put the sewing basket away and went upstairs. He waited until the main news was over, and went up to shut the suitcase and generally get ready.

But when he went into the bedroom, Vinny lay in the middle of the bed, without a stitch. Perhaps the lampshade gave flattering light, but she appeared incomparably beautiful, and lying down emphasized the lines of her body, and her breasts had always been shaped to fill a champagne-glass with not a bubble over.

"Yes, Hamie?"

"Yes. Decidedly yes."

"You won't mind if you miss your train?"

"There's always another."

"I'm so glad."

"Why should there be any question?"

"You haven't been awfully interested lately."

"Well, there are times and moods and so forth."

"Yes, I know. Perhaps I haven't been as affable as I might."

"You're always that."

"I know there's nothing—I mean—Beryl and—darling, don't be angry. But I got the most awful feeling."

"You shouldn't have."

"I know. Like this, darling. Just like this. That's wonderful. I've been so lonely without you."

"Don't cry, sweetheart. That's not my Vinny. Listen to me. I won't go. I'll get a later plane."

"No, no. I'll take you in for the one after eleven. You'll be in London after midnight. But you mustn't be late tomorrow just because I made a complete nonsense of myself."

Again that feeling of unutterable tenderness without beginning or end, shapeless as all desire. Never had she been much more than passive, that over a period had perhaps bred an answering passivity in himself. But she behaved as if everything had to be tried, as if there were no time to waste, and everything were uniquely important.

"This is early days again."

"About time, darling. I felt so old and married."

"Never!"

"But nobody's going to take you away from me. Nobody. Or if they do, they'll get what I leave them. Nothing. I'd kill you first!"

"This is the death. Now?"

"Yes. Now. Now——"

It was a pleasant surprise to see Charles Roff's eyebrows and lenses glimmering amazement in the line of passengers at the Air Terminal getting baggage weighed, but more than a shock to see Louise Hamble. Charles said that she and another girl, a Miss Dykes, were with him to attend an endless conference that dealt with one thing after another, and confessed he had forgotten its original purpose, but he liked the trips and hoped they would go on and on.

That was like Charles. He was always a little vague about what he did, and yet very few worked harder or got more done.

Louise Hamble, early thirties, shortish and well pulled in, rather heavy chin and grey eyes fringed pale that gave her a somewhat Christmas-cardy-angel look, always dressed well, but she had a penchant for hats made of feathers that blew about her face and gave her an appearance of something Triassic ambling out of the wood. Her eye was merry but demurely controlled, giving an impression of being an Nth short of outright coy. But it was more than made up by her attitude, sharp and decided, and a grande dame voice that issued from her nostrils with certain pullings-down of the mouth, permeating her sentences with plenty of air, and an accent that could always have found its way back, blindfold and flatfooted to the inner sanctum at St. Margaret's.

Seeing her might have meant rather less had there not been two telephone messages from Myril waiting at the hotel when he arrived just after midnight. The porter assured him they had come in that evening, the last not long before. That morning he found she had telephoned twice more after his arrival. She might, of course, have called on the off-chance of his still being there. But he could not remember telling her where he was staying, and he was certain she knew he had been going home. He asked that no calls be put through to him except from Beaconsfield, and after speaking to Vinny he went to bed, worried. But he was far more worried that morning.

Charles sat beside him on the plane. They rattled newspapers until Paris. During breakfast, Charles talked of the situation in France, and said he thought the Frenchmen were conducting themselves with superior intelligence. He was very pleased with them, and finely contemptuous of their critics.

Between bites at poached eggs and salvage with fingers of bread and butter and gulps of coffee from a slopping cup, Charles said that at a time when hopelessly helpless people were being fobbed with talk of a re-armed Germany and its wondrous effect on the European situation, a few astute Frenchmen had succeeded, by prodding the ulcer of the Saar, in bringing into broad daylight the hidden faces in the German political undertow suborned by the Americans. The moment they came to power, there would be no Europe, but a Pan-Amerope, with one mission, to obliterate Russia, and next Great Britain. Western Germany could outproduce France. German Communists had strength, certainly, because Marx, Engels and Hegel had written in German and the Germans were on the whole a thinking people. But most Germans hated the Russians. And because Communism for some meant Russianism, and since the mixture meant a threat to private property, there was little danger of Communists being voted into Government, at least for some years. Seeing strength in talking to the Russians from behind a reinforcement of a dozen or so German divisions was much the same as fortifying a bathing suit with a pair of cotton mittens to interview a swarm of hornets. Much more serious to contemplate was the result of freeing vengeful Germans as first line of attack on the American strategic perimeter.

"We've got to go in with the Americans, or we'll lose control in Europe to the Germans. That's why the Frenchmen will have to sign. It's less dangerous if they've got somebody there to keep a finger in the pie. If they stay out, and a war started, with or without help, France becomes a radioactive desert whether they like it or not."

"That's our fate. Thing is, who'll start it?"

"The Americans. They won't wait for anybody else."

"I'm for a third bloc."

"So am I. But it won't do us the slightest good in the event of war. Do you think the Americans would respect European air or waters? Or the Russians? Then again, but much more important, by appealing to German nationalism and everybody else's crapulence, we impose that tremendous defence burden on the German economy. Most of their goods now being produced will stop coming into the market. Basic industries will turn over to production of war matériel. That means our markets won't be cut into by a lot of industrious Germans. There'll be much more chance to sell. Our people are gambling on that."

"And if it comes to a scrap?"

"My money's on the Americans to win in the first week. If they don't, for the next fifty years it'll be on the Russians. If the last Russians have to fight with pointed sticks, they'll win. The American is a pioneer and a poker-player and a bargainer. The Russian isn't. It's a nation of chess-playing martyrs. With a religion. There are more of them. They also have brains, and they don't hesitate to use them. We accuse them of blather. But if you read the blather we give back to them, one's forced to the conclusion that our blather is the poorer quality. We have nothing to offer them, at all."

"I wonder. Don't we want the highest standards of living consonant with conditions?"

"Flapdoodle, Hamish. If you'll forgive me. I've listened to it since I was sixteen. I've yet to see it put into practice. Let me hear somebody—especially an American—say that the first thing to do is to pay the European workman the same wages as his counterpart in the United States."

"Difficult to do."

"Not difficult. Dangerous. There goes the fallacy of the American way of life. There'd be no more boasting from that quarter."

"You don't seem very enthusiastic."

"I'm over sixty. That's too old for enthusiasm. Too young for optimism. Too experienced for pessimism. Old enough to be thoroughly unhappy. How was your breakfast?"

"Impersonal, thanks. Where's all the taste gone in things?"

They put out cigarettes and adjusted seat belts because the sign said so. Ears popped, and the plane bounced along the runway.

Geneva had never struck him as being much more than a lakeside market town made accidentally superior with the gift of a site for the League of Nations, possibly in act of conscience by the shrewd governors of a country that performed as a cloakroom, if not as a gentlemen's convenience, during one world war, and was lucky enough to be holding the concession, and taking the fees, during a second.

Charles went off to stay with friends. It was embarrassing for some reason to find that the two girls had rooms on the same floor as himself at the hotel. There was a difference in scales of allowance, but Louise Hamble could well afford a room and bath. He supposed she was sharing with the other girl. An official car took him out to the railings, the trees, and the flat-blocks of the Palais des Nations. The same old feeling, as if he were entering a factory, afflicted him. All the corridors were lined as ever with doors bearing the names of the world's telephone directories. The side-salons were filled with people listening to speeches read from script.

The conference sub-committee had just finished its detailed agenda when he arrived. There was nothing better to do than to get a light lunch. The coin came down tails, which meant a bite on the roof-terrace instead of going back into town. He went down to the book-stall to get something to read, and while he looked through the stacks of newspapers somebody cackled, and he found Bejian Emyenkov looking at him over his glasses. Beji said he was attending as delegate on a Displaced Persons committee to protect musicians and composers.

Frolla was upstairs, and he accepted Beji's invitation to join them. She sat with three men at a centre table in the restaurant, and held up her hands in a kindly motion of surprise to see him. She introduced Rodolphe Mavritz, a French Civil Servant, dressed in the continental fashion of tight tailoring, with a red rosette in his buttonhole, tall, thin, dark, with black hair parted in the middle and oiled to the shape of a narrow head, rimless octagonal spectacles that made his eyes the size of a black olive, an extremely guttural flow of expensive English, and boots in two sorts of leather done up with buttons. Franzik Drechat, a professor of economics from Prague, fair, thin, wore a pale blue sports jacket and blue flannel trousers, rubber-soled ski-shoes, multicoloured socks, and a scarf with a check shirt. Vissarion Arkhiv looked about seventy, so massive that he sat on the chair's edge perhaps because he might otherwise never have stood up without help, hairless, with a peremptory pale blue ball-and-socket eye, black suit, starched linen and a folded-over grey cravat with a large pearl tie pin, a gold watch chain of large links, and a large ring on the large little finger of each large hand. He sat throughout the meal, using a fork with one hand and resting the other on a walking stick.

Frolla said that he was a professor of philology, preparing to go to Brazil to study the languages of the more backward Indian tribes for the sake of posterity. Professor Arkhiv rolled the ball-and-socket eyes, and said in perfect English that he hoped posterity would thank him.

People were standing at the back of the restaurant and the terrace was crowded. It had always been a sore, though unspoken, point that other delegates seemed able to afford the best restaurants and hotels and never appeared to question the bills or attempt to save on them by cutting down on the tip. Bejian and Frolla were neither of them more than attachés, but they wined and liqueured as if they were ambassadors on unlimited allowances. Bejian chose a cigar and so did Arkhiv. Mavritz was a non-smoker but Drechat burned something palpably French that made a sufferer ask a waiter to open a window. They spoke at length about the difference between modern Russian law and the Roman, and agreed that the death sentence was as freely to be given in the one as the other, and for the same crimes. At about three minutes to two it was time to go back to the conference room. Bejian asked him to have a drink that evening at their hotel, and refused to let him pay for the packet of cigarettes.

Charles Roff waited in the corridor looking like an angry sealyham. He said the food was rotten in the staff canteen and the smell of cooking all over everything had got into his clothing. He preferred the buffet on the ground floor. It was rather lighter on the pocket, too. Swiss money, he thought, was a highly improper because expensive token on what was nothing more than international territory. He was quite of the opinion that the United Nations should have its own currency exchangeable at favourable rates with all Governments, which would give any poor devil having to work for them a chance of eating a square meal. As it was, some currencies had a far greater value than others, to the gross disadvantage not of the wealthy but of the typists, clerks, and lowly Civil Servants generally.

Getting up and making a speech took little trouble and less gumption. There was not much to say that had not been said many a time before. It was difficult to see what else was to be done. Everybody had been told to say what they had said, and if any agreement came about it was an accident of language, rather than admission of argument or desire to agree. Some delegates had to retire to consult their Governments, and others stayed on to talk.

At about four o'clock he strolled out to have a cup of tea and met Mavritz in the corridor.

They took their cups to a table and passed each other sugar and milk, and sat back.

"I think it is a waste of time, here,"—Mavritz, in that rhotacized stream dammed by a mouthful of sugared bun—"I stay four days listening to talk, talk, talk, and what? Nothing."

"Pleasant holiday?"

"I am forty-four years. Why should I live a holiday?"

"If your Government doesn't want to do anything, what's the use?"

"My Government would like to do something. But other Governments, no."

"It's the same with everybody, I'm afraid."

"I am also afraid. Very afraid. We are fools."

"We?"

"We. Men like you and me. Like most of the people here. Fools."

"I don't quite see that. We're doing what we can."

"So is the fat lady making to swim in the sea. She is on holiday. She is doing her best. But we? We are men. We have a position. Imagine to come here, talk, talk, with others talk, talk. And what do we do? What have we done?"

"We don't control policy."

"It is right. We don't. Why not?"

There appeared very little to answer there. A look about the noisy, bare place filled with dozens of men and women yapping among the crumbs, and tea and coffee puddles.

"We see what we have to do,"—Mavritz, leaning forward and tapping the table top—"I will not speak less for my country, you will not say less for yours, no? But we come to an agreement. This is so? Of course. Why can we not? Because we are sent to talk."

"I sympathize. But I don't think we'll get very far thinking along those lines."

"Why not? We are men. We have brains. It is our duty to think. Otherwise, what we are, Mr. Gleave? What, tell me please, what we are?"

"No more than what we pretend to be. Representatives."

"Representatives of what?"

"Of our Governments, presumably."

"Presumably? Is there some doubt?"

"Not in my case."

"And not in mine. Then if you have no doubt, and I have no doubt, what is presumably?"

"Rhetorical, perhaps."

"A correct word, here. Correct!"

It was rather uncomfortable having to talk in the gabble and clatter, and it was time to get back. In any case, the subject was a little too near the bone. Mavritz's contempt, and the glazed look of distaste in his eye demanded argument. Unfortunately, there might have been uncompromising agreement.

The committee still droned, sent things to sub-committee, referred back, postponed, argued, appealed to the Chair, quoted, read extracts, took a vote, and adjourned until the following morning.

"Excellent!"—A representative, laughing, and gathering papers any-old-how into a case—"I thought that cretin would never finish to speak. Now I get two hours the golf before the sun go. You play, of course?"

"Yes."

"You should come one afternoon. It is a beautiful course. I like very much."

136

Walking along the corridors looking at door-plate names, all of them talking and papering on monetary dues paid by Governments and taken from their peoples. Passing a hall filled with people listening to someone talking from a rostrum backed by a rank of flags, each flag meaning a separate people, each separately taxed, each separate representative sent to say something separate and nothing else. And each separate something each separate representative said was translated into four languages at the time it was being said, so that instead of one representative talking, there were as many as the number of languages being simultaneously translated, and they all said the same separate thing but in different words.

Taking the streetcar back to the station there was time to look at the Swiss housewife and the children coming home from school. The women lacked the style of Vinny, and none of the children started looking like Robert and Hamish. But there was a dressed, fed, and cleansed look about them all that might have been hard to find elsewhere in Europe, or for that matter anywhere. Phlegmatic though they might be counted by the more envious, there was a certain common discipline in the way they carried themselves, and an air of living properly and at peace with all things.

Strolling down from the station, and looking in shop windows for something to take home for presents, and watching people talk and laugh, it struck him that the Swiss appeared to have found a solution to the art of living quietly without any help from the demagogues. He had never served in Switzerland, and he surprised himself by failing to remember the name of any Swiss minister. He knew a few Swiss diplomatists, and he also knew that the country was divided into Cantons that had unified under one Government during the thirteenth century. And that was about all, except for a broad acquaintance with the best hotels, and the ski-meets, railway and plane routes, the lakes, and all the roads from end to end.

He walked across the bridge, wishing Robert and Hamish were there to take them for a row around the Jet and wet them in the spray. Remembering Vinny, he wished she were waiting for him at the hotel just as she had been last night. Myril's telephone calls had worried him. They presupposed knowledge he did not believe she had, on top of her mentioning James Wittard as a friend. She might not be anything more than she said she was. Running over in his mind all she had told him about herself, it was barely possible to imagine she might have lied. But there was no way of finding out. It was all a miserably I-spy affair, and he knew better than most that very few could be trusted, although it was difficult to think anything of the kind about her. His knowledge of the Russian language was sufficiently good to detect a flaw in her accent. It might have been accounted for by her lack of early schooling and drifting all over the place with servants, which, of course, gave basis to her story. Security would get at the facts quickly enough. But that was giving the show away.

The café he chose was opposite the flower market. Women were packing the blossoms for the night and roping the covers of their stalls. He ordered coffee, and bought a *Paris Soir*, and the local evening paper.

He read through the news, and drank the coffee, and sat there, looking at colours, and trees, and people, thinking over what Charles Roff had said, and trying to guess what Mavritz might have said had he been given an opportunity. He was not altogether in agreement with Charles about the French. Far from believing them to be victims of a superior intelligence, he felt that most of them had approached a point in pseudo-democracy where every man believed that his opinion counted for just as much as any other's, and refused authority to any except those in perfect agreement, delegated half-authority to those in half-agreement, and none to those with none. Governments could be voted out overnight, and so often were, and dependence rested upon the loyalty of a singularly ill-paid Civil Service and the self-interest of trades unions to keep the country functioning. It was that semblance of order which so often provoked the outsider into saying that there was nothing wrong that a few more years of peace would not ameliorate or eliminate. Unfortunately the seethe remained, of a people stimulated by advertisements of all kinds into wants beyond their private means, by colonial misadventure into debts beyond their national means, by internecine politicking into a flux beyond the means of the best minds among them to restrain, much less to remedy.

An area of appalling discontent seemed to have appeared in every type of European mind. Mavritz had merely begun the introit.

His own mind, he knew, suffered, although he rarely permitted himself the luxury of self-examination. There was something unhealthy about such a process, and deplorable, in that nearly always at the end, reasoning came out at loggerheads with the course of duty, which so often seemed to have no basis in reason at all. For a long time, certainly over a period of years, he had been aware of a mounting disinclination to think in the same terms as certain others, notably, of course, Mr. Flap. The conception, the framing and the implementation of most of the policies were, in his opinion, not only useless, but out of all keeping with the requirements of the day, and at root, undignified. The pro-American policy was only one example. It could lead to nothing more than Britannia's having to put on a skivvy's cap to play housemaid to Uncle Sam. As events were going, it must happen, because Uncle had the productive capacity, and the only real medium of exchange. The policy toward Germany could only result in the German waiting his opportunity and bolting toward the East, for the very good reason that nowhere else were German brains and goods needed more, in larger quantity or at a better price, simply because in addition to the Russian there was an entire Chinese market to satisfy. All the Soviet literature that he had studied throughout his time in the Service gave a fairly accurate picture of the national scene, not only from what was printed, but far more significantly, from what was carefully left out. After thirty years of revolution, and retrenchment, and a war and its outgrowth, their universities and technical schools had begun to graduate tens of thousands of well-trained adults, all with a fairly durable philosophy both of living and of working. That annual strengthening of the common stock in every part of Soviet territory could not but have effect in outlook, in terms of work and enjoyment of leisure. Brains and effort, directed by an authority insistent on discipline of a particular kind, would solve many an economic shortcoming with greater ease than at any period before because all the blueprints were in front of them, tested and made to work by other men's trials and errors. Whether Russian teaching was biased or not in this or that direction, it would be idle nonsense to claim on that account that their minds were less able, less constructive, or less creative. The material evidence was mostly to the contrary. There was little enough proof of any incidence of discontent. The people seemed to have made up their minds that what they wanted was on its way toward them and they were willing to wait for it. Europeans, on the other hand, seemed to have made up their minds that what they wanted was not only not coming their way, but was far beyond their reach and going further away with every moment. It was not dread of war, and neither was it the failure of political systems which was turning the majority of the world's working people toward Russia.

It was, in fact, their discontent.

That special discontent which he discovered in himself, and which he knew tormented Mavritz and how many others, was not simple to formulate much less to specify. It seemed at times nothing more than a desire to do far more than was permitted within the scope of the daily round. To do more, live more, have more. More seemed to be the talisman. But only the American system of economy had so far, and demonstrably, produced more for every class of people, white or coloured, although solely within the American hegemony. Certainly that example had inspired many in Europe and elsewhere. But in Europe there seemed a hiatus between desire and fulfillment; possibly because so many governments required so many groups of politicians, each with their own ideas of what should be done that would leave them in charge, and so many currencies, none of them of much value in themselves and all of them of little value beside the dollar. American economic strength appeared to come from a Federal Government and one currency for a diversity of people and many States. European weakness was manifest in many Governments over a lesser area with twice as many people and as many currencies as there were governments. Russian economic strength appeared to be based on the same principle as the American, with one Government, and one currency, but with greater land mass and three times as many people. On the surface, what had taken the Americans almost two hundred years to achieve could be equalled and perhaps surpassed by the Russians in fifty. They had the people, the material, the will, and the faith. By contrast with the American or Russian, the indigence of the European scene disgusted and, in a small way, terrified because of a prevailing sense of helplessness, and the resultant permeation of an extraordinary discontent.

The kiosk became twice as round, and people had to go out of their way to allow a large figure to tuck a walking stick underarm and choose from a handful of notes the requisite amount for a roll of newspapers and magazines. The kiosk lost half its width, and Arkhiv, in a large grey homburg, leaned on the large handle of the malacca stick, looking pleasantest though mild, even innocent surprise.

"A most fortunate meeting, Mr. Gleave. I take my little stroll as it becomes a good temporary citizen of Geneva. I find this time of the day most agreeable to my constitution."

"I find it so myself. A remarkably good coign for a little light thinking, this. Shady, no dust, and quiet. Pity one can't work in a comfortable café."

"I have often had some such impression. Our offices are beginning to be released from the industrial curse. It is remarkable the progress since twenty years in design. We find out there is no need to work in prisons. Surroundings are most important for mental activity. And these flowers, they are the spiritual food."

"One of life's smaller pleasures. Curious, one often finds a hunger for colour."

"I grow chrysanthemum and orchids. Colour!"

"My wife grows a few, too. But we haven't quite reached the orchid level. Won't you sit down?"

"I shall be most happy, my feet most of all. They have much work. We go to Bejian after? I have my car around the corner. So pleasant, this city, I find. You have known Bejian long?"

"Not very. A year or so."

"I knew him in Russia. In Moscow."

"You're a Russian?"

"Yes. I am Russian. Not White Russian or Red Russian. I am Russian. You prefer I go away?"

"Rubbish! Bejian's a friend of mine."

"I hope he will play tonight. I bring with me a young Russian violinist. He makes a tour of Europe to see, to hear. Very fine."

"Good. What will you drink?"

"At this time I prefer champagne, thank you."

There seemed no way of saving money. A bottle of champagne in Swiss francs was a large sum. However, there it was.

"I think perhaps I will come to Geneva when I retire."

"I thought Russians never retired?"

"Oh, but certainly. I have a villa on the Black Sea. For many years. But Geneva has a quiet . . . "—waving the large hand in lieu of a word—"I find I am peaceful here."

"Isn't Russia peaceful?"

Ball-and-socket pale blue eyes swivelled in a smiling stare.

"Certainly it is peaceful. But here I meet so many friends. I can speak my languages. It is nice for an old man, this. Not to think he is old and going to die. Go home and shut the door. No. In any case, the world is made for men. Not one place. I die where I am. But I live where I choose."

"That used to be the order, but not any longer, I fear."

"Why do Englishmen always say I fear, or I am afraid? This is curious in a race with a reputation of the bulldog?"

"I suppose it's a form of reticence, perhaps?"

"Or apology for an immodest mental attitude? As a student of languages I am interested in the terms of speech and how they are used. I have many theories about the English."

"I happen to be a Scot."

"You speak English in the English manner. You do not think in this way?"

"I suppose I do, yes. What is the English manner?"

"Look in the literature for this. A combination of Micawber, and Sherlock Holmes, and Long John Silver, and Robinson Crusoe.

Examine this penurious humbug, and this expert in petty detection, this good-natured murderer and this resourceful hermit. There is the fundamental Englishman."

"Interesting. I think you forgot Mr. Pilgrim."

"And Shylock."

"But Shylock isn't English."

"An English conception. As English as the others. A Jew cannot be English?"

"He can be British."

"It is a matter for thought, this. A man can be an English Roman Catholic, or a Methodist or something else. . . . But a man cannot be an English Jew?"

"He may call himself one. All loyal subjects are British. There is no English passport. Or Scots, for that matter."

"So it is wrong to describe yourself as Scots?"

"Not at all. My family is Scottish. But Scotland is part of the United Kingdom of Great Britain. We are embodied as British."

"But there is a British Jew, and an English Roman Catholic?"

"There are English families. They live in England. If they happen to belong to a particular church, say the Roman, then they're English Roman Catholics."

"But not English Jews?"

"I haven't the faintest idea. How about Russia?"

"Everyone is born a Russian. He may think what he likes."

"That's not commonly believed."

"But it is a fact. If your nature demands mysticism, there is a church open to you. If you require revelation, there is a Bible for you. If you need speech with a god, your knees are attached to your body."

"But the Communist is atheistic?"

"All Russians are not Communists. I am not. I have been too busy in my life with other studies."

"But you're happy with the regime?"

"I am allowed to do my work. I have everything I require. Why should I be unhappy?"

"Don't you find people interfering? Aren't you told what to do?"

"If I conduct myself in a proper way, no."

"What is a proper way?"

"As a norm in a lawfully-appointed community."

"We should then discuss the norm. An imponderable. A lot of people aren't sure the Russian communities have anything very lawful about them."

"It is better you go there to find out. Your friends at the Embassy do not complain?"

"They seem happy enough. But happier to get back."

"A different question. Why do you not go to Russia, Mr. Gleave?"

"I go where I'm instructed.

"Aha. You are also told what to do?"

"Naturally. I'm a Civil Servant. But my private life is my own."

"In this, there is no difference with the Russian."

Arkhiv spoke of the work he was doing, and the vast area covered by the study of phonetics. He said it was a tragedy that the English language had to suffocate inside twenty-six letters and five vowels, a result of the invention of the printing press, and unlearned printers' impatience in symbolizing instead of phoneticizing.

Six o'clock struck, and at Arkhiv's sign, the waiter came to clear away. But there was no bill. Arkhiv smiled and waved the large hand.

"It is my honour,"—raising himself by resting his weight on the stick—"I have an account here."

"But I must insist. I invited you, Mr. Arkhiv."

"Dear Mr. Gleave, I have been coming here for fifty years. It is understood that everybody is my guest. Please allow an old man his idiosyncrasies."

"Then thank you very much. May I say how much I admire your command of English?"

"I am flattered. But if we did not make a close study of languages, how should we know what you say about us? How should we reply to you? It is a tragedy I must say such a thing, that a language must be learned for invective, even vituperation?"

"I think it the greatest pity our countries have grown apart. I'd be very happy to see English become the second language in Asia."

"Ah, Mr. Gleave,"—the large hand, up in the air, palm out— "who wins that battle gains the greatest victory. English is simpler

in the mouth than the Russian. It has that practical advantage. There
is great opportunity. Why do you not work for it?"

"Civil Servants can't afford expensive hobbies."

"It is individual action that is important."

"Does your Government think so?"

"Very decidedly. It is why I am here. Why many of our people are
here. They do the work they want to do. The Government permits
it because it has a use."

"To Communism, of course."

"Naturally. Would your Government send somebody to do something harmful?"

There was indeed a car around the corner. A chauffeur held open
the door, of a large black limousine manufactured in Russia, Arkhiv
said, and supplied to him by his Government. Two more of the same
make of car waited outside Bejian's hotel. They were shown up to a
suite on the first floor, and knowing a little about prices, it occurred
that Bejian must be paying more for each hour of his tenancy than
the entire hotel bill for the two secretaries and himself over three
days. He wondered how it was done. But the party was just as surprising. A buffet's linen, silver, flowers and heaped dishes took the
whole wall of the drawing room. Four waiters carried trays among
about fifty people. Frolla met him in her happy way, and started
introducing delegates of one kind and another, directors of opera
houses, professors of music and heaven knows who.

"I thought I was coming for a quiet drink?"

"It is very quiet, Hamish. You like to drink by yourself?"

"No. But I don't usually attend parties."

"Then this is a privilege for us. Please stay for dinner. Only six of
us. Downstairs."

There was everything to be said for that. He knew any number of
people in Geneva, but he was in no mood for old-times conversation.
An early night, he thought, and the morning session over, he could
catch a late plain to Paris.

Arkhiv brought over a young man in a tweedy suit too big for him
and clumsy brown shoes and a shirt that might have been rescued
from the wash and put on to dry. Arkhiv explained that he was a
student from Moscow. He looked harmless enough. But when he

started tuning a violin, and Frolla clapped her hands for silence, and Bejian sat at the grand piano to accompany him, the young man became a positive fire-eater. The room hummed with the violin's tone and even the glassware on the buffet seemed affected. He got an ovation, and played something so quietly that it was possible to hear the lady in front's stomach rumbling from a yard away. More cheers, and Arkhiv tapped his walking stick, and laughed a large laugh.

"You like music, Mr. Gleave?"

"Very much. I'm not sure I understand that sort, though."

"Is it necessary to understand music?"

"It's supposed to have an idea, isn't it?"

"Emotion has no idea. Otherwise it is not emotion. Music is emotion made practicable. Many people fear emotion."

"I don't doubt it. A little too deep for me."

Frolla had the young man firmly under her wing. It took a couple of minutes of barging and being barged to tell her that he was going back to the hotel to change and that he would meet them in the restaurant. The hall porter met him in the foyer and said that Monsieur Arkhiv had ordered the car to drive him back. There it was in the street, chauffeur holding the door open, ready. Silly to refuse it, and anyway it was a fair walk back to his hotel.

The car ran not quite as silently as the Rolls-Royce, he was happy to notice. But the fittings and everything else were highly satisfactory. And the chauffeur bowed on opening the door, and clicked his heels, and pushed off without waiting for a tip.

Miss Hamble was in the foyer waiting for the lift. They exchanged "Good evenings" and went up together without word. She turned left, and he right, but all the way down the corridor he wondered if she knew of the affaire with Myril. The look she gave him—that he had seen in the door-glass—implied that given the slightest opportunity she might become talkative. But there was a level to be maintained and familiarity was never wise.

A packet of stuff from London came in by messenger. He dealt with some of it, and after a bath and a change, he took the rest downstairs and had it put in the safe.

There was the car, waiting for him.

He asked Bejian about it when they met in the restaurant.

"What is more simple to send a car?"

"How did the chauffeur know when to come for me?"

"But he was instructed, of course, to wait on you. You don't like to be seen in a Russian automobile?"

"Heavens, it's not that! But there seemed to be a great deal of staff-work going on."

"Not staff-work, Hamish. Friendliness. You have a suspicion?"

"No! About what?"

"Nothing, my dear friend. We speak of it no more."

Dinner turned out pleasantly enough. The young violinist spoke in good French of schooldays in the Ukraine, and a couple of years at Moscow University, and from all he said there seemed little difference between his life and that of any British student of his age.

"It is true,"—Frolla, in her mild way following a potato round her plate—"Everybody learns the same wherever I have been. A school is a school. A university is a university. Eat, drink, play the sport, what is the difference?"

"The sort of things they're taught, perhaps?"

"Teachers are not so much different, Hamish. The subject is a subject. You can teach mathematics differently? Yes. But any given equation is the same in Russia as in Britain. The same answer."

"The liberal arts side might be given a little twist here and there politically?"

"How is it that everything must be a suspicion?"—Bejian, frowning, and looking at Frolla, at Arkhiv, and cutting into some very good roast lamb. "Should we not also have a suspicion? In the teaching at British schools and universities is there no political twisting?"

"Not that I was ever aware of."

"Everybody except the British has this political twist in their schools? It is a discouragement. You see what a handicap we must overcome before we can do anything?"

Arkhiv put down his fork to wave the large hand.

"Exchange of scholars, technicians, students, all young people,"— glistening ball-and-socket eyes staring about the room—"More travelling. More books. More film. This generation, and perhaps the next, is poisoned with their doubts. An important medium arrives with television. Twenty years, the world has all the world alive in its kitchens."

"Not in mine,"—Frolla, laughing—"Nothing in my kitchen but cooking!"

"But, Frolla,"—Arkhiv, holding up the large hand—"Most of the human race are born to spend time and leisure in a kitchen. How many can earn enough to afford a house with a dining room?"

"The poor mother! She is always the cook."

"Except Frolla."

"I cooked for my family. Now I have other work. But I shall cook again when I go home. What is greater pleasure?"

"A lot of women who don't like cooking might not agree with you."

"I think not many, Hamish. Those women who cannot cook, they have a derangement."

"A what?"

"A derangement. Something is the matter with them. Their bodies. Or their lives. Their love."

"That's a new one."

"Not so new. It is like a man who does not like to work."

"Must be any number of deranged men."

"It is true. Look at their faces, and what they do. They are not good men."

"What do you call good?"

"Useful."

"Can't somebody be good without being useful?"

"No. What is bad is useless."

"What do you call bad?"

"Something that has no reason for existence."

"But surely badness is a matter of degree? Who are we to judge?"

"We do not judge. We prove."

"A very tall order. I think I prefer a less utilitarian outlook. There's a little of everything in everybody."

"Find what is best and improve it."

"I'm half-inclined to agree, but I don't like it put so baldly. I think it wrong to regard life as a sort of schoolroom for making the pupils better."

"Then you are not a Christian?"

"Decidedly. Why not?"

"Is this not the object of all Christian teaching? To improve a condition of original sin?"

"I regret I'm not qualified to debate it with you. I suppose it is, yes."

"Then how can you support badness?"

"I'm not supporting it. I'm saying it has a right to exist."

"By whose authority? Your own will?"

"Yes, I suppose so."

"Have you always found it trustworthy, this will?"

"I don't think we'd better take this any further. I'm well out of my depth in the matter of philosophy."

"But is it such a thing as philosophy?"—Bejian, waving his fork—"Isn't it what you want? Good or bad? If you want to be bad, or if you have a bad thought, then you advocate a right for badness?"

"I wouldn't advocate it. I simply don't like the puritanical tone, that's all."

"You prefer the Christian compromise? Sin if you must, but come and tell us and be sentenced?"

"No, Mr. Arkhiv. I don't think that's the attitude at all. They recognize human fallibility. That's what I'm getting at."

"But this fallibility is profitable."

"That's a very old one. There is that side of it. If you want something, I suppose you have to pay for it."

"There is great profit in sin? It is curious to worship Something which can alter its decisions by gifts of goods and money. Even now there is still a bargain for a Pharisee."

"I think you forgot that apart from anything else, any Christian sect believes in the forgiveness of sins. Forgiveness is only that. It doesn't require gifts or the word of any priest. It's a matter of penitence."

"But Mr. Gleave, this self-exculpation absolves the criminal?"

"Not at all. He's a criminal because he's committed a social crime.

But he isn't a criminal in heaven. In the eyes of God, he's a sinner. I hope there're quite a number of ex-sinners up there."

"I wonder what I shall do if I find myself in heaven?"—Frolla, helping herself to salad—"Or perhaps in hell?"

"Won't be much use quoting Marx."

"His value is chiefly as historian of poverty,"—Bejian, cutting meat from the chop bone. "But according to Christian belief, did not God give him life? His brain? And his pity? And his anger? If Frolla comes before this tribunal in heaven, I hope she will say that our eldest daughter died in a prison camp. I hope she will say we spent four years apart, also in prison camps and apart from our children. If it is a God, it is already known how we think. For me, it is enough we have work to do on earth. What is after, we shall see. What is this God that would like to burn people? The same as this one with the oven at the camps?"

"Beji, Beji!"—Frolla, leaning over to tap his paunch a couple of times—"No good to become angry, and eating. You get a bad stomach, please——"

"So let us speak of something pretty,"—Arkhiv, nodding the large head, waving the large hand—"I have at my apartment in thirty minutes, Chinese and Viet dancers. You like to meet them, Mr. Gleave?"

"I'm going home to bed, if you'll forgive me."

"Now, Hamish!"—Frolla, putting her hands together—"Half past nine, you go to bed? Think the digestion. Come to see the dancers, fifteen minutes. The car takes you home, ten o'clock."

"Come, Hamish. You will hear my work. They go to dance in Paris. Music by Bejian Emyenkov. Then, we hope, the Opera House, London. For this night, I drink!"

"Oh, Hamie, please!"

"Frolla, you're irresistible when you pull that sort of face. Very well."

They all got into the limousine and drove for a few minutes to a block of flats on the lakeside. Arkhiv led the way to a lift, and a uniformed man bowed them up, and another bowed them out on the first floor. A butler in knee breeches and medallion of office opened the door, and a footman took their hats. One room opened into another, filled with tapestries, pictures and furniture that might not have come amiss in any museum. The room they sat in was restful and thoroughly comfortable, modern in design and furnishing with some good pictures by people he had never heard of, mostly Mid-European and Russian. Arkhiv somewhat redundantly said that where there was no interchange, there could be no knowledge.

Beji was halfway through a little spasm of odd notes on the piano when the guests arrived. Arkhiv and Frolla went out to meet them in the main salon, decorated in the Chinese style, set about with pottery and hung with some fine portraits and calligraphic panels.

"Our host seems to be a wealthy man, Beji?"

"No, not wealthy. This belongs to the Government. It is lent to him because it is proper to his work."

"He's lent all this?"

"Why not? There is plenty more."

"Could you get a place like this?"

"If I explain why I must have it. If it is agreed, I get it."

"Ah. If it's agreed."

"Yes. If you ask for more salary, it is agreed or not? Or you can walk in and take it?"

"Do you mean that any Civil Servant can live like this?"

"Certainly. How does a British Ambassador live?"

"But Arkhiv isn't an Ambassador——"

"He is the best ambassador. He is a scholar. His name, his work passes the frontiers in his lifetime, and far beyond. But Civil Servants also live well. Frolla and myself, do we suffer?"

"I must confess, not that I'd noticed."

"So?"

There was very little answer to that, but he was not quite satisfied. It was hard to swallow that the contents of a museum could be ransacked for the aesthetic benefit of anybody, scholar or not.

Frolla presented one after another of the most exotic-looking Chinese girls in silken robes, all young, some darker than others, some much shorter, from Hanoi and Saigon. It was surprising to find how many of them spoke English. A group of men squatted with drums, pipes and stringed instruments and played for a suite of dances, as singular for grace as for the dancers' immobility. The salon seemed to have filled up with a large number of people, but Frolla made no attempt to introduce anybody, and that suited him down to the ground. It did occur, and not once or twice, that his presence there was something of a tactical error, especially in view of the security check. But he shook the thought away. He was not going to act as though he were in commission of a crime. If people wanted to play the spy, well and good, and they should have a run for their money. There, the thought of Calton-Islip's offer was reassuring. He could always tell anybody to go to hell, and follow the generals and admirals and all the rest of the easy-money boys along the strip of scarlet to the gilt-edged gates of commerce, an in, to enjoy the gilded increment.

Frolla brought over the leading lady of the troupe to say good night. If Babs Porrit had a camellia-petal skin, Miss Hsiu Tieh had the heart of the bud, with not a speck of make-up, and the tiniest voice he had ever heard. She said she came from a village in Szechwan, and trained in Peiping. She hoped to study dressmaking in Paris and go back to China to open a school of tailoring. He asked why she would not continue dancing, and she said that many younger girls were ready to take her place, and helping to dress a nation was more important. Frolla said that each member of the troupe had a subject to learn, and while they studied they would also perform their dances and leave memories of China with the audiences they entertained.

"Seems a pretty good way to scatter a petal or two of propaganda."

"Why is it propaganda? We admire Greece for its sculpture. Is this sculpture propaganda? What is the use to think like this?"

"Accustomed to it, I suppose. Sorry, Frolla. I'll say au revoir until London."

She asked him to give her love to Vinny and the boys, and Bejian came across to see him as far as the door. Arkhiv got in the lift with him for the journey down, and said he had been honoured with the visit of such a distinguished gentleman, and he would be further honoured to meet him again. It was no use trying to waffle something or other in reply. Arkhiv was plainly sincere, and when the lift stopped he held out the large hand.

"Good night, Mr. Gleave. Please remember that I have also an apartment in Paris that is entirely at your disposal at any time. It would be a privilege. Perhaps tomorrow you would care to go there?"

"No, thank you. I have a room reserved for me."

"Then another time? Sir, good night!"

The lift doors closed before there was time to say anything else. He stood there, looking at the dark square of the doorway, feeling an icicle sprouting out of his spine, and trying to imagine how Arkhiv could have known that he would be in Paris the next day. He was certain he had said nothing to Bejian or Frolla. Nobody at the conference knew anything about his movements. Air Reservations were the only people.

He had quite a creepy feeling, walking down the steps of the building. But it was suddenly magnified by the appearance of the chauffeur, holding open the door of the limousine.

He shook his head, and walked across the road to a cab stand. Stupid, he knew. There might be a perfectly rational answer.

But there it was.

Toddy called the Embassy a gloomy den, a sort of half-finished heterotopia, and hoped to God that enough funds would soon be voted to make the place habitable. A series of conferences had gone on during the day, and everybody, including Kevin, seemed grossly out of sorts. It was a toss-up whether to dine alone, or suggest they dine à trois. They both accepted, and agreed to meet him at nine o'clock in a little Alsatian place off the Champs Elysées, where everybody chose from tables piled with fresh meat and fish and vegetables, and if they liked could watch it cooked, and follow in procession back to the knives and forks.

A chicken broth with a raw egg slowly cooking in it, and a paper-thin steak, barely touched to the grill, a salad of beetroot and watercress, with a Chambertin, made things almost worth while.

"Feel much better,"—Toddy, looking about—"Ghastly day. Another tomorrow. I'm retchingly sick of the whole business. Only the military have plans. Trying to keep their jobs, poor things. We've got nothing. Not even a valid suggestion. Raggle-taggle bobtail patchwork."

"Going to resign?"

"I'm not. No. I shan't at any rate until I'm sure of a date for the General Election. Doesn't look ripe, yet. I'll hang on and learn a little more about the art of keeping one's temper."

"I don't think I'll last six months,"—Kevin, watching the oil in his wine glass—"I'm thinking in terms of a scavenger's job, somewhere. Far more self-respect."

"You two appear deliriously happy?"

"You'll get it all in London. I sent you a bundle tonight. You'll get another tomorrow. If you want to know, we're standing with our feet on the shoulders of La Belle France and Uncle Samivel. The slightest wobble by either, and we're on our heads. I don't believe for a moment the Frenchmen will play. They'll pretend to, because they want dollar aid, and the comfortable feeling of a battle fleet in the Mediterranean and another off Indo-China if they're needed. But what they don't want is the Boche tooling about again. And they don't want any Russian bombers, either. That's their problem."

"What's the betting?"

"Very simple. Hold out until they can talk to the Russians. Get their bargain, and thumb their noses. They constitute a far greater problem for the Americans. A pro-Russian France creates a pro-Russian Italy. What happens after that? Chaos."

"But we're such a weary lot!"—Kevin, almost grinding his teeth—"We know perfectly damn' well, win or lose, we're finished if it comes to a battle. It isn't lack of guts or anything else except lack of any cover against three or four bombs. That's all. But we're talking as if we were still in the days of Metternich. I don't understand it."

"The Russians aren't worrying overmuch,"—Toddy, starting on the lower knuckle. "If they're bombed it'll do far less damage than the same amount elsewhere. They've got all the time in the world to rebuild."

"If there's anything left."

"There'll be just as little in the United States. I had a distinct feeling today that everybody around that table was insane. They were talking as if this were all a fable. Death of millions, destruction untold, desolation itself was merely academical. As if the airmen themselves hadn't said that's what would happen. As if the soldiers didn't agree. Though they try not to. Poor devils, I'm sorry for them. Their livelihood's finished."

Kevin ordered coffee and the cognac bottle.

"Thing is, what can we do? It's pathetic to have to sit here or anywhere else, gibbering like this. What's there to be done?"

"Hamish, if I knew I swear I wouldn't waste a moment,"—Toddy, thumping both fists lightly on the table—"I'd be out and about, shouting my head off. I'd spend every penny I possess to get it across. I'd use every method, tried or untried. The thought of our poor people going about their jobs from day to day, with this pack of poodle-fakers leading them into a furnace, is really more than one can stand."

"Which poor people?"

"Our people. The people I happen to know, among others. The people on my own estate for a start. And all the others. I feel deep responsibility for them. Good, loyal souls. They're the backbone of the Country, Hamish. The good-hearted working man. They've got to be protected. I know so many. They're really the people I work for."

"How could you help? That's the question."

"I wish there were some way of a rapprochement with the Russians. I'm convinced there's something to be done. But it's frightfully delicate. We're halfway there through India."

"There's plenty being tried."

"You don't think we're going to let Nehru lead us, do you?"— Kevin, staring, mock-outraged—"An Indian leading the sahibs? A jailbird? Unthinkable! But he's the only real statesman we've got. The selachians we're burdened with prefer the Gulf Stream, and a flow of nice, warm dollars."

"We'd be finished without them."

"I don't think we intend to be anything of the kind for any reason." —Toddy, sitting back, smiling—"All the eventualities are very well sewn up. No nonsense about that. With the number of ex-Service men and women in the country, we'll have no factional trouble whatever happens."

"Factional? You mean extra-political?"

"All that part of it's well taken care of."

"The entire Government's semi-military in any case, Toddy. We're going into military despotism as fast as we can go. Do you like the thought of a soldier as Prime Minister? The days of Cromwell back again?"

"I prefer it to the alternative."

"Then you believe that between the militarists and the rest, there's nothing? Not even us?"

"We don't appear to be very able, do we?"

The waiter served coffee. While the black pool formed in the third cup, there came a thought of three bombs, one each for Vinny and the boys. Some taint of insanity, as Toddy had said, infected all of it. But it had to be thought about.

"I had a chat with one of the U. S. Air Force officers with tendrils of silver creeper crawling over his cap,"—Kevin, dipping a cube of sugar and watching the colour spread—"He was quite sure they'd degut Russia inside a week. We'll take 'em out, said he. Depopulate and totally disinfest. And what about the United States? says I. Why, says he, we'll maybe lose all our top cities and a lot of good land. But when the cities get burned up, we'll lose all the tenements. But we'll get a better job than Jerry did on yours. We'll have the chance to build real cities the way we know how. The city populations we can do without. That isn't word-for-word, but that's the gist. Some of them are banking on a cold-blooded clean-out. Watch the exodus from Washington when it starts."

"It'll be just the same here,"—Toddy, snapping and unsnapping a cigarette lighter—"I only hope some of the more bloody-minded among the survivors find them out and crucify them. That's the most annoying part about it. Tragedy's fellow-travellers probably won't be alive to be shown their handiwork. Nobody'll have the satisfaction of saying You see? We told you so!"

"A lot of people are beginning to think as we do. Why is it we can't get together?"

"But Hamish, what in Christ's name can we do when we've met? Take a vote and go home to tea? We have no power. We can't push the people at the top who can't be pushed. They like their jobs. If we push too far, the electorate gets panicky. That'll probably mean another dose of the Labourites. Who'd want that?"

"Is a Labour Government less preferable to extirpation?"

"Barely less. I prefer to hold on and see what we can do with a little prudence."

"Prudence?"

"Yes, Hamish. You appear to possess it abundantly."

Kevin spoke for a little about the chances of teams in the coming Rugby season, and hoped New Zealand might come up to play the champions. Toddy said he had decided to enter a couple of horses in some of the American races, but they would go by sea instead of air. He thought something happened to them in planes. They never seemed to run as well. Kevin said it might be for the same reason that obstetricians barred would-be mothers from flying. A lack of oxygen, or too much pressure or something, interfered with the unborn child. Toddy asked where he picked that up, and Kevin said he heard it from somebody at a dinner.

Toddy shook his head, and went back to the lower joint.

"Here we are talking like this, and we may go up at any time. Any time at all."

"It's up to somebody to make a move."

"That's like saying we've all got to become Prime Ministers."

"Well, why don't some of us try?"

"That's anarchy."

Kevin sat back and stuck his hands in his pockets and laughed at the coffee pot.

"Anarchy, you say, Toddy. What have we got now?"

"A form of democracy, surely?"

"I'm glad you said 'form.' There are quite a large number in this form of democracy who hate the Tories just as much as you hate the Labourites."

"I don't hate them. I despise them. If they came in again, I don't think I'd stay in the country. I'd sell up and clear off."

"Where?"

"Don't know. Never thought about it very much. Canada, perhaps. Africa, somewhere. Spain. I don't know."

"Somewhere at any rate where you'd have a chance of saying a word or two about the way things are being run?"

"Not even that. I wouldn't care how they were run as long as people could live decently."

"Which people?"

"People. Just ordinary people. Ourselves, perhaps. What's this for?"

"I wanted to find out more or less exactly where we stand on things in general. Parliamentary rule by a Government elected by people making a choice in a free election, we all believe that?"

"Yes, Kevin. What's wrong with it?"

"There's nothing wrong at all. But you've just said that if an election—a free election—favours the Labour Party, you'll clear off."

"I'm not forced to stay in the country if I don't want to. And I wouldn't want to, because a Labour misfeasance would not reflect my opinion. I've had enough, both of them personally and their policies."

"Then you believe in the divine right of Lord Berrish and his fellow peers to govern?"

"I'm not anywhere near saying anything of the sort. I'd rather say that what I want for the country is far better for it than anything the Labour people want to give us. There are quite a number of people of my belief, and we'd do a very fair job if we were left to ourselves."

"Not democratic, so much as oligarchic?"

"Rather better than autarchic?"

"What's your opinion, Hamish?"

Trying to make matters plain without alienating friendly opinion carried with it a lot of difficulty. Looking at Toddy's face, and realizing by the fixed cloud-blue eye that a good brain was alert to hail its fellow or expose an enemy, there was additional cause for discretion.

"I think it's a waste of time to worry about what sort of Government we're going to have or might have. What we have to do is find a way of using the one we've got."

"I'm entirely in agreement there, Hamish. Now, what can we do?"

"A démarche to the Russians."

"Only on terms, Hamish. On past experience, I wouldn't trust them a millimetre."

"If they think the same as we do, how's anything to be done?"

"Wait until we're in a strong enough position."

"But that's what we're doing. Yet you've said you're retchingly sick of the whole business."

"I am. But I don't see anything else. One's helpless."

"A word to the right man in the right place——"

"Without permission?"

"By the Ambassador."

"Sign of weakness. There they'd be, with their terms, agree, or take the consequences. I don't think we'll get anywhere like that. Besides, the moment they get a say in things, we'll have a roaring time with our own Communists. The Party'd grow overnight. They could probably win most of the Labour seats. No, Hamish. That's a hole in the dyke."

"Then I confess I don't see much to do, either."

"So the weary thing drags on. It seems to me that only the Americans have anything to say. And everything to do."

"If we all think like that, I don't see what we have to complain about. Uncle Sam's the boss, and that's the whole contemptible story."

Kevin scraped his feet on the chair legs, and nodded for the waiter to pour another verre.

"I purposely took no part in that. I don't agree with either of you. I don't think we'll get anywhere with this Government, any more than with the others. Or with the Labour people, for that matter. They're merely a lot of jumped-up trades unionists eking out a living. When it comes to foreign policy, they're all completely at the mercy of what advice they're given by the admirals and generals. Where they're not, they're bussing the backsides of anybody in Burke's. They're the sort of people who've always loved the peerage anyway. Look who they put in the Upper House."

"They tried very hard to denigrate the peerage,"—Toddy, distant, austere. "They couldn't touch education, or outlook. They stabled cab-horses with race-horses, that's all. Perhaps it did the cab-horses a great deal of good. It certainly toned them down. At least they learned to use napkins at meals."

"All of them aren't like that, Toddy. I disagree wholeheartedly with you. There are any number of extremely well-educated men among them. And I don't think my lineage any the worse because my grandfather wasn't a peer. I believe I could show you a longer line of ancestors——"

"Kevin, please don't misunderstand me. Perhaps I was led into saying rather more than I meant. What I meant to say was this, that I can't stand the pretensions of those Labour chaps. That's all."

"Then, is this all we've got to look forward to?"

Looking at one another, faced by a poser. There were many ways of answering, on head or heels, and none mattered very much.

"I don't quite understand what you mean, Hamish,"—Toddy, biting at the lower joint, studying an empty cup, an empty glass, and the smoke from his cigarette. "If you mean check and mate, I'm inclined to agree. That's why it's so enervating."

"But supposing the Labourites and the Communists don't think so. Supposing they believe this to be a very fruitful period."

"I'm quite sure they do!"

"Then supposing they made a move——"

"If the Communists by some unthinkable means took power in our country, I'd feel perfectly justified in shooting as many as I could."

"In other words, free elections or not——"

"They'd never win a free election. It would be a revolution. I'd be out in the streets, putting them all up against a wall. And so would you. Life wouldn't be worth living for anybody. Look here, I don't know about you two, but I've got an early day tomorrow. It's time for bed. Could I drop you?"

"I feel like a walk. The Metro's only round the corner. How about you, Hamish?"

"I was thinking of a stroll, myself."

They paid Dutch, in spite of Toddy's desire to be almoner, and they saw him into his Daimler, and watched him drive off. The night was cold and fresh, and a moon sheeted the roofs in silver, and brought mouths black in pale faces lounging in doorways.

"Toddy's a fustian-wrapped old die-hard at times, isn't he?"

"Yes. It won't get him far, though. His day's gone. I'm sorry he can't see it."

"I don't think it's a case of 'can't.' It's fright. He likes people to bow, and call him 'My lord,' and he doesn't like people who won't even bother to say 'sir.' Plain Mr. Todderton Berrish wouldn't amount to much. The very thought of somebody coming along to take it all away terrifies him. He'll put up a hell of a scrap."

"We're so hopelessly divided. There's no real honesty of purpose in any part of us. It's a constant jockeying. One form of life against another, upper versus lower. Gentlemen versus players. The Americans aren't weakened like that. They know the worst that can happen to them is a Democratic or a Republican majority. And that's their healthiness."

"They're climbing up the walls about the Communists, though."

"I don't believe anybody's lost a moment's sleep over it. Fancy trying to overcome Government agencies in forty-eight States. What an opportunity for the weekend hunter. There'd be a lot of fancy duck-shooting here and there, I'll bet. Texas, Kansas, Virginia, Wyoming, with Communist legislatures? Never mind the White House. Isn't worth thinking about. Unless, of course, they're overwhelmed in the deluge. That's a moot possibility."

"I was totting up today what I have to offer Mary if she comes over here. Do you know it's not even four thousand dollars a year? She gets more than that for pin money!"

"That's another problem. Money. Their typists get as much as I do. Americans aren't hidebound, whatever else they may be. They're very far-seeing. I think the Russians have borrowed some of their technique."

"I'd very much like to hear what you think about things, Hamish. I believe you've got a little pot boiling somewhere, haven't you?"

Walking along a broad thoroughfare, watching neons and café lights glittering through the trees and listening to Frenchmen talking, and remembering processions of troops, and visits of murdered and exiled and present royalty, and Maquis battles, and the tourists of many a year trying to have a high old time and finding it just about as dull as any other city street and perhaps even duller than most, and striving to formulate words into some sort of a reply.

"I think we ought to get to the Russians, one way or another."

"So do I. How?"

"Why do you want to know from me? I'm not for a moment being offensive. But there's such a thing as Security. Even as far as we've gone, we'd have a lot of explaining to do if the talk we've had tonight were reported in the right quarter."

Crossing over the Rond Point, and lighted orange-glass traffic signs throwing Dantesque masks over people's faces and dusting their clothes with a hideous pollen. Sensing Kevin's resentment and wanting to dry it at source.

"It's never safe to say very much. One never knows where it'll go."

"Yes. But I'm sorry you feel I might be one of the sneaks."

"I don't. I'm simply playing a straight bat. I've got a family."

"I'd love to have one. I don't see any hope the way we're going. Fancy asking Mary to pay her own fare to be my love over here on less than four thousand dollars a year. Their gardener gets more than that."

"The more we think along those lines the nearer we are to getting things done."

"How?"

"Individuals are always at the root of any change. Some of us must decide what to do, and do it. Never mind what the consequences are. I mean, to ourselves."

"Those who take the risk? I'm ready.'

"For what?"

"Any course that seems to me to be workable. Unlike Toddy, I'd stop this side of shooting people. I don't think that's any solution at all. But anything that'll let men like myself earn a living and support a family properly, I'm for. I'd like to hear of something that'll put a little more money in everybody's pocket. Mine included. I'd never thought much about it until I had to write to Mary, yesterday. That dished me. Really did. We'd rub along. But good God, Hamish! She's been used to a great deal more."

"You've got a house, though, haven't you?"

"I had, yes. You didn't know? My father died only a couple of years before my beautiful mother. The house went in death duties. So did most of the rest. It's since been knocked down. I can't imagine it. Every time I think of it I could sit in the middle of any road and howl at the heavens."

"I quite understand. I think I'd rather speak about this at some other time. Bang in the middle of the Place de la Concorde is hardly the place."

"I'm probably a little too eager. Although, that's where they chopped off dear Marie Antoinette's pretty napper in the middle there, isn't it? Poor little thing. As if she had the slightest thing to do with it. Told 'em to go and eat cake, didn't she?"

"Or somebody. What was it, innocence or cynicism?"

"Regal ignorance. Doesn't matter what one's told. One's got to go through the hoop to find out. If you'd told me a couple of months ago I'd be thinking as I do today, I'd have whacked you one. Here's the Metro. Three stops from a lonely couch. Come back with me for a goodnight whisky?"

"No, thanks. I've got to call Vinny."

"Dutiful Hamish. See you before you go, though?"

"I'll be there sometime before noon. Sandwich round the corner?"

"Splendid. 'Night!"

Length of dark suiting, bowler hat and umbrella going down the station entrance, making way for a woman with a basket, and reaching out to buy a paper. Unthinkable that Kevin could be persuaded to work against Authority. Not, it seemed fair to think, by having been forced to use his brains in terms of money. Up against the facts, he had been made to think of and for himself and what he was doing, and whether he was prepared to carry on, or try some method of change with a hope of making things better. Turning Toddy inside out and exposing him for a selfish addlepate had not by any means been a revelation, but another guide-stone along the way to go. All the Toddys relied upon all, including all the Kevins, and certainly all the Labourites, to keep their balloons up and sailing. Their conception of duty was nothing more than a settled determination always to keep their own particular pride of place. Unprejudiced self-aggrandisement, and at any price, and well in the shadows of Patriotism and Duty, bright escutcheons catching the public eye and blinding common reason with sentimentality's moist unhealth.

At the hotel, in the writing room silent with the memories of a thousand pens, drafting, and tearing up, and then being satisfied with a one-sentence resignation for reasons of health, and having the honour to be, sir, your most humble and obedient servant H. T. Gleave, Calton-Islip, here I come.

Calton-Islip's manner on the telephone was pleasant enough even though it was barely 8:30 A.M., and his All right, fella, lunch at the Ritz, one o'clock'll suit me fine, seemed a fair way of launching a £10,000 a year career.

The next call, to Vinny, brought her out of her bath to yodel delight at his being home with a resignation in his pocket, and a yell each from Hamish and Robert and a great deal of chatter gave him more than a usual appetite for breakfast. Over a quick tea-room boiled egg he looked at the paper, diverted to see that Our Special Correspondent had written about the conference as if something really useful had been done. He thought it might be instructive to print exactly what each nation had spent for little more than to give its representative the opportunity of identifying his colleagues' tonsils.

He took a bus along Queen Victoria Street in a light fog that had a chimneyish taste with the same effect of welcome as a sniff of the trees' mould in front of the house at Beaconsfield.

But Miss Relph had a minor surprise for him in a message on the blotter. Mrs. Blaise Cramer had telephoned to say that her husband was ordered to bed for at least three days with a severe chill. That, of course, meant no luncheon with Calton-Islip, and at least three days of double work, to say nothing of a daily dose or two of Mr. Flap.

He took the chair at the morning conference, and went up to present the reports and take instructions. Mr. Flap proved to be in fair humour, and they went through a mound of paper without a hitch. At the end of a report from Japan, Mr. Flap enquired after Vinny, and what she thought of the transfer. It seemed a heaven-

sent chance for putting in motion the first stage of the move to resign by repeating word for word what Vinny had said. Mr. Flap was
good enough to sympathize with the inconvenience, but he said
there were ample allowances, and also, in view of the promotion, a
substantial increase in salary.

"You've had the American desk long enough, Gleave. You're going
away as Minister. Do you find that prospect satisfactory?"

"Highly, sir."

"I believe you're the sort of man I'm looking for. You think for
yourself. A bit craggy, sometimes, but I don't mind. I'm craggy myself. Anything else?"

"No, sir."

"Thank you."

Walk out and shut the door, and stand there, pretending to look
in a file case, brain in such a buzz that nothing connects. A Minister-
ship could only mean that a little more time and the luck of one or
two deaths or retirement would bring him an Embassy.

He telephoned Vinny and told her. In the silence that followed
he could almost hear her thinking how near Mumsy's Victoria was
to being Lady Gleave, wife of H.B.M.'s Ambassador to Wherever-
it-was, and what a lot of fun the social side of things would be, and
the joy of increase in salary and allowances, and how superior her
life by comparison with existence as mate and housekeeper of an
employee of Calton-Islip Holdings Incorporated, £10,000 a year, a
house, a car, and all the exes.

"Not simple, is it?"

"I think I'll take this upstairs with me after lunch. You won't do
anything——"

"Nothing at all. I shan't move until you feel perfectly happy."

"Hamish, you're a darling. I love you so much."

"That's not the sort of conversation I should be listening to. But
I rather like it. I'll be late tonight. Let me know what you decide?"

Calton-Islip had been on the telephone twice since Miss Sells had
called to cancel the appointment. She said that he sounded grumpy.
He was not used, he had told her the second time, to having his
luncheon engagements cancelled. Miss Sells pulled a face when she

got through again, and handed over the receiver as if it held something nasally significant.

"Listen, Gleave,"—gutter-rasp, with extreme clarity—"After I been good enough to make an appointment, I don't want to have somebody ringing me up and saying you're busy. I'm busy, too——"

"I was at a conference——"

"I know all about 'em. I've been to a few. Listen, if we're going to do business, it'll have to be on different lines, I can tell you. Now, are you coming to lunch or not?"

"You must realize that I wouldn't have cancelled unless it were a matter of some urgency——"

"All right, Gleave. Others can get urgent, too, y'know——"

And that empty singing along a line when a receiver goes down.

"If that gentleman should telephone again, put him on to somebody else."

"Very well, sir."

Two more interviews carried him over the luncheon period. Mrs. Cramer telephoned when he was thinking of ordering a pot of tea. Blaise was a little on edge, and wanted to see the morning's reports and the doctor had said he might have a visitor for no more than half an hour.

"Would he like me to slip over for a few minutes?"

"Oh, Hamish, if you could! He's getting worse, lying up there worrying. It won't take you more than ten minutes to get here. He merely wants to be assured that everything's going well."

It took little time in Blaise's official car, a well-preserved, highly polished and extremely genteel old lady, dimpled by many a bumping and hammering-out, with the seats of all the mighty outlined in her cushioning, and withal running like a sylph. But different in more ways than one from the car Arkhiv had used.

Dorothea Cramer, white hair wound around her head, in a mauve frock, grey stockings and buckled shoes, led the way upstairs, holding her skirts in one hand and the bannister in the other, to the bedroom overlooking Battersea Park. Blaise sat against a pile of pillows, shaven, but he looked about twenty pounds thinner and his voice trembled. Dorothea went away, and Blaise lay back, closing his eyes, listening to a recital of the day's business. From time to time he made impatient movements with his hands, and at the end he stared at a Watteau on the opposite wall.

"Most extraordinary position."

"It is, indeed."

"I think Washington's taking more or less the same position as we should in the same circumstances."

"I suppose they are. But it isn't much help. Blackmail doesn't go very far."

"I don't like the word. We've used the substance on more than one occasion. In different terms, of course. Has to be done, Hamish. We're up against it."

"I'm wondering how long the Germans and French'll stand it. How long are we supposed to endure it? That's what it comes down to."

Blaise raised himself on both his fists and lay back. His eyelids looked dark against his cheeks and the moustache glinted ends of silver wire.

"There is no health in us. But Thou, O Lord, spare us miserable offenders. It's not by any means hopeless. I dislike that word as much as any. They have their country to safeguard, and I think they're doing a remarkably good job. If we had their advantages, I'd like to think we'd do as well. Great pity the Russians undid that bomb-puzzle quite so soon. We could have done with an extra five or ten years. Made all the difference between what we wanted and what they're prepared to give us."

"I think we're in a much better position to lead. The Americans can't do without Europe. We can very well do without them."

"Under certain circumstances, I agree. But there's an overriding question of loyalty. We've got to stand with them."

"I can't for the life of me see why we've 'got to' do anything of the sort. We're just as responsible to ourselves. If there's any saving to be done, it's got to be for us and on our behalf. I'm getting a little restive under this constant whittling. We're simply making an exhibition of ourselves. A lot of marionettes speaking very good English with Uncle Sam's accent. We'd do far better with the Russians. There're tremendous markets open there, and even more in China

that'll never be open to us in the United States. We're not an
Empire any longer. We're not even a sound Commonwealth. Another war, and we'd have neither Canada nor Australia. India's in
another world. Even if we survived another war, we'd be lucky to
come out with a whole island. We'd still be a small-sized Japan, with
far greater day-to-day needs and a far less disciplined population.
There'd be more than labour trouble here."

"That might very well be. But I don't think there's any danger. In
fact, if there were trouble, I'd be rather glad. We'd find the ring-
leaders, at all events. And in finding them, we'd get rid of their
more enthusiastic followers. Weed them all out. The best pacification
the country could possibly have. There are far too many people with
curious ideas running about."

"Then you sympathise with quasi-military rule?"

"If it's for the general benefit, yes. I've been rather pleased with
the election returns, lately, haven't you? Quite a number of young
ex-officers are getting into the House."

"Legislation by pistol point, if necessary?"

"Well, at any rate they'd be reliable."

"Where does that leave us?"

"Us?"

"Blaise, isn't it people like ourselves who really run things? Without us, who'd represent anything? Who'd report? Who'd instruct?
Who'd advise? Others like us?"

"Why, most certainly. I don't expect to live forever."

"Then why aren't we controlling as well as running things? Why
must we everlastingly have to accept policy instead of deciding it?
What makes us little more than office-boys for politicians who've
never been outside their own back doors? Why shouldn't we decide
foreign policy in the same way as the General Staff decides strategy?
In other words, since we know what we're doing, why aren't we
allowed to do it?"

"Two things, I should say. And they're at the root. It's a popular
vote that produces a Government, and it's that Government's sole
right to decide policy. If the voters aren't sufficiently well educated,
then we get that sort of Government. The other thing is, of course,
that we're servants of the State's needs, and not masters of its opinion.

Our privilege is to help in moulding and bringing into being, but it doesn't go as far as decision. We have the great privilege of putting into effect, of helping our people, all of them. Every one of them is our responsibility. It's our privilege to make the day, or at least to save it. Not for any pride in ourselves, but for pride of Country."

"What's your conception of the Country, Blaise? Ever thought about it in any way?"

"You're not to suppose that I haven't. To my mind, it's a state of peculiarly British duty, loyalty, wisdom and justice under the Crown, mental in essence, to be put in conditions of work by those of us who acknowledge subjecthood. Where one or other of those qualities is offended, then all subjects, the Country, and the Crown suffers harm."

"But you're not unhappy to be the privileged anonymous? You don't want the responsibility of power to act?"

"I'm satisfied to be what I am. It's not given to every man to speak for his Sovereign, anonymously or not. Every time I've been that anonymous voice at the Foreign Office they talk about in the newspapers, I've never been able to resist a feeling of great pride. They're my words. Written on my own desk. Spoken into my own telephone. Speaking for my Country and the Crown. What greater honour does any man want?"

"And if something should happen to the Crown?"

"Far too well protected. Does it worry you?"

"Things have to be thought about."

"I agree. But the Crown is quite safe. Very well looked after. I don't altogether like some of the people in office. Some of them have been guilty of heinous conduct at times, and for the most venal reasons. But that's the human element. It's the greatest single national asset we possess. Why? Are you doubtful?"

"At the turn of things, yes."

"I've seen it all before. A great deal of talking and nothing much happening. But every word spoken is time gained, and lives saved. There's not much wrong with what we're doing. That bomb's frightened all the soldiers. It's put the Royal Navy in a position of running a lot of floating holiday homes for young men who'd be better off in useful employment. A few hydrogen bombers, rockets and fancy-free missiles is all we'll require. Enormous savings, of course. What's going to happen to the officer class, I really don't know. They're just the type to make good settlers, though. A few thousand good hearts every year going to Canada or Australia would tighten many a rope."

Dorothea came in and said it was time for medicine and sleep. Blaise kept the files, and asked for them to be sent for that evening. He said he would try to be back in the office before the doctor had said he might. Dorothea picked up the tray and went out saying that he would move from that bed before the three days were up only over her dead body. Blaise waited for the door to close.

"What do you know about Kevin Chalmers? Anything to his discredit?"

"Nothing at all. Bit young, of course. Had a great deal of trouble when his parents died. The entire estate went in two bites for death duties. He's rather bitter about it."

"That sort of law, taking away birthright to satisfy a State debt, is thoroughly bad. A citizen's turned into an Ishmael if only in his thoughts. There's no longer any reason to feel bound to uphold the instrument of his deprivation, either. Still, that's neither here nor there."

"Something wrong?"

"I'm not sure what's happened. The night I left the office there was a report from Washington. I sent it up. Mr. Flap didn't say anything this morning?"

"Not a thing. What was it?"

Blaise seemed most ready to put his head back and nod off to sleep.

"I suppose you'll have to deal with it before I get back. But I'd like to be made conversant with any move that's made, Hamish. His father was a friend of mine."

"Very serious?"

"Apparently there was a charge outstanding against him in Washington——"

"Charge of drunken driving? But he was fined for it. Nothing else, was there?"

"It's very sad, altogether. I do hope there's some mistake. I'm afraid there isn't. He was introduced to the Service in 1939, you'll remember? He never sat for any examinations. Brought in through the side door, as it were. By none other than the late Mr. Wittard. I fear the charge is well founded."

"But what charge?"

"Soliciting."

"Soliciting? Kevin?"

"Soliciting a male person."

Vinny had asked a couple of times the night before if anything was worrying him, but he told her nothing about Chalmers, preferring to let her think he was studying the Calton-Islip proposal, and whether or not to resign. She left it entirely to him to decide. As far as she was concerned, both careers offered advantages, the one diplomatic and social, and the other pecuniary that had an attractive further prospect of a well-padded and comfortable old age.

He took an earlier train to the office, and found the desk filling up with the morning's correspondence. But nothing from Washington about Chalmers, and no message from Mr. Flap.

"Hamish?"

"Yes, Toddy."

"There's an extremely ugly rumor walking about here. I got it from our friends. Very unfavourable to Kevin Chalmers."

"I know about it. We're waiting for facts."

"The Ambassador doesn't want to wait for anything. He wants him sent home immediately."

"There's not a spark of evidence——"

"I was at some pains to point that out. Made no difference. I'll give him a special despatch to take with him. Let somebody in London break the news. Disgusting business. If that sort of chap's a bad 'un, I'm dashed if I know what to think about anybody."

"I'll let you know the moment the report gets here."

"Do. Meantime, he's booked for an afternoon plane."

Two conferences ticked off details and minutes, and during a third, Miss Sells came in to bend over and give him a sniff of clean hair and a message that Vinny would like to speak to him as soon as he conveniently could about something urgent. She added that Mrs. Gleave sounded most awfully upset.

A thought that something might have happened to Hamish or Robert pulled him out of the chair. Connection to the house took a few moments, but even so he had time to study an entire catalogue of misery in phases of running blood, broken bones and half-size shrouds. But Vinny seemed to have pulled herself together.

"Darling, I'm so sorry to bother you like this, but the most terrible thing's happened——"

"What?"

"That poor little Mrs. Lindley's dead."

"That's a relief, anyway."

"Oh, Hamie. Don't say that! She died of heart failure in the kitchen. She must have been chasing those wasps, or something, and she tumbled over."

"Anything I can do?"

"I've arranged with the Cottons to take Hamish and Bobby. I'd like the funeral to be from here."

"What are you talking about?"

"She was a dear little soul, and she's not going out of my house by the back door. And the family can't afford a proper funeral."

"Neither can we."

"We can use some of our £10,000 a year."

"Darling, be practical, for God's sake——"

"I'm being very practical. She was sweet, and she shall have what I can give her. Couldn't you possibly come home and arrange things?"

"Vin, are you feeling quite well? Don't be absurd——"

"I'm not absurd. Please come back and help me. We've got to get a plot in the cemetery——"

"Why the devil should we have to do anything so stupid of the sort?"

"Because! That's why. She's not going to be flung into some hole or other just because they've got no money——"

"There are all sorts of allowances——"

"I tell you she's going to be buried from this house, correctly and decently. Are you coming home to help me?"

Counsel, common sense, persuasion, nothing supervened against

Vinny, because when it came to sheer mulishness everybody might just as well decide they were whacked to a frazzle.

"All right. I'll see what I can do."

"Darling, I knew you would. Come soon, won't you?"

He sent a message upstairs to say that a domestic contretemps called him home for a couple of hours and that he would return and work late that night. It was fortunate that nothing of any great importance was toward, and lucky that Blaise's car was available, since it cut almost an hour off the journey.

The house looked quiet enough. Vinny came to meet him with an expression which said I-know-perfectly-well-I'm-doing-something-howlingly - imbecilic - but - I - don't - care - and - in - any - case - I'm - rather-proud-of-it, and kissed him, and said he would never know how happy he had made the Lindley family. They were all so frightened she was going into a pauper's grave.

"That sort of thing doesn't happen any more."

"You'd better have a talk to the Vicar. He has to be paid for his services, you know. And the grave-diggers, sacristan, bell-ringers, choirboys, organist. It costs money to send people nicely up to God."

"I can't see why we should have to fork out for this——"

"I do. Something simply won't let me have that poor little soul taken out of my house and sold to a medical school to be cut up."

"One step further in surgical progress?"

"Not out of my front door. Now, I'll go to the church and arrange everything there, and you go down to the village and see the family, and ask what time they want the carriage to pick the old ones up——"

"Are we letting ourselves in for burying the entire damn' family?"

"Wait until you see them. There's the address. Then go to the undertaker's and pay them. Here. And then go to the doctor and get the death certificate. Meantime, I've got to find another maid."

"And I'll have to work late tonight——"

"Poor darling. But you'll feel all the better for having been kind, won't you?"

Salter's Humby took a little time to find, through side roads and over a wooden bridge and around a duck pond. The Lindleys' cottage was one of a dozen all built alike, with gardens in front rich with wallflowers and ramblers and splashed with pink and white hollyhock. He went along a narrow path that smelt of honey and leaf-green, and tapped on the open door. A woman opened the inner door and let out an odour of boiled washing and gross stews. She was another Mrs. Lindley, less tidy in her person, blear-eyed, and chinnily minus teeth.

He went in at her chattered invitation. A baby slept in a wooden crib beside an iron stove covered with saucepans dwarfed by a kettle. A table spread with newspaper held a basket of clean washing and a bowl of water. Eight wooden chairs stood about the walls, and a sofa, heaped with baby's clothes and a sewing basket turned to the fire. Plants outside and inside the one window screened sunlight that shone on a tiled floor, in points of metal on the stove and on the wheel of a sewing-machine. Everything was clean, rickety, and smoothed with usage. And the smell of many a generation of hearty lives in a room without air, except when the door was open, got up in the head and suffocated.

A businesslike approach shortened her thanks, dried fresh tears, got the information he needed, and he was able to leave a moment or so before he was quite sure he must be sick. He got out in the sunlight and stood in the road for a moment. Several women, in shades of black, leaned over their front gates, all of them looking very much alike, grey-haired, hollow-cheeked, with swollen hands, and all in the same stare, as if somebody had dropped something, and he was it. He got in the car, and told the chauffeur to go to the cemetery.

In a greystone coop that looked like a cross between a lych-gate and a Gothic signal-box, and decorated on one side by a great heap of rotting flowers, an old man showed him on a map where the plot would be, and what would be charged for this, that and the other. He had no wish to argue, and less to go and see what he was buying. But his cheque-book brought a shaken head and a wise grin. No cheques, by order. Be surprised what some people got up to. Cash before digging, that was the order. But it was after three o'clock. The banks were shut. Sorry, must have cash.

He bribed the village grocer to cash the cheque by deduction of the current account. The chauffeur took the money back to the cemetery, and left him at the undertaker's on the way. The smells of raw wood and French polish were preferable, because sharper, but sickening just the same. A stout man in shirt-sleeves, aproned, with tools stuck in the bib, scrawled figures with a flat carpenter's pencil on a plank, asking if the coffin should be lined, quilted, braided, tacked or studded, and what type of coffin he was looking for, if it was in elm, or in oak, or walnut, or mee-ogony. A thought of Vinny came, and he could see her nodding her head.

"Let it be the mahogany. But it's got to be this afternoon."

" 'Tis ready, cep' for a go-over. Made for her, that 'un. We'll be up at th' house inside the hour. She's laid out, so no time'll be lost. 'll the fambly be there?"

"I doubt it."

"Ah. Where'll they have their sightin's, then?"

"Sightin's?"

"A sight o' her. 'fore she goes off, like."

"I really don't know. Do you take cheques?"

"Cert-ny, sir. Got a pen, have you?"

And, Great God Almighty, the glory of pure air, even with a smirch of Diesel fumes from a passing bus. He walked along to the doctor's house, ivied, with an old-fashioned red lamp on an ornamental iron bracket, and collisions of disinfectant and iodoform inside a waiting room with the WELCOME almost worn off the rubber mat. A girl in a white overall gave him an envelope through a pigeonhole and said that Doctor Gill was on his rounds.

"He wanted to tell how glad he was poor Mrs. Lindley was going to have a good funeral. He was her doctor for years."

"Thanks. It's an extraordinary process, burying people, don't you find?"

"Yes, it is, rather, Mr. Gleave. Everybody makes a bit out of it except us."

"No charge?"

"No charge. Good afternoon, sir."

The car came along and the chauffeur put his head out.

"I'm sorry, sir. The old bloke up there, he wouldn't take the money, not without you go up and sign some papers or other. Yearly upkeep and what-nots."

"All right. Back we go."

The withered flowers were still there, and another funeral party walked its black measure toward a pile of earth. Birds twittered, and women sobbed, and Deah-leh Belov-ed, We Are Geth-ahd Togethah sounding like some blighting travesty of itself.

He signed what he had to and paid for one year's upkeep and thankfully went away. The sum he had spent surprised him. If there were not, as Arkhiv had said, profit in sin, at least somebody made a penny or two out of burying the sinners. Yet he had paid for nothing except essentials. However, Vinny would like the polished mee-ogony, and it surprised him to feel that Somebody might be approving his order for polished wood rather than the original in its created state.

Vinny had been crying when he met her inside the church. She said that the Vicar was out burying someone else, and that only he could give permission for the body to lie in the church, and as far as anybody knew, he was not going to allow it.

"Why shouldn't she be taken to her own home?"

"She didn't have one. She had a room in one of these shacks at the back here. Would you care to see it?"

"No, thanks. I've seen enough."

"You mean her sister's place at Salter's Humby? That's a palace compared with it. A palace!"

"Why can't she go there?"

"With five children in the house? And a baby? And four grown-ups? And two rooms upstairs?"

"Are we turning into social workers?"

"After the little I've seen today I could turn into anything. She was always perfectly clean and tidy, but God knows where she had a bath. No bathroom, and the lavatory made me quite ill, poor little thing. If you'd seen her clothes—!"

"All right. That's enough. Is there anything else I can do?"

"Just hold me for a moment. I haven't been inside a church since Bobby was christened."

Standing in brownish shade, tapestried by colours from the stained-glass windows, among rows of pews hassocked and numbered, leading down toward a lectern's brass eagle with open beak, and a silken bookmark hanging out of the Bible, and along to the altar's white marble and glinting brass candlesticks.

"Shall we say a prayer? That nobody ever has to pray for us? That we don't have to rely on somebody's heart? Not even that. On their pocket——"

"You've done quite enough crying for one day, my girl. You're coming straight home, and you're going to make us a cup of tea."

"All right. I'm sorry, Hamie. Really and truly, darling. But I'm sure you've made her happy. I hope the Vicar says yes."

"She's not going to stay in the house——"

"Where else can she go? She hasn't anywhere——"

"I never heard anything so insane——"

"Hamie. Please listen,"—calm, unlike herself, a new and strangely bright-eyed Vin—"That poor little thing was never so happy as when she worked for us. She told me so. She loved Hamish and Bobby. She couldn't do enough for them. She's not going to be carted off to some hole or other——"

"But are we going to sleep in the same house with it?"

"If the Vicar won't let her come here, where can she go?"

"But Vin, the children——"

"The Cottons are taking care of them——"

"But what about us? Are you suggesting we sleep——"

"Stay at an hotel for a couple of nights. I'll stay with the Cottons——"

"Vinny. I don't want to quarrel——"

"Neither do I. But that little thing's going to rest in peace. That's all!"

Not a bit of use feeling angry, and he knew that if he flung the body out of a window, she would pick it up and bring it in again. He followed her out. For many reasons he was finding something profoundly excellent in ordinary fresh air that day. And coming through the gate was the Vicar, tall, quite young, flat hat on the back of his head, wheeling a bicycle and smoking a pipe, looking as if he kept himself in fair trim.

No, Mrs. Gleave, he was afraid not. If he allowed it for one, think what would happen. A peepshow all day long and every day. The undertaker, of course, would keep the body for the requisite period.

He was very glad to have met her, and of course Mr. Gleave. On the two occasions he had called at the house, the maid had told him there was nobody at home. He was glad to find they were parishioners. Perhaps he could look forward to seeing them at the usual services. And so on and so on.

Vinnny hurried after him and took his arm.

"Hamish! You were awfully rude to leave like that."

"I lifted my hat and I said good afternoon, did I not?"

"Yes. But nobody could possibly mistake your tone."

"Good. Now, do we call at the undertaker's to ask them to collect the——"

"Yes, I suppose so. You mustn't think I liked the idea of her staying in the house. But if the undertaker's where they're taken usually, then all right."

"And we get a cup of tea?"

"Yes, darling. The best you ever had. And I love you for being so patient with me."

"Funny. I love you for being such an old fuss-budget. But a little of it goes a long way. As it is, I'd like the house fumigated. I don't like what I've seen today."

"Do you think I did? People seem to like living like pigs. Send the car on, and I'll drive you."

The undertaker was out c'lectin', a boy told them at the shop or whatever the undertaker called the place, and they drove on. An empty hearse stood in front of the door, and when the car stopped they could hear the telephone. Vinny's side was nearest and she hurried in. He told the chauffeur to park and come in for a cup of tea. But Vinny's face changed all that.

"London's been trying to get you for hours. Extremely important. You won't wait for a cup of tea?"

"I'll wait long enough for a small kiss. How's that?"

"Don't forget to telephone, darling. I'm simply torn to see you go without even a cup of tea."

All the way back to London, thinking of Vinny and her late Mrs. Lindley, and trying to imagine having to live in Salter's Humby all his life, and what he might do to escape, and realising there was no way except as Mrs. Lindley had gone, turning her head to cough into her shoulder, uh-hum, par me, and loping off in her black felt slippers. All the cottages and the rows of houses they were passing, full of Mrs. Lindleys, washing, or hanging out washing, or serving somebody or only their families, though God knows where they got a bath, because there were no bathrooms, and the lavatories would make you quite ill, poor little things.

Miss Sells, bless her, shut her eyes in a sigh of relief to see him, and took his hat and coat. He went up in the lift, and walked down, wondering if instinct were correct or not. Kevin Chalmers came firmly in mind.

Mr. Flap stood at the window, looking out. He wore approximately the same suit, and it looked as if the same bootlace trailed. A Washington bag lay open on the desk, and a sheaf of reports heaped on the blotter.

"Hear you've had a bit of trouble at home, Gleave?"

"Yes, sir. A maid died. Heart failure."

"Dear, dear. Sorry about that. Everything all right now?"

"Yes, sir, thank you."

"Good. I believe Lord Berrish spoke to you about this man Chalmers this morning?"

"Yes, sir."

"There's no doubt about it. I've looked into it very thoroughly. If Mr. Cramer wasn't feeling poorly, I'd ask him to go to Paris and kick him out, neck and crop. As it is, I must ask you to go. Immediately, please."

"Yes, sir. You won't allow him to resign?"

"I'd thought of it. Mr. Cramer told me about his father and all he'd done for the Country. All very fine. But that man was willing to drag all of us down. Paint us all with the same brush. When I think of all the people I'm proud to work with, slaving away here, day and night, doing their level best, and then to have somebody like that making them a laughing-stock? No, Gleave. I'm giving you direct instructions to see that man in Paris, and discharge him. He's to get out of the Embassy, there and then. That's all I've got to say for him."

"Yes, sir. It's a very severe shock to some of us."

"I don't doubt it. But can you explain how the same night he gets arrested for soliciting—soliciting, mind you!—he goes out and gets drunk with some girl in a car?"

"His fiancée, I understand."

"His what? Look. This head's a bit too old for that sort of thing. He did it deliberately. Remanded and bailed and pleading diplomatic immunity on the first charge, he had the cunning to go out and get arrested for drunken driving. He knew he'd come up at a night court. He knew he'd get fined, and he knew he'd get sent home the next morning, bag and baggage. He never said a word to anybody, did he?"

"No, sir."

"You see? Slimy-sly cunning. Like all of them. Let anybody in for it. I've told the Ambassador you're going over. I'll send my apologies to your wife for taking you away so much. I'll write her a little note. Thank you, Gleave."

Toddy put his hat on and went out, leaving his office to be used, he said, as a private though temporary abattoir. The Ambassador had gone to the Quai d'Orsay, leaving instructions that Chalmers' passport was to be collected and that he was not on any pretext to remain in Paris after that evening except as a private individual. Toddy let go his Parthian shot while he straightened his tie.

"Did you know this fellow's been in touch with the Russians?"

"Where did you get that?"

"Our friends. They seem smarter than ourselves at picking things up. Why?' '

"More dollars. More agents. More gossip."

"I wouldn't call a report of that sort gossip. But now we've got the long glass on him. We might get a shock or two we won't like. I'm quite prepared to find my sainted and very dear grandmama popping up in the reports as a super Lesbian at any moment, and of course, in the pay of the Romanoff pretender. Living in a weird age, aren't we?"

Toddy's question seemed to twist in the air long after he had gone. Garden and trees were dark, and foliage against an evening sky waved like the trees in front of the house at Beaconsfield. He wondered if the basket of clean washing on the table at Salter's Humby was all put away. A couple of knocks brought in a messenger to turn on the lights, and announce Monsieur Chalmers, at your disposition.

Kevin came in with his overcoat over an arm, carrying an umbrella and bowler, and in such high spirits that it seemed a pity to shatter them.

"Hamish! Delighted to see you again so soon. You wanted to speak to me, but——"—an envelope out of a side-pocket flipping across the desk—"I think I know why, and that's my resignation."

"It's unacceptable——"

"I shan't argue. I've no desire to stay on, in any event. Mary's joining me here in a couple of weeks' time, and we shall be married. Then we'll start living."

"I'm glad for your sake."

"Thanks. I don't want any sympathy, though. Matter of hard luck, that's all."

"I must ask you to leave as soon as possible——"

"I don't intend to embarrass you. The chap I was arrested with I'd met at a party. He asked me along to his place for a drink and got a little chummy on the way. That's all. Stupid, unexpected, and fait accompli. No defence, nothing."

"If you're implying you're innocent, why didn't you say something when you came back to London?"

"Many reasons. I have indulged, in fact. No use blinking it. Started at school. Messing about in the dormitory——"

"I don't wish to hear about it."

"I'm sorry you're taking it like this. It's very ordinary, really. If you can once disregard the moralistic side of it. Grow up, in fact."

"My growth in that respect has been singularly stunted. I'm waiting for you to go."

"Not even a wee doch-an-dorris? Ah, well. We'll meet again."

Going out whistling, and breaking off to call Good Night to somebody, and whistling again across the courtyard, and silence.

Sitting there thoroughly shocked and a little amused and wondering how anybody could put such a face on complete personal disaster, and then remembering James Wittard. And another memory of a weeping brother. But that was a different face. Hamish and Robert running white socked and flap-shirty to meet ice-cream man and Vinny tipping out her purse to find change enough and saying Now wait a minute, you two monkeys, wait a minute will you? Oh Hamie, have you got a shilling please, and damn it, to think of those two falling into the same mire, messing about in a dormitory, God Almighty.

Taking up the receiver and getting through to London almost without a pause, and a sense of small wonderment that machines and wire could produce instant communication between two or many more beings, though without a moment of understanding except by desire, and trying to assess the meaning of desire. The operator's voice, and somebody answering, and a click, and Mr. Flap himself.

"Thanks, Gleave. I'm very glad that's over. Any trouble?"

"None whatever, sir."

"Yes. Well. I think you'd best stay the night and attend this meeting at the Quai tomorrow. As an observer. You'll get your instructions. If you can get back in the afternoon, all right. If you can't, Mr. Cramer's going to be here in the morning. You can get back the following day. Then you can take a couple of days off. Thanks for all you've done. G'night, Gleave."

Another Calton-Islip talking to another office-boy. Go there and do this, and stay there and do that for sheer politics, none of it of much lasting value or intended to be. And all for little more than hope of future small-glory and a present salary earned by many a typist elsewhere.

The operator said there was no reply from Beaconsfield. He asked her to try the Cottons' number. A cheerful woman's voice said that Vinny had gone up to Town with a friend. No, oh-dear-dear, no, a woman of course, not entirely sure who, haw-haw, yes, and the two boys were in bed ahrs ago, really no need to worry, yes, do let's meet soon, oh, Vinny's a darling, yes.

The woman, he judged, would be Delia taking darling Vinsy-Wins to the theatre for a night out. Nothing wrong with it except that he wished he were there. Perhaps there might have been some errancy abroad in the Parisian night, but there came a sudden and surprisingly fierce want, and without effort he was thinking of Myril, although it took much more in the way of effort to replace her with Vinny and even so she went slowly, regardant, leaving memory of bracken-sweet, and a blunt breast that meltingly grew a soft, firm spindle, without taste except to sense.

He went into the hotel and looked at the dozens of people waiting in the telephone bureau. If he gave a false name nobody could trace him, though if her telephone were tapped, and it might be, he was simply asking for trouble. He went into the bar, and sat down for a philosophical drink, prepared to think over his misdeeds and generally consider his position.

He knew quite well at the back of his mind that he had never had any more intention of accepting Calton-Islip's offer than of volunteering to serve ten years in a prison. Hopping to the tune of a gutter-rasp was not on his cards. Panama had a lot to say for it, and so did a free house and all the rest. But the notion of helping in any way to enrich Iv's collection of jewellery was most unpleasant.

But there was little pleasure at thought of staying on in the Service. He knew beyond any doubt that a time must come when he might speak too plainly, either to Blaise, or more easily still, to Mr. Flap. That would be the finish.

There had to be something to put in its place, a hope of some future chance of proper use of time and ability. Even as Sir Hamish Gleave, H.B.M.'s Ambassador to somewhere, there still would be a Mr. Flap in London, pulling strings and do-this-and-thatting, or perhaps somebody like Toddy with a brusque piddlededee manner borrowed from the cheaper type of staff officer, but without any notion of what constituted true diplomacy, and no regard at all for the natural ambition of any born below the peerage.

A page-boy put a salver down and showed a card. Rodolphe Mavritz, advocate, of Paris, presented his compliments and wondered if Mr. Gleave would care to join a small party. First inclination was to plead an appointment, although there was no good reason why he should have to give an excuse of any sort. He asked the waiter to bring his drink, and followed the page to a table in the corner.

Mavritz sat with a young woman and two men. Miss Jessica Morse, from London, looked tired and unhealthy. She wore a grey suit and a turtle-necked grey jersey, and her dark hair was uncombed, she frowned, wore no lipstick, picked matches apart, and whistled under her breath. She merely disarranged her face in greeting and lapsed. Jocelyn Retford, about thirty, tall, in loose blue with a loose collar, dark-eyed and dreamily remote in a Cantabrigian manner, nodded his greeting with one moccasined foot on a chair. George Taylor-Dutton, an Englishman, wore a drab corduroy jacket, flannels and a shirt that might have cleaned a window or two in its time, and a wrinkled foulard bow, and spent most of his time fingering his hair, touching his spectacles or pulling the bow in place, and in between sipped a glass of beer.

Mavritz said the three had motored back from a Moral Rearmament meeting in Switzerland, and the journey was beginning to tell. Miss Morse said in a monotone that it was much more spiritual exhaustion than anything else. She was still uncertain about everything. She wished she really knew. It was all very well people talking, but there was such a thing as surety, and one really had to be sure. She had done as much for the time being as she intended to do, and she had watched everybody coming and going, but it seemed to her that some people did all the work and others enjoyed themselves. It was just like everything else. If you had the money you could do as you pleased and life was easy. But if you had no money, then life was all rather jumblesome and grimy, never mind how you believed or what religion you followed.

"Not if you apply the absolute standards,"—Retford, looking seriously at the olive in his martini—"of absolute purity, absolute honesty, absolute unselfishness, absolute love, and live by them——"

"I've been watching all of them for five months from my little place under the stairs, making beds and carting buckets and slopping about like some old char. Not a hap'orth of thanks, and not a penny in return. All for love. Just look at my hands. Where're your absolute standards?"

'You mustn't confuse things, Jessica"—Taylor-Dutton, gently and rather fondly, over a sip of beer—"or be childish. Besides, you're rather tired. I think you'll feel better about things in the morning. Ask yourself during your quiet time——"

"I've done too much asking. I never get any answers. Sitting there, getting cold as ice, with a pencil and a piece of paper, I can never find anything to write."

"Write what comes into your head. I've told you times enough."

"Buckets, pans, towels, brooms, soap, and what else?"

"Doesn't that tell you how much more you ought to put your back into it?"

"Look here, Jocelyn, you men make me sick. How can you dare sit there and say that to me, considering what you did all day? You've never done a hand's turn in your life and you'll see to it you don't. You're best at sitting in the Ritz talking M.R.A. and knocking back martinis. Don't worry, dear. I've seen it all, thank you."

"I don't think we're being at all kind to Mr. Gleave,"—Taylor-Dutton, laughingly, though a little annoyed—"He can't possibly be interested——"

"Quite the reverse. I'm very interested. Any sort of religion making an attempt to explain——"

"Oh, but it doesn't attempt to explain anything—"—Taylor-Dutton, spectacles alight in movement—"It clarifies immediacies rather than explains anything. It makes no attempt to deal with any phenomena other than the self. And it's not a religion in the accepted sense. There's no ritual. You can't join. You can't resign. It's a commitment. It tends toward an inspired democracy. Every man not for himself, but for all others."

"And the women do the housework. Just as it is anywhere. It's entirely a man's religion. Women get nothing out of it. Do they, Jocelyn?"

"Nothing, Jessica. If that's all you got out of it, then nothing's the answer."

"It's all so beastly unfair. Why don't men use a bucket and broom now and again?"

"Jessica, you're making it into a dirge. Like the Song of the Shirt —'work, work, work, my labour nevers flags, and what are its wages? A bed of straw, a crust of bread, and rags.' You're not subordinate. That's really your trouble. The old elements of impurity are still in charge. You simply don't like to think of yourself as a charlady. The choice of the word shows what you think of that sort of work. You don't mind somebody charring for you. That's their place in life as far as you care. You only did it to prove to yourself that you could. But when people took it for granted what did you do? You felt hurt. Dear Jessica counted no more than any old char. And a good old charwoman could have done it all much better without any hulla-balloo. That's why you feel down-in-the-mouth."

"None of that's really right. I hate housework, yes. I couldn't feel I was doing anything really constructive, that's all."

"There's nothing more constructive than making people comfortable. After that, they can work."

"Is the basis of Moral Rearmament so materialistic?"

"No, Mr. Gleave, it's not,"—Retford, with perhaps a soupçon of pity—"It's completely of the spirit. But we don't try to disguise the fact that someone's got to feed the brute in us, and give it enough to spend. Then we believe it might take some intelligent interest in the things that matter. Even Christ fed the multitude, you know."

"Where God guides, He provides,"—Taylor-Dutton, nodding and smiling at Miss Morse. "That's the root of our faith. But Jessica prefers a cheque-book."

"It's really not true! I'm so dying to throw myself into something worthwhile. To give myself wholly for—"—hooking fingers at the ceiling, shutting her eyes, a female Agonistes—"for something, anything I can believe in. Really believe in. I've confessed in public. I've told things about myself that are utterly revolting. All true, of course. But awful to think about. I was so sure I'd feel wonderfully cleansed afterwards. As everyone said I would. But I didn't. I merely felt most shockingly let-down. I couldn't look at people. Then I thought well, never mind. They've all thought and done the same things, but they wouldn't have the guts to stand up and say so. What does it matter——"

"But Jessica, it does matter most dreadfully—"—Retford, leaning toward her in a somewhat cope-and-mitre manner—"We feel absolutely responsible for you——"

"Jocelyn, you mustn't be, you can't be. You know you can't. You're married."

"Makes no difference."

"Oh, but darling, it does. You know I want your baby——"

"Jessica, please,"—Taylor-Dutton, straightening the bow, looking away—"Hardly the——"

"We must be honest with ourselves and our friends—"—Miss Morse, tearily watching Retford—"And I never intend to be anything less than utterly honest in private or public. Is there anything dishonest in the desire to have a child? In love? Some women get them by insemination. I'd rather have the primal contact. The freedom and beauty of sexual union——"

"It's so easy to be misunderstood—"—Retford, less ecclesiastical and a little rosy under the eyes—"Mr. Gleave might not appreciate our sort of openness——"

"I find it very interesting. Other Christian sects have had their troubles, too. I didn't know you indulged in psychiatry."

"We don't. We believe in open confession, a complete recital of all the things we're ashamed of, reprehensible personal habits, hates, resentments and so forth. When they're out of the system, then we believe there's room for God to work in."

"Then you believe in God?"

"Implicitly. Why should you ask?"

"You spoke of guidance. How do you know which guidance has control? If there's a God might there not, on the principle of black and white, be a devil?"

"We believe the devil has no power when we are once given to God."

"That's a tall order, Mr. Taylor-Dutton. Any radio operator can be confused if there's no call-sign. How do you know whether it's God or the devil? Do you know your Bible?"

"Not awfully well. Is it necessary?"

"I should have thought so. Where else do we get the Word?"

"You're in the older tradition, though. We distrust the churches. They're businesses. Money-grubbers, for the most part. Money for anything under the sun. Fire insurance. Not that we blame them. It's the way the world's made at the moment. We want to change all that. Moral Rearmament is a race with time to remake men and nations. It must go to every heart and home throughout the world. It's the ordinary man's chance to remake his world more as God intended it to be."

"But if God made it in the beginning, how did it go wrong? And if it's gone wrong, how do you know you can put it right? Are you greater than God?"

"Oh dear me, no!"—Mr. Retford, a negligent turn of the head in rebuttal—"But we have the advantage of being here, with a capacity for work and a desire to do His Will. 'Were the whole realm of nature mine, that were an offering far too small. Love so amazing, so divine, demands my soul, my life, my all.' That's our belief."

"But they don't have to do any cleaning, or scrubbing out bathrooms, you'll notice——"

"Jessica, life isn't entirely a round of cleaning bathrooms——"

"Oh yes, it is. For those who have to do it. Wait until you have to clean up after a couple of queers——"

"Jessica! You'll really have to learn to drawn the line somewhere——"

"Absolute honesty, George. That's what's asked for, and that's what you're getting. And weren't they queer? You know who I mean. Suede shoes——"

"Everybody who wears suede shoes isn't——"

"Green shirts and silk hankies——"

"No reason at all——"

"One of them had a green suit, and the other wore a green jacket all the time he was there——"

"Do I understand that suede shoes and the colour green have some significance?"

"Yes, Mr. Gleave."—Taylor-Dutton, touching his spectacles between the eyebrows with the tip of a middle-finger—"Green's been identified as a colour most favoured by the pervert. Suede shoes have always been almost a brand, of course——"

"One moment. All the Irish aren't perverts, are they?"

"But that's a national colour, isn't it? That's a little different."

"How about the Knights of the Most Ancient and Most Noble Order of the Thistle? Their robes are green. But it happens to be a Scottish Order. How about the Clans wearing green in their tartans? What would you say of the Rifle Brigade? Their uniform's green. Who's your authority?"

"It's rather well known, I should have thought——"

"Well known by whom?"

"Does it really matter?"

"Yes, Mr. Retford. It must matter a great deal. If you think in such a haphazard manner about items that aren't very important, why should you expect to be any clearer in things that have real substance?"

Miss Morse stood, brushing splinters out of her lap, and made rather a meal of picking slivers from the region of the mons veneris.

"I'm going to have something to eat, and bed."

"I think you're very wise. Meet you at seven, ready to go. Don't be late."

"A lot you'd care, Jocelyn. Aren't you even going to offer to see me over there?"

"I suppose I could——"

"Don't if you don't want to——"

"It's not that, Jessica——"

"Supposing we both go——"—Taylor-Dutton, a sudden fervour—
"We could all have dinner at a little place I know——"

"Oh, all right. Come along to protect him. Absolute purity——"

"Don't mock, Jessica,"—Taylor-Dutton, putting down his glass—
"If you can't believe, if you must recant, don't trample on things you know are sacred to us——"

"Now George, you know I didn't mean it that way. You're so touchy. I say the things I think. The bad things. I get rid of them. That's the proper way, isn't it? To say the things one's ashamed of. Say them openly. Fearing nothing any more. I want Jocelyn's baby. That's what I want. Why shouldn't I say it? I've said it. Still it doesn't make me feel any better, or make me think I don't want to. I do. Terribly——"

"That's because you're forever thinking of yourself—"—Taylor-Dutton, putting his arm about her, tender, protective—"You've got to learn to forget yourself. For the sake of others."

Taylor-Dutton looked about and shared a smile of orbicular primness between his host and remaining guests, and walked on, head close to Miss Morse's. Retford chewed the olive, a little at a time, and sighed.

"Sorry about that. She's rather a problem. We'll get her to a doctor tomorrow. She needs a rest."

"The lady was very nervous, I think."

"Yes, Mr. Mavritz. Very nervous. Anything can be made fun of.

But it's impossible to discuss anything with someone as ill as that. She went rather far. And losing a weight of sin is like losing fat. Take off too much in too short a time, and there's bound to be trouble. Still, we pray for her. She can't possibly come to any harm. Lovely girl, really. In herself, I mean."

"And was she, indeed, a femme de chambre as she said?"

"Yes, she was. We all did some work or other. We don't much care what we do to help."

"I expect we shall meet again in London."

"I'll hope to see you there, Mr. Mavritz. Au 'voir, Mr. Gleave. Please don't think of us as advertisements. We try, that's all. Others are more successful. We hope to be. 'O, God, to us may grace be given, to follow in their train.' Good night."

Wealth murmured in the bar, glassware clinked, a woman laughed oo-hhoo! and men chorused, and a cash register rang. Outside a newspaper seller gobbled the headlines.

"I am sorry if my guests disturbed you, Mr. Gleave,"—Mavritz, polishing his spectacles, large black eyes a couple of inches from the handkerchief—"I am a friend of the father of young Retford. So we meet. But I shall say, for me, it is difficult to understand the young men of your country today. The mother of the pioneers, what is happening? It is like Spain. What shall I say?"

"They'll grow out of it."

"I think there is something more strange in them."

"Of course. The Reformation was that sort's fault. The Roundheads got their strength there, too. Blinding about for something they think they ought to have. Doesn't last long. The search keeps them happy. It's the Grail of one kind and another all over again."

"You are not troubled in this way, Mr. Cleave?"

"No, I'm not. I've never felt that need in myself. I'd rather use time on the more practical aspects of living. The absolute standards they talk about may have considerable value for some people, I suppose. But while they're getting recruits for their commitment, there's a lot of social engineering to be done. People are still starving, and they'll go on starving. I'd much rather hear what they propose to do on a national scale, financially for example. Rather more useful to the rest of us."

"But how can they? Who can do this? Even the powerful Roman Catholic State does not dare venture so far. The most the Vatican can decree is that human beings were lifted bodily up to heaven. Without oxygen or any necessary paraphernalia, up they go. By decree. But the Pope, poor man, suffers such a human complaint as the hiccups."

"It's an article of faith. If you're ready to believe, then you've got to believe the lot or nothing. When they've got enough people believing like that, they've got a steady fundament to work on."

"But think what a dis-balance in the human brain. The mathematics of fission and space on one hand, and the flight of solid or ectoplasmic bodies through areas patrolled by the spirit on the other. How does a Roman Catholic mathematician control himself? He cannot work as a man and worship as an infant?"

"Lest ye be as little children——"

"Ah, but Mr. Gleave, no, no! That had to do with pride, and who should be the most important in heaven."

"Isn't it 'Except ye be converted and become as little children'——?"

"Certainly. Of which time? Ours? These precocious monsters, feeding on cinemas and television? It is much more the pure in heart, the childish purity. What has a child to do with a corpse raised up in space? This is an adult and wholly diseased conception."

"Not strange from men who've never known a woman or fathered a child except by word of mouth——"

"But they use women. Without conscience. The mother and child symbol is good advertising. Something beautiful for prayer. You British people are becoming more Roman Catholic every year. Desire for theatre, colour, candles, incense. It is the more fashionable fascism. Contra-Communism. When your Royal Family becomes Roman Catholic——"

"That's impossible——"

"But members of it have certainly known the Last Rites——"

"I'm sorry, but it's beyond all discussion——"

"With you, perhaps. But not with others——"

"It's the worst sort of scandal——"

"It has a great bearing on what is thought elsewhere, remember.

For example, if a revolution or a cataclysm should destroy the Vatican State, where would be placed the papal throne? In London? The last European stronghold? Or in New York? Washington? San Francisco? Where? Rio de Janeiro? You think there are no plans made?"

"I don't see where they concern us——"

"Then you underestimate the power of zealots. Others have made the same mistake——"

A page-boy stood in front of Mavritz and lifted his thumb off a salver to release an envelope. Mavritz smiled, surprised, changed his spectacles for an even heavier pair, tore open the envelope and read the card. Finishing the drink, feeling ready for dinner and undecided where, and still, formlessly present, a desire to call Myril.

"Mr. Gleave, I don't wish to shock you, but you are being followed."

"How do you know?"

"This card tells me so."

"Your informant may be mistaken."

"Possible. We shall find out——"

"What interest have you in this? Why should you be told?"

"I am also employed by my Government, Mr. Gleave. You would like to know or not?"

"Yes."

"Very well. Maxim's is a public place and not far away. We will shake hands. You will go to Maxim. I shall book a small table in your name from here. I shall let you know soon after, and you will be good enough to tell me what you would like me to do."

"What could you do?"

"Many things."

A look at black pupils magnified at least two or three times, without light, and certainty freezing that any number of things could happen.

"I'd prefer you did nothing at all. If it's not a mistake, I'd only like to know who it is."

"As you wish, Mr. Gleave. I have enjoyed your company."

"Now tell me why you invited me to join you. Not to meet Moral Rearmamenteers——"

"Because you are a friend of Frolla and Bejian. Is it good manners, or hospitable to allow a friend to drink by himself? Are we not friends?"

"I suppose we are. We will be if you find out who this shadow is."

"It will be simple to find out who she is——"

"She?"

"It is a woman. I shall soon be able to tell you her name."

Strolling through the bar, wondering who the devil she could be, wildly thinking it might be Myril and mentally kicking himself, and crossing the foyer to the long gallery, stopping now and again to look in showcases filled with the sweetmeats of all daydreamers' watering mouths, glancing in mirrors, stopping to ask prices of saleswomen, seeing nobody he knew and nobody to attract suspicion, and walking out to the Place Vendôme, a little angry, and except for memory of Mavritz's eyes, willing to write it all off as moonshine. A cab wheeled off the rank without signal, and more surprising still, the cabman smiled and leaned out to open the door. The cab smelt of Paris, of used saddlery, warm newspapers, and a whiff from an old perfume bottle. He looked around at the long row of the Rivoli's lights. The roadway was clear. He sat back and felt for the right change, trying to read the meter. The cab pulled up, and he paid the fare, tipped for the smile, and went in. The old Moroccan coffee-maker kissed his hand in welcome, and a maître showed him to a table in the corner of the small salon.

Choosing his dinner, as the maître observed, with a fine fork, two of the simpler dishes, and a half-bottle of the sommelier's own reserve for the more exacting client, took time without detriment, except to a crusty roll, torn apart and dipped in the wine, as the sommelier advised, to cleanse the palate and praise the Holy Ghost.

Two shrieks, two women bent in laughter, coming toward the table. Unbelievably, Vinny and Frolla, holding on to each other.

"Darling! I knew we'd find you. We went to the Plaza, the Ritz——"

"But how on earth did you get here?"

"Frolla had an extra plane ticket. We're going back tomorrow afternoon. Isn't this wonderful? Paris! A whole night free. Oh, I'm so happy!"

Frolla explained that she and Beji were flying back to London, but at the last moment Beji had been sent to Bonn. She had gone on to London, had telephoned Vinny about the party in Geneva, found her in the middle of the Lindley details, and invited her up for an afternoon's shopping. When the office told them that Mr. Gleave was in Paris, Frolla persuaded her to use Beji's ticket, stay overnight at a friend's flat, and fly back in the afternoon in time to cook the dinner.

For all its simplicity, and Vinny's excitement, he sat there pretending to enjoy the meal and trying to make himself agreeable, lost and damned in a state of quiescent misery.

He had a feeling of storm behind the hills, of a rumour of drums, of silence before tocsin. Something was happening that he did not altogether understand, trust, or want. He was not averse to Vinny's accepting invitations, or flying to Paris, or staying overnight. He was glad for her sake. She needed the holiday badly. But it was the timing, the sequence of events, that he distrusted. Instinct was against it, and there was no earthly use in argument.

But he said nothing and listened to clothes talk and fashion chatter. Frolla knew everybody in all the dress establishments worth knowing, apparently, and the afternoon had been an enormous success. Vinny's new coat had cost about a tenth of the price she expected to pay and three dresses she had chosen were together just half the cost of one of the same quality in London, and the silk lingerie she bought was less than the price of nylon. In the morning she was going to buy a suit, shoes and a handbag. Fortunately Mumsy had given her a cheque which she would probably have to use to satisfy the blasted Customs going in. However, she was revel-

ling in every moment of it, and she had her eye on something
simply scrumptious for the boys, and, of course, something for
Daddy, and she was also taking things back for the Cottons and a
couple of people in the village.

Frolla had tickets for the theatre and wanted to get one for him,
but he said he had work to do. Whether or not Vinny should go to
the hotel with him or stay at the apartment with Frolla was settled
when the hotel receptionist confirmed over the telephone that there
were no vacancies at all. Vinny was delighted, she said, because the
apartment was simply wonderful, and the bathroom in her suite was
all pink marble and mother o' pearl, with huge mirrors, and a hot
room for a good sweat, and she had always so wanted to feel like
Cleopatra before the asp.

They left to reach the theatre in time, and much to his disgust,
arranged to meet him at the Bal Tabarin for the midnight show.
Vinny wanted to see something naughty because this was Paris, and
she could do with a little fun, and she could hardly tell the Cottons
she had merely creamed her face and turned in.

He saw them as far as the cab, and went back to the table. The
bill lay folded on the plate, and lying on top, an envelope addressed
to him. Your follower—written on the card inside—is Miss Joan
Thiery, employed by the Wemster Private Enquiry Agency in London. She stays at your hotel, Room 247. If you wish anything done,
this is my number. M.

He went to the telephone box and dialed. A switchboard operator
answered, and put him through to an extension. A woman asked him
to wait a moment, if he pleased, and Mavritz came on.

"Gleave here. I don't understand this at all. I'll find out about it in
London."

"There is nothing you would like me to do?"

"Pack her up and send her out of the country. But you can't!"

"No? She will be on a late plane from Orly. Examine the passenger
list if you want. The man who took her place is now in Maxim's,
near the door, blue suit, grey hair, reading a newspaper. He is
French, of a Paris agency in partnership. He will not be a nuisance
to you and I would advise you take no notice. As for me, I am always
at your service."

"Could you find out through the Paris agency who put these
Wemster people on to me?"

"Certainly. I shall leave a message at your hotel."

"Thank you."

"My compliments to Madame. Good night."

The man in the blue suit sat there, right enough, reading a paper
propped against a carafe. But there was another little surprise at the
table. The maître said that the ladies' dinner had been paid for. No
need to guess. Frolla. The Moroccan served an extra cup of coffee
with a dash of orange-water, kissed his hand again, and pocketed
the tip in one endless motion. On the way out the man in blue
looked up. Then was the time to incline the head, murmur Bon
Soir, and take away satisfaction of seeing carmine suffuse a rather
pale, lined and long-nosed face.

He walked back to the hotel, trying to take stock of his position.
Think as he might, he made nothing of a private enquiry agent. He
could attend to it later. The matter of Frolla and Beji, Vinny and
himself was what really worried him.

It seemed that they must either break altogether and get back to
the safe and sane humdrum, or he must go on being discomfited by
doubts about their probity. Analyzing the doubts, however, brought
a few doubts about himself. As Bejian had said, they were very
ordinary people working for a Government of a type considered un-
desirable by some, but apparently enjoying a majority vote inside
its own country, whether by force or not was matter for pro- or anti-
propaganda. As an established fact, the Government was in being,
had authority, and was properly represented. And Bejian and Frolla,
and others he had met, were by no means bad representatives. They
were good-natured, honest as far as his experience went, lived well,
did well, and generally comported themselves as reasonably civilized
human beings.

His doubt appeared to rise from their very friendliness, yet they
did no more, certainly, than any friend of his might have done in the
same circumstances. If they were inclined to be lavish in their
hospitality, that was because they had the money to do it with. Compared with any diplomatic standard of hospitality in earlier times,
what they did might have been looked upon as a skimp.

Perhaps, too, there was more than a little envy at base of his doubt. He would very much have liked that scale of allowance and that style of living. It went solidly against the grain that Vinny had to buy a coat at a tenth of its value by Frolla's help, rather than be able to walk in and order it at its proper price, by herself, in a manner becoming to his name and place. Anything less had smack of the worst sort of charity.

The same wormwood as having to hire toggery and return it. The same forgery of values. Almost the same disgusting pretence.

But it was ridiculous on the face of it to tell somebody he no longer wanted anything to do with them because they had more money and were too kind-hearted, or because he imagined they were using the friendship for some ulterior purpose of their own. Perhaps his doubt was really nothing more than a camouflaged fear that some demand might be made upon him. It would be simple to pass their names to Security and have them deported. They knew him well enough to know that they could expect to take no liberties. He questioned whether they would be such fools as to run the risk.

But something about the entire business rankled, made him uneasy and resentful.

Miss Thiery had left a short time before, the receptionist said. She had arrived from London that afternoon, but nobody could remember what she looked like, tall or thin, old or young, anything. If she had been following him, it was difficult to see how she could have known he was going to Paris. Unless she belonged to Security. But if she did, Mavritz could not have had an easy time in getting rid of her. Nevertheless, she had gone. There were several mysteries one on top of another, but all they meant was that Mavritz had exceptional influence in the Government. Not many men had the power to expel anybody, much less an agent of a friendly power. He began to wish he had asked for an interview with Miss Thiery. There would have been some relief in knowing who she was.

He asked for a call in a couple of hours, and went up to his room to nap before meeting Vinny and Frolla. There was plenty to think about, and a music hall was about the last place he wanted to think in. Thought of Chalmers occurred, but there was no pity of any kind. Punishment had been condign, and proper, he felt, in the interests of the Service, although he regretted the loss of a good legal brain and years of first-class experience.

The telephone rang, kept on ringing while he watched it, hating it, thinking of a dozen people he had no desire to talk to, wondering if it were London, or just Vinny ringing him in the interval, as she often did, to see if he were thinking of her. He took it off the hook.

"Hamish, sorry to disturb you—"—Toddy, matter-of-factly—"I've got Bob Abbatt with me. Remember him?"

"Very well."

"We'd like a short talk. Not in the room. I don't trust these places. Never know where there's a mike. We'll find a little café somewhere. Knock heads over a table."

"I'll be down immediately."

Toddy appeared relieved to see him, and Abbatt's handshake was surprisingly cordial. They went out, along the Rue Rivoli, and Toddy led the way to a comfortable little café and took a table on the pavement behind a screen of shrubs.

"This is how it is, Mr. Gleave,"—Abbatt, speaking in a whisper barely heard over the traffic—"And I'm sorry to take your time about it. I've been handling a pretty damn' touchy project lately. Not even my secretary knew a thing about it. As far as I know, right this minute, the Ambassador's the only man in Europe outside the Commanding General and some of his staff, British, French, and Beneluxers, who've got a line on it. What happens? I went to this party tonight. Some very important men were there. I'm talking to this Deputy, his name's Crivande, Jules Crivande, and he asks me in so many words what I know about it. The whole thing. I gagged. I tell you, I thought my drink was doing things. I'm just plain lucky I swung my head the right way. Thing is this. If any part of it gets in the papers I'd have to do some pretty tall explaining and I just wouldn't know how. You can't explain something you don't know. What I want to know is, how'd it get out?"

"Lucky guess?"

"No, Mr. Gleave. I'd thought of that and worked on it a little. But you don't guess the unguessable with one hundred per cent accuracy.

You don't guess it to the one guy in the entire place who could know. You do it because you've either been told to, or else you've got your own reasons."

"Did you find out which Party this man belongs to?"

"I certainly did. He's a Communist. Beat that!"

"Damn them, and thrice damn them!"—Toddy, leaning back, looking up at the sky—"They're wickedly clever. When does this reach us?"

"It probably reached London through your NATO top echelon yesterday, or maybe the night before. That's why I wanted to talk to Mr. Gleave. If you'd be good enough to verify who's seen that file on your side, it's known as WA101, whose hands it passed through, and they can't be many, all the way back to NATO, I'll check from this end. I don't want to get Security on it in case I'm wrong. I keep on hoping he made a guess. But he didn't. Take it from me he didn't."

"I infer it's a plan or series of plans of some sort. Do they concern us intimately?"

"If they got published, they might toss your Government out. That's how intimately."

"You mean by public outcry?"

"And how!"

Abbatt promised to send an aide-mémoire to London, and took the Beaconsfield number in case of emergency.

"Who can one trust?"—Toddy, asking the rear light of Abbatt's car, taking him home to a cold dinner and, he said, a wife getting kind of sick of this European stint. "It's getting to such a pitch one's almost afraid to say a word to anybody. When Abbatt told me just now, I quite thought it was some sort of trap for one of us——"

"What do you mean?"

"It's been done before, you know."

"I'm well aware of it. But who'd want to trap us? For what reason?"

"Part of the Security programme?"

"Ridiculous!"

"Not half as ridiculous as some of the tricks they've tried. But I agree with you. That's why I fell in with his suggestion and called you. I shall be very interested to read those documents."

"So shall I. Another plan by Uncle S. It makes me wonder what our own planning staffs are doing."

"Preparing training exercises without troops, I'll bet a pony. Where a young gentleman with a red flag, over there, pretends he's ten divisions of Red Guards, and another young gentlemen, over here, with a blue flag stands for a corps of their rocket artillery. A platoon of ours, using our superior tactics naturally, goes through the lot of them like twaddle through a goose, and at about four o'clock they all fall out for a good old brew-up. I don't know what there is for the poor devils of planners to do. If it starts, the airmen'll take their plans, and their troops and the country itself, and annihilate the lot."

"Isn't much we can do about it."

"Appalling thing is, it's possible. Sometimes I have to ask myself if I'm sleeping or drunk. I'm neither. Simply bad-tempered and disheartened. There's no longer any room for diplomacy. It's raw bargaining and nothing else. Bazaar dickering. Prime Ministers, Foreign Ministers, all sorts, shooting off here and there to chitter-chatter. What's the use of an Ambassador? They used to have a certain status. Now they're nothing but managing clerks. A Minister's not much higher than a messenger. I wish to God I could go back to the City. Unfortunately, I don't need the money, and it's much too late."

"And in any event, you prefer to be on the inside knowing the facts, rather than grubbing about on the outside for juicy gossip——"

"Doesn't make me any happier. How about you?"

"I'm not happy, either."

"I thought so. I shall be taking a few days off in a week or so. Why don't you come down to Mappersley and let's talk about this? You know Charles Froweth, don't you?"

"Lord Froweth of Ablady? I've met him——"

"He'll be there. And one or two more. In confidence, we're thinking of forming another party. We think it's time British dynamism were given its head."

"British—?"

"Dynamism. The true national spirit, in other words. We've been held in too long. Time some of us produced a programme that might appeal to the younger people in the country. We've been victims of a gerontocracy for far too long."

"Putting what in the place of the old men?"

"A Government of the more progressive type of young business-man. With a high sense of duty. Each with a sound commercial record in his own sphere of action. No politicians of any kind. No hangers-on. Every man pulling his weight. We're already promised a large central fund by the City. It'll take about twelve months, we think, for the programme to soak into people's minds. We'll put up our candidates at the first General Election. I believe we'd romp home. People are utterly weary of the more nigrescent type of Tory. As for those Labour sweepings, we'd put them all firmly in their places——"

"Bit steep, with half the electorate voting for them."

"We're confident we'd take a lot of them away. Most people have voted Socialist from sheer exasperation. Now that things are looking a little healthier economically, we believe that if we presented them with something even better, even with a sense of advnture, we'd attract the younger vote, and the largest part of the thinking artisans, too. They all want a car. Equal pay for women, of course, would give us tremendous strength."

"You may be right. Do I come into this?"

"Most certainly, or I shouldn't be talking to you. We've had an eye on you. If we came to anything, you'd get the Colonial Office."

"As cut and dried as that? Who'd be Prime Minister?"

"Charles. Magnificent war record. Knows as much about finance as anybody. Great name in the City. Couldn't look for a better man."

"And Foreign Secretary?"

"I was rather hoping I'd be offered it. I've got what I think's a fairly comprehensive plan worked out. I don't doubt I could put it over with the slightest luck, and that's all it wants. Particularly for India, China and Japan. We want those markets."

"I'd like to hear more about it."

"I was hoping you'd say that. Can't tell you how glad we'd all be

if you joined us. Whole thing's very sub rosa at the moment for
many reasons. We'll meet before you go?"

"I'll have to report to the Ambassador. Does he appear in your
plan?"

"One of the first I'd put out to grass. Anaemic bumpkin. I must
say I prefer a bit of dash about people. No use without it. 'Night!'"

Watching the Daimler go away, and thinking of the sort of
Foreign Secretary Toddy would make. The whole idea of Lord
Berrish trying to knock his kind of sense into the new type of Indian,
Chinian and Russian, or of coming to a slither of grips with the
emergent European, ripped open the imagination and left a void
blown with an echo of Calton-Islipian laughter. As Colonial Secretary, there was prospect of lasting about a month in that company,
and then enforced resignation. But there were elements of unreality
about it, taking into account that he was plodding toward a French
music hall to indulge a wife in a ravage of bawds which schoolgirl
tradition bolstered by an Anglican conscience impelled her to think
of as naughty and something to giggle about. Decidedly there was
some aspect of unreality in discussing Cabinet structure along a
Parisian side-street. Yet the same conversation in a bedroom in
Downing Street, or in the Carlton Club would have been considered
at least climatically proper.

Light rain fell, and rather gratefully he took a cab. Women selling
nude rubber dolls bent them in suggestive postures for his amuse-
ment in the crowded foyer, and sheered off when Vinny kissed him,
and pulled a face at them. Frolla had reserved a banquette, but
refused on any account to let him share the bill even though he
threatened to stamp out, and might have done but for Vinny's eyes
which said she was a little sick of arguing about money and she
cared nothing anyway. A bottle of champagne appeared, and when it
was finished, another. By that time the show was almost over, the public danced a few waltzes on the raised stage, the stage had sunk into
the floor again, and tableaux of a couple of dozen young women, as
their parents had produced them, except for jewelled lorication of
the pubic area pranced, bawled a ditty, and went off as if their
feet hurt. It struck him that some of the matters he had dealt with

that day, the Chalmers business not least, were far more immoral than anything taking place on the stage.

They went out in a crowd. It was still raining, and he had to leave them and walk a fair distance uphill to find a cab. Coming back, watching for them, he realized why Toddy was tired of what he called the more nigrescent type of Tory, obviously, because the Black families were of somewhat longer line historically, by their standards better bred, closer to the Royal favour and inclined to treat any Toddy Berrish either as an upstart, or as a particular kind of monied, if titled, joker, useful in many ways, but not a person to cultivate. Under Parisian lamplight he caught a glimpse of that realm of castles, manors, and grassy demesnes owned by a breed ready to confess itself Somebody and never at any time to be taken for Anybody, requiring a bend of the head and body in personal address, and some mark of respect in speech and demeanour by any they considered less than their kind. Toddy's impatience was understandable. He, too, liked the limelight, the tile, the respect, but he disliked having to give it all to somebody else. Toddy thought there was no need to go any higher than Arthur Gregory Todderton, Baron Berrish. Those above him according to the College of Arms thought differently. In, of course, what was acclaimed as a classless society.

One grasshopper balking at a jump over another grasshopper's back.

The girls discussed the show in the cab, and agreed that either could have taken off their clothes and given the leading lady or for that matter any of the others a run for their money as far as their figures went. Vinny said that if she could earn a couple of hundred a week by parading about in a little leaf, she was quite prepared to show what she had to anybody, at a reasonable distance. She did the same thing in a bathing costume. Frolla said that in many parts of Europe men and women bathed in the nude and who took any notice, nobody. Vinny said she had been shocked at first to find the nicest men and women in the public baths in Japan, but nobody else seemed to mind, and after a little while she thought her attitude childish and perhaps gauche, really, and she was rather disappointed to find that nobody looked at her except, possibly, in the eye, because it gave her no right to look at anybody else.

The apartment was not far from the Eiffel Tower and on the same side of the river, in a new building with a foyer of quite portentous luxury in carpets, striped silk chaise longues and wing chairs, and vases of chrysanthemum that looked real, and very likely were. The lift went by itself and hoisted them ten flights in a jiffy.

A footman opened the door, and a butler, in white wig, knee breeches, corded frockcoat and starched linen ruffles, led them into a salon and asked Frolla in the third person whether Madame had something to demand. Vinny said she would love some water with ice in it, but Frolla said that after all, this was a special night, and there ought to be a bottle of champagne to drink a health in, because Beji would have been outraged at anything less.

A Cézanne flower painting occupied a few minutes, and brought a memory of Calton-Islip. In turning to a Bonnard, he had to look across a desk furnished with a silver inkstand, a speckless blotter, and a large photograph framed in plain silver.

"Lovely place, isn't it, Hamie?"

"Yes."

"Can you believe this is their Government's idea of the way they ought to live?"

"Meaning their Diplomatic staff?"

"Not only us, Hamish. Everybody representing our people, or doing our work."

The girl in the photograph looked directly at him from the mists of a new technique, where lines and features merged in light and shade, but nothing could disguise a smile he knew very well. He felt caught in a plague-ward.

"Frolla, is this the apartment Mr. Arkhiv offered to me?"

"Yes, Hamie. It is the same."

As if there were any doubt about it.

"Hamie, come and see my boudoir while I do my hair. I'll show you how the other half live. Remember Salter's Humby?"

"Extremely well."

"Good. This is owned, Frolla tells me, by one of the proletariat. See how you like it."

"Anything to make you happy."

And any mortal thing to get away from Myril's terrifying smile.

A cab got him to the Air Terminal in time to catch the airport bus as it started. He felt grateful, first because he detested all the playing about with luggage and tickets, and secondly he was able to sit quietly and listen to nothing more important than the bruit of passage. The morning turned out much as London had warned him, with a lot of people talking, most of it too drearily well known, unimportantly little of it fresh. Notes and the transcripts bulged his coat pocket throughout luncheon, a vol-au-vent and a glass of wine around the corner and some conversation with a Greek delegate about home rule for Cyprus which the Greek thought ridiculous, and the return of the Elgin Marbles, which the Greek thought mandatory. The afternoon yawned by in one speech after another, all read as if they were Third Form compositions. The folded transcripts stuffed his other pocket. At about five o'clock, an adjournment of fifteen minutes for instruction on questions relating to defence of the Saar was asked for by the French delegate, but it spread out in some extraordinary way over three hours. A little after eight o'clock the French declared themselves ready, and two of them went into speeches lasting an hour and a half, the first setting out the position as everybody knew it, and the second offering no solution or any hope. At about ten o'clock, the meeting adjourned for top-level discussions, and he was able to sit down, classify notes and data, write a report, shove the lot in his case, collect shaving kit, pajamas and dirty washing at the hotel, and scramble bag, bumbershoot and bowler into a cab.

Few passengers meant he might be able to talk winningly to the stewardess and get the forward compartment to himself to polish up the report during the trip instead of having to get up a couple of

hours earlier in the morning. Lit brasseries and corner cafés swerved
and swung by in all the wild certainty of French bus-driving, without
accident, and no comment except from a stout lady in front wanting
to know how'n hell they kep'm on the roads.

But the aircraft from Rome was thirty minutes late. That meant
time for a philosophical drink, and a long moment to speculate on
the meaning of Myril's photograph in Arkhiv's flat, and what she
meant to him, and what sort of a game everybody seemed to think
they were playing. He had not stayed very long after seeing Vinny's
suite, truly a Levantine's dream, with a white and bottle-green bedroom, and a bed that Vinny said required a referee, a blue and
copper sitting room and of course, the mother o' pearl walls and
pink mirrors of the bathroom. One glass of champagne after that,
and he was away, gladly. Frolla appeared not to know anything was
amiss and said nothing about the photograph or anything else except that she was sorry he had to go before Beji's call came through
from Bonn. Vinny telephoned after lunch to say they were flying
back on a plane which would get her to Beaconsfield with any luck
at about seven, but she was not looking forward to a night in the
house all by herself, and expected she would ask the Cottons if she
could use their divan.

More people were in the waiting room than he had expected, but
he managed to get a table in a corner, out of the lights, and not too
near the chattier type of conversationalist. But when the waiter put
his drink down, amazement shocked to recognize Kevin Chalmers
laughing at him not far away.

"I'm waiting for Mary,"—waving, calling across—"Want to talk
to me or not?"

"No reason why not."

"Good."—getting up and coming over—"I was hoping you'd say
that. It's rotten losing a friend."

Giving an order to the waiter, pulling up a chair, and time to
notice excellent French, not too schoolish or too refined, easy.

"I cabled Mary what had happened to me, and she cabled back
she was catching the next plane. So here I am. Take us a little time
to get things fixed up, but she's going to stay with friends, and I'll
go over to London to wind everything up. She wants a few days

there for the honeymoon, buy some clothes, I suppose. Then she wants to go to India. I'm all for it. Rather useful having a wife who can do as she pleases."

"Financially."

"Oh yes. And it won't take me long to get on my feet. I don't intend to be a lotus-eater. I'm going to use the trip to find things out from the civilian point of view. The pleasantest way, I may say. Lots of things going on in India, China——"

"Not Russia?"

"Yes. Russia. There more than anywhere."

"Why?"

"I think they've got most of the answers."

"You surprise me."

"Really? I've thought so for a long time. They're running rings round the rest of us. Give them ten years, that's all. In twenty there won't be any doubt."

"Any idea what you'll do?"

"Only thing I know a little about is International Law. As it affects diplomacy, of course. I believe I could be rather useful."

"You ought to know the form by now. Useful where?"

"Anywhere, should I say, where my services might be appreciated?"

"In Russia?"

"I don't say so. But why not? They're extremely weak in their English section. Nobody's got any style. Very poor translation most of the time. And in quite the wrong sort of English to appeal to the people they ought to be getting at."

"Who?"

"Us."

"How do you mean, us?"

"Or should I say canny Scots dissenters and their Lowland confreres? And all the others like us? Wasting our time."

"How put it to better use?"

"Surely, Hamish. Would you call your career well spent until now? Even if you do make a go of things in Japan, what will it bring you?"

"How do you know I'm going?"

"People talk."

Not many could, because not many knew, and he was ready to
bet his hat that Kevin could not have spoken to any of them. He
suspected it had been said deliberately, a gambit in hope of opening
a wider discussion. All it really did was to irritate him to the fiery
quick that an ex-official, far his junior, should know State business
of a highly confidential nature reserved for not more than half a
dozen heads of departments. It also spun its weight of warning.

"You bear your specialized intelligence lightly enough."

"It's fairly common of its kind."

"I'm not sure it is. It comes under the Official Secrets Act, as
you're probably aware. May I ask how you knew?"

"You may."

"But you won't tell me."

"Absolutely right. Isn't it the medical profession and the Fourth
Estate who won't divulge sources of information? Number Mr.
Chalmers among them. But will you honestly feel any better than
you do now when you're a somewhat gone-at-the-knees Ambassador?
Considering what a few of them are? Thinking of the type you might
have as a Foreign Secretary? Won't be much of a look-in for us, will
it?"

"Us?"

"As I mentioned before. People like us. Where do we come in?"

"It may have evaded your attention, but as far as your own Government is concerned, you don't come in at all. I see no use in
pursuing this——"

"I wasn't talking about the Government. Why waste time on
cadavers? I'm speaking of people like ourselves who possess thoughts
a little beyond those given adequate expression by the social order we
happen to live in——"

"Because you've put yourself outside it?"

"I don't think I have. Whatever you and others may think. I
shall marry and I shall have children, I hope. They'll be citizens of
one country or another. But they'll have a happier life than I've had
because I'll take a little time and trouble about them. Mary agrees
with me completely about that. But what sort of society are they to
grow up in?"

"What do you suggest?"

"I'm not sure. I haven't seen enough to make up my mind. Not in the United States, in any case. Certainly not in ours. European, no. Canadian or Australian, perhaps. Even there they don't bear gladly with new expressions of thought without trying to destroy them in embryo. Enlarged suburbias, unfortunately. There are very few countries in the world and just as few people who'll have anything to do with something new in the way of thinking. Unless there's a bit of profit involved. Then they get the advertising chaps on it and up she comes. Like the jets. It took a couple of crashes to bring them to their senses."

"I still don't quite understand what you're talking about when you say new expressions of thought. What, for example?"

"I shan't bother to give you an example. I'll simply ask you to consider how we're to develop, sandwiched between what some call the wur-kuz and our variety of higher-up? Where do the rest of us breathe? If we didn't sustain ourselves, where would they be? Why don't we drop those on top, and shovel the others out from underneath?"

"How do you drop them on top?"

"Abolish them. We've got a House of Commons——"

"But you couldn't make do without the workers——"

"Couldn't? We might even make a lot of thoroughly decent people out of them. All they want is the right sort of schooling. Where would they be different from anybody else?"

"You sound anti-pretty-well-everything. Is that because you resent being sacked?"

"Not a bit. It's been steaming for a long time. The consequences of a little male love made no difference one way or another——"

"I dislike intensely the use of the word love in that concept."

"Oh, I don't know. It's about the same as a woman, isn't it?"

"No. It's not."

"Well, as an easy gal might say, it's the same old bang——"

"I deny you the right to say it. In front of me, anyway. You're not even going to be permitted the suggestion that it's on all-fours with a drive at a particularly leprous sort of female prostitute. And God knows, that's little enough to do with love——"

"Aren't we becoming rather wee kirk o' heather——"

"Nothing of the kind. That sort of thing's nothing more than a vicious disgust. Any attempt to excuse it to my mind's insufferable. Any sort of humour about it is only further incursion into nausea. If your thinking's poisoned in that manner, you've no right whatever to suggest any changes at all. Until you change yourself. I hope your wife—— "

Loudspeaker warning of a flight in arrival from Los Angeles, New York, Shannon and London. Kevin held the glass between his cupped hands watching the prisms flash. Age seemed to have got him, and a thin kind of sorrow, bringing out little wrinkles in his face, never seen at other times, a monkeyish dejection, hardly compatible with the cheerfully robust Mr. Chalmers.

"I've said this before, but I'm sorry you adopt that sort of attitude. I'd have thought one had to be rather more sophisticated—— "

"We're at odds. It's not sophistication that you're talking about, but a mental slop and rot. Don't confuse understanding with condonation. It was the misuse of English I resented. Isn't this the plane you were expecting?"

"Yes. You wouldn't care to meet Mary, would you? I've told her quite a lot about Vinny and yourself. I was wondering whether I mightn't suggest dinner one night while we're in London—— "

"It's kind of you, but it'll be a domestic problem more than anything else. If you can get her here before my plane leaves, I'd be glad to meet her."

Montreal- and London-bound passengers please go to Gateway 6, over the loudspeaker. Picking up a case, umbrella and newspaper and hurrying to have a talk to the stewardess. But among the crowd in half-light already at the barrier, a woman in a feathered helmet turning, looking at him, half-turning away, and looking again, half-smiling as if ready to go unrecognized, and the entire airfield turning into a large groan.

"Good evening, Miss Hamble."

"Good evening, Mr. Gleave."

"Mr. Roff not with you?"

"He's gone on to Brussels, sir."

"Been over here since I met you coming out?"

"Yes. It's been rather long, this time."

"Enjoyable, I hope?"

"Oh, we've had a marvellous time. Lots and lots of work, though."

"Good."

Relief, anyway, that she was alone. There was still a chance of getting that compartment to himself. But a pace behind the stewardess and gaining on her, Kevin, with a girl almost as tall as himself, light shining in fair hair drawn back from mid-parting, grey eyes smiling excitement and a beginning of dreams, a beautiful mouth, even in shadow some aura of grace, and perfumed fur exhaling the unmistakeable American Eve.

"Mary, this is Hamish. Mary Edwards. I wish Vinny were here."

"I've heard so much about you, Hamish."

"Not as bad as all that, surely?"

"No! I think you've been wonderful——"

"I? What have I done?"

"Giving him the help he needed. I'm taking over from here on in. I hope we can count on your friendship?"

"Well, yes, certainly——"

"I know all about everything,"—a look at Kevin—"and I'm just not worried. Not worried at all. We'll get along fine. I'm sorry we had to meet this way and have to talk here. But I think it's the best thing that could have happened."

"I think he's very fortunate to have found someone——"

"But I'm fortunate, too. It's a modern world and we've all got modern problems. Why wouldn't we have? We've just got to face up to them the modern way, that's all. I hope we meet in London——"

"We shall. Goodbye——"

Through the gate, turning to wave, watching a long scarf float, and up the stair to the stewardess' smile, and a neat head shaking regret. Two people had the table on one side of the compartment, and a lady had a seat at the other.

He could have named the lady without hesitation.

But at least he had a seat and a table. He emptied the case, smiling at La Hamble's sympathetic wry, and sorted the transcripts while the aircraft ran up to the start line. La Hamble lifted a portable typewriter from under the seat, took off its cover, slipped out of her fur coat, took a cigarette out of a gold case, and lit it, and pfffd a sickly-sweet grey plume across the table. At intervals she swallowed smoke —pwhah—and gulped—ngk—and pffd shadows over the light. Until the lead paragraph was written he said nothing, and made no move to dispel the frequent clouds of nicotinous monoxide bathing his head with the malodorous waste of her lungs and trachea. But he sensed her eagerness. She leaned on the table watching him, a created phoenix waiting in its ashes, that appeared never to fall anywhere but in its lap. There was no point in refusing her offer, mute or not. She typed faster than he could scribble, and within forty minutes she gave him a report ready for presentation.

"That, I may say, was a piece of luck. Thank you very much indeed."

"It's really nothing—pfff—I couldn't very well sit here——"

"Any number of others would. The classic style of working hasn't many followers today. How long have you been in the Service?"

"Eight years, sir."

"Just long enough to have known the spirit of the old days, at any rate."

"Yes,—pwhah—I must say—ngk—I don't very much like the sort we're getting—pfff—lately. At least one used to have the feeling one was working in good company. Even that's being denied us at the moment—pffff—I think it's far more the way one's brought up and the people one comes from that matters, rather than the examinations one's able to pass, don't you?"

"Somebody's got to find out who's got a brain."

"Yes, I know. But I don't think it's awfully useful finding out who's got a brain when they can't speak the language—pwhah—it's not—ngk—frightfully impressive to others, and hardly—pffff— fair to some of us having to work with them. One's often made to look rather cheap."

"You've passed all your examinations, haven't you?"

"Sailed through, thank heaven. But I've got Myril to thank for the last one. You know Myril Gislan, don't you? Absolute wizard. —pwhah—Brilliant. Love to—ngk—see her in the Service—pffff."

"Any chance of it?"

"Mr. Roff's mentioned it. We haven't many people who've got

Russian and Chinese and six European languages all letter-perfect. She'd be an enormous help. Especially now."

"Something going on?"

"The new trade approach, and things of that sort."

"Known her long?"

"I've taken lessons three times a week for about a year. We've become rather good friends. Of course, she's a peculiar sort. All foreigners are, I suppose. Pffff."

"How peculiar?"

"Hasn't many interests. Doesn't go to the theatre, won't go near a cinema. Doesn't read anything. Rather difficult to talk to."

"If she hasn't read anything where did she get her knowledge of English?"

"Mr. Wittard, remember? Who died? He taught her for about five years."

"I didn't know she'd been over here as long as that?"

"Mr. Wittard knew her in India. But you've met her, haven't you?"

"Yes."

Deep water, and ample notice of warning. Myril had never said anything about meeting Wittard in India although there had been plenty of opportunity for saying so. The pwhah-ngk-pfff went on, thumb-tip against the wet end of the cigarette, finger-tips touching chin, eyes pretending to see something out of the window, attitude more than suggesting it was his move.

"I was going to her place from the Terminal, as a matter of fact—" —pffff—"I suppose you wouldn't care to join me? I know she'd be glad to see you——"

"Unfortunately I must go to the office——"

"I could easily wait. I've got a couple of lovely bottles and some of those crunchy things with foie gras——"

"Very tempting. But I'm going to catch that last train if I can."

"May I say I met you?"

"I see no reason why you shouldn't."

Stewardess putting her neat head in to ask them to adjust their seat belts and put out their cigarettes. During the final pwhah-ngk-pffff he wondered if Kevin's information about the appointment to Japan had come through La Hamble. She was in the right position to know. Arkhiv, Myril, La Hamble was a fairly complete chain. Toddy had said Kevin was known to have been in touch with the Russians. But it was more than difficult, watching a self-possessed, almost voluptuous struggle into a fur coat to imagine it. There was, in any case, one certain way of finding out.

"Thank you for being so very helpful, Miss Hamble. I'll talk to Mr. Cramer and try to get you at least two minutes off——"

"Delighted to have been of the slightest help. I've got a car waiting. May I lift you to the office?"

"I'm quite sure a cab will relieve you of all sorts of inconvenience. And he can wait to take me to the station."

Carrying her typewriter down the steps, across the tarmac, making the pace, knowing perfectly well she wanted to say a great deal more, but she had to hobble in high heels to keep up, and talk was held at a minimum. Out in the foyer, handing over to a porter, raising his hat to a breathless nod, goodnight and thank you again.

Quiet black-blue-grey streets in London's lamplight, entirely different from anywhere else, subtle perhaps, in some way more delicate, kinder to ugliness, more flattering to the mediocre.

Rounding the corner, hurrying to the entrance, and up in the lift to the office's familiar smell of quires of blotting paper and new lead-pencils. Miss Relph answering the telephone, calm, assured, authoritative as if the Country itself was speaking.

"Mr. Cramer dealt with most of your work, sir. Mr. Porrit took over this afternoon. But there's still a great deal here for you. There's also an urgent personal from Paris. It just came in——"

"Read it for me, will you, please?"

"Certainly, sir. From Paris, 1027, Official. Message reads. Agency reports client's name Delia Hall. Regret was late. Regards. Signed M. End of message. That is all, sir."

"Thank you. One more great favour, Miss Relph. Would you please find out for me exactly who Doctor Rodolphe Mavritz is? He's something to do with the legal department at the Quai d'Orsay. I'll spell it for you——"

Waiting, thinking of dear Mumsy, darling Delia Hall, the Delia Hall Foundation Scholarship for prying into other people's affairs, especially a son-in-law's, and I must send you a cheque. He disregarded any thought that the private enquiry might have been behind Vinny's trip. That kind of deceit was a long way beneath Vinny. He was certain that she could never have looked him in the eye or kissed him as she had if there had been any doubt of him in her mind. Therefore, it must be Delia, dear Delia, darling Mumsy-Wums doing it all on her highly poisonous own.

Vinny, truest of all trust, ever, utterly, and the telephone bell struck a sounding line all the way under it.

"Doctor Rodolphe Mavritz, Mr. Gleave. Born in Ivry-la-Bataille. Educated——"

"What is he at the moment? I mean, what's he doing?"

"Doctor Mavritz is secretary to the Council of National Defence, sir."

"Council of National Defence?"

"Yes, sir. Perhaps a shade higher than our Imperial General Staff."

"Quite an important gentleman, then. Could you also tell me if there's any record of a document, WA101, either from H.Q. NATO, or the War Office, and where it is now?"

Thinking of Mavritz's lazily enormous eyes and acknowledging that without doubt he could make any number of things happen, and pitying poor Miss Thiery, whoever she might be. He wondered if Mavritz were part of the Arkhiv pattern. The two knew one another. Both were friends of Beji and Frolla. It seemed impossible that Mavritz, in his position, could openly consort with an Arkhiv. But even more impossible to conceive was that dear Hamish Tyrwhitt Gleave, in his position, had consorted with them all, in the friendliest possible manner. However unthinkable in terms of Security, it happened to be the fact and it was idle to deny it, and neither did he want to.

"The document came in yesterday morning, sir. Mr. Cramer has it at the moment."

"Does the file show where the copies have been sent? Has the Council of National Defence had one?"

"Yes, sir. All Governments represented at NATO H.Q."

"Thank you, Miss Relph. What would any of us do without you?"

"Oh, Mr. Gleave, really. You're too kind. Will that be all, sir?"

The document WA101 on perusal was
an orderly and indexed formulation of air, sea and land deployments
for the defence of Europe, secret of its kind, of use to himself only
in the numbers it gave of U.S. personnel to be based in Great Britain,
but all the other ground had been surveyed many times before. Its
chief interest for the layman was the change it showed in military
opinion over a period of a few years, and a note in the preamble
warned that the plan would come into operation only if theatre
commanders could assure their Governments that thermonuclear
warfare would not be waged. Secret or not, that made WA101 obso-
lete if not still-born.

Toddy laughed over the telephone and said he was sure Bob Abbatt had played it a little too strongly, and in any case, most daily
newspapers had published as much with excellent maps in support
and all sorts of other data. But in the dither of nervous hypochon-
dria their State Department was in, the poor chap could hardly be
blamed. He had three children to think about, and any smallest
mistake could cost him his position if not his career.

Mr. Flap had merely scribbled his initials on the dispersal tag.
Blaise thought that Abbatt might have had a drink too many and
said something or other to somebody and might be trying to cover
himself. In any event it was Abbatt's duty to report the incident in
the proper quarter. There seemed little more to be said about
WA101, and he put in a note to Intelligence about the meeting
over the café table and let it go at that.

But uncertainty remained in thinking of Abbatt's tone of voice
and the expression in his eyes. Senior officers rarely made dramatic
issues of anything unless there were ample reason. Nothing in

WA101 deserved to be called touchy in the most secret sense. In ordinary conversation about the day's news, it might have been possible to mention quite a number of the matters it covered so fully. But perhaps Abbatt's sense of the touchy was a little different from others'.

There it was.

He had five fairly pleasant minutes with Mr. Flap, and took the graciously offered day's holiday without a qualm of conscience. He called Vinny and said he had a couple of things to do, and would find his own way home, and she asked him to bring some fruit and a carton of cream because the village stuff was dreadful, and she wanted a little surprise for the boys.

He found the Wemster Agency in upstairs rooms off the Strand. An elderly gentleman with a pronounced Scots accent listened to his enquiry and regretfully shook a white head. No employee of theirs had gone to Paris, Joan Thiery was unknown to him, neither had he any record among his clients of a Mrs. Delia Hall. If it would help in any manner the books could be produced for inspection on the spot.

Mystery. Unless, of course, Joan Thiery were an alias, and Mrs. Delia Hall had used another name, or that the agency had decided that the case was a little too explosive for comfortable dealing. But he had not the faintest doubt that Mavritz's information was correct. The question was, whether to go to Delia and ask her, or let Vinny do it. He decided to let it lie for the moment.

The night before he had slept on the couch in the office, a comfortable enough berth, used many a time before and nothing out of the ordinary. But he looked forward to a hot bath and old clothes, and a thoroughly lazy day.

Vinny was out shopping when he got there, and a young woman met him with a dustpan and brush, and said Mrs. Gleave asked him to use the boys' bathroom because she was expecting visitors and wanted the house to look presentable. He wondered who the visitors could be, damned them anyway, and had his bath and got into flannels and went out in the garden with a book.

An unusually fine day, and the scent of flowers, and bees playing

Puck set him in a nod. He woke up to somebody shouting and a lot of people joining in. It came from the Cottons' place, and he went along the path, through the orchard, and got through the hole in the fence delighted to find that Vinny was an incomparably superior gardener.

A woman in tweeds he took to be Mrs. Cotton stood on the doorstep facing half a dozen men and women, all angry, and one of the women, hair all over the place, barely able to speak for sobs, was being held up by a couple of men. He called out his name and Mrs. Cotton came running to meet him, whitish, and her eyes were bloodshot, and when he took her hands they were ice-cold. She was tall, brown-grey hair under a fur cap, rather solid face, freckled and no make-up.

"Oh, Mr. Gleave, these people followed me from the village——"

"Who are they?"

"I went to the local Council meeting last night to complain about the state of the road. And what do you think? I was told I had no right to complain and we wouldn't be here much longer because we're all going to be turned out to build a school——"

"Just a moment. Who's going to turn us out?"

"The Town Planning people. It's a Government affair. It's perfectly true. I've seen the map."

"All right. We'll discuss that later. Why are these people trespassing on your property?"

"I said last night I'd see them and their Town Planners in hell, first——"

"Good."

"And that harpy over there—she's the wife of a Councilman—insulted me in the street this morning, so I told her what I thought of her. She went off, and when I was coming home, she and this lot followed me. So I slapped her face."

"All right. Now, will you telephone your husband, first. Tell me when he's on the line. Then do whatever you've got to do, and leave the rest to me."

She went inside, from her waddle, rather glad to be gone. He went toward the group with a curious feeling that had the men been in the women's clothes and the women in the men's it would have been impossible to tell their sex. The faces were as hard, as lined, as hateful. Earrings and lipstick made the difference.

"I don't want to cause any trouble. But I'd like to know what you're doing here——"

A man in a felt hat that had seen a lot of work in the fields hunched himself inside a raincoat, holding the folds into the groin with both hands, staring steadily at the front door.

"We want the bloke 't lives here."

"Mr. Cotton's in London."

A woman reached out and took the man's shoulder.

"Come on, Ed. Won't do no good. We'll get 'em some other way. Chuckin' their weight about——"

"Leave us alone—"—a shaken shoulder—"That cow in there, she walloped my pal's wife——"

"She could take out a summons for assault."

"I can do some assaulting——"

"Very foolish. Might mean hard labour for a few months——"

"Oh, admitted. But that cow'd get off all right, wouldn't she?"

"Take it to court and find out——"

"What're you stickin' your snout in for? Who are you?"

"I own the property on the other side——"

"You won't for long——"

"Doesn't worry me in the slightest——"

Vera Cotton brought the telephone to the front door. He took the call on the steps. Frederick Cotton bad-temperedly shouted that he would take it as a great personal favour if those bloody toads were warned that there was a loaded shotgun in the house and that he would use it. He had made it his business to look into this piece of Town Planning crookery and had talked with some burglar at the Ministry, and it was quite right about the school and playing fields. Most of the property in that area was zoned for a satellite town, a dormitory for London. There was no decision when it was to be built. But judging by recent events, owners of the marked property would never get half their outlay. And no private buyer would look at what was nothing more than a condemned site. They might be

turned out at any moment. It seemed to him that all the property
owners ought to pay into a fund to retain a lawyer, but it was doubtful if anything could be gained. They were up against the State. And
if those Labour bastards got in again, that was that.

"I think if you call the local police, they'll take far more notice of
a call coming from London. Simply say your wife's got some callers
she didn't invite. I'll wait here until they come along."

"Really most grateful to you. Can't say how much. See you tonight."

The group had not moved. The tearful woman leaned back, resting
on a foot and a heel, doing her hair with her hat tipped over her eyes.
He had an odd sense of Myril trying on Toddy Berrish's bowler.

"I don't know about you, but I'm feeling hungry——"

"Get that cow out here."

"I wouldn't use that sort of language——"

"Told you before, keep your snout out of it——"

"Listen to me. Is this worth it? You're trespassing on private property. Threatening bodily harm. You're an unlawful assembly. That's
three charges. They may sound funny from me, but they'll sound
much worse in court. Why not go home——"

"She ain't going to walk away with this. We can do something,
too——"

"Of course you can. See a solicitor...."

"Come on, Ed. It's only going to get you——"

"Will you shut your blindin' mouth, will you? Eh?"

"A'right."

A blue car came along in a cloud of dust and skidded, and a constable swung open a door and made a sitting leap to his feet in a flash
of polished black leggings.

"All right, what's going on here?"

"Nothing at all, sergeant——"

"We just got a signal there was something wrong here, sir——"

"A little private misunderstanding, perhaps. The lady of the house
is inside. I'm on my way home next door. I suppose everybody else
is?"

Everybody looked at the man with his hands in his overcoat

pockets. Under the hatbrim he looked at the car, and sidelong at the doorstep, and smacked his mouth as if he had a nasty taste, and from the colour of his tongue that was possible.

He turned and the others followed him down the drive.

"Sergeant, there's a bottle of beer at the back door—"—Mrs. Cotton, speaking through the window— "and a sandwich if you'd like one."

"No thanks, 'm. We'll follow these down the road."

"There's no charge made against any of them, sergeant."

"I know, sir. But this area's my responsibility. That man's a local nuisance. Trouble-maker."

"What is he, Socialist?"

"Hasn't got the brains for it, sir. Just likes a bit of trouble. There's a lot of them about. Good day."

The car went off. He felt he ought to say something to Mrs. Cotton, but he could hear her weeping. He went along the path toward the hole in the fence, watching a movement in the shadow of a holly. Vinny held out her hand, and he put an arm round her. She said she had been frightened by the same man the day before. He had come to the house with some of the Lindley family asking for money in lieu of the burial grant allowed by the Government. She had given them five pounds to get rid of them.

"Five pounds?"

"Don't make any fuss about it. I don't want to hear another word."

"But that's extortion by threats——"

"Hamie, it wasn't extortion. I flung it at them. And I said I didn't want to hear another word, please."

It was done, insanely or not, and there was no use shouting about it. She said that Charles Roff had telephoned to say that he was bringing Zena down for a few days, which made her feel rather better toward the world in general. The boys would be home from school at four o'clock, and they now had half an hour's homework. They were babies only yesterday. Now it was homework, if you could believe it. There would soon be a question of school fees for Hamish. That would be a sad bite.

"If you bury many more people at our expense and fling five-pound notes about, there'll be nothing to bite at."

"They've got to be shown at times that money isn't of the first importance——"

"Oh, for God's sake, Vinny——"

"It isn't. They have to be shown that some people have principles——"

"They don't give a damn for you or your principles. Money's what they wanted and that's what they got. Through being irresponsibly soft——"

"I told you I didn't want to hear another word about it. I'm sick and tired of this everlasting talk of money, money, money. Shut up about it!"

"Would you mind telling me how we're going to live if you——"

"I'll ask Mummy. If you must know, the five pounds came out of her cheque. Should we choose another topic, d'you think?"

Charles Roff's old car bumping down the drive prevented a first-class row. Getting him a drink while Vinny took Zena upstairs chased rancour out of the system and got everybody more or less on speaking terms.

The telephone interrupted Zena's delightful story of her adventures on skis, and Vinny came back with her It's-London-Again shrug. Blaise said he hated to be an infernal nuisance but there was a very urgent matter just tabled, and there was no help for it, and he would send the car if necessary.

Charles had to go back in any case, and the few hours out of the house would do nicely to clear away all the bad feeling. It had always been tacit that disagreements should never be heard by the children, and neither should they be exposed to the harrowing aftermath of a quarrel.

He told Charles about the Lindley affair on the way up. Charles said that although it was a little difficult to understand, he entirely sympathized with Vinny's attitude. Every woman had the right to play Grande Dame at times, rightly and at whatever cost, because in that time she shook away a lot of the little unlikeable things about herself that collected unseen like barnacles on a hull, and emerged as her true self, one she could respect, and look back upon as source of future strength and decidedly of spiritual comfort. No, by spiritual comfort Charles meant nothing to do with religion of any kind. He had little real faith in a God, although if there were not one, there most certainly ought to be. He disagreed that there was any necessity to invent one. He was going to wait until he was a little older before he gave any thought to it, for or against. He believed in a spiritual strength as an integer of the human make-up, a sort of projection of the life-force stronger in some than in others. But whether that spirit or force or whatever you liked to call it came from, or was sustained by, an Almighty God was an interesting postulate. He had never in his fairly long and varied life seen anything either to disprove or corroborate it. Matter of penny-plain or twopence-coloured.

"Londoners have the fitting expression. Them as 'as it, 'as it. Them as ain't, ain't. If anything happened to Zena I suppose I'd crawl about on my hands and knees looking for it. I hope I wouldn't though."

"Awful to think of anything going wrong with the children!"

"Indeed. And not only with the children. Hamish, would you think me unforgiveably presumptuous if I offered you a piece of advice? Not advice in the usual sense. From a heart, you must know, full of gratitude to Vinny and yourself?"

"Of course."

Charles' eyes appeared to go back a yard at a time behind each of smaller and smaller bright concentric rings in the lenses. Under the white brows they held all the menace of an aged ferret.

"You met the Emyenkovs in Geneva recently——"

"Yes."

"They're no longer friends of mine. Normal diplomatic contact and nothing more. I'd have nothing more to do with them if I were you. I believe that's what you've been called back here for. Suitable warning?"

"Taken. But our meeting was quite by chance——"

"They all are. No plan, no forethought, no go-betweens, nothing. You don't believe that, do you?"

"No. But I can't see what they'd get out of me."

"Everybody uses almost the same methods. Impossible not to like them. Great hands with the odd bottle and bowl of soup, aren't they? Settle down for a couple of hours with your cigars and liqueurs. An expression of opinion on some matter or other from a man in your position? Very innocent? Very little said. But even your caution's enough to tell which way the wind's blowing, isn't it?"

"We talked about very little. Religion, I remember."

"So they know more or less your opinion? There'll be further religious discussion next time. Religion and politics aren't far apart."

"I'm rather too long in the tooth for any of that rigmarole."

"I'm glad. Because you met a past-master of rigmarole at their dinner party. There probably isn't a more dangerous man in all five continents. To us. A great scholar. Linguist. Patron of the arts. Compelling old codger, isn't he? Do you know the man I'm talking about?"

"Vissarion Arkhiv?"

"I didn't mention that name. Neither shall I know you knew it."

"Very cloak and daggerish."

"We're part of the business, aren't we? Do please take my advice."

Blaise, Leonard Porrit and Hatton Dail were in Mr. Flap's office, and nothing about them suggested that the meeting had been anything but thoroughly unpleasant.

Mr. Flap said that there was no need to boil potatoes twice. The whole thing was that very secret information had somehow got into other hands. Fortunately, nothing had yet reached London, and no representative of Great Britain knew anything about it officially. It was an "Eyes Only" document. Seepage must have come through an American, so the fried egg was in their laps for a change. At the same time it was his wish to do anything to help his friends. Lord Berrish had told him over the telephone about a cup of coffee with Robert Abbatt in Paris. Now, Gleave, he wanted a second account of that meeting.

He got it, in very few words.

Blaise said that Abbatt had been in a most unenviable position as one of three or four men in Europe with any knowledge of a particular matter. He could hardly go to Security and give away the whole show and, in any event, he would have had to get prior permission from Washington. Taking two senior officers of the British Service into his confidence was a compliment and ought not to be regarded as anything else.

Dail said it sounded fine the way Mr. Cramer said it, but the State Department thought differently about it. Poor old Bob was on his way to Washington and he doubted if he would ever be allowed to do anything more important than lick stamps back there. If he was allowed to stay in the Service.

Leonard said it was a pretty harsh way to deal with anybody as conscientious as Bob Abbatt. Mr. Flap surprised everybody by saying he would do exactly the same thing. A man in that position had to keep his wits about him. He should have gone to his Ambassador instead of yapping in cafés. The Ambassador was out of Paris at the time. But there were plenty of cars and planes. There was no excuse.

Hatton Dail stood up and said he was glad to have had the pleasure, and apologized for the absence of his own Ambassador, also en route to Washington, and hoped he had caused no undue inconvenience. Leonard Porrit went out with him.

Mr. Flap tapped an ebony ruler on the blotting pad for a few moments.

"Gleave, why didn't you report the conversation that night?"

"We were asked to verify a certain course, and we did. I didn't think it necessary——"

"Not necessary? When a man in Abbatt's position tells you he's been milked——"

"He didn't say so. He said he hoped it had been a guess——"

"A highly secret matter that might affect us. Both you and Lord Berrish. Why didn't you report it till you got back?"

"It was fairly late that night that he told us. I caught the first flight——"

"It wasn't too late for you to go to a theatre with your wife, was it? And this Emyenkov woman. Gleave, do you allow foreigners, employees of a country not too friendly by any means, to buy clothes for your wife?"

"That's a monstrous thing to say——"

"Just a minute. Mr. Cramer, give Gleave those bills to look at, will you?"

Blaise took about a dozen slips out of an envelope and lined them along the edge of the desk. All of them were addressed to Mme. Victoria Gleave in account of Mme. Frolla Emyenkov. The total dried his mouth.

"Well?"

"It's perfectly all right, sir. She used her own money. She was introduced to these places by Mrs. Emyenkov."

"I don't want to make this more painful than it is, Gleave. I'd like you to take these things with you and compare them with her cheque-book. Then consider things. She's not allowed to spend that amount of money outside the country to start with. It's a serious offence. If she didn't spend that amount, who did? That's all I want to know. See the position, don't you?"

"Yes."

"Thanks. That's all."

Talking to Vinny was an ordeal, far worse for her, he realized, because Zena was still downstairs and he hated to think the child might notice signs of distress, and in any event there was Charles to think about. Quietly as he might he read out the bills and the amounts, and at the end he asked her if they were correct. The items were, she told him, but the amounts were not. She could tell him to the penny what she had spent, and what she had paid in duty to Customs. Not a red cent of it had come from Frolla, of that she was certain as she stood there. She asked him where he was and he said at the Club. She told him to stay there until she had spoken to Frolla.

During the time he waited he ran over what might have happened. There were several ways of looking at it, but before all he knew that Vinny could not be telling untruths. Therefore, either the bills had been falsified, almost an impossibility with houses of such repute, or else Frolla had paid the balance in each case. If she had, it might have been through some mistaken and unforgiveable idea of friendly service, or as a means of putting Vinny under an obligation. That led to all sorts of surmises, none of them less than intolerable. The more he thought about it the gladder he became that he was not at home, because he knew perfectly well that in that state of mind he might easily have burned every rag first, without thought of the children or anything else.

Vinny called back and said that Bejian and Frolla were down at their bungalow outside Seacray, on the coast. Frolla had denied the whole thing, and was quite prepared to come to London, immediately. She was waiting to hear.

"Tell them I'm going down tonight. It's got to be thrashed out before the morning."

"Then I shall come too. I'll use the car——"

"What about the children?"

"I'm sure Vera won't mind. I couldn't stay in the house. I'll meet you there. And we'll drive back together perfectly satisfied. Or I'll throw myself in a river——"

"Vinny, listen to me——"

"I mean it. If I've been made a fool of and—oh, Hamie, what a dreadful thing——"

"Pull yourself together. Remember the children. It'll take you three or four hours——"

"I shall be there. I'll say good night upstairs for you. You trust me, don't you?"

"It's the only thing I'm holding on to."

Fortunately he was in time for the express. Dinner took an hour's tedium away, and he managed to doze the rest in an empty compartment. A taxi took him to the place, and he got out in a dip above the beach. Lights came on when he pressed the bell, and Bejian came up a rock stair to meet him without a word except to send the taxi away. Frolla took his hand inside the door and led him through an entrance hall, down a stairway, and into a library modern as a next breath.

Bejian took the floor. Without raising his voice, and using a musician's gestures, he offered £1,000 to any charity if it were proved that his wife had acted in anything but an honourable manner. He would allow her to say nothing. The bills could be explained only by the principals of the companies concerned. It was late, but they might call Paris to see if a few could not be reached. Frolla had most of the private numbers, and she started well by talking to the first woman she called.

Bejian gave him an extension so that he could listen. Yes, a Madame Romsmaillenne agreed, a gentleman had come in that morning to enquire about purchases made by Madame Gleave. He said he had authority and showed her a sealed paper. She had a copy of the bill made out for the full price because she could not run the risk of showing a rebate on a model. But certainly, she confirmed the price paid by Vinny. There had been no other payment.

Out of eight calls, Frolla spoke to three people and they all said

232

the same thing, and the description of the visitor tallied in every case.

Bejian poured drinks, and sat down in one of the leather armchairs, more comfortable than most beds, and put his feet on the stool.

"So, Hamish. You still suspect us?"

"No. I don't understand it, though."

"It is of all things most simple. It is thought that you take gifts, I think."

"I'd rather not talk about it if you don't mind. Vinny will be here shortly——"

"Vinny?"

"She's coming by car. You can imagine what this did to her——"

"Frolla, you hear? We shall be hungry——"

"I go to make something good for the appetite. I hope you say what you have in the mind, Hamie,"—Frolla, at the door, holding up a fist—"Who talks about a police state?"

"Frolla, who asks we don't speak any more? Respect, please."

Bejian took him on a tour of a dream of a house, nothing like a bungalow except that on each of four levels going down to the beach, there was a single floor of one, two or three rooms.

The house and everything in it except the books was new, furnished in sprightly but comfortable style and bright without effort or tawdriness. Bejian said that although the choice of design had been Frolla's and to some extent his, they had been fortunate in having the best advice. There were no better architects, designers and workmen than the British, and every advantage had been taken of their knowledge. He supposed the initial cost was high, but considering the house had a life of at least fifty years, its cost per year was low, and during all that time it would give pleasure and every comfort to its occupiers. The house and all the furnishings, of course had been provided by his Government, not in the form of a loan and not as a gift. It was his country's property, to be used by its servants during a tour of duty.

Thinking of penny-wise upstarts in the House of Commons debating Foreign Service spending, there was relish in an outlook that brought pride and dignity, if not contentment, to those amerced of more profitable livelihood by service in the Country's interest.

In the beach room, lit by the sea's phosphorescence, a light flashed near the telephone, and Frolla said over a loudspeaker that Vinny had arrived and that she would meet her and garage the car.

Vinny lay on the wide divan with her shoes off, looking as happy as she had ever been, but in a new, more confident manner that was hard to define. She appeared to have acquired new strength, certainly not physical, because she could barely keep her eyes open. Frolla brought in dishes of small sandwiches and pastries full of meat, just what was needed for the time of night. Bejian said that obviously they could not go back to London, and a room was ready for them.

But it had to be explained that there was something far more important than sleep to be thought about.

"I'll catch the next train up. There'll be a brief interview about this in the morning——"

"Not too brief, Hamie. Tell them what I'd love to tell them. After all the blah about freedom and liberty? I hope you'll go rather deeply into that side of it. And surely to God you'll throw your resignation at them? Is that lot really worth a moment's thought?"

"We'll have to see."

"But Hamie, if you resign, what do you do? You become a lawyer, perhaps? Or——"

"No, Beji. I'm something of an international lawyer, I suppose."

"Oh, listen to him! Blaise told me himself you were head and shoulders——"

"That's tales out of court, Vin. Nobody's interested in that sort of thing."

Bejian filled the wine glasses and remarked that the South African and Australian wines were very palatable, and Frolla said that in America they had been surprised by the quality of the home-grown, even from New York State. Bejian said that excellence came always from the most surprising places. For him, the best part of living was always the surprises, good or bad was the same stimulation for the adult mind.

Frolla said she would love Vinny to bring the children down for the weekend, fine or not. The beach was wonderful, and there was plenty of room in the house, and bathrooms for everybody.

"Don't you wish our Government did this sort of thing for us, Hamie?"

"I do, rather. Much better than mortgages and so forth——"

"It's the truest form of investment, with benefits to people, land and property at the same time."

"But Beji, I thought you Communists didn't believe in private property?"

"Not your kind of private property, Vinny. We learn not to nurse things for ourselves. We don't like to take a weapon and stand over things and say this is mine, keep away. We are not like animals with a carcass. We use what there is to use. The more we produce, the more we have to use. This property is not mine. But I use it. I take good care of it. When I move, and go to another place, the same thing. Why is it necessary to say This is mine? If I die tomorrow, is it mine?"

"But it's rather nice to be able to say you've got a place of your own——"

"We have a beautiful place. When we finish our work, we go back. It is there waiting. On Sunday, I open for you a bottle of wine from our own vineyard. Small, but such grapes!"

"I'm not sure we can come at the weekend——"

"Hamish, of course we can! Do you mean to tell me I'm going to give up two blessed days of sea and sun in this lovely place? Are you still under the impression we have a maid? I've cooked three meals a day——"

"I cook for everybody, Vinny. You come, you bring the children, you rest, sleep three days. Enough, Hamie. She comes!"

Bejian drove him into Seacray to catch a milk train up to London. They said very little on the way, but at the station Bejian told him that he looked forward to seeing him with Vinny, and he hoped that this experience had deepened their friendship, or at least proved that he could trust the word of foreigners.

"Have no fear of it, Beji. I regret to have to tell you that I have more respect for you than I have for any of the people I'll have to talk to in the morning."

"That is unfortunate, but it is good. One day everybody thinks in this way. Then all people like Frolla and myself shall smile in the spirit."

"I wasn't aware you consider things in terms of the spirit?"

"Of the human spirit, certainly. What else could strengthen us against the ill-will of the Christian spirit? The Mohammedan, the Buddhist, the Hindu, are they our enemies?"

"That's begging a question. Good night, Beji, and thank you for everything you've done. I'm quite sure you prevented some sort of tragedy."

But if the milk train clattered and jolted hour after hour, or age after age, he cared very little. In between naps a wickedly-happy sense buoyed him that an answer was ready for all the Mr. Flaps.

But he was very far from feeling certain that it would be anything like the end of the matter. Charles Roff's warning had been a little too offhand for comfort.

London was still dark, and cold squalls blew paper along the platform. There were no taxis in the forecourt. He felt the need of a hot bath and bed. But it seemed sheer waste to pay an hotel bill for less than a night's sleep. A thought of Mr. Flap comfortably in the sheets, careless as a raindrop, put him in a distinctly bad temper. He felt the need of satisfying a wish to show contempt not only for the scheme of things that gave authority to such a creature, but also for the underlings and particularly the spies that had to be relied upon to retain control.

There was nobody outside the station or in the ticket entrance. He went along to the line of telephone booths, and steadfastly put pennies in the slot and dialed Myril's number.

"Hallo?"

"Myril?"

"Who is that?"

"Please forgive me. I've got the wrong number——"

"Oh, no, Mr. Gleave. This is Myril's. I'm only here for the night. This is Louise Hamble——"

He put the receiver down, and walked out in the rain, trying by anoesis not to think of the consequences.

Above all—dear Father!—for God's sake be careful of women.

Unfortunately Mr. Flap had gone to Chequers to attend the Prime Minister. Blaise dealt with the matter in the most perfunctory sort of way, and said he was glad everything had turned out well, and so many things that happened these days were perfectly obnoxious, but considered necessary in certain quarters, and therefore had to be borne, he supposed, though he would be glad to see the end of them. There could be no apology, official or otherwise, since the enquiry had been made in the normal course of duty by a responsible officer.

Going next door and sitting at the desk facing trays of incoming reports and correspondence, it occurred that certainly such things were to be borne, but only by those that had lived through years of restricted conduct, war-mania and general hysteria, though never by any of an older generation reared to speak their minds. He was brought to appreciate the change in himself by the effects of an acquired habit of static thinking that produced a general torpor, especially of outlook. Reports from abroad, primarily from the United States, had always been combed for facts and figures relevant to his department. So many of the items might have caused a real sensation in the popular press that the news served to the public day by day rarely held interest, except for private commentary among colleagues, always jokingly superior, as if his opinion were prophetic rather than the essence of all that had been learned from fact restricted to the very few.

He thought that perhaps taking too much notice of Father's early advice had done a great deal to acclimatize his mind into a state of recipiency without sift or winnow, and with no volition other than to do what his official duty prescribed. The outcome was a mentality that swept a series of limited orbits, at all times capable of sound decision based on fact and past experience, with a unique record of having never made a mistake either in method or in policy.

But if only by impugning Vinny and causing her distress of mind, to mention nothing of any insult to himself, his entire attitude toward the system came under bleak inspection. He felt like a sleep-walker suddenly prodded awake in a familiar house, frightened of his condition, grateful that nobody knew, and sitting down to adjust himself to knowledge of gross aberration, and assessing all things, thoughts, and feelings by a new awareness of mind. Never at any time had there been conscious effort to arrive at a lucid summation of the whole. That, of course, had been left to Mr. Flap and his kind, with, unquestionably, the most pernicious results. The same wickedly-happy sense of advantage that had filled him the previous night began to occupy his mind almost with the strength of an oath to make somebody pay for Vinny's humiliation and his own excoriating sense of helplessness.

He began to examine the correspondence item by item as if he had never before read a report or a letter. As he worked he became aware that he had never assessed any information cohesively as it affected the Country or the rest of the world. His outlook had always been segmental rather than comprehensive, an amateur more taken with the prowess of the village team than the importance of the game itself. It was, indeed, a sudden reveille, like waking on those cold mornings when they first took the house and finding that the car had frozen and having to walk through the slush to the station, cursing himself for not keeping a few sacks over the radiator. It was very much like that. A quiet sense of sheer surprise that he could have been so unspeakably dense, or to give it the right word, stupid.

Leonard Porrit came in to give him a résumé of the work done in his absence. There was a good deal of it and it took a long time to run through. But every moment of the time his mind functioned in a new way. As if a new sort of light were switched on he became aware of things he might never have seen before. When Leonard finished there were several pages of notes, and a growing conviction that for most of his adult life he had been not somnolent, but obtuse.

"If this goes on, I really don't see why the President of the United States shouldn't rent Buck House, and put somebody in the Speaker's chair. If the Commons got to know about this, there'd be Christ's own blast about it——"

"They won't, Hamie, thank God. It'll all unwrap itself in time. They talk far more than they dare do. They're adept at fighting all sorts of dragons on paper, aren't they?"

"I wonder if there's any inch of Asia that's worth the tip of an Occidental fingernail. Much less its cities. This type of big-bellied hypocrite loves to talk of winning wars with other men's sons and substance——"

"Is this a hangover from the Paris jaunt? Dr. Porrit's Pink Mixture for you, my boy. How about coming out for one?"

"I've got this lot to clear up. When did you start going out for one?"

"Recently. Wish I'd started before. Puts everything in a most considerate sort of glow. I can even imagine I'm doing something fruitful. See *The Times* this morning?"

"No. Why?"

"Kevin's marrying his Mary at Caxton Hall tomorrow. Three P.M. Going?"

"I thought they were getting married in Paris."

"Quicker here. I'm now going to act as host and father-confessor to a couple of gentlemen from Bonn. Be surprised what Doctor Porrit's Pink 'un does for them. We straighten the European situation with the first. During the second, the Lion and the Eagle sit down together in Red Square licking blood off chops and talons. With the third, we're uber alles. I've never had time for a fourth. I suppose it'd mean a disembowelled Lion."

"Is this the Deutsche eagle or the one on the dollar?"

"My dear Hamish, what a question. The dollar-boys vanish after the first sip. The laddies from Bonn smile in their cagey way and beg me to wait until they have a Luftwaffe. That's all. Just wait until then. So I think I'll wait. At least the pink 'uns'll make the wait worthwhile."

"What's the answer?"

"I think we're history's bloodiest fools, and nothing less. But a pink 'un'll cure that, too."

Miss Sells came in to say that Mr. Calton-Islip was on the telephone asking for Mr. Gleave. She showed a list of a dozen calls over three days, and refusal to speak to anybody else.

"Ah, Hamish? This is George. I've missed you lately. Iv' was only saying last night she couldn't make out where you'd got to. What about some lunch? Manage today, can you? Or you got some more conferences?"

"Thirty minutes is my limit today."

"Oo, dear. Busy man, eh? All right. Thirty minutes. Sandwich and a glass of beer do you?"

"Excellently."

"My car'll be outside at one sharp."

It was, and George was an affable companion through a chicken and ham sandwich and a glass of cold lager standing up at a pub buffet. He said among other things that the offer was not only open but gaping, and that if Panama was too far away he might consider the head office in London. That, of course, would mean taxation, but there were ways and means of getting round it, and long trips abroad would always count for a lot. The thing to do, as he saw it, was to get the Gleave nose into everything at the Foreign Office that might be useful in the future. Make strong connections with the people in other departments so that when he wanted info, all he had to do was pick up a phone. Never knew when they might come in useful. Every country in Europe meant money one way or another. America, well, with all the inside dope, and knowing everybody, there was no doubt about what would happen there. Give it five years, and Hamish Gleave might easily count his first million. Big deals meant big profits. Oil, ships, foods, there was no end to it. He was getting very interested in this uranium stuff. Much better than gold, more of it, easier to sell, and not too many people knew anything about it. So, Gleave, it was up to you, fella. Get the old nose in there, boy. And make up your mind when you want to serve king George. I don't ask you to duck your nut, though. Just use it for our benefit, that's all. Eh?

Fortunately there was far too much of a crush and far too much noise for any adequate reply, and in any case a scene in a place like that was not quite the thing. Happily, too, Mr. Calton-Islip saw somebody he knew, and because it was almost one-thirty, it was simple to pretend hurry and go.

The walk back gave ample time to think over what he must do. He knew that had he said anything in the bar he might have hit first and thought afterwards. There was no possibility of having a thought in common with George Calton-Islip, much less of sitting down in cold blood to work for him, with or without the millions. Vinny must be told, and he would have to put up with her disappointment and even her complaints if she made any. But £10,000 a year would never palliate a crawling sense of dishonour. Get the old nose in there, fella. Eh?

Without surprise he found a note on his desk that Miss Hamble would call him, if she might, when he returned from luncheon. He suspected she would try before Miss Sells came back. Correct.

"Mr. Gleave, awfully sorry to bother you. This is Louise Hamble. You did call Myril last night, didn't you?"

"We were cut off——"

"I think that's because Myril tried to take the phone. I'm really terribly sorry. Wouldn't you care to come for a drink tonight——"

"Much too much to do——"

"Then may I call again in a day or so? Myril's dying to see you as you can probably imagine——"

"If you'll take less interest in what people imagine or don't imagine where I'm concerned, I shall be most grateful."

"Oh. I beg your pardon, sir."

Pull up a chair, and start on the day's work again. Blaise came in about a couple of things, and when they were done, he hesitated, looking like a well-bred if not inhibited terrier pretending not to be nosing about for a buried bone.

"I don't think you'll go to Japan after all, Hamish. I don't know with any certainty. But that's how it looks at the moment. I thought you ought to know."

"I'm making no move in any direction until I'm given a date. We're going to have a devil of a time getting rid of the house. Who's taking over here?"

"In all probability Toddy. But there again, I don't know. He's not particularly anxious. He'd like to go to Germany. It's quite possible he'll go to Japan in your place."

"He won't like that much."

"That's probably why he'll get it."

There was no need for Blaise to say any more. He was being kindlily cryptic in his own way for the express purpose of conveying that Lord Berrish and Mr. Gleave were both in hot water.

"I gather we're not very popular with the Management."

"Oh, I don't think I'd go as far as that. The Abbatt affair was a little viscid, of course——"

"Why? Could you tell me? The thing he told us about wouldn't get two lines in any newspaper——"

"He knew what he was talking about. What he didn't know was that a change in cipher altered the nomenclature of the despatch. It's extremely inflammable. It's being discussed at Chequers at the moment. I can't blame Mr. Abbatt's superiors for getting rid of him——"

"In Abbatt's place, I wonder if I wouldn't have done the same thing——"

"Of course you wouldn't——"

"He took the best sort of elemental precaution——"

"It was not a precaution to let anybody else know that such a thing was in existence——"

"It was on its way to us, I understood. Are we or are we not allies? Are we not to be trusted?"

"It wasn't meant for that sort of discussion. It won't be seen by anyone below Cabinet level——"

"Extraordinary that a Mr. Flap can be regarded as a higher form of life than either of us."

"I'm surprised to hear you say that. I should have thought he was distinctly higher because of his responsiblity. Is he not the Minister?"

"He is, by virtue of Party politics, unfortunately."

"Whatever fortune may have to do with it, I'd be far happier to hear a more restrained tone. One becomes rather sick of this all-encroaching indiscipline. Whether it's in thinking or speaking it's improper to a degree. I shall be obliged if in future I am not subjected to what I can only refer to as an extremely ill-conceived attempt to belittle the Minister. He has his faults. We all have. He also has authority. We have not. I hope I make myself clear without offence?"

"Perfectly, thank you. But I must say I'm a little bewildered to find you defending politicians. Merely because they happen to have achieved Cabinet rank? By accident?"

"The electoral vote is a matter of single efforts resolved into a majority and a minority. As perhaps you are no doubt aware. It is never by accident that a man is elected. It is never accidental that he becomes a member of the Cabinet. At least, not in my experience. Is this something new, Hamish?"

"Not by any means. I've always regarded politicians as only that, and nothing more. If they say anything as officers of the Government, it's from our mouths. If they think anything, it's from our brains. They merely embroider. That's my experience——"

"Which I don't share——"

"I'm sorry, but that's exactly what I mean."

"Hamish, I've felt there's been something wrong with you lately. May I ask, is it domestic? If I'm on a tender floor, do forgive me——"

"Not at all. I'm simply fed to the teeth with the way things appear to be dealt with generally——"

"I'm afraid I can't help there. I agree there are matters that seem to be more than usually troublesome. But hurried work is always excessively bad. The sanatory properties of time can often work wonders."

"Have we the time?"

"I think so."

"I wonder. I'm not worried about others so much as ourselves."

"This country?"

"No. The You's and Me's. We're in a cleft. Can't for the life of me see how we'll escape."

"Which cleft is this?"

"Knowledge of duty and compulsion of fact."

"Oh lord, I don't deal in that sort of thing, Hamish. Gave it all up years ago. There's duty, yes. I agree. As to compulsion of fact— didn't you say?—yes—we're not asked to judge. That's done for us."

"I'm worried about how it's done, and how it's being done. Do you really like the idea that your future's being decided by a Mr. Flap and his colleagues? Not only your national future. Your economic and social future, which are just as important——"

Blaise walked to the window, and turned, very much as if he were deciding whether to lose his temper thoroughly, or slip the edge of his tongue some distance out of its sheath.

"Look here, I've no wish to discuss or debate that type of subject. They don't arise. But I'd like to know what you're doing here if that's the way you think. I know something about ambition in young men, and I know, or shall we say, I think I know, some of the attendant poisons. Among them is the swollen head. I've never noticed anything of that sort in you. But there is such a thing as a swollen mind. That's a much worse danger. If you feel that your future's not being safeguarded by the Minister you serve, you have only one alternative. You're wasting your time here, and your boundless sense of duty, I don't doubt, must urge on you the necessity to resign and put up as a candidate for election, win your seat, and fight him in the House. With your knowledge and ability, who could possibly stand against you?"

"It's a misfortune, but there aren't enough of us——"

"Us?"

"And too many of them. Labour votes."

"I've always thought that extremely healthy. It's a very good thing to know that the moment a Government goes against the public will, it's out and finished. It's a salutary check—and any Minister knows it—that the moment he offends and steps over the line, he's in the gutter. That's the best safeguard of all."

"But haven't you ever wondered if the electorate has the necessary knowledge? Do you believe the majority fit to vote? On any issue?"

"Probably not. But they have a vote. Are the majority fit to live? By many standards, probably not. But they have life. They produce and they consume. They form the economy and the body politic. Why shouldn't they manifest their will? Without them there'd be no manifestation of any sort at all. Why don't you go into Common's, Hamish? It's extremely rough and tumble. Nothing like these cloisters, this limpid backwater——"

"But the cloisters produce the decisions——"

"They help. It's our privilege. And our duty. The decision is National——"

"That's where we disagree. Duty is one thing. But problems require thought and decision. Duty doesn't decide what's right or wrong."

"The decision, as I was careful to explain, is not ours to make. It is for those responsible. If you wish that responsibility to devolve upon yourself, you have your expedient. Isn't it rather strange to be talking in this manner?"

"I suppose even we in the cloisters sometimes mature——"

"Very good thing to make sure the maturity doesn't become overripe, I should think. However. Would you be so good as to take my place at the four o'clock conference? And preside over tomorrow's meetings? I shall be at Chequers if I'm required."

Blaise looked as if he might want to say something else. Instead, he slapped the paper on the desk, and went out, and the door thumped behind him.

The business in Paris, coupled with Charles Roff's warning and now this, were all signs that something was wrong. Undoubtedly reports must have been circulated, although, had they been derogatory in any manner, there would never have been any chance of his being asked to preside over the daily meetings.

Even so, the thought that he could be chivvied in the same way as a refractory prefect at school rather got on his nerves. Leonard Porrit came in again, pinkishly deliberate, and blear, and inclined to smile into corners.

"Something I forgot, sorry. Did you know Mr. Calton-Poop-Poop's going about saying he's got a pipe-line into the Service? A gusher, according to him. The name's Gleave. Isn't he going to sit you on some golden eggs or something?"

"When did you hear this?"

"Day before yesterday. Blaise was frightfully annoyed. Took two of us to put him back in his garter-belt, poor dear. Yes, came up at the morning chibber-chobber day before yesterday."

"Thanks for telling me. There's absolutely nothing in it."

"I hear that with the greatest regret. I quite thought that at last you were using a little of that stored intelligence. I wish to God some-body'd offer me £10,000 a year. I really don't know what for——"

"Even the salary was mentioned?"

"Oh, yes. Everything's in the report. Can't move an inch, can we?"

"It's certainly becoming difficult."

Waiting, hiding impatience until Leonard had gone.

That, then, was the reason for Blaise's suggestion that he resign. He thought it strange at the time, but it was less strange now. It was apparent that had the conversation taken place in Blaise's office, considerably more might have been said, but in a far different tone of voice. Underneath the humour and, as it were, the light touch there was much more than a courteous dummy. Behind his own desk, Blaise was a martinet of the old school. He gave the impression of a dear old well-combed sheep-dog, always delighted to have his ears scratched, the sort that became a ravening monster the moment the flock was in any kind of danger. A calm, and a perceptive, and a very dangerous man at any time. If enquiries were to be made, there was only one thing to be done for self-protection, and it had to be done immediately.

A deep breath, and a ring for Miss Sells.

"There's a department of Inland Revenue dealing with people who don't pay their taxes. A sort of investigation branch. Find the super-intendent or whoever he is, and put him on."

"Yes, sir."

He introduced himself to a voice that seemed to know it was talking to the Foreign Office, and sounded as though it had been recently gargled with an inferior brand of margarine.

"Over a period, this section has given the chairman of Calton-Islip Holdings Incorporated certain figures relating to various commodi-ties in bulk. There's a strong possibility that those figures will be used as a basis for tax returns. They're official, but they don't com-pare with the market. They're far too high. As far as tax is concerned there'd be a vast difference. The same methods may have been used in other transactions."

"That's very interesting, Mr. Gleave. We've been thinking some-thing of the kind for a considerable time. But he's a very foxy one. A very fly man with a piece of paper."

"I'd like to think the rest of us had earned a little relief."

"We'll put him in the squeezer, don't worry. Will you instruct the messenger to give the papers to me, personally? I'll get on to it, right away."

Then a call to Vinny, but she laughed at him, and said she had never even dreamed of it, really, and not to think about it in the slightest. After all, £10,000 a year, poked away in Panama, full of mosquitoes and heaven knows what, how on earth he could ever have given it a thought she had not the remotest idea. Besides, there was far more self-respect in being what he was, and in a little while he would be the best Ambassador the Country had ever had, and she would be so proud of him, knowing what he had sacrificed, and how Hamish and Bobby would love to see him in his dress uniform, and what a great deal of good it would do them at school.

"Have you said all you've got to, now?"

"Yes, darling. I did rather give you a neckful, didn't I? What time are you coming home?"

"I'm catching the six twenty-seven——"

"I'll meet you. Do you think you'll be too late to buy some bath soap? We're down to smidgix. And if you can remember, a packet of curlers. I lost half of them doing the washing today——"

"Washing?"

"Of course. Who else do you think?"

"Can't you get somebody to come in?"

"Yes, darling. Droves of them. And that's all they do. Come in. Hamish?"

"Yes?"

"I love you. Look out for me."

On the morning he had arranged to take off for the visit to Mappersley, Vinny got up first as usual to shovel coal on the boiler and put the kettle on, and came upstairs soon after to whisper that Mr. damn' Blower could always be relied upon to go wrong when common decency demanded best behaviour. Mr. Blower, the boiler, had been bought secondhand as a bargain because the man said it was the best, and they never got made like that any more. Many were the times, and for minutes on end, when he had used plain Anglo-Saxon to congratulate the nation on its fortune. It meant at least thirty minutes of digging out clinkers, brushing a flue, laying, lighting and watching the fire until the gauge started going up. After that a cold bath because the children needed the hot water, and a shave in a kettleful that Vinny always, with thought for his feelings, brought in on tiptoe with a third cup of tea. It also meant that he had to miss a ride with the milkman and walk to the station because Vinny had to take the boys to school, and she could hardly go with him and drive it back or they would never get any breakfast. She was doing everything herself, again. The maids she had tried were all useless. They wanted too much money, did too little work, disliked clearing up after the children, refused to do any cooking or washing, and they preferred scrubbing from a vertical position with a wet broom, which Vinny said was cat-licking and not washing a floor.

He got the boiler going, had his bath and shave, and left the house almost an hour late, in a spitting temper, with hands like a coal-heaver's. The train to Oxford ran late and the connection to Mappersley ran even later. Instead of getting there at ten o'clock as he should have done, it was nearer noon. Mappersley, glorious in red creeper and cypress, piled two floors of grey stone with leaded windows and gables around three sides of a square garden, with a fountain and cross walks, and stunted rose trees in clumps of colour, and borders of flowers that had the swollen, cared-for look of properly-pummelled bolsters.

A butler took his dripping hat, coat and umbrella into a cloakroom without a vacant hook, and led him through the hall, hung with tattered regimental flags between suits of armour, animals' heads and racing trophies under glass.

Toddy opened the door when the butler knocked. His eyes plainly said that God Almighty was in conclave and it might be better if he came in and sat down in the first available chair without distracting too much of the divine attention. The room looked like a barn from the days of Hereward the Wake, though without the rushes, hounds and bones, but it had a crested chimney and half an oak was on fire inside it.

Charles Froweth, fourth Baron Ablady, stood at the head of a refectory table spread with books, files and paper. He was tall, fairish, of porty complexion, quite the self-assured City man in appearance, but slightly-staring eyes, that might pass for blue, appeared always to be covertly on the lookout for something which might be said, looked or thought to his disadvantage. The vocal quality was a mixture of All Souls, company balance sheets, and adenoids. His lordship made an almost grammatical pause of sipping from a glass of water, though it was noticeable that thirst attacked generally after some allusion to the courage and gallantry required, that must be part of, that should always be inherent in, all they did. His lordship was known to make a bullish business of courage and gallantry.

He drank his water, and went on to say that the people required leadership, not, in all conscience, of the sort of jack-booted braggartism they had recently been called upon to kick back in the gutter, but one, he would say, of blood, of family, of proven reputation, and, he thought he should say, of tradition. Everybody listening to him knew what he meant, and he would not pursue the matter. The people wanted somebody they could trust, in other words. They were tired of the sort of mountebank who came before them offering all sorts of things they could never in this world get. The great majority of decent people wanted nothing more than to be left alone to work. It was only when these people went among them that they stirred up all the trouble. An end must be put to it—(Hear, hear, knocks on the table)—Thank you, and it would take courage and the most superhuman effort to make those people see where things were going and get the country back to normal. That was the well-spring of his policy. To get back to normal living. The sort of thing, they knew what he meant, of being able to live as England had always lived. It was simply unbelievable, the way things had been allowed to drift. There must be no more of this knuckling under to deputations from all over the place. They must set their faces and tell the people if necessary, that every factory in the country could close down. That should and must be the answer. Close them all down for a month or so. A little starvation would bring them all to their senses and additionally provide a sense of reality. The General Strike of 1926 showed what could be done. All the loyal, decent hard-working people had instantly come to the rescue of the Government. In times of stress every Englishman rallied. That had been proved throughout our history. Fortunately, and he called to mind the glorious days of 1940, the people always responded to the truth. All they had to do was tell them the truth. Never coat the pill. They were a nation of hard-headed realists. They could always be counted upon to do their duty. He relied on that spirit. As for himself, he would lay down his life in their service, and he wanted no more of posterity than that it should be said of him that he served the noblest ideal of all, that England should be the home of the free—(more knocking, Hear, hears)—and he had no doubt that his sentiments were shared by all within hearing.

During a pause for consultation with somebody in charge of paper, Toddy explained in a whisper that the previous speeches had been absolutely first-class, and that the meeting had resolved to commit itself to the financial responsibility of forming the new party. No, they had not yet chosen a name. Charles was giving them an outline of his personal views, nothing more, but reading between the lines it was fairly easy to guess what the policies might be. It was all tremendously exciting, almost a revolution, he thought.

"Gentlemen, among the first things I would try to do is to insure everybody,"—Lord Froweth, talking at the shield on the far wall— "not as hitherto, by compulsory payments to the State, but through established insurance companies. A much better actuarial scheme could be worked out privately with great advantage to everybody, exactly as it's done in the United States, and look at the wealth of that country. It's only when the cheaper type of politician is allowed to enter in the financial workings of a nation that things begin to go wrong. Insurance and pensions for everybody all financed through proper insurance methods would take an enormous burden off the Exchequer, with a consequent and gratifying drop in the rate of income tax. I need say no more. Secondly, while I rather disagree with my friend, Lord Berrish, over the question of armaments, I'm fairly certain that it's no longer necessary to go on arming and spending money for the convenience of the Americans—(Hear, hear)—I'm glad to welcome support. They'll be told so, and upon that, knowing me, you may depend. What I foresee is a Missile Force, not even dreamed of yesterday, and there's no doubt in my mind we've got the answer. Nobody can beat us when it comes right down to brass tacks. We've always proved it. Nobody can deny it. We're absolutely right on top when we start using our common sense and get down to business. That's half our trouble. Thirdly, I shall rescind the present educational act. That might sound a little Draconian, but I mean what I say. Here we have a country, gentlemen, and I ask you to look at what fifty years or more of mass education have done for it. It's not good enough. Far from taking people out of uniform, I'll put more in, men and women. Give everybody a few years of real discipline, and teach them to obey orders instead of what we have now, utter chaos."

If he expected applause, and he stopped as if he did, he was disappointed. The eyes looked about, not at anybody, but at everything else.

"I make a differentiation, of course, between those who've enjoyed the benefit of a public school education, and those who've not. Those who've attended one or other of our public schools are very well prepared for all that life has to offer. Nowhere is discipline more severely maintained than in the public schools. It's an incul-

cation which lasts throughout life and leaves its stamp. In my opinion
it's the basis of all that's worthwhile in the entire country. Our sons
will be trained to command—(Hear, hear)—and nothing less, and I
shall fail in my duty—but I don't think I shall—if that part of our
programme falls short. All, of both sexes, naturally, will be exempt.
The rest will go into uniform at sixteen and emerge into civil life
at nineteen or twenty, thoroughly well-trained workers in whatever
field they were found to have been most suited for. Because, of course,
that period of service will be used as a pre-factory or professional
training period. From that pool, the employers will be able to draw
semi-skilled labour. There will be no talk at all about trade unions.
There'll be no need for them, first of all. Trades unions came into being because of malpractices. Those times are over. Everybody will
be paid for what they do, and not for the time they spend ostensibly
at work. In that way, it should be quite possible to get at basic production figures. On those figures a mass over-all wage can be based
so that everybody who does any work will get a fair share of what
they've helped to produce. That, in my opinion, is the only way
to run a country on modern lines. Basic pay based on basic output.
That's my contention. Any other way is simply taking the short cut
to bankruptcy."

Watching Toddy biting the lower joint, and the raptness of the
other faces, some of quite elderly men, nearby, and trying to realize
that these were a few of the coccyx of the new party, he could almost see Vinny on her hands and knees with a bucket and scrubbing brush with no thought of basic pay, and losing her curlers in the
wash and along came a blackbird and pecked off her new coat that
she had sworn she would never wear from loathing, and Hamish
watching shadows appear under red light in his little shed and
Robert grunting with fury because the crane would hoist not even
a few matchsticks without falling over.

Listening, suddenly, to words without looking at the man.

"Then again, gentlemen, what is it we want out of life? Isn't it
the knowledge that what we have we may use as our own instead of
having people who have no right to it forever making demands upon
us? Why are they enabled to do so? Isn't it because we've always
been too idle to think for ourselves? Or too lazy to deny them? Or

too vapidly chicken-livered to fight? Are we, the truly educated, unless, of course, I've mistaken the meaning of the term, the people born with a sense of duty, to allow these nonentities to take leadership away from us, take away our sustenance, the lands we inherited after so many generations of struggle? Are we not ashamed to admit that there are among us certain people who are quite willing to lie down and be trodden on with the excuse that times are changing and that duty to the Country demands their obedience? What duty and which Country, I want to know? We must beware of clever propaganda from whatever quarter it comes. I, for one, never listen to it. I have an absolute sense of duty and I intend to see it through to a successful conclusion. Or, as I've said, perhaps at risk of being thought sentimental, which I assure you is quite untrue, and you may ask anybody who knows me personally if I'm given to sentiment or not, I will die, and willingly. Though not, I might add, without a fight. Now I make no pretence of being anything but what I am. An Englishman with a profound sense of the English tradition, but no orator, although I must confess I very often distrust those with the silver tongue. I prefer plain English from men who speak their minds. That's all I've tried to do. If I've sounded a little high-flown at times, I'm sorry, but one can, on these occasions, be rather led away. I suppose it's patriotism and nothing more. All we need is the high courage, and that sense of selfless gallantry that has always marked the finest traditions of our race. I feel no shame at having said that. None."

An outburst of cheering loud enough to startle in the stony confinement brought Toddy to pull his chair closer, and pause to finish clapping, and turn an eye that had lost distance for a gain of watery blue.

"Don't you agree, Hamish? Isn't he our man? Listen to them. They aren't cheering someone out in the street. There must be about fifty millions of capital in this room from all over the country. He's what we've needed for a long time. He's not a spell-binder, thank God. The country's sick of them. He's what he says he is, plainspoken, with considerable ability and a lot of brain. What more could we ask?"

There was no opportunity to reply. Toddy looked about to nod at the butler, and in a trice a line of footmen appeared with dishes, plates and cutlery, and everybody turned to his neighbor.

Possibly because it was almost unbelievable, it took a second or two to recognize Dr. Rodolphe Mavritz smiling from a nook beside the chimney.

"Am I permitted to notice your surprise, Mr. Gleave?"

"I apologize, but you're about the last person I'd expect to find here——"

"But why? We have the same problems in France. If strong parties in the two countries had an alliance, many things would be possible."

"But could you get the votes with anything based on that programme?"

"Could you?"

They had luncheon together. Mavritz was very good company. He knew most of the people in government in Europe and the United States and he spoke sensibly of many things, not the least of the troubles of the family man. He had two daughters and a son, all of them going to school, and confessed that without private means he could never have afforded it. However, they had to contrive with the times. A question about the prospects of the new party brought a look from lenses that appeared black in their entirety.

"What shall I say, Mr. Gleave? Everybody has a wish to do something. Some have ambitions beyond their ability. Opium is not needed by such people. They manufacture their own opiates inside their heads. One must feel sympathy, I think. They have power in a room filled only with themselves. It is a pity."

Lord Froweth came around with Toddy to be introduced. His manner was that of the oracle making itself known to neophytes. A glance meant to penetrate, a spreading of facial muscles, an extension of a hand as if it were going into a sack, a 'd'ydo, and on to the next.

Mavritz got warm welcome as representative of his party, and promised to make a full report to his chairman.

"This is Hamish, whom you'll remember, Charles——"

"Oh, yes, rather. Glad you were able to get down. What's your opinion of the possibilities?"

"With the right programme, I don't think there's a doubt."

"But you think I've got the right programme?"

"I think it needs a lot of work——"

"Oh, well, naturally. I think when you hear the details you'll be rather more impressed——"

"I don't doubt that I shall——"

"Hamish, for God's sake. He's not always as stuffy as that, Charles. But you asked his opinion. Quite the wrong thing to do."

Fortunately there was a train to catch at three-ten. Toddy begged him to stay on, promising real fireworks when it got down to the industrial discussion. But it was appreciated that Leonard was looking after things in exchange for an early day, and a car was ordered to take him to the station.

On the express to London he refused to think of the morning's waste of time, and picked up a magazine in the buffet car. Thought of Lord Froweth as head of a Government got between him and the pictures. A mixture of Froweth and Berrish as guiding lights was stuff of bad dreams. But it was a little worrying to think that many another with a seat in the House was not much better or worse.

It was a relief to get to the office and to find the machine still at work, steady as ever. There was something almost comforting in being able to sit at the desk and to feel that so far, things were better than they might be.

Work went easily, but with the same sense of surprise that even a few days ago he might have missed the significance of much that crossed the desk. When he had finished, Miss Sells went home, and he changed to Leonard's office to finish off the day's work. He took everything out of the safe, sent for all the files he wanted, and instead of working found himself having a most enjoyable time fitting together pieces of a jig-saw.

Out of it all, while the pencil covered the pages, a scheme took line and crept into movement. The substance spread and set, and he had to concentrate on the file under review to deprive his mind of the luxury of implementation.

Big Ben struck eight o'clock almost unbelievably. It meant another late night getting home, no dinner, or something in the oven by the time he got there, and a walk from the station unless Vinny got out of bed to bring the car to fetch him. A look at the couch, and thought of an hotel room, and from that to Myril was barely a step. But the Hamble incident had almost cured him.

The telephone rang. Dr. Mavritz said he had called before to say how sorry he was not to have had the opportunity of saying good-bye at Mappersley, but had asked the secretary not to disturb him. He would be so happy if Mr. Gleave could join him for dinner.

"I shall be happy to accept your invitation, Dr. Mavritz. Except that the dinner will be at my Club, and I shall be host."

"I am a great admirer of London clubs. I am privileged to accept. My car will wait for you."

It was a little late, but the steward managed a fair grill in the quiet dining room, and a bottle of wine that seemed to enchant Dr. Mavritz, not into wine-bibber's cant about neat ankles and bruised elbows, but into noting its name and saying that London clubs had the best wine in the world, not only because of shrewd knowledge in buying, but because of love of the best. In few other countries in the world was the best regarded with such affection. In other countries it was possible to find the best mixed with the rest. But not in Great Britain.

"I'm afraid that's considerably changed. There isn't the money for it. We have to take what we can afford, or do without."

"And you do without. This again is a British quality. But it has a very important effect on markets. It begins to affect economy. But why should we speak of such things? Tell me, Mr. Gleave, what is your opinion of this morning's meeting?"

"Too firmly nebulous to be an opinion."

"You agree they have no chance? The press would be violent, and also the parties. They can spend all the money they like——"

"I am sorry to disagree with you. That type of programme's gain-ing strength throughout our side of Europe. It's a shadow, but the shadow falls long before the body arrives. Consider. We all have eighteen months' or two years' service for youth. Why? Emergency? Of course not. To take them off the labour market. To keep that number of older people in work. The intakes are trained for certain tasks. When they leave the Services, naturally they go into the work they've been trained for. That's the beginning. Between that and the full programme Lord Froweth spoke about, is it very far? The school bill requires a little driving, but when the propagandists deal with it little by little, with promises of free scholarships, new universities, technical colleges, all open to young men and women in uniform, can't you see what will happen? Lord Froweth, remember, was not speaking his own ideas. He's a figurehead for a lot of very clever men."

"I think I know them."

"From Intelligence summaries? But it was interesting to see them in person. I didn't know you held such an important position, by the way."

"No? Of its kind it is important. But as far as action, it is nothing. Talk and more talk. As we said at Geneva. It is time to do something."

It was an opening, and he let it go as he might have stepped across an open drain.

They strolled along Pall Mall, with the car going on to meet them at the park, speaking of the change in European cities since the hansom cab and brougham days. Mavritz wanted more change and quicker. He resented that fine buildings stopped outside the suburbs. There should be, he said, fine buildings as a reminder to people that they had something to show for their work, good to look at, to live for. The old idea, that only the wealthy should possess beauty, was in all senses repugnant to him.

"This talk today about the public schools. We have the same problem. People like to think their children will have the advantage in life. It is a natural desire. But it has several penalties for the rest of the nation. If children are educated apart from others they will have another outlook on life. Why should they think or work or live as others if they are taught differently? They speak a different kind of the same language. They have pity for those who do not speak as they do. Pity is near to hate. How can a people function well in such a broken condition?"

"We seem to have done very well so far."

"So far? How far is this? For the entire world, where have we arrived? Exactly to the point where there is danger of eradication without defence."

"How would a change in system alter that?"

"Mr. Gleave, I think you speak against your thoughts. Did not that system cause it? I say that all children must be educated on the same level. Not necessarily in the same way. On the same level. Then the best scholars should have the advantage of the better teaching. The rest will not miss it."

"I doubt very much if you'd get very far with that. It's not merely the upper class who'd be after your blood. The entire middle class wouldn't like it, either."

"Mr. Gleave, what is the middle class? In the middle? Of what?"

"The titled and the labouring classes."

"By titled, you mean the ladies and gentlemen who do nothing to dirty their hands. Does the middle class dirty its hands?"

"Generally I suppose no. More of them are having to, though."

"Because they want to?"

"Indeed not. But the laboratory and the engineers' bench aren't being considered as lowly as they used to be——"

"Because now it is not a matter of hands and mechanics, but of brains and the hard work of experiment? And better salaries? The legal profession will not change, you agree? But more and more scholars will be required to unravel those complexities. The medical profession will become more and more a matter of electrical engineering in the day of the passing nostrum. Clerical work, accountancy, statistics will go to skilled operation on the machine. Factories will work automatically. So? What shall become of labour? Which class will this be? And when profit can no longer be made out of a mass of labour, who will support the idle? The State? Who is the State?"

"There's many a long year yet——"

"No, Mr. Gleave. Yesterday I was twenty-one. I remember my celebration. I remember my family. They are all dead now. But it was yesterday. Today, I am forty-five. Twenty-four years. There are not many years for us to do anything. We may live and disappear. Shall we bury ourselves in mud like the crocodile, and drop our tears when we are reminded of what we might have done? Should have done?"

"What do you suggest we do?"

"Our best."

"A wet squib. What d'you call best?"

"I should say this duty which we know we must do. With the full possibility of the gifts we were born with, that most of us never use. From timidity. From fear of what others might think. From desire to enjoy their esteem. From cowardice, moral and physi-cal——"

"How physical?'

"Assassination is the last resort of the desperate. What the brain-less ones have no defence against, they kill. There will be many assassinations before we have our way——"

"We?"

"We. Men like us, who must endure banality from above, and incapacity from below."

There again, the opening. But no takers. Mavritz, being what he was, could have been the nastier type of spy, a planted talker, the friendly sort that squirmed into friendship, encouraged culpability by precept, and stank its way back to its den to squeal.

"I'm afraid I'll have to be getting along to the station, Dr. Mavritz. I live a long way away——"

"Do you not have a car to take you? It is a pity a country has such small regard for public servants. It is a species of obscurantism. In-ability to endure decency."

"I don't think it's altogether that. The tradition in this country is that anyone who goes into Government service has something besides salary. We don't any longer. And people are quite ready to believe we don't do anything for our salaries. And we earn too much anyway."

"Perfectly European, ignorant, of the mass."

"You don't like the mass?"

"Human beings, yes. The mass, the product of our deficiency, our lack of mental accord, no. It is a constant rebuke. We have not pro-gressed——"

A tall constable with legs of extraordinary length, like stilts, came into lamplight over the bridge. He slowed, looking along the dark path, and turned, smiling, sandy-moustached, unlined, alert.

"You gentlemen having a bit of an argument?"

"No, constable. Just a discussion, that's all."

"I could hear you the other side of the lake."

"With profit, perhaps?"

"Not the words, sir. Voices carry a long way. They could have heard you up at the Palace."

"Might start something——"

"Not very popular at night. People like getting off to sleep. Even the ones in the bushes——"

"Oh. These bushes?"

"Lots of people sleep out. Big place, London."

"Must be rather cold for them."

"They're all right as long as we don't turf them out."

"I don't think I've ever seen very many."

"You want to walk about at night, sir. You won't see many in the day. The no-goods. Themselves or anybody else."

"They get some sort of dole, I suppose?"

"I don't know, sir. Most of them get along all right. Pitch you a yarn. Touch you for a couple of bob. Get your tale right, you'll never starve in London."

"That's useful to know. Do they give you any trouble?"

"No, sir. Not that kind. Petty thievery, begging, quarrelling, nothing much else."

"What keeps them alive?"

"God knows, I don't. I don't reckon I'd last a couple of weeks living like they do. Still, that's their lookout."

"You haven't much sympathy?"

"Well, you can't help feeling sorry for some of them. But there's no need for it, is there? You've either got to pick out what you want to do, and stick to it, else go under. That's all I say. And if I'm found down here instead of up where I ought to be, I'll be under too. Good night, gentlemen. Just keep it down a bit, will you?"

Lamplight turned Mavritz's lenses into golden octagons.

"Where would you put this policeman in the strata of society, Mr. Gleave?"

"Fairly high."

"There would have to be something very attractive to make him turn against existing authority——"

"Almost impossible."

"But in order to control, it would be necessary to command the Police."

"You'd do it constitutionally, or not at all."

"But the Froweth people would have no trouble? Because he is a Lord and others with him?"

"The Labour Party had no trouble——"

"But I speak of a time when a party takes power that is not popular in certain circles——"

"I'm sure they wouldn't get very far. That sort of party sounds a little too furtive——"

"That is only one of our problems, Mr. Gleave, to rescue ourselves from fundamental error."

"Which error are you talking about?"

"The error of contempt for poverty."

"I'm hanged if I'm contemptuous of it. I hate it."

They walked out of the park, and the car followed, temptingly. The ride back would be a restful doze, and that two mile walk in the dark could be laughed at.

But the warning held.

"Incidentally, Mr. Mavritz, the agency here had never heard of the name you very kindly sent me."

"It had been heard in Paris. On instruction from London——"

"I don't doubt it. I got a blank denial."

"If you told your Security people——"

"They probably know in any case."

"We must be very careful where we go in our times, Mr. Gleave. It is strange in this country to be followed."

"It goes on everywhere. If there's anybody behind me tonight, he'll get a run for his money. Two miles walk at the other end, pitch-black, no train for hours and nothing's open."

"You will go to Seacray next weekend? I spoke to Beji tonight."

"I believe my wife may go about Friday with the children. I don't think I can."

"This will be a great disappointment. I was going to suggest I could take you down in my car——"

"It's not certain I can get away——"

"Perhaps you would allow me to telephone next Saturday morning?"

"No harm in that. Thanks for a very pleasant evening. Good night."

Three others and himself occupying a train, it appeared, and a car going back to a garage. Another hour and a quarter on another train, and the walk home with owls along the telegraph wires to ask him Who're you—Who're you, as Robert told him they did, and sometimes finding himself almost unable to reply with any real confidence.

It began to be a cause of private worry, trying to decide whether the inner man could be seen from the outside. The inside, he knew, was changing almost until he could feel himself exuviating from some sort of husk. When it would happen, or what he must do to protect himself when it happened, or how the change might make itself known, were all causes, not of fear exactly, but of a curious kind of excitement, not unlike the wickedly-happy feeling of being able to defeat Mr. Flap, and certainly not far from that euphoria which came to instant perception of a strategy, virtually unthinkable, that even now he hardly dare put on paper for close study.

All you have to do is to think your way forward and make the right decisions. For God's sake be right. Take informed opinion, ask advice, enquire, read everything and give yourself time to digest it. Remember that British statesmen have made a reputation by doing the unexpected successfully.

Remember that, Hamish. Stifle your feelings and say nothing, do nothing, unless you're told.

Dear Father.

But there it was.

Leonard went to Kevin's wedding and came back to report a most beautiful bride—"a real fizzer, I give you my word. Never been so struck. Married too long, perhaps"—and that anybody caring to meet the blissful pair should be at the hotel on Friday at six for cocktails. They were seeing nobody until then, and really one couldn't blame them.

Blaise said nothing. With that look there was no need. Even the moustache looked like a piece of umbrage.

A couple of fairly active days had settled down to a succession of meetings with nothing much happening. There was time to read what he wanted of the reports, think as he wished, and he did both with gratifying results and pages of notes. Hatton Dail rang him a couple of times to make enquiries and sounded a much happier being. Nobody had heard from Bob Abbatt. Mrs. Abbatt and the children were going back to the States. Yes, it was a rough deal. But that was the way it was.

Blaise said nothing at all about the visit to Chequers. He appeared to have had a tiring passage, and that, despite the day's rest before coming back to the office. His secretary was still away, and so were two of the girls upstairs. So there must have been a great deal of paper about something or other, although nothing had yet appeared in the Registry. He had come to a small determination to find out what could have been discussed at the Chequers meeting which might have frightened Abbatt and panicked his superiors. The original WA101 had travelled a closed circuit of heads of departments for their information and comment. The new hash apparently was considered too secret even for that, and there was plenty of room to wonder what new meats, scientific, social or economic, were being ground for unpopular consumption.

It was also a little amusing to consider that at any time before he would certainly never have taken the slightest interest in anything that did not concern his department. Work, that had been a specialist occupation, rather pridefully acknowledged as Governmental in the highest sense, was now much more an all-encompassing hobby, at once enjoyable and utilitarian.

Getting back after tea, he found a small cellophane package on his desk with a clove carnation inside, and a card, Amo, Ami, please come, M.

In the clove scent he had quick thought of her, of Louise Hamble, of the telephone, of the rattle of a doorchain, the lenses of Mavritz's spectacles, and a rat's shadow, and dearest Mumsy-Wums.

He threw the flower in the wastepaper basket, took it out again and put it in the drawer, tore up the card trying to think how to telephone with least risk, and decided against it. Let the shadows waste their time.

But anger stayed at thought of Delia. He very much wanted to indulge himself by doing something about her, but that, too, held risk. The best thing was to let her go on spending money for nothing, and choose an opportunity at the right time, in his own way, to tell her all that had been omitted on a previous occasion. A thought came that this might be her revenge for the things he had said all those years ago. Built like an elephant, she might have the memory of one.

He was glad to find all at home entirely peaceful, and gladder still that Vinny had waited to have dinner with him. She was tired though not sleepy, and excited at thought of going to Seacray, although he suspected that it was a couple of days freedom from the stove and bucket that excited her most. She went with him down to the village to get the car filled ready for the trip, and while he was at the garage, she waited for him at the Flower of Fortune. He got back to find her in the saloon bar talking to the proprietress, a Mrs. Wentworth, stout as a cask, red-faced, jowly and jolly, with a mass of grey hair stuck with combs at the sides and falling out of the top like a frothy glass of her own beer, which, she said, got her cooled down because it was that there dratted ot, she couldn't ardly abear erself.

Vinny said there had been new trouble about the Town Planning thing, and there was a summons out against Mrs. Cotton. Mrs. Wentworth was certain it might cost fifty quid time she finished. She said that what with these Planners doing their dags, all she might have left when the new town got built was her publican's license. She might make a bit on selling that. But nobody knew what was going to happen about the property, or what price they might get. Still, it turned out all right for some. Look at this bloke Harry Manders, the one had the row with poor Mrs. Cotton. Stonemason by trade, he was, got a fine job with the surveyors, he did, putting up stones, don't rightly know what for, and going about boasting he was marking the graves of all them as never had no rights there. He swore as he was going to dig the first pick in all the cottages as had to come down, and what was more, he was going to be the first one to start tearing the roofs of all the houses like the Cottons'. Yes, he talked very big about it, he did, and she had no doubts, mark you, as he do just what he say. Local mad, he was, and never liked no strangers, never worked for them neither. Hard-mouthed, he was, but there, took all sorts, she supposed, have to put up with 'un. Sorry if she gave them a mite more worry than what they come in with, but better they knowed than not, eh?

They drove the long way back because Vinny wanted air. She leaned against him and he thought she might be asleep, and he took the ruts a little easier.

"There's another payment this month on the mortgage, Hamie——"

"Yes?"

"And heaven nows how many more until it's finished."

"Yes."

"Darling, I hate to worry you, but a couple more very small cheques and we shan't have a penny——"

"I'll arrange an overdraft——"

"That means we go short on the next one——"

"I wouldn't worry about it——"

"I was wondering if you'd allow me to talk to Mummy——"

"No."

"I only wanted to help, that's all. I'd pay it back in a rather more leisurely manner——"

"I said no. I'll get on to the house business tomorrow. We can't pay off a mortgage if the damned place is as good as gone."

"Vera said there's no way out——"

"Can't be right. The Government can't rob people——"

"From the papers recently, it can have a jolly good shot at it. Vera said poor Freddy's going cracked. If he takes a loss on the house, he's finished. They've put too much into it——"

"Worry about your own affairs. What's going to happen to us?"

"I've thought about it. I really don't know. We haven't any money, and whether you're sent away or not, we're apparently not going to be allowed to have any property, and we've got two great lumps of boys to send to school. I suppose the next appointment might help a little. But where's it to be? I'm almost ready to go to Japan. At least we'd have some gems as servants——"

"There goes another dream. We shan't be going to Japan, I'm told."

"I didn't think we would. Had a feeling. Then where?"

"God knows, at the moment."

"In any case it'll mean a little more salary——"

"Don't bank on it."

"I could kill myself for spending anything at all on clothes——"

He braked hard enough to rock the car, turned, put his arms around her, and held her, and there was a feeling that he was holding the perhaps more judicious side of himself with all its warnings and tremors of conscience, all the elements he had to subjugate, as yet ascendant, but ceding little by little to encroachment and duress.

"You're not to speak like that. I won't have it. They're your clothes. I bought them. You were very happy with them. Is that enough?"

"Yes."

"I'm utterly, murderously sick of this damnable way of wasting our lives. We do nothing, we're allowed to do nothing with any sense of self-respect. I'm sick, sick, everlastingly sick of it."

"Yes, darling. So am I."

"Is there anything we can do about it?"

"Only a way I'm rather frightened of——"

"No! Not that, of course not. Don't be an old pudge, for God's sake. I mean some other way——"

"I don't care what it is. Honestly. But anything to stop this day and night dreary dree about money, and housekeeping, and servants, and that bloody boiler, and school fees, and what we're going to do——"

"You're not blaming me, are you?"

"Oh, darling, how could you say anything like that? Please, Hamie, don't. I can put up with it for years. I'm as strong as a horse. Once the boys are in school it won't be so bad. But to go away and lose the use of the house and the garden, even if it's still ours, and to have to do it all over again——"

"Don't think about it. Let's sleep on it."

"That's just what I needed, darling. Let's."

But the officer he spoke to in Finance the following morning was far from certain that anything could be done. Town Planning was notoriously dilatory, and the scheme might take ages. That would not mitigate against prompt payments. When the amount was settled, and if the matter ever came up, that would be the time to make a claim. Doubtless they would get a very fair bargain. There was nothing to worry about. Simply let things take their course.

Arranging an overdraft was simple as ever, apart from some quite unnecessary questions that made him feel rather like a counter-jumper making his bow for an eightpenny rise in the quarterly stipend.

Vinny telephoned from Seacray to tell him the weather was glorious, the house was divine, she could stay there forever, wait till he saw the kitchen, and except for him, she would give anything to change places with Frolla. He promised to get there as soon as he could. It was only after he had put the telephone down that he remembered Charles Roff's saying he was no longer friendly with Frolla and Bejian. Taking Zena there might cause some trouble. He was undecided whether or not to tell Vinny, but then it seemed ridiculous. The child was having a couple of healthy days by the sea.

Charles was in Cairo. After all, there could be too much fuss made about anything.

Miss Sells came in to announce Mr. Calton-Islip on the telephone. She said he seemed in a strangely happy humour and had told her he was sitting in a deck chair enjoying the sun down at Bournemouth, and he wanted a good reason to stay there, so she could take her time, and so could Mr. Gleave, and he was ready to wait all day if necessary.

"Gleave, here——"

"Ah. Good morning—"—gutter-grin impregnating voice and words —"What a pity you're working. Silly habit on a day like this. Iv's having a splash in the pool, and yours faithfully's having one in a great big glass. Don't you wish you was here?"

"Sounds most enjoyable——"

"Oh, it is. Yes. At twenty-five guineas a day, it ought to be. That's only for the rooms. Grub and drinks extra. 'Course, you couldn't afford it, could you?"—desire, almost ineluctable, to stretch through the line and smash, break off the gutter-maw—"If you was working for me you could, though, couldn't you? Eh? Twenty-five a day, you could do that how you liked. Put it on the old expense account. You know the game, don't you? Oh, here's Iv'—"—away from the mouth-piece—'This is your pal, the Scotchy'—and her voice saying something indistinguishable—"Yes," into the receiver—"She says to be sure to give you her kindest regards, best she's got——"

"Please reciprocate for me——"

"Reci—want a receipt, did you say?"

"Reciprocate. Return them."

"Ah, I see. I'll do that. Listen—"—taking out the cigar made it clearer—"Did you ever take singing lessons when you was a kid, did you?"

"Singing lessons?"

"You know, doh-ray-me-fah-soh-lah-te-doo-oo-oh! I ain't got the wind for it."

"I didn't, no——"

"You done a lovely solo for the Inland Revenue people though, didn't you? Eh? Thought you'd drop me in it, did you?"

"I think it most interesting you should know——"

"Oh, yes. Most interesting, is it not? Think you're the only one with any brains, do you? Where else them figures come from? Going to deny it?"

"I haven't the time——"

"That's all right. You go on back to your conference, Scotchy. Kilts and all. Just remember you've made a friend for life. I'm going to be very kind to you, Gleave. When I'm Lord George Calton-Islip —won't be long, now—you'll be my pet. I've spoke to Charlie Froweth about you. You'll get the job all right. I'll see you do. I've got a lot of money in the new one. I think they'll sail in. Can't go wrong. And d'you know what? I'll help you up, and up, and up. Then I'll bring you down. If you don't take the job with Charlie's lot, I'll get you where you are. I'll haunt you. I'll dog you. I'll break you as no man's ever been broke in this life, you dirty, rotten, low-down toe-rag——"

Enough can sometimes be a great deal more, and all the files can sometimes appear to float in blood.

But there it was.

Going out for a pink 'un with Leonard Porrit did some good, and a second and third took off a lot of edge as well as an appetite. During the afternoon he refused any calls, and devoted himself to work that was suddenly even more important, notwithstanding the ends he foresaw, but as a weapon to be used against Calton-Islip and others of that indecent phylum.

A little after six o'clock, Leonard came in to insist on going along for a drink with Mary and Kevin. The room was fairly crowded when they got there, and Leonard said how fortunate Kevin was to have found someone to put a bar always at his mercy. People were taking flashlight pictures and it seemed wise to lie low until all that was over. A photograph in such a company might have earned a black mark from the Management. He saw a lot of people he knew from the Diplomatic Corps, a few school friends, quite a lot of Fleet Street, perhaps because of Mary's father, and little groups of the Chalmers family, not entirely at home from the way they held their glasses.

Mary was free at last, beautiful as he remembered, and, she said, out of her mind with happiness. They were leaving for Paris that night, and then on to India. She had no idea how long they would be away and refused to think about it. It was joyous, it was heavenly, it was all she had dreamed of and she knew she was right. She only wished her father would come over to her side, and then everything would be ecstatic. Kevin asked him particularly to give Vinny their love, and thought him an absolute curtain-ring for not bringing her.

Kevin was a little unsteady and a trifle loud, but otherwise tip-toe. He wanted them both to stay to dinner, but Leonard had promised to go home, and in any case, the party looked as if it might wash them out to the airport.

A hatful of feathers, pink this time, smaller than last, delightful anyway, brought Louise Hamble through the crowd. A kiss for Mary, a glass from the waiter, and a hug for and from Kevin was all he required. La Hamble was the last person he wanted to see, and he made as certain as he could, given the crowd, two rooms and various pieces of furniture, that she had no opportunity of seeing him. Leonard went off to forage for a waiter, and Kevin came over happy as the drinks are long.

"Looking for you two, Hamie. Cracking show, isn't it?"

"Hullo? Learned to speak NATO?"

"I speak damn' good Russian——"

"I wouldn't say that too loudly, if I were you——"

"Why not? I'm perfectly free. Well, free's a benedick can be. That's what Mary calls me. Jolly. Terrifically happy."

"Good to hear."

"Yes. I'm the luckiest chap I ever heard of, really. Can't believe it, simply can't."

"I didn't know Louise Hamble was a friend of yours?"

"Louise? Oh lord, yes. Several places. At least, she dropped in now and again. Very good value. I'd like as many pounds as I've helped her with her reports. That was half the job in Washington, keeping them happy——"

"I thought so, too. She's one of them. Class by herself. Everybody loves her. Security. M-I. Reigning toast of the O.S.S. Best agent we've got. Nobody like our Louise. Why? Surprise you?"

"No."

No, not surprise. Something cold forming inside that made an iced drink seem tepid. Mr. Flap evidently knew more than he had told. Blaise's indecision and unusual humour might have been caused by knowledge, and a desire to warn. Charles Roff might also have known, not only about Arkhiv and the Emyenkovs, but about Myril. La Hamble and Myril. La Hamble and Myril and the late Mr. James Wittard.

La Hamble, Myril, and the late Mr. H. T. Gleave.

In no time at all, though, so far, for very little reason.

Perhaps a desire to give anybody behind him a little exercise in the study of a virtuous husband took him all the way home to dark rooms, impersonally cold, and damp draughts in the bedroom, almost unnoticed when Vinny and the boys were there, and he began to understand what she had meant about noises. The place was like a ghosted barrack.

With the exception of his chair and Vinny's sewing basket, there was nothing, as Vinny had so often said, to suggest a home. It was little more than a house, a convenient place to stay and bring up the children, flatteringly large and made bearable by the garden, nothing else.

Whether it was compassion, or fondness, or pity for the trapped, he was unsure. But the argument going on in his mind was undecided except that he had to help Myril. If she needed help. If she were friendly with La Hamble it could mean two things. She was a colleague. Or she was quarry. Either way, talking to her meant risk. It was fairly well established she had some connection with Arkhiv. Perhaps a word to Bejian might help. No decision. Risk ruled.

The solution to the entire problem, he saw quite clearly, was not only simple, but it carried a considerable hope of quick promotion and certainly kudos of the rarest kind.

All he had to do was to let Intelligence know that he had a feeling he was being scrutinized by agents of another country or countries and with official sanction contrive a meeting between Arkhiv, Mavritz, Emyenkov and himself on home soil, and denounce them. Whether they were, or were not spies, would be entirely up to the policemen. The hints given by Charles Roff, and the antecedents of La Hamble pointed to it. His own opinion could be kept to himself. Nothing could be simpler. He could imagine his interview with the Secretary of State and the heads of departments, not least, the Director of Personnel. He saw the flush of intense pleasure in Blaise's face that trust, at least, was vindicated. He could almost read the head-lines of the newspapers with his name large in all of them.

All he had done, the entire Vinny episode, every alleged indiscre-tion, would be most happily explained by a singular, close-mouthed devotion to duty, and an absolute determination to put a nest of spies in the bag. He could even hear Mr. Flap apologizing, and that, in itself, was worth the money.

Yet. But.

Calton-Islip's threat was in being. There would be no mercy. It took small effort to imagine the coals heaped on by Iv'. That thin-boned clothes-horse with the kestrel's screech would always find a way to rub a nerve. Georgie would keep the promise if only to earn her wide-mouthed, adoring smile. It was very easy to imagine them opening a bottle a moment or two after his head had rolled. And no comment. You got my lighter, dear? Eh? Where's yourn?

Conversely, and apart from a triumphal return to diplomatic fa-vour, there was also a simple remedy for the Calton-Islip imbroglio. He could very easily get in touch with Calton-Islip, and act the mortally-wounded friend by explaining that Inland Revenue had first made enquiries, got the answers wrong as usual, and that, in his position, he was unable to do anything except be silent until he got an opportunity to put things right. And that could very easily be done by telephoning to the official at Inland Revenue, if necessary, from Calton-Islip's own office, so that the conversation lifting all blame from Georgie and listing another set of official figures might be overheard and approved. Then would follow the reconciliation, with, probably, renewed offers of £10,000 a year and all the exes, including hotel suites at twenty-five guineas a day, grub and drinks extra, and of course, now I can afford it on the old expense account, you know the game, don't you, Scotchy?

Vinny's delight, kilts and all.

And all very well.

But in either case, he was proven a traitor of sorts. Not that he minded, particularly. The word was becoming slightly shopworn in his mind, he found. The sharp corners were being blunted with use. He wished he could remember that epigram Wittard had quoted.

"Treason doth never prosper. What's the reason? For if it prosper.
none dare call it treason." That was it. And so very true. If it prosper.
He wondered what Father might have to say. For God's sake be sure
you're right. That, anyway. But none dare call it treason. That, too.
Time was the master.

The telephone awoke him. He had to get up and blunder downstairs in the dark.

"Hamish? Blaise. Look here, I'm really very sorry about this, but
there's an urgent telegram from Cairo here. It says 'Rely on you
instruct Gleave return my daughter Zena to my sister Elsa Greig
15 Harriston Gardens Kensington without delay. Charles Roff.' What
does it mean?"

"She's down at the seaside with Vinny and the boys for the weekend——"

"Oh, dear. I thought something quite dreadful had happened. I
suppose it's some family trouble. But why not telegraph you direct?"

"Probably thought he'd get you quicker——"

"Ah. Yes. Brain's not working yet. Sorry to have got you out of
bed——"

One or other agent, or perhaps La Hamble herself, too plainly,
had more than a finger in the pie. It also looked as if either Vinny
had been followed, or the Emyenkovs were under surveillance. If
they were, it gave further point to Charles' warning. It also meant
that the visit to Seacray was off. Plus, of course, the most almighty
rocket from Charles when he returned.

He went out to the kitchen to make a pot of tea, and shaved,
dressed and stamped about wasting time until seven o'clock.

Beji answered the telephone and seemed to get the gist as much
by tone as anything else. He was going up to London that morning,
fortunately, and would deliver the child at the front entrance at
about eleven. Yes, he would explain to Vinny. Family trouble. Such
a great pity, beautiful little girl, Frolla would cry so much to lose her.

He telephoned Mrs. Greig from a call-box at the station. She
sounded very concerned, but she promised to take Zena, although she
was at loss because Charles knew perfectly well she had no room with
three people in the flat. However, she thought she could manage.
So tiresome. No consideration for anybody. Really.

Half a mind to telephone Myril and chance it. Flung, suddenly, deep in the dream, watching the crowds outside the booth, the continuous umbrella-crowned crowds, the anonymous dun pharaohs, watching the wet pavement flash beneath their feet.

But if the telephone was tapped, there was risk.

He got to the office before Miss Sells. Blaise was not in. Leonard Porrit's office was empty and so were all the others he looked in, and none of the secretaries had arrived upstairs. Mr. Flap's office was shut.

It seemed a fair opportunity to visit the Registry for a glance at the index. Several recent files were marked by new numbers. The senior filing clerk said they were all out. That meant they could only be with Mr. Flap.

Not much to be done about that. But at least it was an odds-on bet that those were the files on the Chequers meeting. He sent a message of thanks to find Robert Jerome Abbatt of the flimsy curl for an unexpected windfall of most valuable information, if not of a pass-key, wondering if Mrs. Abbatt felt less irritable now that her husband was no longer permitted to do anything but lick stamps. If that. Or what the poor devil might say to her in excuse of himself.

Just after Miss Sells came, the door thwacked open, and in came Toddy, tweeds, little bag, on his way, he said, dammit, back to Paris. Something was on, probably a move, no earthly idea where to and neither would anybody tell him, but he hoped Germany. Lot to be learnt there and it was all useful to know. Just came in to say au revoir, that's all. Dined with Charles Froweth last night. Rotten dinner, but very good talk. And by the way, Charles mentioned that George Calton-Islip, oil and so forth, had made a great fuss of our Hamish, thought him this, that and what not. Great future, terrific admiration all round. Very useful, Charles said. The man was the most awful stithe himself, of course. Nobody wanted him anywhere near them. But he was the sort of chap one had to keep in with. Hardly pick and choose. Powerful. Very. Enthusiastic about the new venture, too. Lot of backing. An Earldom would keep him quiet. Seemed a pity, but there were no heirs, thank God, apparently no family at all. Which was all to the good. However, love to Vinny.

"I suppose you never found out what Abbatt was so worried about, did you?"

"No. Not a word. You heard anything?"

"Nothing."

"Well, they've got their Flaps, too. Miserable little thing that is. Delighted to tell him what I think of him one day. I hope, in the House."

"Power to you——"

"Take care of everything, Hamie. 'Bye."

Goodbye.

Mrs. Elsa Greig, Charles in skirts without the specs, provided the touchstone. She made up her mind to get there early, she said, because she had some shopping to do in the West End and she hoped Zena would get there before the shops shut at one o'clock. He made no attempt to question her reasoning, but he asked if she might be going near South Audley Street. She said she could, without any trouble. He asked her if she would give a note to somebody in Chotouille Ltd. His wife had a sports coat there, and if they could deliver it to him to take home that afternoon, think of the excitement. No trouble about that at all, and he gave her a note to Myril, asking her to meet him at Mansion House Tube Station at four o'clock.

Bejian arrived almost on the dot. Zena had been very good about everything, loved Seacray, called Beji Uncle Bij-Baj, thanked him again for his thoughtfulness in buying theatre tickets for her aunt's family and herself that night, and went off in highest feather.

"Beji, it's becoming very dangerous for us to meet or to be seen together. Dangerous for me, as well as for you. I'm extremely sorry, but there it is. I think we ought to have a final luncheon together."

No surprise, no change in the smile, no movement.

"It does not matter if it is public?"

"It's too late to worry about that."

"The Ritz, one-thirty?"

"Splendid. Could you reach Dr. Mavritz?"

"Immediately."

"Please tell him I can't go to Seacray. And not to telephone me."

"Very well. He can come to luncheon?"

"Mavritz? All right. And Mavritz."

Work went the merrier after that. He found himself in song a couple of times, and Miss Sells said it was almost worth coming in on a Saturday morning to listen to.

Blaise sent his compliments from Mr. Flap's office, and asked Mr. Gleave to present himself. Expectant, ready for anything, and not a fear in the world he went up, a little surprised to remember other days and a funny sort of quiver above the knees that always had made him wonder if anybody could see his trousers shaking.

Mr. Flap stood at the window, in an unbelievable new grey suit. But old habits seldom die. There was the bootlace, drooping behind. Blaise sat, without turning his head, knees crossed, hands in pockets, looking at the desk.

"Gleave, I'm not quite sure where to start—"—Mr. Flap, looking out of the window, and no invitation to sit down—"I've got a two-page priority from Charles Roff, there. He says he warned you about a man and wife called Emyenkov——"

"That is correct. About his daughter. But my wife's arrangement to visit them for the weekend was made, and the child went with her. It would have been unreasonably rude to cancel. It won't happen again——"

"That's all very well. Just run your eyes over that Security report, will you?"

Blaise picked up a dozen sheets of typescript and handed it across without looking.

Dates, times and places. Himself, the people he saw, had spoken to, their identity, appendix showing who, what they were, telephone calls in and out at the office, at home, the butcher, baker, candlestick maker, every detail. But nothing about Myril. No mention.

"I had an idea they'd been busy——"

"What made you so friendly with these Emyenkov people?"

"They're friendly people——"

Except that the humour was anger, Mr. Flap looked in humorous surprise at Blaise.

"What do you make of that?"

"A very curious thing to say——"

"Curious? Gleave, you must be mad."

"Care to tell me why, sir?"

"Hobnobbing with people like that? A man in your position? What's your answer to that report?"

"A record of a normal day-to-day round of activity, I'd say. Didn't Mr. Cramer, on two occasions recently, dine both with the Soviet Amb——"

"Neither here nor there. That was part of his official duties. It wasn't part of your duty to go gallivanting about in Paris, getting your bills paid——"

"I resent that and won't accept it——"

"You won't? Would you like to see a few dinner and lunch bills?"

"That's normal——"

"Normal, is it?"

"I'm not going to quarrel over bills——"

"I'll do it for you. Fancy having to talk to a man in your position like this!"

"Then why try? You're being deliberately rude for a purpose. What is it?"

Mr. Flap took his hands out of his pockets, and drew in a deep breath, and looked at Blaise.

"I don't want to lose my temper—"—sitting down—"You talk to him."

"Hamish, it's more a question of a number of rather disquieting reports. But the most innocent things can well look frightful in print. For example, you met and were entertained on three or four occasions by a Mr. Vissarion Arkhiv. Have you ever bothered to find out who he is?"

"Apart from what he told me, no. I never expect to meet him again."

"Your wife stayed at his flat in Paris."

"Taken there by a friend——"

"Madame Emyenkov. Mr. Arkhiv is no friend of ours. He's considered by some to be the mainspring of probably the best espionage system we have the misfortune to try to controvert. The Emyenkov couple are part of it, from our information. Dr. Mavritz, you know?"

"Yes."

"Not the wisest choice for a dining companion. From our point of view, you'll understand. Did you receive an offer of employment from a Mr. George Calton-Islip?"

"Yes."

"You didn't consider it necessary to inform me?"

"No. I didn't take it seriously."

"The point is, of course, that he did. Which rather reflects upon you, unfortunately. And you also attended a meeting at Mappersley, did you not?"

"Yes."

"But you didn't think it necessary——"

"Certainly not. My political beliefs are no concern——"

"I fear you're misinformed. Mr. Calton-Islip is known to be financially interested in the Mappersley group. He also occasionally relies upon certain officers of the Foreign Service for information of, shall I say, first importance? Do you follow the implication?"

"I do. But it's unfounded."

Mr. Flap got up, and put on his spectacles. Took them off. Bit the ear-pieces. Put them on.

"Gleave, can you tell me one good reason why I ought to let you stay in your job a second longer?"

"You don't expect me to answer that——"

"Don't I? I tell you straight, I don't like any of this. It's a very hard thing to say to a man like you, Gleave. But I don't think you deserve promotion. On this showing, you've got no recommendation at all. You waltz about the place, no sense of responsibility, no attempt to find out who people are. When people suddenly get pally with me, d'you know what I do? First thing, Security. Why didn't you?"

"I really don't know. There's nothing in my record of a little over twenty years——"

"I'm talking about this—"—waving the summary—"These people. Dangerous people. And you. In your position. I'm thinking of that man Wittard——"

"You're not putting me——"

"I said I'm thinking of that louse. What he did. That's what I said. Cramer, what's your opinion, here?"

"Undoubtedly, there's been what might deserve to be called gross carelessness, but not, I think, of an improper nature. Reckless, perhaps. Overconfidence, let us say. Far more, I suppose, familiarity with a certain type of——"

"Just a minute. I want to know what you think?"

"This will serve as a warning to be far more careful in future——"

Mr. Flap threw down his spectacles and kicked back the chair.

"Careful! Christ Almighty! Telling a man like that to be careful? Who are we supposed to be talking to? Any idea what'd happen if the Opposition got to hear about this? Or if somebody on a newspaper got his nose in it? It's the Service that'd suffer. It doesn't deserve to. Whatever reasons you've got, I don't care what they are."

"It seems a great deal of fuss to make simply because I've made some friends among the people we're supposed to work with——"

"I've never heard that we are, Gleave. At least, work, yes. In a particular way. That's not to say we hobnob."

"I wasn't aware that I had hobnobbed. Any more than you hobnob if you happen to speak to an Ambassador——"

"Gleave, there's a bit of a difference——"

"I'm speaking of the liberty of the Subject. We aren't political prisoners——"

"You can thank God for it, too. If you came from some countries I won't mention, would you have the opportunity——"

"The whole point is that I don't. I therefore have opportunities denied to others. Shouldn't I make an issue of showing my advantage? Doesn't illustration teach lessons?"

"The illustration you're giving now is that you've got no idea of the scope of your duty——"

"I won't accept that. I resent it——"

"I don't care what you resent. I'm telling you for your own good. If I could see something down in this report where you've been friendly with an American or two, I'd have more to say for you——"

"We may hobnob with the Americans——"

Mr. Flap picked up his spectacles, and in the same moment flung a lot of papers off the desk. Blaise made no movement.

"That's enough, Cramer. I'm having no more of it. I think I know what we're dealing with, here. Listen, Gleave. Go away. I'll

send for you Monday. I'll have your future seriously in mind between
then and now."

"Thank you."

The gauntlet clashes to the stones, as Father always said when
events had reached a time for challenge and outcome. To be or not
to be, and there was no question about it. With Mr. Flap as head
of the Service, there was no possibility of promotion. There was
every sign of demotion, in fact, to some forsaken spot in Portuguese
East or somewhere equally benighting. And no hope of a Sir Hamish
and Lady Gleave. Plenty of scrubbing, buckets, though, and lots of
overdraft and mosquitoes, presumably. That is, if Mr. Flap had his
way. He doubtless would, and there was nothing to prevent it.

Except by a denunciation of the Arkhiv lot. That would do it. But
Mr. Flap had looked and sounded as though the mists might cling,
whatever happened.

For God's sake be certain you're right, dear Father. There was
excitement in wondering what Father might have said about this.
About Mr. Flap, there was no doubt what he would say. The idea of
such a creature taking charge of Foreign Affairs. A thought of Sir
Mathew Kyle among his rose bushes intervened. I can't think what
you fellows in Whitehall are doing. But the fellows in Whitehall, or
those making the decisions, were going to be there for a long time.
It was all very well to talk largely of elections. But if the vote on the
other side was larger, then Mr. Flap could be followed by another
from the same stable, and so the business would drag on. No promotion, probably. Years of chair-polishing. And nothing at the end. An
aging Vinny, growing sons, no school or university for them on
that scale of pay, and a Gleave family dropping into the limbo of
ex-Civil Servants on an in-between pension. In between rigorous
self-denial and virtual starvation, not only in food and drink, but
certainly in the civilized pleasures, whether they happened to be
owning a car, or visiting a theatre or concert now and again or even
going for a holiday.

All for duty. So that all the Mr. Flaps might supervene.

Taking Blaise's advice, and resigning to fight for a seat in Commons might have been a solution if the bank had held enough to
make it possible. Even if it had, he required the backing of a Party.

But after the money and the backing was got, and the seat won, there was still no opportunity of service as a Minister until the Party was called upon to form a Government. And even then, there was no guarantee of his being called. The Froweth Dynamist Party he thought might collect a fair-sized vote. But they could never hope to withstand the strength or penetrate the fortress of the trades unions. The workers of the Country must win in time. There were more of them. Not only must they win, but go on winning. There were more of them being born. Elections could see-saw this way and that for a few years perhaps. But the end was well in sight. Labour, and only Labour, must win.

In that event, there was no place for a Gleave, unless, of course, he closed his ears and eyes to fact, and went on serving from a sense of Duty. What that Duty was, or what it was to, he was not concerned to think. It seemed to be to the Country. But the Country appeared to be nothing much more than a succession of Mr. Flaps, governing a mish-mash of Flap voters by their will given expression at the poll.

A crowd of oafs, voting for nothing more than the right slogan. The workers. The pay-envelope boys, the pay-up or down tools mob, we want our rights.

Mr. Flap and his colleagues in the House of Commons represented nobody except the Maw, the many-headed nestling to be fed and fostered by effort of the few and prevailing industrial circumstance, and where those failed, by charity. They spoke for the neo-mendicants, that by guilding and unionizing had achieved commercial influence never by brain but by dead weight of the strike-threat, and national power by rationalization of want and a merest head-count, in a system which mistook the vote, a legal because political gift, for valid expression of the adult will.

There was no Duty there, as far as he was concerned, and no prospect of living any sort of life at home or abroad except that decided for him—and for Vinny—by Mr. Flap.

In those circumstances, dear Father, there was only one thing to do, and that was to find a Duty which could be undertaken with a clear conscience and worked through to its conclusion, one, moreover, that would supply an agreeable social life, and reasonable pro-

vision in old age. Rather more, in fact, than either dear Father's or
Sir Mathew's later generation had enjoyed in their most helpless
years, and very much more than poor Blaise and Dorothea or
Leonard and his Babs might expect.

That decision taken, it had to be acted upon, and there was no
time to be lost.

Miss Sells had gone. There was plenty of time to pack the larger
suitcase with the documents, files and notes he wanted, and lock
it in the cupboard. On the way out to luncheon, Blaise passed him
in the corridor.

"Hard going, that, Hamish."

"Was, rather."

"Shouldn't take it too much to heart. He'll come round."

"Don't doubt it. Thanks for all you did——"

"Must do something, mustn't we? Think I'll watch some cricket
this afternoon. Have a happy weekend."

Into the pub, order a drink, go to the telephone, call the Ritz, and
talk to the porter. See if Dr. Mavritz is there, certainly, sir. Mavritz
rolling those French r's down the line.

"We can't meet there for many reasons. D'you know Paddington
Station? Take a cab. Buy a platform ticket. Go on the main No. 1
platform. Take the underground passage between platforms 2 and
3. Meet you there in fifteen minutes."

The station's smell of old milk and drains full of sooty rain
brought a sudden thought of Hamish and Robert admiring the
engine on the day they went away for their last holiday. If he were
right or wrong, this was the time to think. For their sakes. For Vinny's
sake. I shall have your future very seriously in mind between then
and now. Go away, Gleave.

It was splendid advice. Mr. Flap had reached eminence on the
Maw vote. A mob of inarticulate stentors had put him and his colleagues in power, and would in time keep them there. In that vote,
and nowhere else, was the secret of power over the mass. To direct
that vote, and to have the means of controlling it was all that was
needed to reign, possibly lifelong, or at any rate until retirement.

That, in all its implications, meant that the Gleaves and the Porrits and Cramers would, indeed, go away. They would be sent with-

out volition. They had no recourse. Their property and assets must go little by little in taxation. Their schools must go little by little to the more fortunate because higher-paid, worker-earners' sons and daughters. Their universities must go in exactly the same way for the same reason. Then the Gleaves would stop going away. There would be none left to take that advice, or any advice at all.

The Gleaves would no longer exist.

But the Flaps would still be there.

Floreat Flap.

There it was.

He held out the ticket to be punched and went down the steps under the platform. He saw the lenses reflecting before the man came off the wall. Bejian hurried from the other end. Careful men.

Words, words, a few words, handshakes.

"You must go to Seacray with Beji this afternoon——"

"I can't——"

"But Arkhiv is there——"

"In Seacray?"

"To meet you with your wife. It was his desire. You must first of all talk to him. Imperative."

"Very well. But not in the house. My wife mustn't know. Yet."

"I will make a rendezvous."

"What time for Beji?"

"When it's dark. Six. In the forecourt."

He advised them to go out on different platforms, and went on to the local end and caught a train to Westbourne Park, the next stop. A cup of coffee passed a little time and gave opportunity for watching the people round about. They all appeared to have dropped from the same worn womb, and smoothed, like the sticks of furniture in Salter's Humby, by the same process of dilapidation, whether in spirit or the mind, or from lack of any proper nutriment was not to be told, although from what they were spending their money on, and from what there was to be bought, small choice was theirs and smaller good to come. Floreat Flap and the Flappy vote. That was the true power. Government of the inarticulate, for the inert majority, by the opportunist.

Floreat.

But nobody looked at him, nobody waited.

Back at the office he telephoned Blaise. Dorothea
answered, said she was sorry, but Blaise had gone out and probably
would not be back until late, and that she was going out, in fact,
she was almost putting her hat on. What? Blaise's keys? She supposed they were upstairs, yes. Mislaid your keys, oh dear-dear-dear! I
say, how simply. What? Oh, of course. Wouldn't dream of moving.
Expect you in ten minutes.

Dorothea, in a grey cardigan, tweed skirt and hat to match, epitome
of all health, sanity and essential kindliness, was standing at the
front door when he arrived, holding the keys like a bell. Her teeth-in-
lower-lip smile, half-frown and shadowed eyes told him she sympathized with a predicament, and she accepted his thanks and assurance he would have them back in about thirty minutes with a nod of
eternal understanding.

Back to the office, and upstairs to Mr. Flap's suite, and use Key 1,
shut the door. Desk first, all the drawers, nothing much. A prudent
secretary. The filing cabinet, orders of State, despatches, very little.
The safe, Key 2. Key 3. Combination written on the ivorine tab inside
the key case, never can remember numbers, always a nuisance, and
both doors breathing out. Small, cool cavern inside, shelves, drawers,
racks, three crimson despatch boxes, royal cipher innocently brag-
ging side by side.

Prime Minister's notes and memoranda, Secretary of State's notes
and memoranda. European reports, considerations, appreciations,
summaries. White House dossier, complete. NATO dossier complete.
Moscow, Peiping, Delhi, complete. French-North African report, with
American and European appendices. Soviet, economic and military,
complete. Commonwealth reports, most secret, good. Arctic and
Antarctic survey, complete. Pan-American survey, complete. Drafts

for German, Austrian treaties, for and against. India, China, Soviet, complete. Thermonuclear report in committee, most secret, excellent.

And three despatch boxes. The first, matters for the House, disappointment. The second, luck, bless you, dearest lady, the Chequers discussion in notes, shorthand and typescript. Third, memoranda on conversations with the United States on defence, containment and attack, with figures and dates. Lovely.

Empty red bags were stuffed full, two big handfuls of crushed crimson, little Santa Claus, two despatch boxes emptied, closed, locked. Out, into the office, and pray dear God, nobody comes in. Pile everything on the desk. Shut the inner safe doors, combination correct, outer doors breathe inward.

So far, so good.

Write a note for Mr. Flap's private entertainment or not, that was the question. No. There was every possibility he might be coming in during the weekend, conscientious humbug he was. Open the office door. Nobody in the corridor. Shift all the bags outside. Close the door, and here comes Mr. Hobson, a senior messenger, rubber heels, steel glasses on the end of his nose, moustache cut like Blaise's.

"Hullo, sir. Working late, are you?"

"Yes, confound it. Much rather be out in the fresh air today."

"Ah. You're right, sir. Could I give you a hand with that stuff, sir? Your office, sir?"

"Yes, please. Very kind of you."

"That's nothing, sir. Call a man, might be five minutes getting here. I was just off, meself. Get in a couple of nice games 'fore the sun goes in——"

"Games?"

"Bowls, sir. Clapham Park. Have a very nice time, there. Look after the place, they do. That be all, sir?"

"Yes, and thank you very much indeed, Hobson."

"'mention it, sir."

Big Ben struck three-thirty. The suitcases were not large enough to take everything. Sheets of brown paper off the bookshelves made two tidy parcels. The porter helped to carry them outside and, an additional courtesy, whistled up a cab.

Dorothea seemed to have been standing just inside the front door, waiting. She was delighted to know he had found the keys, in his other suit in the locker, of course, how ridiculous. Such a waste of time, but there, all's well that ends.

Through the taxi's little rear window, a two-horse dray, a couple of lorries, a few cyclists and a bus, all falling behind, nothing following. Turning off on side streets, no traffic, except for a fruit barrow, and children playing on the pavements, and boys using lamp-posts for wickets and bowling a tennis ball. Nothing behind. After all, even shadows could hardly be crystal-gazing, or using some sort of radar. Therefore, there was no need to worry about them.

He chose the corner of Queen Victoria Street to stop. The City's normal Saturday afternoon desuetude brought a steamer's moan to play bassoon for a chorus of pigeons, and the street's shining surface reflected a bus's scarlet, appearing to blush at thought of George and Iv' enjoying twenty-five guineas worth a day, grub and drinks extra, all on the old expense account, but you know the old game.

The station hollowed with a train passing through, almost the sound of spoken prayer in a cathedral. Nobody seemed to be alive. The parcels made a hideous crackle in the silence.

But then heels, and a shadow down the stairway, lengthening across the floor.

In black, Myril, pale, running.

"Ami!"

"Wait. Wait, darling. Listen to me. We shall stay here to see if anybody follows you. Listen carefully. Do you trust me?"

"Always."

"Do you trust Louise Hamble?"

"I trust nobody. Except Ami."

"I believe you're in danger. After this weekend you might be arrested——"

"That was my instinct——"

"You work for certain people, don't you?"

"Certain people?"

"I saw your photograph——"

A laugh, eyes at the ceiling.

"It was meant you should——"

"Then you know Vissarion Arkhiv. I'm seeing him today. I shall come to your flat tonight. You'll leave with me. For good. Save yourself a few years in prison——"

"I understand. I will go."

"Take these parcels. Catch a train to Waterloo. Put these in the cloakroom. Go straight to your flat, and wait for me. Two questions——"

"Tell me."

"Did you ever suspect that Louise Hamble might be an agent?"

Wide eyes, unfrightened, staring inside themselves a moment, a train sighing expiringly, and a shaken head.

"No."

"She is."

"It explains, then. Poor Jimmy——"

"I believe she's already explained you and me. That's why we're going——"

"The other question?"

"When we first met, what made you waste your time with me?"

"I did not waste my time. Is there a better way to be friends?"

"I'm not talking about us. Us two, I mean. What caused you to pick me out? That's what I'd like to know. You couldn't hope to have any effect on my way of thinking. What was the reason?"

"You must ask someone else. But Ami. I could not have effect? La Belle Crachoir?"

"I didn't mean that——"

"No. But Ami. Consider. If you could be taken from your family, for a moment, could you not be taken from other things?"

"You gave yourself to that?"

"And to you."

She was away, hurrying, lumpy with parcels in the shadowy tunnel, an elongated hen, wings outspread and gone.

A couple of elderly women came down from the street. Three or four people come from the train. The sun was warm outside in emptiness. Himself in the entire street, goodbye Mansion House, dear Lord Mayors and all your cocked hats in florid procession, goodbye. Five minutes walk past shuttered shops, and a bus stop, goodbye. A gentle ride through ruined St. Paul's, goodbye, down Ludgate Hill, good-

bye, up Fleet Street, goodbye, the Strand, goodbye. So long, Tra-
falgar Square. It's a long, long way. A healthy walk down Whitehall,
a momentary temptation to take a last chair in the park. But there
was still plenty to do.

No telephone calls, and no messages. He put in a call to Seacray.
A maid answered. The family was out, she was sorry. They were
having tea in the boat.

Blaise's office gave a little information about a number of things,
and he sent up to the Registry for files on other matters he knew might
be useful. From some he took notes, and from others the documents
themselves. At a few minutes to six, both suitcases were full. He
telephoned the porter to send someone up to fetch them, and went
for a wash.

The suitcases were gone. Nothing to do but lock up, goodbye
everything, take a few coloured pencils for the boys by habit,
straighten the top of the desk until it might pass Miss Sells' inspection. Goodbye Miss Sells, nicest and best, and goodbye, good rid-
dance to everything. Let the door thump to Blaise's office in exactly
the same way as it would on Monday, and Tuesday, years and years
from now.

Goodbye to Blaise's office, straighten the files, put everything in
order, must do the right thing, mustn't we, and off we go, goodbye.

Bejian was there, the bags were put in the car, and the porter had
to be persuaded to take the tip.

"Nice weekend, sir."

"Thank you. Goodbye."

"Goodbye, sir. It's all clear."

"I'm sure it is. Goodbye."

Bejian went over the bridge while Big Ben flung six farewells in
bronze diapason, and strangely, his thoughts were of Blaise and
Dorothea.

They drove south, and Bejian spoke of Vinny working in the
garden at Seacray, she said, for her keep, and the great pleasure it
would give Frolla and himself to look after her while he was away
and until the family could join him.

"But I thought they'd be coming with me——"

"A moment's thought, please. It takes less to hide one man than a family? From the moment you are gone, there will be a search. You must go first. Nothing can happen to your family——"

"How is Arkhiv in this country?"

"By an excursion from Boulogne today. He leaves tomorrow——"

"Fortunate for me he's here——"

"He came to see you. For what other reason should he come to Seacray?"

"Beji, how did you people know about me?"

"It is not my duty to say. But if you know a man, and his wife, and you know what he says of certain things, and what she says, then you know how they think. When you know how they think, it is possible to tell if they have a place or not. You have a place, Hamie. A superior place."

"How do I know I'll be accepted?"

"I ask you this. Would Mr. Arkhiv interest himself if it was not thought you would be acceptable? But certainly not."

"Good to hear, Beji. I'm trusting people like Arkhiv and yourself——"

"And we trust to you."

"Why?"

Night, stars, and oaten wafts from the fields, and lights in houses, and a woman drawing curtains, the same as it would all be if he were only going home. The sameness of everything, like the door going thump.

"For some men it is possible to change. For others, impossible. They are the revolutionaries. They are themselves all their lives——"

"I'll be called a traitor——"

"It has a price and premium not known before. It is a twisted word. By some the traitor is a hero. He is paid with gifts. And remember, the French Revolutionaries, the Americans, the Russians, traitors everybody. In whose mouth is this word?"

"Why? I want to know why?"

"This I think you must ask to Mr. Arkhiv. For me, it is because you cannot be somebody except yourself. You will sacrifice. Family. Career. Everything. Why?"

"Impulse?"

"No."

"Looks like it."

"On the contrary, no. It is severely planned in your mind. Every step for weeks, or months, perhaps for years. Or why did you make no approach to me or to somebody else long before?"

"I won't bargain——"

"There can be no bargain. You knew you must be accepted, and you are accepted. So?"

Beji turned on a driveway and went toward the lights of a small hotel. They went through parked cars to a side door, and Bejian unlocked it, and led up some stairs and knocked. The place seemed full, and voices and music came through the floor and all the woodwork shook with people dancing.

Mavritz opened the door wide in a flourish of welcome.

Vissarion Arkhiv took up most of the room, resting on the stick, right hand held out, half-bowing. But if the ball-and-socket eyes smiled in greeing, they were hard, perceptive, not part of the roly-poly social Arkhiv, but aids to a working brain. Suddenly, that was better, more agreeable, certainly flattering.

Mavritz and Bejian bowed to Arkhiv, and went out.

"Mr. Arkhiv, is this a suitable place to speak?"

"It is not. But we shall make the best of what we have."

"I wish to join your Foreign Service."

"First, why do you make this decision?"

"I believe I shall have more opportunity to do what I want to do."

"And that is?"

"Work for the sake of everybody like myself."

"Bourgeoisie——"

"I'm not. Don't make that mistake. That's one of the reasons why I want to join you. Your own command of English is superlatively good. But English is the one language where even an Englishman can make mistakes——"

"It requires the scholarship of a Scotsman to correct them?"

"I'd much rather correct your Government's. Your English section is deplorably bad. If you're going to deal with the English-speaking people, and you'll have to sooner or later, you'll want people who understand how to write English. Not merely how to mistranslate Russian."

"But, please, you must tell me, why is bourgeoisie wrong in this sense?"

"Go back to history. I belong to what is generically called the Middle Class. It was in being long before any bourgeoisie. Originally it was peasant. The better trained of the populace left in the country when the Roman forces withdrew from Britain after almost four hundred years of occupation. They were a society of landowners and seamen. They provided judges and magistrates in the Roman tradition. They framed the law on Roman law. They officered the Navy and the Army. They led freebooting abroad. They owned the shipping. They directed commerce. They discovered and fought for, and governed colonies. They amassed land and fortune. They founded and controlled banks and exchanges. They dealt in commodities. Napoleon called us a nation of shopkeepers. That was the cynicism of a failure, a half-wit. The Middle Class did not shop-keep. It entirely controlled commodities at source. The world over. No other country has a Middle Class in our sense, or with our meaning. It ranked below the aristocracy only in precedence at Court. Its patronage created the artisan and the mechanic. It stood between the courtiers and the labourers. It governed by its knowledge and its care for trade and investment. Its commodities created the Bourgeoisie. It was they, the stall-keepers and journeymen, setting up business and congregating in the towns, who became the Bourgeoisie. But don't confuse them with us. Even today."

"Is it your purpose to seek Government office?"

"That's my training, yes. Preferably in Britain."

"We shall discuss this later. First, you come freely to offer your services where we consider they shall be found most useful."

"Yes."

"Secondly, you are willing to be trained in our methods."

"Yes."

"You are prepared to spend a period of time at a university to make yourself completely at home with the Russian language, with Soviet law, and with our social philosophy."

"Yes."

"You must allow me to ask why?"

"I suppose that's not so simple. For twenty years I've been reading everything that's come in from our people about you. I've also read a lot of Soviet material. For the past five years I've been watching the effect of your diplomacy. During the last couple of years I've studied the whole thing very carefully. Recently I came to a conclusion. I believe Europe is bound to go to you. After that, everything else. I don't think you'll have to fire a shot. I'd prefer not to see any shots fired here. No bombs, no destruction. I'll do my best to prevent it. Everything we could possibly want for the matter of taking control of the Government is here, ready and waiting. Half the electorate is completely in the hands of the Labour Party. Of the other half, a fair proportion can be swayed very easily by an appeal to their stomachs and pockets. Supposing—I say supposing——"

"I follow very carefully, Mr. Gleave."

"Supposing, then, that at the proper time, we were to produce an economic and social plan that went further than anyone else's? To the disadvantage of nobody except the landowner and millionaire. Supposing that the plan incorporated a message that seemed to be in the finest tradition of the British free-thinker——"

"A free—?"

"Somebody who doesn't belong to any party. The floating voter. That's the most influential, because it's decisive. It gives a majority. Get them on our side first. Approach it historically. Stress the fact that all progress in Britain has been by revolution, from Magna Carta to Peterloo and after. Once you've got his nod on that, you're on fairly safe ground."

"But the British are radically opposed to Communism——"

"They're radically opposed to anything presented as stupidly as Communism has been. But I don't for one moment doubt that given time and the right assistance I can rectify even that. I happen to know a little about formulating policy for the mass mind——"

"That, of course, we had already deduced. It will be an enormous advantage, naturally. What you say of the Middle Class is also profoundly interesting. It is a matter of supreme importance——"

"More than that, Mr. Arkhiv. Until you have the Middle Class with you, or unless they're extirpated in their entirety, you'll make no real progress in Europe, and you're at a dead end in Great Britain. I hope it'll be my job to frame a policy aimed solidly at the Middle Class——"

"But not Communism?"

"Let's call it Reformism. Reform is an English word. Extremely respectable. And a great vote-getter. That's what I'd like to go for. I'm sure it can be done. Desperate people aren't particular, you know. And the British Middle Class is desperate. They'd snatch at anything more substantial than a straw. When the day comes, I'd like to come back to supervise. If it's not in my time, I have two sons to carry on my work."

"You wish them to be educated in Russia?"

"Yes. I distrust the educational methods here. From all I've seen of your top people, they appear to have gone to good schools. That's all I want for my sons. They are my guarantee. I mean what I say. I warn you that I am not of the Proletariat. My sons are not of the Proles. I didn't produce them merely as gifts to the State, either for work or for wars, in the manner of the historical Prole. I present them, as we of the Middle Class have always presented our sons, to work and to flourish for the sake of a common dignity. Marx was not a Proletarian, was he? Lenin was not. Stalin was not. None of your present Government are of the Proletariat. You are not. Peasants, yes. But the peasant is far from the Prole. Each one of you comes from what might be called the Middle Class. Brought up in decent homes, properly-mannered, well schooled——"

"Proletarian is a mistranslation, you think?"

"What else? And worse than that. Who was so foolishly ignorant as to permit the use of the term Communist in English? Bad judgment. Poor scholarship."

Dr. Mavritz put his head in the door, looked his sense of hurry, and shut the door again.

"Tomorrow, you will leave for France, Mr. Gleave. A car will call for you. A friend of yours will drive. You will catch an excusion ship which leaves at ten-thirty in the morning. When you reach Boulogne, you will go to La Melpomène, a café to the left of the quay as you leave the gate. Somebody known to you will meet you. Follow him to a car. You will have further instructions there."

"Very well. La Melpomène, on the left of the quay. I should tell you that I thought it proper to advise Myril Gislan to leave the country——"

"Myril?"

"Your very beautiful far-from-wooden duck. That exquisite canard. How did you know she might attract me into putting up a blind?"

Arkhiv tapped his cigarette, and dabbed his walking-stick.

"We did not know. We did not hope. But she has charm, I think. Not beautiful, but a woman. More important——"

"But how did you know?"

"I did not. But I was most pleased, I may tell you."

"Is anything she told me true?"

"What she told you were instructions. What did you advise her to do?"

"I wanted to take her with me to Beaconsfield tonight. The search may start tonight or tomorrow. She'd be about the first arrest——"

"She will return to France with Mavritz. For what reason do you take care of her?"

"Not the romantic or the erotic one. I don't want a certain Miss Louise Hamble to mount any dunghills and cackle. Let me give you some useful information——"

Arkhiv took down every detail of La Hamble in microscopic script, and noted that perhaps the photographer at the Chalmers wedding might provide a few pictures.

"I am told you thought the Mappersley group has some chance——"

"Yes, I do. There's more than enough snobbery left lying about in the country to be attracted——"

"But a Lord cannot be a Prime Minister——"

"Except in certain circumstances. A revolution could provide an opportunity——"

"You think it is possible?"

"Give it a little time. France goes. Italy goes. Austria. Germany. How long? Did you hear, perhaps, about a recent meeting at Chequers?"

"Yes. I have the greatest interest——"

"I have the papers, complete, in the car."

Mavritz put his head in and cut Arkhiv's panegyric to a whisper. The old boy looked really beside himself, and in any case he was large enough. He leaned on the stick and the top of the large bald head gleamed almost as if the flame of a prayer were alight inside it. He seemed to be talking to himself, but when he looked up he was convulsed with an enormous laughter, silent, rather awful. Some kind of a presage of things in store, perhaps. For God's sake, be sure. Yes, dear Father. But this is not your day, unfortunately.

They all went downstairs without seeing anybody. The music and the dancing went on. Mavritz put the bags in his car, and Arkhiv got in the back.

"We meet soon, Mr. Gleave. Be assured. Nothing will fail."

"I'm sure of it. Good night."

Plenty to think about on the way back with Beji driving, and not much conversation until they reached the lights and the traffic.

"I am instructed to pay Vinny £2,000 in the moment you reach France, Hamie. She will be taken care of. Any debts will be settled. Also the mortgage——"

"You know about that?"

"Oh, yes. The Englishman's mortgage is his castle, no? The driver of the car tomorrow will have your expenses with him. The ship is a day excursion. You will not need a passport. One will be provided when you arrive in France. There is nothing more except to wish you our hopes for your work in the future."

"Take care of Vinny."

"I promise."

"I'll write to her at the first opportunity. God, what a hell of a way to say goodbye to one's wife——"

"You could telephone——"

"She'd hear it in my voice. I'll leave a note for her. Au revoir."

Turning again at the entrance, perhaps with some thought of another glance at one lucky enough to be meeting Vinny quite soon. But there was only Bejian's spectacles glooming through the window. That wave was a lugubrious thing, unwanted, better unseen.

He got out at Hyde Park Corner, glad to be free of a rat warren under sewers and slums, spitting away a foetor of mouldering humanity. Women's whispers reached out of whitish blobs of faces

in the wall's shade, a hand in pluck at his sleeve, a tip-tap of heels
for a pace or two, You looking for me, dear? Oi, how about a bit
of kutchy-kutch? Anything you like, dear. You peasy bastard, you.
The whispers, the ladies, and a distant wonder why that type of
heel-tap could always be told from any other.

A car waiting on the corner of the mews. Worry of turning an
ankle on the cobbles, and silence all the way down there, and not a
light. During the wait, after pressing the bell, a thought that he
might have a bath and a drink, and take her for something to eat in
one of the restaurants near the station, and catch the eleven-some-
thing down.

Light shining on the frosted glass, and the shadow coming down
the stair.

But no rattle of a chain. The door opened wide.

"Hamie? Thought it might be you. Come in."

He had to look, and look again, trying to see somebody except
Vinny. But it was she, looking up at him with the light behind her,
and he knew she was budding her mouth in that well-well-well-
caught-you-at-last-have-I smile, though with that glacial hint he had
dreaded since the beginning. There was nothing he could do about
it.

There it was.

Myril, in a black dress, sat curled on the divan. She smiled at him, once, without confidence. She looked gaunt. Vinny introduced a woman unnoticed in the bathroom passage. Miss Thiery, forties probably, neither one thing nor the other, long coat, handbag, umbrella, and brownish flowered straw hat. A shadow. She asked Vinny to identify her husband and the co-respondent, and Vinny laughed and told her not to be so silly, and please go. Miss Thiery went creakily downstairs, and the door closed as it ought behind a shadow.

Vinny said she had a marvellous opportunity to play the jealous wife, but she was hanged if she could, and if she tried she might spoil it all by laughing at herself. That would never do. She was jealous, yes. And she supposed she felt murderous. She did actually. If she thought of the little boys, she might do something rather serious. But it was so silly, because really and truly she knew there was nothing to get in a frightful tear about. She thought Myril was only having a bit of fun in her own quiet way, that was the long and short of it. Lots of girls went about doing the same thing. Other peoples' morals were their affairs. But when they interfered in her life she felt entitled to say something about it. Not in a virtuous sort of way. It was simply no use talking about virtue these days, because people simply laughed at one. If a girl wanted to go to bed, that was that. She could always find somebody hard-up. What she really objected to was a girl who deliberately opened her legs to a married man. Children or not, he had an oath to keep to his wife. The oath was taken, the words were said. If they were meant, well and good. If they were not meant, it was still a filthy trick, she thought, to shake the branch. That kind of apple dropped so easily.

He was listening, but without hearing in a funny sort of way, and he thought Myril might be doing about the same thing, for the same reason. It was far more comfortable to listen rather than hear.

Let her go on. Say nothing to stop her, or alter her method of thinking. Let her say what comes into her mind and get it out of her system. Stop her, or argue and break the flow, and she might lose her temper and start screaming, Vinny-fashion. She might also throw something at Myril. Let her talk. Let her tire. Let her go away thinking that she behaved in an entirely proper manner, spoke every word she had to say, silenced all opposition, and in general achieved a complete victory without once raising her voice. More than that, no woman, especially Vinny, could ask.

A lot of people blamed the girl instead of the man, Vinny's voice went on. She was inclined to agree with them. The girl had to undo one or two things, nearly always, at any rate, and pull other things off, and she had to take up the loading position. It all took time. It was not a spontaneous matter. If it were, she might forgive what had happened. But human beings were not cats. They had all sorts of defenses, and a knowledge of time. She saw that Myril wore a watch. It never seemed to remind her that there was such a thing as a sense of doing things the right way with time, even for a watch, or it would never tell the right time. Of course, human beings were not watches, but they had hands and faces, and they decidedly had to do with time and nothing else. You were born, you lived, you died. It was all time. What made her so sick was that some of her time had been stolen from her. All she could do about it was get a divorce, if she wanted one. She had no intention of getting one. The nicest parts of her time had been stolen behind her back. With two children and the house to look after she had no chance to fight. And she had, she supposed, ten years disadvantage in the way of age. She hardly wondered the apple fell off. She felt there was a wonderful speech in the whole thing somewhere. All about virtue, and modesty and chastity, and that sort of thing. But if people were ignorant of the meaning of words, it was not a bit of use talking about them. Virtue for most people simply meant you were to keep your hand on it, modesty meant you were not to let anybody see it, and chastity meant you

were not to let anybody touch it. If that was all they meant to some
people, she had nothing more to say. But there was still the question
of her husband, and the wrong done to her. She supposed she might
call it a wrong. It seemed a silly sort of word for what she felt. A
man who could break an oath of that kind, break it, take his time
about it, because after all he had to take his trousers off too, unless
he was the kind that liked discomfort, and she was quite sure in
saying it did not apply in this case, that sort of man was not much.
Really not much. A man who could break his oath to his wife could
break his oath to anybody. And he was welcome to think that one
over. She meant it. She had never thought him dishonourable before.
It was that, more than anything, that hurt. Lots of people thought
nothing much of honour, the husband and wife kind, anyway.
Nothing about oaths, or keeping their word. All stupidly old-fashioned
stuff. Now, we all had to do as we liked because we liked, and somebody would let us. And it was all beautifully democratic, and everybody was so free. And so sordid, and disgusting inside themselves.
And untrustworthy. She wished to God she had the words to say
what she really meant. But it was no good, she never had been very
bright at anything. It was awful to find she was no good in bed,
either. That was perhaps what she meant. No good. Somebody else
got it.

"Vin——"

"Shut up!"

"Vin, please——"

"Don't you dare come anywhere near me. When I let you, you'll
go down on your knees and beg my pardon. I wouldn't trust your
word countersigned by a dozen archangels. You never had the
decency to come to me and say you were a little tired of the same
old thing. I'd have understood. I feel tired sometimes——"

"Darling, if only you'd let me——"

"Don't talk to me. You've taught me a lesson, and I'll use it. I'll
beat a sense of honour into your sons, be certain of that. They'll never
break their word. Especially to women. Out of my way!"

"Listen to me——"

"I'll listen to nothing. Take your slut, and dishonour her. If she
can be. She can't, of course. That's what's so maddening——"

"Vin——"

"I'm going to my mother's and I'm going to tell her exactly what I think of her for daring to interfere in my affairs. If she hadn't put these beastly people on your slimy track, I'd know nothing about it and I'd still have an honourable husband. Aren't I an ass? But I'd have preferred it. So I'm going to tell darling Mummy that I never want to hear from her again as long as she lives. That ought to keep her out of my business. I shall drive back to Seacray tonight. If you're going home, you might thank Vera for sending the wire to me. I wish she'd broken her neck first. Good night."

She had nothing with her, hat, gloves or bag. He followed her down the stairs, but she threw his hand away and opened the door herself, and went hurrying along the cobbles.

"Vinny, darling, please listen——"

"Shut up."

"Would you please let me tell you something——"

"No."

"Please try to——"

"If you lay a hand on me, I'll scream for the police. I'll give you in charge. I mean it. Get out of my way."

She opened the door and got in. It was Delia's car. The door slammed. The engine turned over.

"Go back to your slut. Go to hell."

Not a shake in the voice, not an eyelash out of place, bone-dry, emotionless, at ease. The car went off, braked at the turning, and the rear lights gave him two clear rays in scarlet farewell.

He went back and shut the door, hearing Myril crying. She leaned, bent, hands to her face, against the wall.

"Better get ready."

"No."

"The police may come here at any time tonight or tomorrow morning."

"I don't care."

"You must. We're very fortunate. She might have caused considerably more trouble than that."

"Why didn't you say something? Why did you let her say those things to me?"

"Probably because she had the right. In any case what did it matter?"

"Matter? You can listen? It matters nothing?"

"Compared with what it could have been? Nothing at all. Besides, what did she say that wasn't correct? Guilty people haven't a case——"

"You feel guilty?"

"Of course. Don't you?"

"No. Until now, no."

She stood straight and shook back her hair, and dropped her hands. The watch attracted her. She took it off her wrist, and threw it at the coal scuttle.

"It is finished. Please go."

"I'll get in touch with Mavritz——"

"I will——"

"You're sure?"

"Quite sure. Leave me."

"Give me the voucher for the parcels."

While she looked in her handbag, he was not quite sure whether to take her at her word, or if he ought to try one more plea. There was, after all, considerable danger.

"Myril, I wish you'd just forget what's happened for the moment. There's a great deal more to worry about than this, you know."

"If you will worrry, good."

"But be reasonable. Fun's fun. If it catches up with you, it's no use throwing watches away, and all that sort of nonsense——"

"Here is the ticket. Leave me——"

"Myril. For the last time, please come with me——"

"Leave me, for the last time. Go."

There was tension about the line of her body that warned him she might hit him with something if he came too near. Then there might be a real scene.

"Goodbye, Myril. Sorry about things. But there it is."

No word, and no movement as far as he could tell going downstairs. He walked up the mews and into the turning, and looked back. Not a sound, and goodbye. A lucky cab took him to Waterloo for the parcels. No trouble. Another cab to catch the train home. A

drink in the buffet made him feel rather better and a second touched
the spot. The journey down was considerably shortened by a fast
train and a longish nap, and further, by a sense of good fortune that
Vinny had done no more than bruise feelings. Had she pulled the
stops out, she might have put the lid on everything.

It was almost a festive occasion to be back in the house, dark,
damp, ghostly or not, because it all seemed decked in trappings of
fond farewell. He even went downstairs and gave the boiler a crack
with the poker for luck. He packed a small bag, put out the one good
suit, linen and tie, socks and shoes, ready for the morning, and sat
down to have a drink.

There were several minor worries afloat. First, there might easily
be a spot check of all documents that night. One could never tell
when Security might pounce. Or Mr. Flap might take it into his head
to do some work after dinner, as he very often did. Or he might go
in early in the morning, another careless habit of his. La Hamble
might visit Myril. Anything might be said during a little tête-à-tête
between a couple of bosomy friends. But if the lines were tapped
here and at Seacray it would be very silly to risk a call. He might have
thought of that before leaving London.

Either he was dreaming, or a car was coming down the drive. It
might be anybody. But it was too late for chance callers. Too late
to turn off the light. Too late to run. The car stopped outside the
front door, too practised to be a stranger.

A key sliding and turning, and a weight of relief.

Vinny came in, and let the door swing shut, and threw the keys on
the table.

"I thought I'd done enough damage for one night, so I came home.
Where's that girl?"

"In London. Why?"

"She told me you were coming for her——"

"For some dinner, that's all——"

"I don't want to hear a word about it. Are you seeing her again?"

"Never. And you may take that for what it's worth. Never."

"We'll see. I ought to ring Frolla and ask after the children."

"Little late for that, isn't it?"

"Don't be too considerate of people's feelings. You'd disappoint me. I'm tired. I'm using the boys' bedroom. What time are you going in the morning?"

"Quite early. Don't bother to get up. Use our room. I'll use the boys'. If I must."

"You must. I shan't want our room for a long time."

But she leaned over the top bannister.

"Would you mind telling me why men do this sort of thing? Never mind the children or anything else. Why do they do this to their wives who aren't, well, not too bad, I suppose? What's the attraction? If it's bed, and I don't doubt that's it, what is it? A change of vegetables, or what?"

"Curiosity, perhaps. And the wiles of Eros."

"Oh, balls. I don't think I'll ever feel comfortable with you again. I'll feel you're doing a rush job with me and thinking about the high jinks you're going to have with her."

"That's not fair——"

"Don't talk to me about what's fair or not. Isn't that the girl you danced with at the Grosvenor?"

"Yes."

"Finding out quite a lot tonight, aren't I? Trust Beryl to be absolutely right where that's concerned. Takes a slut to tell a slut."

"Vinny, I wish to God you'd listen."

"Go to hell."

Consolation, or some sort of balm came with a thought that he might at least be able to tiptoe in and kiss her goodbye in the morning. He set the alarm for six, and got into bed. With all the excitement, there was no dream of Myril, no tautening. Mind went blank, cool, no stirring. Not a sickening, not revulsion, not anything. Blank.

Rapping on the door woke him, and the room was light. He could hardly believe he had closed his eyes. It was six-thirty. He must have slept through the alarm. The church bells rang, and the milk cart drove off while he was going downstairs. The kettle was already on. Vinny was in the basement lighting the boiler. But she wore a pair of rubber gloves.

"Get the milk, will you? Are you going away this morning?"

"Yes."

"You weren't going down to Seacray at all, then?"

"No. To London."

"If you're going to the office, why do you need a bag?"

"I might have to stay overnight——"

"At the office."

"Yes. At the office."

"I'll bet if I telephone, I shan't find you there——"

"If you're going to be a nuisance——"

"Don't worry. I'm not. I simply want you to know, that's all——"

"Know what?"

"How much I trust you. Will you get the milk?"

He reached outside the front door and brought the milk bottle in. A cold bath, despite Vinny's saying she had lit the boiler for him, put life in the dead, and the shave was boiling hot, which was all to the good. No doubt about it, when Vinny lit the boiler, she lit it.

The papers came about seven. He took them out in the garden with a cup of tea. Vinny came out, dressed, and stood arranging a piece of veil on her hat.

"I'm going. Better now than chance being snailed in the Sunday crawl. I'll start back with the children fairly early, too. I'll get the small room cleared out tomorrow for me——"

"There's really no need——"

"There's every need. If you can do without me, I can more than do without you."

"Vinny, please let me tell you how I feel about it. I'd crawl——"

But while he was speaking she was walking away, and into the house, and her slam of the back door nearly shivered the panes out.

He went in, and stood watching while she looked at herself in the hall glass, putting the hat on.

"If it's no use saying anything, I hope you'll try to remember that I've often not only regretted it, but I've been completely disgusted with myself. It hasn't happened for a long time. Won't again——"

"If I told you I'd been having an affair with the milkman, or any of the other rather good-looking young men who come here, and who could easily put me on a bed with lots to spare, what would you say if I said I often felt disgusted? Don't talk rubbish."

Her hands were still above her head, and she listened to a car coming down the drive.

"This is probably yours——"

"We'll at least accompany you part of the way——"

"Who's we?"

A set trap, beautifully taken, and who, indeed.

"You're the lady of the house. Why not look? You've got to listen to this. I'm going away."

Vinny turned her back with her feet together.

"It hasn't anything to do with last night. It's got nothing to do with anything except what we've talked about so often. It's highly probable the police will be here sometime today. If not today, certainly tomorrow. There'll be Intelligence people with them. You'll have to answer questions. I shan't tell you anything. You'll therefore be able to tell them very little they won't know. When things settle down, I'll hope you'll come to me with the boys. Your neighbours may not like you after this. The boys might be victimized at school. But it won't be for long. And it will be for the best. I'm certain of it. Do you understand?"

She nodded.

"Sums of money will be paid regularly. There'll be no need to fear about anything. You'll have no worries. That's one of the things that decided me. There'll at least be a little leisure in your life——"

"Hamie——"

"Here's somebody on the step——"

Vinny put her fists to her face and walked slowly toward the door. She looked back at him, but the short veil hid her eyes.

A second ring.

Vinny straightened the carpet he had kicked up coming in with the milk, and opened the door wide.

Kevin Chalmers' large smile turned almost to horror.

"Kevin! I thought you were on your honeymoon!"

"Well, yes. I sort of am. But Mary's gone on to Paris——"

"Kevin's driving me to London."

"I've just come up from seeing some of my people——"

"Come in and have a cup of tea——"

"Vinny, I'd love to, but we're a little pushed, I'm afraid. I should have got here earlier——"

"Vin, you'll come with us a little way, at least——"

"No. I don't think I will. Don't forget the bag. And the parcels——"

Kevin put them in the back. He had no luggage.

"Off we go. Goodbye, Vinny. Mary sent ten thousand messages——"

"Double them from me. Shall I see you soon?"

"Very soon. Lord, yes. Half a mo'. I'll turn round."

Vinny stood on the top step with her back to the white pillar. Her mouth might have been smiling but the veil hid what she thought.

"I'm not going to let this sound like 'wull ye no' come back again.' But I'm too obliterated to feel anything properly. Are you quite sure you've done the right thing, Hamie?"

"Yes. And when all the poison's blown away, you'll see that I did. And you'll follow me?"

"Do you want me to?"

His arms went round her easily enough, but it was rather like holding a caryatid. Nothing gave. He tried to kiss her hand, but she took that away, too.

"When we meet will be plenty of time, Hamie. I'll keep everything going here. Whatever it is you're going to do, try to remember me——"

"You're one of the reasons I'm going. You know it. The other two are Hamish and Robert. They don't want a nought for a father. I don't want noughts for sons."

"And I don't want one for a husband. Or any nought habits. Do you remember what your father once said to you? About remembering who you are? What rules to follow? How you should comport yourself?"

"I'll have plenty of time to remember other things as well. Vinny, a kiss——"

"No. That's how I feel."

"I shan't say goodbye——"

"There's no need! Kevin's waiting. Write to me——"

Nothing else to do. A walk to the car, and a glance before getting in, and wait for Kevin to finish waving, and watching Vinny getting smaller, and the drive going by, and out of the gate, and goodbye. Goodbye.

"God, I never had such a shock in my life to see Vinny. Mavritz said she was at Seacray——"

"How did you get here?"

"Planning this for months. We're going as far as France together. Then you go one way, and I go somewhere else——"

"D'you know a girl called Myril Gislan?"

"No. Who's she?"

"Somebody who should have come with us. I'm worried about her——"

"Let Mavritz look after her. I shan't feel comfortable until I'm in France——"

"Why? You're in no trouble——"

"Not at the moment. Wait till they find out. I'd had enough a long time ago. Sucking up to that lot over there. Loud-mouthed heap. They're quite sure they can get everything done by pounding a desk and God-damning. Their own chaps may be used to it. I didn't take to it. I thought we could put up with it for a little while. But it got worse. We were all going about like a lot of tadpoles in a jam jar. Feed for the bigger fish. A lot of damned sore-eyed lazars. Then I had to sell the house. So I said to hell with the whole thing. There's a better way than this. I began looking into the trade and loan side, collecting names, dates and facts. Commerce and banking. I had the right job for it. The results might surprise you. I had a stack that high when I came away. I'd been in touch with a couple of chaps over there, and they put me on to Mavritz in Paris. I told him what I'd got, and what I wanted. Then I waited. And here I am."

"I thought you were going to Paris a couple of nights ago——"

"We were. But Mavritz told me things were moving. It was on. So I changed our minds for us."

"Didn't you take a frightful risk lugging that stuff about with you?"

"Oh, lord no. The night I got to London, remember, the night we met? I got in with it all right. Diplomatic passport then, of course. But I didn't know how long I'd last. Question was, what to do with it. Banks shut. So I called a chap I know in Uncle Sam's joint, here, in Grosvenor Square, and asked him if he'd look after it for me. Told him it was family business, deeds and so forth. He was delighted to be of assistance. So I rolled round and got it yesterday, and delivered it to Mavritz last night. Great rejoicings everywhere——"

"Do I know this chap by any chance?"

"Doubt it. Rather too junior. He's a molecular small-fry assistant to Hatton Dail."

"Probably kept it in the safe for you."

"Don't doubt it for a moment. They're awfully careful."

"What about Mary?"

"She doesn't know yet. But it'll be all right. She's rather fed up, as a matter of fact. Got a cable. Daddy's sawn off her allowance. Not the sort of thing to get up to in the morning."

"Do you feel all right about this? Sure of things?"

"Certain. I'll tell you why on the ship. My job's always been commerce, more or less the legal side of it. That and Intelligence. Plain as a pikestaff what's going to happen. But you don't think our bloody fools are going to wake up till it's on top of them, do you?"

It started to rain, and mist hid anything the rain left open. All the villages were a grey Sunday street, with not a soul anywhere. All rather defeating, but even a little symbolic in its way. Empty streets, misty land, no people and pouring rain.

He explained about the parcels, and Kevin pulled up at the harbour station and waited while he put them in the cloakroom, folded the vouchers in an envelope with a message to Bejian, stamped it, and dropped it in the pillar box.

"Trusting soul, aren't you?"

"When it comes to the Post Office, yes."

"Not worried the boys might be opening letters?"

"I doubt it. I put nothing below those people. But I don't think it's come down to that."

They freewheeled the hill to the harbour, and Kevin parked the car, locked the doors, and said that somebody was coming for it.

"Hamie, I hope to God they haven't cancelled the trip because of the weather. That'll bitch everything."

"You're very nearly guilty of criminal slander. When's the British

tar turned back from the streaming seas? When's the tripper fore-
gone his misery?"

A surprising number of people seemed determined to try their
stomachs on a most unappetizing sea. The tickets were on sale and
they went aboard without the slightest trouble, and found a couple
of seats in the bar. Kevin seemed unable to sit still. He went off to
look at the winches, he said. But when the siren boomed goodbye,
and the gangway clattered up, back he came, all smiles, to say he had
just watched the car backed out and driven off. Mist came down, and
there was nothing to see except the end of the harbour going past.
It was warmer in the bar.

Kevin said he was delighted, in such agreeable surroundings, to
open a session of the Chalmers school of economics with an informal
polemic on the behaviour of Messer Topsiturve when snagged in the
elastic and inelastic laws of supply and demand. Under present
fiscal laws in what was quite properly referred to as the Old Country,
nobody, not the greatest industrial genius, could keep much more
than £3,500 a year honestly, never mind how much he earned. It was
a thought of considerable magnitude that no boy, whatever his
propensities for service, would ever, the way things were going, be
worth more than a couple of thousand a year, more or less. Great
industries were not built by wage-earners. Undertakings were not
captained by starvelings, or brought into being by politicians. There
was no legerdemain. There was only brain. It was a natural law that
the donkey travelled faster with a bunch of carrots in front of him.
But they had to be real carrots when he caught up with them. Not
plastic. Some said that a plastic carrot of £2,500 was quite enough to
live on. That sort of moron could never hope to earn it because with
the kind of brain portended by such a remark, he would not be
worth it.

The Country's past supremacy had been created by the few who
earned, and kept, vast sums for themselves, and by application of
those riches to work created opportunities for others. It was no use
talking about equality. Some had brains and some had not. In past
days, some could reach up and have the moon, and others could only
yelp for it. Under the present good old democratic chase-me-charlie
system, the yelpers could reach out and take it off the boys who got

it because there were more of them. By the same principle, pirates once took possession of everything they could get their hands on. With the oncome of that legalized piracy, robbery and barratry, the country got into debt, was still in it, and nobody, apparently, could see any way out, or any way of getting straight. From year to year various cooks got together with the books and produced the annual budgetary bellyful, which the yelpers, always so careless of their figures, could be relied upon to swallow with or without the traditional pinch of salt. The yelpers had the further advantage of being able to sweeten their sufferings with a dessert of schadenfreude by thinking of those who should have lumps of moon robbed of everything but the pips, with not one drop of the oil of satisfaction to ease them down. It went on year after year until it became rote, part of established procedure and like the Book of Common Prayer, not to be tampered with. But the thing to consider was this, that without the debt, the Country could never have advanced as far as it had, and neither would the yelpers have been in any position to yelp, because they, the book-cookers and the country would long have gone to pot.

By sheer brainlessness and other evidence of Bedlam, sciolism, and outright malversation, debt had become something to buy and sell, or set off against, or create loans for.

But to give things their right name, debt was nothing except amenity. Without that amenity, nobody could move, nothing could function. It represented the advance of the empiricist over the pragmatist, the moon-reacher doer over the yelper dullard. But the yelper had a majority of votes, and gabsters to represent them. And progress went about in the sheep's clothing of the hire-purchase system, and the yelper never saw that his debt was his amenity.

"I'm waiting for a peep at Messer Topsiturve."

"Coming up. He's never far away from us. As with any other god, we never see him. But we can always tell where he's been. The last time he laid about him was in 1929, you'll remember. Poor Mr. Hoover was blamed for it. Wasn't him at all. It was good Messer Topsiturve. About that time the Americans were owed about thirty thousand million dollars in war loans here and there, and private investments all over the place. It was all kept going by fresh loans to pay the interest on the old 'uns, and for exports of all sorts. But the moment the Government clamped down on the issue of foreign loans, the countries who owed the money had to try to pay the interest and capital in goods, and goods had to pay for their American imports, too. System of under-the-counter barter. But at that point, Messer Topsiturve sent a gentle-man named Hawley into the Senate with a tariff bill. Everything coming into the United States was taxed. That was to prevent the home market from being swamped with cheaper foreign goods so that the home product could be sold and factories kept at work and thus the American in his job. The foreigners' goods were priced out of the market, their paper money was worthless, so they turned to gold. The more gold they wanted, the more they had to pay for it. Every dullard in the world wanted gold. The more they paid for gold, the less they got for their goods. The less they got for their goods the less were produced, and the less men were wanted for work. That was when Messer Topsiturve came on for a bow. The Americans couldn't get money for their goods abroad. They couldn't sell the goods coming in. They couldn't get any dividends on their investments. They couldn't get any interest, much less capital pay-ments on their war loans. Everything was stuck, dried up. The stock market broke. Everybody wanted to sell, but nobody was buying. Businesses closed, banks went bust. Millions starved. Messer Top-siturve yelped 'Slump' instead of 'Howzat' and took game and match. Mark this. As things are, the moment the United States has to stop lending abroad, there'll be serious trouble. If the yelpers win, and they manage to build their tariff wall again, you won't find Kilroy peeping over the top, but our pal, Messer Topsiturve. Where we're going, they use money as a tool, not as an instrument of power. When they're able to export goods, where will the rest of us be? And it won't be long."

"Do you know Charles Froweth?"

"I know of him. Chairman of all sorts, master of nothing. They'll all fail. If that sort of chap didn't have a staff of first-class accoun-tants, he'd die. It's the accountants more than anybody else who keep things going. While you're looking at one book still warm from their ministrations, they're cooking the next. It won't stop until Russia and China enter world commodity markets. With India mak-

ing a bid, too, that's the other half of the earth's population creating
a demand that's never been known. Misuse of privilege, poverty, and
foreign devil's pittances didn't allow it before. Prices are going to
rise at least five hundred per cent. What happens to Europe and
America's wages, rents, and all the rest? That's when the whole
rattlekettle hits the buffers, snap goes the elastic, and hoopla for
Messer Topsiturve. And we'll be in the right place to see it. Knock
out one pin, and the lot comes down. Along with that, remember
that Uncle Ivan has always produced a great deal of gold but he's
never spent much more than a dribble. What happens when he un-
loads the yield of thirty years?"

Sunshine on a beach, and red roofs behind the dunes, first glimpse
of free land and first strong doubt of safety. Kevin drank another
straight, and went out to lean over the rail, watching. Fishing boats
were harboured by the dozen, taxis waited outside the gates, people
strolled along the promenade, Sunday-calm and lassitude over all.

A sudden whiteness felt in the face at the top of the gangway.
But the crowd going down was rather comforting. A couple of policemen stood on the quayside. The white batons hanging from their
belts looked safe enough. Nobody bothered to ask him what was in
the bag. Everybody roamed along in no hurry, perhaps glad enough
to enjoy the feeling of being able to walk on something steady again.

Kevin held out his hand.

"Good trip, Hamish. Good luck. See you in the droshky, or whatever it's going to be. Just occurred this moment. Are we British over
here?"

"Must be, yes. Can't exactly resign, can we?"

"Hardly, I suppose. Again——"

" 'Bye."

Turn to the left, sniffing the sea, watching a troop of little girls off
somewhere with a couple of nuns flapping white wings in rear. La
Melpomène, written in script across a café's awning, and a waiter
polishing ashtrays among the tables outside.

There was no mistaking the man with folded arms on the corner,
looking toward the sea. In the blue jacket, and paler blue trousers and
possibly the same socks, the man he remembered as something-or-
other Drechat, one of Bejian's Geneva luncheon guests, gave no sign,

and made no attempt to sit down at a table, which was rather a pity in a way.

Nothing to do but follow, around the corner, and down a street that brought much too much in the way of reminder of Robert's gappy teeth. All the houses appeared to have been started by people with half a mind, and there they were, all halves of houses, of three storeys, with half-a-house space in between. Which said rather a lot about half-minded people. At the same time, a very small plot of ground provided quite a lot of house. That said rather more.

Drechat opened the rear door of a new car and bowed an invitation to enter. The little bag was put in front. There was nothing to say, and they said nothing, and that seemed to suit everybody. The overcoat made a pillow on the seat. A nap was in order, and in any case fewer people would notice him if he kept his head down.

He woke up a couple of times, the same roads, trees, villages, signs, and went to sleep again, thinking of Vinny, hoping that Myril got away, wondering what was happening to Kevin, and over all, a pleasant sense of surprise at evidence of smooth planning and a hope that it kept to standard.

Drechat awoke him in traffic. They were outside a railway station, on a slope, with a terrace. A distinctly provincial tang. Wood smoke.

"Monsieur Gleave—" leaning over the front seat, extremely cautious, and most respectful—"inside this envelope you will find a ticket for the express to Paris. The money is to use as you wish. Please go to the restaurant car. You will find somebody waiting for you. I hope I have been of some assistance."

"You did splendidly, thanks."

Time to waste, a wash, a drink, and the express came in while he bought a paper, although he was hardly conscious of what he thought he was looking for until he found himself disappointed not to find his name in print.

He was shown to a reserved First Class compartment in the carriage next the restaurant car, and when the train was well on its way, he went toward the smell of the kitchen.

But he stood in the restaurant car doorway, wondering what sort of magician he was dealing with.

Arkhiv, voluminous in grey flannel, sat in a corner seat. The large head nodded, and the same perceptive look was in the pale ball-and-socket eye, but even its pale-blueness seemed modified by laughter.

"Now, Mr. Arkhiv. I insist that you tell me. How the devil did you get here?"

"Mr. Gleave, I do not know how I can impress you with our great joy. Such riches you brought to us. I am still in a dream. Non compos mentis. Then what shall I do? I must take everything with me. Mavritz has friends——"

"I'm sure."

"Oh, yes. We flew late last night to France. Miss Gislan, you must know, is safe in Paris——"

"Delighted to hear it——"

"Mavritz took the baggage, and I flew to Lyons this morning to catch this train. Originally we should have met in Paris. Now I accompany you——"

"Flattery?"

"No. Admiration. We shall go to Paris now. There you will have your passport. You will go to Stockholm, to Helsinki, and to Moscow. You will have a welcome, my friend, I promise you."

"I'd like to drop my wife a line——"

"Certainly. It will be posted in England. Mr. Gleave, you took exceptional chance——"

"What was I doing, in any case? I determined to get the paper work away, or who'd have believed me on your side? Would anybody believe those schemes existed? Nobody can make plan after plan, Mr. Arkhiv. The best plan is the best of many. I took all I could that I thought could never be bettered. They can ring changes, yes. But what I've taken were basic. If you know those, there's nothing much anybody can do about it. As important, it'll cut a channel between ourselves and the United States. Almost more important than anything else, as I see it."

"We are in accord, certainly. Should I ask, Mr. Gleave, why you approach us? Instead of the United States Government?"

"Very simple, really. There are too many Toms and Dicks over there. Too many voices. Far too many opinions. Jack is himself and his master. Pseudo-individual. There's no popular discipline. I like discipline. Without discipline there's nothing."

"That is, I think, correct. Obedience, or chaos. It is an insult to the cosmic mentality that chaos comes, disregarding obedience or disobedience, with the thermonuclear bomb technique. To think of the complete anguish of this human race——"

"I don't wish to see the hydrogen or any other kind of bomb used anywhere. I want to see brains used for a change. I think you people use your brains. Particularly in controlling the mass. There you excel. That, I'm convinced, is the secret. Control of the mass. You seem to have made a science of it."

Arkhiv told the waiter to open a bottle of wine.

"Let us now drink our first toast in the Russian language together. Felicity of translation depends far more upon a mastery of the mother language than the widest knowledge of the other. I could not translate this toast into English. Let me test your competence, if you please."

"I'll have a shot, certainly."

"Here is the toast that defied me. Listen to the conjugation. 'Yà più za stchàsti zhìzni, a tàkzhe v seznànyi, tchte blagodarià nam, i dreegìm zhizn dast bèlshe ràdostei.' Let me hear how you translate?"

"Well now, let's see. 'To the enjoyment of life, with the further enjoyment of knowing that because of us, others have promise of more enjoyment in their lives.' "

"My compliments. Superb. I must write this down. May I ask, has enjoyment of life any place in your philosophy?"

"Is there any better reason, do you think, that might bring me here?"

"Agreed. I wish I had my years again. You have much to learn. Wide studies. Much to experience. I drink to the day you will work with me."

"With you?"

A large nod of the large head. A glimpse of ball-and-socket eyes through the claret in the goblet, smiling, perceptive, and something more, unapprehended, distant.

"When that time comes, you will be ready to return. This will be the end of our duty together. And the beginning of yours. To this we drink."

"An entirely philosophical drink, as my father used to say."

"If you permit, then, in addition, to his memory."

"To his memory, though not to his memories, perhaps. He hated the times he lived in. He was pushed into hating his life. He was in many ways among the last of his kind in a period that was beginning to regard the machine as more important than the man. Decidedly let us drink to him. Better still, to the overthrow of an order he hated. I regard it as something of an omen, Mr. Arkhiv, that he should be mentioned."

"I am happy to notice this attitude. It is, of course, essential to think in this manner. I am often amused to hear of people who pretend various sympathics and still can decide to live comfortably among the mores they wish to destroy. Shall the toast be to the enjoyment of life and the memory of your father? Or shall we now drink to the day of your return?"

"I'll drink to that, certainly. To the day of return——"

Crowding now, a wish for that day, long-desired though only from a moment ago, and never more than now, with heartsease and rosemary in the linen cupboards, and Vinny's lingerie on the bathroom line, miracles of herself in puffs of voile, and a ringed stocking on the hall table—oh damn these kids, they don't undress, they *slough*, and darling, do try to catch the six twenty-seven and I'll fly down to meet you, I've been feeling rather yessy all day—crowding, leap and tumble, that desire to return if only for the small delight of eyes and ears, for pleasure in the smell of buses, and the bap of taxi horns, and the quack of a wakened duck across the park and the trees and lights dabbling a gold and black reredos in the lake, and amber lamps shining over polished order in the writing room at the Club, to return and keep it all, unchanged, as it was, as it is now, and will be tomorrow, undoubtedly, though not without help. Never without help.

Remember tradition, Hamish—dear Father!—and never permit the slightest nonsense about change, or any discussion of any kind about relaxing, or remitting, or revoking or repealing. The authors of that type of amendment are all alike. They have no tradition, and having none will make none. Never permit them any encroachment. You have a brain. For God's sake use it. Strive for your proper position, and having gained it, maintain it. Use what ends you may to hang on to it. All means are proper for that purpose. Remember, Hamish, do please try to remember that your first duty is to yourself and your family and others in your position. We are absolutely dependent each on the other. Whatever you do, whatever has to be said, safeguard yourself and them. Never be deflected. Those beneath you can only follow. Those above must move on or be shouldered aside. If we fail it means tragedy for all. Without us, the lower stagnates. The higher crumbles. On our backs are supported the hustings for all that caricature of chivalry, that ignoble ermine and velvet rout miscalled an aristocracy only because women have children. Aristos, remember your Greek, means best in all things. Best implies mastery and leadership, by example, by precept, by thought, by sweat. Those who now pretend to that estate have nothing to recommend them but their genitals, and nothing to preserve them except our toleration. The system is founded and maintained by our brains, our beliefs, our style of living, our work, our decencies. Without us, no order exists because the disciplined will no longer controls. We revert, and the ruffians rule. Set your face and prosecute your will. Never permit yourself to be denied any opportunity of doing your proper duty, or of partaking in any movement to promote our general well-being. Remember that we are the intermediates, battened on, used, maltreated, disregarded. Remember us, Hamish. Remember us. Remember your duty. But for God's sake be sure of yourself, make no move, say no word until you are sure. Where we survive, nothing changes.

A raising of the goblet, a mouthful of wine, and that was that.
There it was.